A *Rose*

beyond a
STAR

A ROSE BEYOND A STAR
Copyright © 2017 by Adams Family Press

Library of Congress Cataloging-IN-Publication Data

ISBN: 9780692964606

Cover Arts & Graphic Designs by:
Dani Sax, danisaxdesignz.com

For information contact:
ADAMS FAMILY PRESS
P.O. BOX 737517
ELMHURST, NY 11373

Email: AdamsFamilyPress8@gmail.com
Website: AdamsFamilyPress.com
Facebook: ADAMS Family PRESS
Twitter: ADAMSFAMILYPRESS @AdamsFamPress1
Instagram: adamsfamilypress

In Loving Memory
of my Mother

DOROTHY JEAN ADAMS

A *Rose*

beyond a

STAR

by
Sha Born

PROLOGUE

MANHATTAN, NEW YORK, 2007

Presbyterian Hospital, although ranked #6 in the United States, it is justifiably ranked #1 in New York State. A ranking, that brought a sense of satisfaction to Senator Thaddeus C. Star, as his driver skillfully maneuvered the Cadillac Escalade through the Midtown traffic. In spite of his hectic schedule, Senator Star along with his wife Roberta, made a weekly visit to the renowned hospital to see his ailing mother Tyra Star, who had recently turned 90!

"Good evening Senator, and Mrs. Star." Greeted the young Hispanic receptionist, whose name tag read; T Garcia.

"Good evening, to you Theresa," said Roberta Star with a pleasant smile. "How's school coming along? "

"School is great!" She replied. "Thanks for asking."

Having gotten somewhat familiar with the young receptionist, more so in passing, the Senator asked, "If my memory serves me correctly, this is your final year, Am I correct?"

Pleased, due to the fact that such an important couple would actually remember even the slightest details of her life, and/or endeavors, filled Theresa with gratitude.

"Yes Indeed!" Theresa answered proudly.

Roberta Star gave a wink to the young ambitious woman, whereas the Senator gave her the thumbs-up sign, while placing his free hand at the small of his wife's back, ushering Roberta towards the awaiting elevator.

The Secret Service Agent, who also served as the Senator's driver, inspected the elevator. Meanwhile, the second agent stood slightly behind Senator Star and his wife, while watching for any suspicious movement(s) within their immediate circumference.

"Excuse me ma'am, do you mind?" The agent who inspected the elevator said to a young lady who suddenly tried to enter the car.

His question wasn't actually a question, but an indication that she'd need to await the next elevator.

"That won't be necessary." Roberta interceded.

"She's fine." The Senator co-signed, producing his trademark smile.

Once recognition set-in, the stranger was totally speechless being in such close proximity of the famous couple. Realizing she was literally staring at the Senator, she spoke for the first time.

"I am so sorry!" She apologized. "Please, excuse my manners."

"It's okay Honey." Since becoming a political family, Roberta was now accustomed to such reactions. "What floor?"

"Excuse me?" The young stranger was obviously (still) star struck.

"Unless you're joy riding, you may want to press for your desired floor," the agent closest to the elevator's buttons said to the young lady. Albeit, uncharacteristic, he did flash what could be construed a smile.

"Oh my God, I am so embarrassed!" She shook her head then laughed as she pressed the button for the 9th floor, not realizing that the 9th floor was also their floor, and had already been pressed.

"I hope you all will excuse me, I feel like a total groupie

right now," she laughed. "Talk about first impressions."

"I understand," Senator Star assured her. "Between you and I, its every politicians desire to have an impression on people."

"Trust me sir, I'm confident I speak for the majority when I say that the people of New York City are *'totally'* in love with you!" she informed the Senator with a huge smile on her face, before further informing him, "My very first experience at the voting booth happened to be when you were running for the United States Senate. I was so impressed by what all you had accomplished as a State Senator for New York, I *'had'* to cast my vote for you!"

Upon hearing such honest and kind words, especially coming from young people, never ceased to please Senator Star. Believe it or not, it had been his pleasure to represent the people of New York, he wanted to tell the young stranger.

Although, it was still quite early in his campaign for the Presidency, Senator Star nonetheless, found it quite overwhelming the amount of support he was 'already' receiving from the American people!

In fact, he was quite certain this young vibrant stranger standing behind him and his wife in the spacious elevator, couldn't possibly know (or maybe even understand) how much *'she'* has actually boosted *'his'* spirit, by informing him that her first appearance at the voting poll was in his honor. However, what really made the Senators day, was that she added "You, or anyone else, could not have *'ever'* told me that my first time voting I'd be casting a vote against my party's candidate." She shook her head at such irony, laughed, then added, "My entire family are die-hard Republicans."

As they all exited the elevator, the secret service agent closest to the Senator whispered in his ear, "Popular fella."

At that, Senator Star gave an approving nod. Yet, he was mindful that 'popularity' did not guarantee a candidate a seat inside the Oval Office. Al Gore and Grover Cleveland were both proof of that, he told himself.

Entering his mother's room, Thaddeus, nor Roberta were entirely surprised at the sight of the huge display of flowers which took up the majority of space in Tyra's room. Besides the flowers, he noticed several greeting/get well cards, as well as boxes of candy, mostly chocolates. Unbeknownst to the Senator and his wife, most of the nurses on the 9th floor had acquired a sweet tooth, as a result of his mother's generosity.

Whereas, Senator Star was accustomed to his share of fanfare, especially during his visits to the hospital. It was no secret that his overall fame was nothing in comparison to Tyra Star's celebrity! Tyra Star, was truly a legend in her own right.

During World War II, while most of the country was focused exclusively on winning the war, and others on migration, Tyra Star was zealously pursuing her Law Degree, at Howard University's School of Law. After being admitted to the Bar, she went on to prevail in a number of cases that would set a precedent in the American Court system. Not to mention travel the country as an associate of the NAACP's Legal Defense Fund, representing indigent clients whose civil rights had been violated. Ultimately, her success as an accomplished Attorney, would be overshadowed by her acts of courage/activism during the Civil Rights Movement. So much so, her actions garnered her national and international acclaim.

"I never understood how, or why, some people were content watching television without any volume." Thaddeus spoke, as he approached his mother's bed, planting a kiss on her left cheek.

Roberta approached Tyra from the right side of her bed, where she planted a kiss on her mother-in-law's right cheek.

"Trust me, I have no problem watching 'without' hearing." Tyra began. "It's such a tragedy, all the senseless acts of violence taking place throughout this country."

No one in the room could argue that point, considering she had spoken the absolute truth.

"I understand that America was built on violence. However, some would argue that most of its wars were tantamount to a necessary evil. Even though, that has never been my personal opinion." Tyra spoke, as she attempted to get comfortable in bed. "This new generation of young folks, need to understand

and realize the number of folks, especially black folks, who willingly and unwillingly gave their lives in order for these kids to have the freedom in which they clearly take for granted these days." She shook her head.

Thaddeus, and Roberta had become accustomed to hearing such talk, therefore they allowed her to go on without interruption.

"Robbing, stealing, killing, and bringing drugs into the community although is nothing new, black folks have clearly lost their way. We may have been guilty of leaving our children, and/or babies unjustifiably with grandparents and other relatives, but never would we have left our babies in a trash dumpster."

With that being said, Tyra aimed the remote at the wide-screen television that was mounted to the wall, turning it off.

"So, how is it that you expect to keep up with the status of my campaign, if you're not listening to the news?" Thaddeus posed his question with a smile on his face.

"Oh please," Tyra shot him a look. "I don't need to watch nobody's news channel to know that you're going to win the presidency." That being said, brought to mind how much Thaddeus had always cherished his mother's support, optimism, and overall confidence in him.

"I could not have said it better myself," Roberta chimed in, she too was wearing a smile as she held onto Tyra's right hand, which she noticed felt a bit clammy.

"Has Dr. Zayas been in to check on you today?" Roberta asked with concern in her voice, not at all caring that she'd changed the subject.

The question, prompted Tyra to roll her eyes.

"Oh please!" she began. "When is that man 'not' paying me a visit?

Only to tell me the same ole nonsense each day. At 90 years old, I'm expected to have a weak heart. That's a conversation he and I can engage in, from the comforts of my home, instead of being cooped up in this hospital." Tyra stared into her sons' eyes as she complained.

"If I'm dying, why does it have to be here?" She added, as tears began to form in her eyes.

"If your doctor felt you didn't need to be here, you would not be here." Thaddeus tried to explain, even though it broke his heart to see his mother lying in the hospital bed, let alone having to leave her.

"Della Mae, is more than qualified to take care of me. I actually trust her capability more than I do any of these nurses here. Which she and I both already brought to Dr. Zayas's attention." said Tyra.

That last piece of information caused Thaddeus and Roberta to exchange a knowing look. Meaning, they knew that it was imperative that one of them, if not both of them needed to have a discussion with Della Mae Richardson, who was Tyra's home attendant for nearly the past two decades.

"I'll have a word with Dr. Zayas. If he doesn't agree to us bringing you home, I'll see if he'll at least allow me to take you out for some fresh air." Roberta offered.

"Thank You. I'd sure appreciate it." Tyra said.

"No problem." Roberta replied, giving her hand a gentle squeeze.

Turning her attention towards Thaddeus, Tyra asked, "Have you decided on a running mate?"

"I still have at least five to six months before I make that decision. However, I have a few potential prospects in mind."

Tyra, realized that 'now' was as good a time as any to reveal a family secret in which she'd been keeping, being that it was only right that Thaddeus learn who some of his family members were. However, she also knew that she'd be running the risk of him being upset with her, more so than actually being delighted to finally know the truth. Above all, Tyra didn't want him to hate her. The thought alone was enough to cause her blood pressure to rise.

"Do you recall me keeping a diary when you were younger?" asked Tyra.

Thaddeus had to give his mother's out of the blue question, some thought.

"As a matter of fact, I do recall you keeping a diary." He did remember.

"Do you even have it still? Let alone, write in it?" Thaddeus asked out of curiosity, being that he hadn't seen it in years.

"Actually, I no longer have the diary. Instead, I decided some years back to turn it into a journal using information that was provided to me by your grandmother Anne Lee, events that transpired throughout my life, and some additional family information that was provided by other sources." Tyra revealed.

"Other sources?" Thaddeus repeated, with a raised eyebrow.

"Other sources as in family members." said Tyra

Thaddeus simply stared at her. He spent his entire life without any mention of other family members. Basically, there had been so little talk concerning family, he grew up believing that Anne Lee and his mother were the only family he had.

He had been told, by his grandmother that his father, a man named Curtis, died shortly before he was born. She'd also revealed that she had migrated to New York City at a very young age, because she needed to get away from the oppression and cruelty that blacks were subjected to in the South. That was about as much as she'd been willing to tell. Out of respect, and not wanting to cause Anne Lee to relive an obviously painful past, Thaddeus never pressed for further detail.

"Is there something you need to free your conscience of?" He eyed his mother. Not suspiciously, but, because he usually could tell by her expression if she was keeping something from him, which he found ironic at the moment seeing how she had obviously been holding 'some' things from him, apparently for years.

"You never told me that mother kept a diary!" Roberta interceded, attempting to diffuse whatever was going on between Thaddeus and her mother-in-law.

On several occasions, Roberta had asked Tyra why hadn't she done an autobiography. At least two un-authorized biographies had been written about her life's story. Albeit, they *both* were really well written, Roberta had to admit, she knew they wouldn't be nearly as interesting as an autobiography of Tyra Star's own account.

"I'm not surprised he didn't mention it to you, or that he'd even forgotten. I stopped writing it ten years ago." Tyra explained.

Thaddeus, however noticed how Roberta had interceded, something she often did, when or if she felt he was being insensitive or argumentative, which he felt he was being neither.

"Why would you stop writing? Aren't journals supposed to cover our life's story and journey?" Thaddeus was somewhat dismayed.

"It seems, to me anyway, that you'd still have a great deal to write about. I mean, not many of us live to see our 90th birthday." He added.

Tyra didn't respond.

"Are you alright mother?" Roberta asked, clearly concerned.

"I'm okay." Tyra replied, in a much lowered, tone of voice.

"A set of events, one incredible, the other devastating occurred back in 1997. It was the devastation that not only caused me to put my pen down, but more so changed my life forever." Tyra couldn't stop the tears as they began to stream down both sides of her face.

Thaddeus was totally thrown aback by the sight of his mother's tears. Not because he had never seen her cry, but because Tyra Star was the least vulnerable woman he'd ever known. The sight of her tears literally broke his heart as he stared into her deep greenish/blue eyes.

"Thaddeus, would you mind going down to the cafeteria?" Roberta asked. "I can certainly use a diet sprite, and I'm sure your mother would love a yogurt."

Looking away from his mother, and into his wife's eyes Thaddeus didn't have a clue as to what was going on. However, he certainly hoped that Roberta would clue him in once they'd left the hospital, he thought to himself as he turned away from the bed and exited the room.

Once he was gone, Roberta brought a chair over to mothers' bed. Reclaiming Tyra's right hand, she held it in between the both of hers.

"This devastating event, I'm assuming it's a person. Do you want to tell me about he or she?" Roberta inquired.

Opposed to responding to the question, Tyra was truly grateful that Roberta had sent Thaddeus on his way. She hated crying in front of him. As a child, it was something he had seen her do maybe once.

In fact, she appreciated Roberta for more reasons then she knew.

"Thank you." was Tyra's response

Staring into Roberta's eyes, Tyra had always felt that her son was indeed blessed to have such a woman as his wife. She and Roberta had hit it off from the start.

Although, Thaddeus and Roberta initially met while they both attended Columbia University, Roberta had ultimately earned her Law Degree/Juris Doctorate from Howard University School of Law, the same school in which Tyra also, had earned hers. That was only one commonality however, Tyra saw a lot of herself in her daughter-in-law.

Whereas, she had mostly practiced Criminal Law, Roberta was General Counsel at a Fortune 500 Company.

"All of what I've never revealed to Thaddeus, or anyone else for that matter is written inside my journal. Till this day, it dismays me why I've withheld such pertinent family information, and history from him. Especially seeing how incredible the stories are pertaining to a number of his ancestors, and what they've achieved."

"By the time I had learned most of my family's history, tragedy struck. As a result, I totally lost focus." A fresh batch of tears began to stream down Tyra's face.

"I need one of you to take the time out to read through my journal. I do not believe in coincidences. Therefore, I honestly believe that fate is about to shape Thaddeus's destiny."

"Where can I find it? The journal?" Roberta asked.

"I have it with me." Tyra revealed. "I had Della Mae bring it to me some time ago."

"You mean it's right here in this room?" Roberta inquired, not bothering to mask her interest. The actual thought of being the first and only person to read Tyra's life story, written in her own words, more than excited her.

Truthfully, Roberta was not surprised at all, regarding her level of excitement. For as far back as she could remember, she had heard stories about Tyra Star. Not including what she'd read. The fact that her mother-in-law had been one of the first African America *'female'* Attorneys in the country, had played an integral part in Roberta's desire to become a lawyer at a young age.

Not to mention, it was legendary. The stories of how Tyra Star had been a fearless opponent of racial discrimination, seg-regation, and oppression. As well as, stood at the front line in the fight for Woman's Rights, to vote, to choose, and receive equal pay in the workplace. It was no secret that the majority of 'sexual harassment' cases she had won for women all across the country, were usually handled Pro-Bono, only added to her legend.

Therefore, Roberta was not only excited, but moreover proud, and honored to call Tyra Star her mother!

"It's in that draw over there." Tyra pointed to the small dresser that sat directly beneath the 52" wide-screen television.

Although, Roberta hadn't delved into the contents of the journal, she was nonetheless impressed by its exterior, as she now held it in her hand. It was obviously professionally printed and binded, she noticed.

On its 'cover' was a Rose intertwined with the word 'Rose', and a twinkling star was adjacent the word 'Star'....

"You haven't said much since we left the hospital." Thad-deus voiced his observation, as they sat in the backseat of their chauffeur driven SUV. Unfastening his seatbelt, he moved clos-er to Roberta, whose right hand he took into his.

"I'm fine dear." Roberta turned to face her husband, before producing a smile to assure him as much. In fact, she met him halfway, when Thaddeus leaned in to plant a kiss on her lips.

It was during such times that Thaddeus told himself not even the victory of the Commander-in-Chief's seat could compare to the Prize sitting beside him.

Leaning her head on Thaddeus's shoulder, Roberta inquired.

"Would it bother you if I read mother's journal first?"

"I was under the impression that we'd read it together." Thaddeus kissed the top of her head.

Roberta didn't respond.

Thaddeus knew how close his wife and his mother were. As a matter of fact, it had been Tyra who'd encouraged him to marry Roberta, at a time when he was mainly focused on his political career. Moreover, the fact that Roberta had lost her biological mother to breast cancer at a very young age, contributed to her bond with his mother.

"Since I have to leave for Washington D.C. in the a.m., I guess you'll have something to keep you preoccupied tomorrow night, being that I won't be back until Tuesday morning." Thaddeus reminded her.

"It's under 300 pages, so it won't take me but a few hours to read." Roberta informed him. Unbeknownst to Thaddeus, she had already decided that she would stay home from work tomorrow, so she'd be through reading it by the time he returned from his trip...

CHAPPAQUA, NEW YORK
Monday, December 15, 2007
10:00 A.M.

Two hours had passed since Roberta saw her husband off (for his trip to Washington D.C.), and their Eleven-year-old daughter Najae Akira, off to school.

"Marvette, I want you to reschedule all of my appointments for tomorrow, I won't be coming in today. Actually, I won't be available at all, so I'll call you this evening to check my messages." Roberta informed her secretary.
With that out the way, she climbed back into her bed with a bowl of mixed fruit in reach, and opened the journal to Page One....

FOREWORD

My name is Tyra Star, and this is a brief 'foreward' to my Journal, "A Rose Beyond A Star", which spans over a century and a half. It is the story of two families that begins in Mt. Pleasant, South Carolina, in the year of 1850.

Although, a great deal of my life's endeavors, trials, and triumphs has become a matter of public interest, and fascination, I assure you all that 'no' unauthorized Biography(s) can truly depict the blessings, the love, nor the lost that has been a part of my Journey.

I, myself have never been a slave. Therefore, it does not interest me to try to learn, or to imitate in my journal the broken English, dialect, and dialogue from that era. I am a very well learned/read black women, who appreciates a well written (non-offensive) story. I've also decided to omit the use of the word *'Master'* in reference to any man or person.

My Great Grandfather, Albertus Addison, was born into slavery, a predicament he decided to free himself from in 1849. Unfortunately, his successful escape from the Addison Plantation, meant having to leave his wife, Arethea, and three young sons (Albertus Jr. 14, Granville, 12, and Thaddeus, 6.)

I realize that in 1849, it was unfathomable that America would ever refer to black men as 'Great' whether it be his place in lineage, actions, or deeds. However, as I write with Albertus Addison in mind, the only word I can think of is "Greatness".

My Great Grandfather's successful escape, was followed by his return to his former plantation to lead over 18 others to their freedom! Unfortunately, his three sons were too young to survive the wilderness, and path that became known as the Underground Railroad. That being the case, his wife Arethea made the decision to remain in bondage. A decision that would not only cost Arethea her life, but also lead to the 'selling' of their three young sons.

Today, as I write with my son Thaddeus in mind, I also see Greatness. However, being that I 'did' say that, this was a brief forward into my Journal, I will let 'it' be my elaboration, as far as Thaddeus is concerned! (Smile.)

A good portion of 'A Rose Beyond A Star' takes place during Reconstruction, Jim Crow, and the Civil Rights Movement. Therefore, it is inevitable that the story is laced with hope, disappointment, tragedy, and struggle.

Yet, you will find that it is filled with love! In fact, when I decided to write my Journal, it was my endeavor to share with the world (in writing) the kind of "love" in which John, Paul, George, and Ringo endeavored to share, in song...

Tyra Star

ONE

CHARLESTON, SOUTH CAROLINA, 1850

Nathaniel Lawrence Pinkney, was a descendant of migrants who arrived in Charleston S.C., from England, in 1670. Truthfully, his family had played a pivotal role in the colony's establishment, considering Nathaniel L. Pinkney rose to become owner of Charleston's largest Rice Plantation.

However, it was his father a man named Charles J. Pinkney, who in 1786, turned 70 acres of undeveloped land in a relatively unknown town named Mount Pleasant, into a thriving rice plantation.

By 1850, Nathaniel was listed among the South's power elite, one of the Great Planters of Cotton, who by then was the owner of over 50 slaves. Nathaniel, his wife Ruth, and their daughter Elizabeth (the couple's son, Nathaniel Jr. would be born later), often vacationed throughout Europe, Asia, as well as spent summers in places such as New York City, Philadelphia, and Boston.

It was no secret that, in his home state of South Carolina, Nathaniel played a part in hand-picking Mayors, Senators, Congressman, and deciding who would run for Governor!

Pinkney Plantation, now surrounded by over a thousand acres of land, and home to over 50 slaves by 1850, was no longer a place of residence for Nathaniel, and his wife Ruth. Instead, he made the decision to become an absentee owner, allowing his daughter Elizabeth, and her husband Andrew, to oversee not only the plantation, but also his lucrative cotton business.

As far as Nathaniel was concerned, his family's plantation was all he'd ever known. However, as his wealth continued to grow he came to the realization that the *'plantation'* no longer satisfied he, and his wife's social and cultural needs. Wealth and success had taught him that social interaction was imperative for longevity.

The Pinkney's regularly entertained bankers, merchants, politicians, judges, and other business associates. Yet, a vast majority of Pinkney Plantation sat on reclaimed swamp land, albeit pivotal for cotton growth made it a breeding ground for mosquitos that broadcast various diseases. So, becoming an absentee owner was certainly in his best of interest, Nathaniel told himself, as he and Ruth relocated to their Greek Revival styled mansion located in the city of Charleston.

Theirs, was a Six Bedroom mansion with three floors, and three and a half bathrooms. Outback, was a Four Bedroom guest-house, which served as their slave quarter.

Unlike Elizabeth, it was in Charleston that Nathaniel 'Junior' was born. The Pinkney's not only treated their firstborn son as royalty, but moreover couldn't help the feeling as though he had been their *'miracle'* baby!

"Our gift from God!" Ruth Pinkney often exclaimed.

Considering, at the time of his birth, Nathaniel Sr. was already 54 years old, and Ruth had already reached 46. Actually, there was an eighteen-year age gap between Elizabeth and Nathaniel Jr. Nevertheless, she loved her younger brother to death. Nor, did Elizabeth envy or display jealousy in regard to his Golden Child status.

"Nate, I think you and I both know that you already know this stuff." Corice, the Pinkney's servant eyed the seven-year-old boy suspiciously. She had been calling Nathaniel Jr. 'Nate' since the day she helped deliver him.

"I think you enjoy hearing me repeat myself is all." She complained.

At that, Nate produced a smile, which usually brought a smile to Corice's face as well.

Corice, genuinely adored the young boy. Who, in spite of all his wealth and special treatment, had been born with a learning disability.

"Okay, if you insist." Nate replied, at the same time reaching for the Bible in which Corice had been reading from.

Corice, actually closed her eyes, as the young boy began reading the Lord's Prayer. It wasn't Nate's small voice, nor its eloquence that brought Corice to tears. But, upon the opening of her eyes, she was basically blown away by the sight/realization of what she saw! Nate was reciting the prayer, word for word, as he held the 'unopened' Bible in hand.

"I've been practicing." He informed her with a smile on his face, before further revealing. "I can also recite some of the Psalms without looking in the book."

Opposed to giving a verbal response, Corice wrapped her arms around the small boy, engulfing him in a 'motherly' embrace. Although, she was not the woman who had given birth to the child, she had only assisted in Nate's delivery, the majority of his 'time' was nonetheless spent with Corice. Just as it was the same with Elizabeth. Corice had been the primary care taker of both the Pinkney's children. Which was why the Pinkney's didn't have a problem with Corice's ambition to learn to read and write, at a time when the majority of slaves/blacks were kept illiterate.

During slavery, it was not uncommon for the children of slaves to become 'playmates' with the children of their owners. However, seven-year-old Thaddeus, had never been separated from his brothers (Albertus, and Granville), therefore, he didn't know what to think or expect, when Elizabeth summoned him.

"Per request," she began, "My parents' driver, Milton, is

coming to fetch you and take you back to Charleston."

Thaddeus simply stared at her.

"Apparently, Ms. Corice heard about you and wants you with her at the guests' house in Charleston. However, I'm inclined to believe that she feels you may be a good playmate for my younger brother Nathaniel." Elizabeth revealed with a smile.

Although, Thaddeus did not return her smile, he genuinely liked the woman. In fact, Elizabeth Pinkney, and her husband were by far the kindest white folks he'd ever known. Truthfully, it was an assessment shared by all of the slaves owned by the Pinkney's.

"I realize, you'll miss your brothers. But, I'm confident you will return here once you're old enough to assist in the fields." Although, Elizabeth didn't particularly like how that sounded, she knew it was the truth.

Considering, the three Addison boys were the offspring of strong parents, neither of them shed a tear as Thaddeus was packed onto the horse-driven carriage and taken away.

Truthfully, Albertus, the oldest of the three brothers, was actually relieved that his little brother was going to reside in a better place (as Elizabeth had called it.) Being that Thaddeus had been too young to experience the tedious hours and hard labor, he and Granville had to endure in the fields. Especially, picking cotton.

Arriving in the City of Charleston, which was separated from Mount Pleasant only because of the Cooper River, Thaddeus couldn't believe his eyes!

Whereas, he had also observed large crowds in Orangeburg, where he and his two brothers had found themselves on an auction block. Also, where Elizabeth's husband Andrew had purchased the three of them, the two cities were nothing alike, Thaddeus thought to himself.

Not only was downtown Charleston bustling with activity. Stores were everywhere, the streets were nicely paved and cleaned, and most of the folks he'd passed were not only well dressed, but also walked with their heads held high. Thaddeus couldn't help noticing as well.

However, it was the sight of all the fresh fruits and veg-etables being sold on the market, that suddenly garnered his undivided attention. Actually, the sight caused his stomach to growl loudly.

Milton, heard the loud growl, but kept his focus on the road.

"So, this is Thaddeus!" Corice spoke in a joyful voice, be-fore giving Thaddeus's left cheek a sharp pinch. Inspecting him from head to toe, yet speaking to no one in particular, she gave her assessment.

"He is so adorable!"

Milton gave a shrug, then turned and left the two of them to themselves.

"Child, they must not have been feeding you much over there in Mount Pleasant. I can see that I'm gonna have to fat-ten you up some."

Nodding her head, as if giving confirmation to her state-ment.

"Nate is already about twice your size." she added, as if Thaddeus knew who Nate was. "Are you hungry?"

Opposed to giving a verbal response, Thaddeus nodded his head up and down, indicating that he was.

"Although, I'm somewhat familiar with sign language, it will be in your best of interest to *speak* when being spoken to. Especially, around here." She wanted to say; around these white folks, but used 'here' instead.

"Yes ma'am." Thaddeus replied, speaking for the first time since his arrival.

"Yes, ma'am what?" Corice eyed him.

"Yes, ma'am I am hungry." He corrected himself." If it's not too much trouble, I'd love something to eat." Thaddeus added, to her obvious surprise.

At that, Corice produced a huge smile. Something tells me that this boy has some real potential, she couldn't help thinking to herself. It actually wasn't her intentions to be hard on him by correcting him, she was simply aware that it was imperative that Thaddeus presented himself in a certain way. Especially, being around the offspring of a wealthy white family, and because it was 'she' who persuaded the Pinkney's to allow him to come live with her.

Taking hold of the young boy's hand, Corice led the way to the kitchen. As Corice watched Thaddeus eat the meal in which she prepared for him, she noticed that although he was obviously starving (being that she had overheard his stomach growl more than once as she cooked) he clearly possessed excellent table manners. Which prompted her to ask a question.

"Have you ever lived with your parents?"

Chewing, and swallowing, the food that was in his mouth before speaking, Thaddeus replied, "Yes ma'am"

Having her answer, Corice decided to let him finish his meal before asking anymore questions. Yet, she wanted to know all about him, and his brothers. Whereas, black families were often split up, especially men, women, and older children. It was quite rare to see such young boys separated from their mother, Corice thought to herself.

Thaddeus sensed that the older, very generous woman wanted to pick his brain. However, his family and upbringing was a subject that he didn't like discussing, or giving detail.

Once he was done eating, Thaddeus stood from the table, and headed towards the kitchen sink.

"Do you have a cloth and soap?" he asked, without turning to face Ms. Corice.

"You can leave it in the sink. Miriam, will be in to wash the dishes shortly." She informed him. "Would you like some dessert?"

"No thank you."

"Are you sure?" Corice asked, before informing him. "I have some blueberry muffins cooling off. As well as, apples, oranges, and bananas." She offered.

Remembering how his stomach had reacted to the sight of all the fresh fruit he'd passed on the market-place, prompted him to respond.

"There was a man selling sugar cane, and a fruit that was

8

bright yellow on the inside." Thaddeus tried to explain.

"You're talking about Mister Moultree. He sells the sugar cane and pineapples." Corice was well familiar with the man he was referring to.

"So, you've never had pineapple?" She asked.

"I have never even seen one before today." Thaddeus admitted.

"Unfortunately, I do not have any here. But, as soon as Milton brings Nate home from school, I will have him go by the market to purchase you and I some pineapples." Corice said with a smile. As far as she was concerned, pineapples would only be the first of 'many' things she intended to expose him to.

"Who is Nate?" Thaddeus inquired, sounding every bit of the Seven-year-old, whom he was.

"Nate, is short for Nathaniel. Who happens to be a very special child." Corice answered with a smile. "Actually, he is the main reason for you being here."

TWO

CHARLESTON, SOUTH CAROLINA, 1853

Since arriving in Charleston, three years earlier, Nathaniel and Thaddeus had become as close as brothers! Theirs was a relationship that was not only influenced and encouraged by Ms. Corice, she also manipulated the circumstances that enabled the two of them to spend as much time with one another as possible.

As a result, Thaddeus had not (yet) been sent back to Mt. Pleasant to plow the fields with his brothers, and most slaves owned by the Pinkney's. Instead, Thaddeus found himself doing various jobs, such as cleaning, landscaping, basic repairs, feeding, and maintaining the horses, at the Pinkney's Charleston residence.

Unlike Nathaniel Jr. (whom Thaddeus preferred to not refer to as 'Nate', being that he could tell the Pinkney's were not at all fond of his doing so) who attended one of Charleston's most prestigious elementary schools, Thaddeus found himself being tutored by Ms. Corice. She had, continued to tutor 'both' boys, however it was Thaddeus whom she had to do so with absolute discretion, considering the Pinkney's (mainly, Ruth Pinkney) was totally against Thaddeus receiving any form of education! Unless, it was somewhat vocational, and had very little to do with reading.

Unbeknownst to the Pinkney's, Corice spent countless hours teaching Thaddeus all that she knew, and some. Never had she'd known or witnessed a young boy devour books the way Thaddeus did. The boy literally loved to read! Not only did he devour any and every textbook in which Nathaniel brought home from school, Thaddeus often found himself explaining lessons to Nathaniel, as well as Corice!

"I hope you know how much I appreciate your generosity, and everything else you've done for me since I've been living here." Thaddeus expressed to Nathaniel, as the two of them made repairs to Nathaniel's tree-house.

"There's no need to thank me." Nathaniel replied, "Besides, you're like the brother that my parents couldn't give me."

At that, they both laughed, even though Nathaniel was being serious.

Not only Thaddeus, but even Corice, had been moved by the fact that Nathaniel, unbeknownst to his parents of course, decided to share his weekly allowance of fifty cents with Thaddeus. Who in return, gave Corice his twenty-five cents to save for him.

"I came up with an idea that will enable the two of us to make some real money." Thaddeus revealed, hoping Nathaniel would be willing to go along with his plan.

"What is your plan?" Nathaniel asked, only half interested, being that making money didn't really appeal to him. Especially, at ten years old. Not to mention, his parents gave him any and everything he asked for.

"I want you to tell Mister Pinkney that you want to start earning your own money, on weekends and holidays."

"Making my own money doing what exactly?" Nathaniel halted, putting nails into the lining of his tree-house, giving Thaddeus his full attention. Not so much because he was interested in what he had suggested to him, but more so because Nathaniel couldn't quite fathom earning any money of his own.

"It's no secret that your father supplies the majority of the old shopkeepers, and merchants in town. But I seriously doubt that anyone will have a problem with me going out there on the market, like old man Moultree, if they knew that I was working for you."

"Working for me? Selling what?" Nathaniel didn't try to mask his dismay.

"Fruits and vegetables." Thaddeus answered him with a smile.

Nathaniel simply stared at him.

"With your fathers' approval, Elizabeth and Andrew can load Milton's carriage up, with fruit, vegetables, flour, and wheat. Which I will stand out there and sell for you." Thaddeus explained, before adding, "Your father is a businessman. Therefore, he will relish the fact that you too, especially at such a young age are showing an interest in the business."

"Actually, most of these white folks around here have a tendency to turn their noses up every time they see you and I doing things together. So, to see or hear that you've decided to put me to work, which I'm certain your parents will boast about, will take care of any conflict of interest, as far as shopkeepers, merchants, and old man Moultree are concerned.

"What if you suck as a salesman?" Nathaniel couldn't hide his grin. "I mean, you only get one chance to make a good impression."

At that, Thaddeus burst into laughter. Even though Nathaniel made a valid point, he told himself. Nevertheless, Thaddeus was glad that Nathaniel seemed to be on board.

"Success is never guaranteed when starting your own business. Yet, the only thing that beats a failure is non-attempt." Thaddeus spoke wisely for his age. "Besides, what do 'you' have to lose? If our business fails, you can also ask that your allowance be reinstated."

At that, they 'both' shared a laugh.

Nathaniel gave thought to all that was said, and ultimately decided that he'd not only go along with it, but moreover certainly would 'not' fail in their endeavor. Even if it meant getting out there on the market, as well.

Just as Thaddeus had predicted, Nathaniel L. Pinkney Sr

was so impressed by his son's request, he not only set Thaddeus up in business immediately, he also provided Thaddeus with more produce than he could handle! In fact, he secured Thaddeus's space on the market place as well.

Seeing that Thaddeus spent less time with her son lately, it was Ruth Pinkney who'd suggested to her husband (who made the suggestion to Thaddeus), that he sell Nathaniel's produce 7-days-a-week, opposed to just weekends and holidays!

Unbeknownst to the Pinkney's, their suggestion was music to Thaddeus's ears!

The only downside to working 7 days a week was that doing so would interfere with his tutor sessions and studies, he thought to himself.

"You and I can always study at night." Corice suggested with a warm smile. Although, she knew she'd be tired, she was nonetheless impressed by how much money Thaddeus had been giving her to save.

They both know that *'money'* was the greatest means to a black man acquiring his freedom...

FEBRUARY 11, 1858

Not even the Pinkney's were as excited as Ms. Corice to see that Nathaniel, at 15 years old would advance to the 12th grade.

"College at sixteen!" Corice exclaimed proudly. She had never claimed the words 'learning disability' as the pediatrician had once diagnosed.

"I suppose." Nathaniel replied with a shrug as he ate his ice cream.

"What kind of response is that?" Ruth Pinkney stared across the dining room table at her son.

"Leave the boy to his ice cream!" Nathaniel Sr. interceded. As far as he was concerned, college was totally up to Nathaniel Jr, whom secretly preferred to come work with him upon completing high school.

Ruth Pinkney however, knew exactly what her husband's thoughts and plans for their son were, which was why she turned her attention towards her husband, whom she now stared at with a raised eyebrow.

"May I be excused?" Nathaniel Jr. interrupted.

Without awaiting a yay or nay, he got up from his seat and exited the dining room.

"What's on your agenda today?" Nathaniel asked, glad that he had caught up with Thaddeus, who spent more time working than anything else, he noticed.

Nathaniel certainly enjoyed the money the two of them were making and saving, as a result of Thaddeus's salesman capabilities down on the market. However, he truly missed how they once spent time together.

"Same as every day," Thaddeus replied. Indicating he was en route to the market place.

"Has it been a good week?" Nathaniel inquired, displaying mild interest.

"Overall, things are good. I'm just thankful that your father allowed my two brothers to come out there and work with me."

"Yes, that was really kind of him." Nathaniel agreed.

"You seem kind of down for someone who was recently advanced to the 12th grade." Thaddeus was truly happy for him.

"The schoolwork, and the homework is much more difficult."

"Is there something that I can help you with?" Thaddeus inquired, at the same time priding himself for knowing Nathaniel better than anyone.

"Well, we're studying the United States Constitution in my history class," Nathaniel began to explain. "We have to turn in an essay in regards to the farmers who drafted the constitution, who was responsible for its 'final' draft, and so on."

"We both know that you already know all of that." Thaddeus too, had read several books that Nathaniel brought home from school on the subject.

"I know, but I was wondering if you'd read over my essay and give me your honest opinion." Nathaniel knew if Thaddeus liked it, his teachers would love it.

Putting his carry bag down on Corice's kitchen counter, Thaddeus reached for the essay that Nathaniel had in hand.

"Did I cover everything?" Nathaniel asked, once Thaddeus was done reading.

"It will do." said Thaddeus.

"I thought I asked for your 'honest' opinion?" Nathaniel knew Thaddeus well enough to know when or if he wasn't totally impressed with something.

"My honest opinion is that it's good. However, it's pretty basic. Meaning, it's what I'd expect the entire class to turn in, being that the facts are in order." Thaddeus explained, before adding.

"Nevertheless, do we really want your essay to be an exact replica of what your other thirty or so classmates are turning in?" He asked.

"Of course not!" Nathaniel answered with a smile. Again, he knew Thaddeus well enough to know that there was 'more' to his feedback.

"The goal, is for 'your' essay to outshine everyone else's.

"True." Nathaniel's smile was still in place.

"We 'are' in the state of South Carolina, are we not?" Thaddeus asked.

Opposed to a verbal response, Nathaniel nodded his head, yes.

"Okay, so along with all of the facts you've included in your essay, you need to also incorporate the pivotal role in which the state of South Carolina played in influencing it's drafting. Your teachers will undoubtedly be more so impressed with your essay, above all the rest actually, if you can do so." Thaddeus produced with a smile.

"How am I supposed to show, or prove that South Carolina had something to do with the drafting of the U.S. Constitution? Whether pivotal, or otherwise." Nathaniel appeared frustrated.

"I think you need to read more into all those books you have laying around." Thaddeus laughed.

Nathaniel simply stared at him, considering he really wasn't in a joking mood.

"In 1663, Charles II, awarded the colony of South Carolina to a man named Lord Ashley. The first Earl of Shaftesbury," Thaddeus began. "In turn, Lord Ashley asked a man by the name of John Locke to write the governing Constitution for South Carolina. John Locke, wrote into the Constitution; certain guarantees among them, life, health, liberty, or possessions.

"Although Locke's Constitution provided a distinct class structure and the incorporation of a feudal system, his ideas on checks and balances had obviously, if not proudly 'influenced' Thomas Jefferson, as well as formed the actual basis for the United States Constitution." Thaddeus explained, thus 'showing' Nathaniel how to incorporate his home state of South Carolina into his essay. Nathaniel however, was momentarily speechless....

MARCH 15, 1860

If nothing else, Nathaniel Sr. recognized *'potential'* from miles away! Truthfully, he had long ago detected great potential in Thaddeus. However, as in the case with his son, Nathaniel Jr, both boys were simply too young for him to truly capitalize.

"Or, is seventeen still too young?" The elder Pinkney asked himself.

Deciding that it was not, Nathaniel Sr. summoned Thaddeus, to inform him that he was sending him back to Pinkney Plantation.

"Elizabeth and Andrew are doing quite well running things. However, something tells me that you son, have the potential to take things to another level over there."

"As far as?" Thaddeus asked with a raised eyebrow.

"As far as the business of cotton is concerned." Nathaniel Sr. answered with a huge smile on his face.

Business of cotton, Thaddeus had never heard of it referred to so casually. Although, he himself never planted or picked cotton, Thaddeus knew it was back breaking, arthritis causing, and certainly led to the misery of countless field-hands.

Unbeknownst to Thaddeus, Nathaniel Sr. was well aware of the war that was brewing between the Industrial North, and the Agrarian South. In fact, the majority of the Pinkney income was derived from cotton, especially following the invention of Eli Whitney's Cotton Gin, which Nathaniel L. Pinkney capitalized from by duplicating, yet, never giving 'Whitney' his due.

Not to mention, he and his associates in the North (Boston, and Lowell, Massachusetts) continued to bring in a fortune from the hundreds of thousands of bales of cotton that was planted, picked, cleaned, bundled, and shipped from the Pinkney Plantation!

Unfortunately, with age, Elizabeth and Andrew had both become quite lax and content, Nathaniel Sr. noticed.

However, Thaddeus had no desire to assist him in his business of cotton, as he so casually put it. Especially, if it meant putting additional pressure on those already working in the fields, sun up to sun down, without pay.

"You stated your desire to send me back to Mt. Pleasant, which I have no problem working the fields or whatever I'm told to do. But, I have no interest in the overseeing of those who I will be living amongst, and working beside." Thaddeus said with sincerity.

"You haven't heard what I expect of you, nor what I'm willing to offer not only to you, but to your two brothers as well." Nathaniel Sr. responded with a confident smile on his face.

Holding the older man's stare, Thaddeus knew he was indebted to Mr. Pinkney, and his wife, for all the years in which they'd allowed him to reside at the Charleston residence (opposed to working the fields.) As well as allowed him to earn a 'wage' from the produce he sold for the market, at a time when slaves did not receive pay for their labor. Ultimately, his decision to hear the man out, was largely due to the mention of Albertus and Granville.

THREE

MT. PLEASANT, SOUTH CAROLINA, 1860

Following his conversation with Nathaniel Sr., Thaddeus had to admit that things not only improved for he and his brothers, but for all those who were owned by the Pinkney family. As he thought about it, his mind reflected back to their conversation.

"For decades now, I've been supplying my associates up north with bales of cotton." Mr. Pinkney began. "Unfortunately, we are all concerned about the tension taking place between those liberals in the North who are being pressured by the Conscience Whigs to abolish slavery, and the Southern politicians who are not willing to relinquish State's rights.

If you want to know the truth, I think they're all idiots, who honestly do not know their asses from their elbows." Mr. Pinkney let out a laugh. "The government is making tons of money off us tax payers. In fact, I pay hundreds of thousands in taxes annually. Do I complain? Of course not." He gave a shrug.

"It's called working together. Trust me, I do not enjoy working with those Northern Yankees, who call themselves my business associates. Especially, those in New York City, who take us southerner's kindness for weakness by charging an exorbitant toll to ship cotton through their ports and harbors.

But like I said, I don't complain.

"In business, we have to learn to make our relationships work for the sake of making money. Unfortunately, our political leaders in the North and South, obviously fail to realize that what's bad for business is also bad for America. Meaning, a war is the last thing we need." He sighed loudly.

"Not only does it have the potential to cripple America, but most of Europe as well." Nathaniel Sr. informed Thaddeus, as if it really mattered to him. Actually, Thaddeus relished the thought of a war taking place between the North and South. Especially, if it meant a potential end to slavery. As far as the American, and European economies being effected, Thaddeus could also care less. As far as he was concerned it was totally unfair how such a small percentage of men, on both continents enjoyed enormous wealth, while the majority of people struggled and starved. Not just blacks, he told himself, recalling that several of his customers on the market had been poor white families.

"Why do you say that Europe would suffer as well?" Thaddeus had asked, simply for the sake of 'acting' as though he was interested.

"Not only is Raw Cotton 60% of Americans export, but us southerners supply over 80% of the cotton manufactured in Britain. Not to mention, two thirds of the world's supply." Nathaniel Sr. informed him with a smile.

"How certain are you, that a war is on the horizon?" Thaddeus wanted to know.

"I'm about to tell you a story, that I want you to keep between the two of us." Nathaniel Sr. stared at Thaddeus in his eyes.

"I'm listening." was Thaddeus's only reply.

"A few years ago, a friend of mine who's actually a politician by the name of Senator Andrew P. Butler, was on the receiving end of some really harsh words. Scorn actually, by a yankee politician named Senator Charles Sumner, while making a presentation on the floor in Washington D.C.

"Senator Sumner, went as far as heaping criticism on the

entire state of South Carolina. Can you believe that?" Nathaniel Sr. shook his head in disbelief.

"Naturally, and rightfully so, my good friend Senator Butler didn't take too kindly to such criticism. Had I been in his shoes I can't say how I would have reacted. However, the following day, a cousin of Senator Butler, who also happens to be a politician, approached that same yankee senator with a full mouth, and commenced to whipping him with his metal cane." Nathaniel Sr. laughed out loud.

Thaddeus, simply held the man's stare. Wondering if there was actually truth to the story.

"I hear, he beat that yankee till he was bleeding and unconscious." Nathaniel Sr. smiled proudly.

Thaddeus noticed that he'd never offered the name of the politician who'd assaulted Senator Sumner.

"Did the man who whipped him get in trouble?" Thaddeus asked.

"Sure did." Nathaniel Sr. replied, before adding, "Had to pay a Three Hundred dollar fine. But, he was allowed to keep his position."

Thaddeus had no comment.

"Anyway, I said all of that to say, the assault of Senator Sumner added fuel to an already burning fire. In fact, the pressure to change the south's position has not only increased, but, it is in my opinion that a war between the state's is inevitable." He explained, leaving out the fact that he had first-hand knowledge that South Carolina was only weeks away from becoming the first state to secede from the Union.

In light of knowing what he did, Nathaniel L. Pinkney had already began putting his plans into motion. He opened an all-purpose store on the market, no longer supplying his competitors.

Nor did he inform Thaddeus that an Illinois Senator, and leader of the new grassroots Republican party, had just won the presidential election, that mans name was Abraham Lincoln.

"So are you going to tell me, how my returning to the plantation fits into all of what you've told me?" Thaddeus asked out of curiosity.

"For starters, I always knew that it was 'not' my son's idea to send you out there on the market to sell my produce. Not only was I impressed by your coming up with the idea, but moreover your potential or rather, ability to awaken the entrepreneurial spirit in my boy. Which I never knew he possessed." He smiled.

Thaddeus however, had to witness Nathaniel Jr's entrepreneurial spirit considering he'd done 'all' of the work. Nevertheless, he was truly thankful that his friend had agreed to go along with his plan.

"Once the war begins," Nathaniel Sr. continued, "The economy is going to be hit hard, which is one of the repercussions of war. Yet, you and I are going to let it be our stepping stone." He smiled, at the same time watching Thaddeus's reaction to what he'd said. Seeing there was none, he continued.

"I have always been pretty accurate in my predictions. Therefore, I want to not only produce as many bales of cotton as possible, but more importantly, it is my intensions to store just as many."

"To enable you to control the price?" Thaddeus asked.

"Wouldn't you agree it's about time I did so? I mean, my associates in the North have been capitalizing long enough, or more so, taking advantage of my kindness, product, and hard labor long enough. I say it is time to turn the tables. Besides, it will still cost me

an arm and a leg, as far as shipment is concerned. But at least, I will be seeing much greater profits for my cotton."

"Something tells me that you already have the issues of shipment worked out as well." Thaddeus commented.

"If you and your two brothers agree to take the helm, however you see fit to handle and increase production in Mt. Pleasant, I'm willing to make it worth your while."

"How so?" Thaddeus inquired.

"For starters, your freedom." Nathaniel Sr. revealed with a smile.

"I believe you completely, when you say that you're pretty

accurate in your predictions. Therefore, I also believe that a war between the North and South is inevitable. That being the case, if the North wins the war my brothers and I will potentially gain our freedom anyway. So, your 'starter' really isn't a great incentive." Thaddeus explained, as he held Mr. Pinkney's stare.

Opposed to giving an immediate response, Nathaniel Sr. continued to stare into the eyes of the young black man, whom he practically raised. Well, not exactly raised, but provided for, he thought to himself. Producing a smile, he also couldn't help thinking how he wished Nathaniel Jr. possessed Thaddeus's overall intellect. Never mind the fact that his son was away at college, what impressed him more was what had 'always' impressed him, which was a man's ability to generate Capital.

"How much money do you want?" Mr. Pinkney inquired.

"Truthfully, money is not what I had entirely in mind." Thaddeus replied. He had saved over Ten Thousand dollars over the years, working the market.

"I'm interested in owning some land of my own." Thaddeus revealed before adding, "Not just any piece of land either. But, land that will enable me to grow my own produce, rice, and cotton."

"That's not a problem." Mr. Pinkney replied.

"Also, my brothers and my 'guaranteed' freedom, regardless to the outcome of the war." Thaddeus added.

"Not a problem." Mr. Pinkney added.

"By the way, I won't be needing any credit from you to buy the necessities I will need to cultivate my land. Whatever produce and cotton I intend to sell, I'd like to eventually make an arrangement with you whereas, you will buy the bulk of it at a discount price that will still enable you to make a profit."

"Sounds good to me."

The two of them sealed their deal with a handshake.

Thaddeus, realized he could never underestimate Nathaniel Sr., who had been totally correct in his predictions. Not only was the state of South Carolina the first state to secede from the Union, announcing that it would 'no longer' tolerate the encroachment of the federal government on a State's rights! But, shortly after, fired on Fort Sumter! Which was a federal garrison in the Charleston Harbor.

The Civil War, officially began when President Lincoln dispatched 75,000 volunteer soldiers to the South. His promise to keep the Union together *'at all cost'* was made obvious to anyone watching!

Over Ten years had passed, since Thaddeus had left the plantation to live with Ms. Corice and the Pinkney's. And although, the Pinkney family was certainly a rare breed, in terms of slave owners and how they treated their slaves, Thaddeus was nonetheless disappointed to find how badly they (the slaves) were actually living upon his return to the plantation.

Ramshackle, was the only word he could think of, seeing the conditions of their wood cabins, which were borderline deplorable!

"I want you to get everyone together." Thaddeus informed his oldest brother, Albertus, shortly after his return.

"Everyone?" Albertus asked with a raised eyebrow.

"Yes, including those working inside of the house." Thaddeus replied.

As Thaddeus went on to inspect the fields, that same evening, he overheard the majority of the field hands singing a song. The chorus, he noticed was; "Steal Away." Unbeknownst to Thaddeus, it was a song that slaves would sing to indicate that, a 'meeting' would be held that night.

As nightfall arrived, Thaddeus counted a total of 31 (apparently abled) bodies. However, that number excluded the elderly, and small children.

"I realize that many of you are exhausted from today's work. Especially, those of you who have been out in the sun tending to the fields." Thaddeus began his speech.

"How would you know?" Someone in the crowd shouted.

"Yeah, when have you ever worked a field?" Another voice shouted out.

"Will you folks hush that noise, so the rest of us can hear what this young man is trying to say!" A woman, whom Thaddeus guessed to be at least 75 years old, addressed the crowd.

Yet, Thaddeus did not know at the time, the older woman's name was Clarice, who was also Ms. Corice's older sister.

"Thank you." Thaddeus thanked the woman.

"Today, I took the liberty to inspect the majority of you alls living quarters, if that is what you want to call them." Thaddeus made eye contact with as many in the crowd as possible.

"It is in my opinion that, the cabins you all are living in aren't fit for 'livestock'." He emphasized the word livestock.

"That aint' nothing but the truth!" Someone in the crowd shouted in agreement.

"Amen to that!" Clarice, Corice's sister shouted.

"As of tomorrow morning, my two brothers and I, will officially be responsible for the overall production of Mr. Pinkney's cotton. I understand that planting, picking, cleaning, and bundling cotton is back breaking work.

"However, I am more than prepared to get out there and do as much of the work, as many of you. Why? Because along with my labor, a vested interest is attached." Thaddeus spoke honestly to the crowd.

"A vested interest for my brothers and I, also meaning a change for the better for all of you."

Not only did Thaddeus have their full attention, no one spoke out in response.

"No longer will there be abled men, and healthy young women doing household chores inside of the Pinkney's residence. Instead, that will be a job for our older women and children who are of age.

"I want all of us who are able and healthy to begin making necessary improvements to our homes. None of you should have to live the way you all have been living." He added.

"I don't think the Pinkney's will take too kindly to your telling us that we can no longer prepare their meals, as well as conduct our usual chores." A black man spoke out, who was obviously a house servant.

"What is your name Ma'am?" Thaddeus asked the older woman, who had hushed the others moments earlier.

"My name is Clarice."

Returning his attention towards the man who had obviously been a house servant, Thaddeus continued to speak.

"As of tomorrow morning, we will let Ms. Clarice worry about 'who' will feed and clean up after Elizabeth and Andrew Pinkney. I'm confident she'll appoint the right person for the position. Isn't that right ma'am?" Thaddeus asked Ms. Clarice

"Ms. Mable will do just fine." Clarice replied, returning a smile.

Truthfully, her 'smile' was directed towards the man named Penceal, who had been the Pinkney's #1 house servant, whom she was delighted to see was finally being taken down from his high-horse. Especially, being that he'd had a tendency to speak down towards the rest of them.

"My understanding is that, the cotton seeds have recently been planted. Which gives us time to work on the re-building of our homes. I also realize that, there are several other smaller chores that will require tending to, but we'll work together to get things done to the Pinkney's satisfaction." Thaddeus added, making eye contact with the man named Penceal.

"As I'm sure you all are aware, there is a war going on. That being the case, Mr. Pinkney's number one concern is his business of cotton." Thaddeus termed it just as Nathaniel Sr. had.

"In closing, I am proud to inform you all that, most of the homes in which we will commence to re-building, will be situated on our 'own' land!

FOUR

MT. PLEASANT, SOUTH CAROLINA, 1862

In 1862, one year after the Civil War began, Confederate soldiers were given the order to torch all cotton fields to render them worthless to invading union troops. In fact, they burned down thousands of acres!

In turn, union troops also set fires to the fields to prevent the South from harvesting and selling cotton, and crops to fund its war efforts.

"I hope you know that most of the neighboring farmers, and white folks in general are labeling Mr. Pinkney a traitor. Some even saying that the man is guilty of treason." A slave named Norman, from a neighboring plantation (which Nathaniel Sr. owned the deed to the land,) informed Thaddeus.

Having already heard such talk, Thaddeus nonetheless feigned surprised.

"Really? And why is that?"

"Because Mr. Pinkney is obviously continuing to sell his cotton to the North, instead of discontinuing its growth or simply burning it. His actions are in contrast to the South's cause." Norman added, speaking as if the 'cause' actually benefitted him.

"I'm confident Mr. Pinkney is not concerned with such gossip. Not to mention, treason is a very serious accusation

Norman."

"I'm just telling you what I heard." Norman responded. The last thing he wanted, was his name associated with gossip.

Thaddeus witnessed, first-hand the staggering amounts of bales (of cotton) in which Nathaniel Sr. was shipping North. Yet, he was also smart enough to know that Mr. Pinkney was inevitably aligned with some equally powerful and/or influential individuals seeing the frequency and effortlessness of his shipments. Especially, in the midst of a war!

It was no secret that the North possessed the majority of the ships, as well as controlled the railroads. The Union Army established effective navy blockades, along the South's seaboard, shortly after the war began. Hindering farmers, and planters from capitalizing off their crops.

Cotton production in the South, plummeted from 4.5 million bales in 1861, to only 1 million bales by 1862, as the unions blockade thwarted large transport. As a result, about 1/3 of Great Britain's textile factories had to shut down, leaving half a million of its factory hands out of work!

Those kinds of statistics only lent to Thaddeus's awe of Nathaniel Sr., a man from whom, he realized he could learn a great deal.

As far as Nathaniel Sr. was concerned, he was not at all concerned with the events nor the suffering that was taking place all around him. Not even 'he' could have predicted the magnitude of economic decline the war would have on the country, and abroad! Yet, in spite of the fallen economy, 'Pinkney' found himself enjoying greater profits then before the war began.

His stores, he'd open at least two more shortly after the war commenced, were thriving. As a store owner/merchant, 'Pinkney' gave credit to majority of the planters, farmers, and land owners throughout the Low-Country region. All of whom, were basically land rich, but literally cash-poor! However, Nathaniel Sr. was so wealthy, it didn't bother him that most of his profits were on the books, opposed to in-pocket.

The merchandise he provided, not only had a 30% to 50%

mark up (above their cash value) his interest rate on loans and/ or lines of credit were as high as 70%! Considering, there being on the 'books' not in-pocket. As a result, that same majority or planters, farmers, and land owners, couldn't maintain their obligation. Thus, found themselves having to turn over their deeds to Nathaniel Sr.

The fact that 'Pinkney' had sent his son Nathaniel Jr. to attend college (Harvard) in Cambridge, Massachusetts, Thaddeus couldn't help noticing, was also a part of his calculated plans. Being that, it was Nathaniel Jr. who negotiated any and all changes in price pertaining to the bales of cotton that his father continued to ship to his associates in Boston and Lowell.

When all of this is said and done, not a single one of the 50 plus slaves residing on Pinkney Plantation could believe how much things had changed, for the better, under Thaddeus's direction.

Although the field work was no less strenuous, especially having to 'carry' the newly picked sacks of cotton (which could weigh up to 200 to 300 pounds) nearly a mile to the cotton gin to be weighed, cleaned, and bundled which was backbreaking work!

Fortunately, the slaves also got to enjoy (new) rewards. Even Penceal came around and seemed to be in much better spirit, Thaddeus had noticed.

Four days out of the week, everyone, including Thaddeus and his two brothers, worked from Sun up till Sundown. Or rather, from Sunrise to Sunset. However, Fridays, were reserved for families to enjoy their time with one another. Saturdays, usually saw everyone coming together to have a good time (dancing, singing, eating, kids playing etc.), even slaves from neighboring plantations were invited to join in. Most slave owners didn't have a problem allowing their slaves to join the festivities taking place on Saturdays at Pinkney Plantation, only because the majority of them were indebt with 'Pinkney' and were willing to do whatever cast them in favorable light. Sundays, of course, were reserved for Worship/Church service.

Albertus, was now married to a woman named Yvette, and

the pair had a 3-year-old daughter named Monique.

Granville, had also married a woman named Sarah, they also had a daughter named Danielle, who was now 4 years old. As for Thaddeus, he was still single.

"I think the only thing you're missing in your life is a good woman. I can only imagine, what you'd be capable of achieving with the right woman beside you." Ms. Clarice gave Thaddeus her honest assessment and opinion.

"It'll happen." Thaddeus replied. "Right now, I'm more focused on building." He told her. Building, included personal wealth, land, business, and whatever else that he felt imperative to the guarantee of stability when he 'did' decide to marry and start a family.

APRIL 9, 1865

On April 9, 1865, slaves throughout the South could be heard in their rejoice! Truthfully, most still couldn't believe the news… General Robert E. Lee and his Confederate Army had surrendered!

"I pretty much knew the end was near, upon hearing that President Lincoln had approved the sending of food to Petersburg, Virginia, for General Lee and his soldiers." Nathaniel Sr. informed Thaddeus.

Thaddeus, however, couldn't fathom the president having to send food to enemy troops. Yet, he also knew not to doubt anything that came out of the mouth of Nathaniel L. Pinkney!

Things did not change immediately for blacks in the South, following the war's end. However, many former slaves did decide to leave the South.

"Why would you entertain the thought of migrating North or West, when we have our own land, homes, and are accumulating money?" Thaddeus asked his brother Granville, who informed him of his desire to leave South Carolina.

"I have some money saved, and I hear that factory jobs are prevalent especially in the North." Granville countered.

"As far as I'm concerned, the ending of slavery is a clear sign of the times to come. I seriously doubt that the majority of black folk who relocated to the big cities are enjoying a piece of the American pie, because them white folk aint' gonna let anyone come in and take their jobs. Most aren't gonna allow you to work beside them."

Granville had no reply, he simply listened as he held his younger brother's stare.

"Independence is nothing without means. It would be really foolish for me to leave what all I've built, for a so-called land of opportunity and promise." Thaddeus added. He knew the transition would be hard for the majority, who'd relocated, considering most had defected with little money!

In the end, Thaddeus was thankful that his brother had accepted his logic and reasoning. Others who had stayed, newly freed slaves throughout the South, simply hoped and Prayed that the Government kept its promise of what was termed; Reconstruction!

Being that a great deal of the war had been fought in the state of South Carolina, most of its cities (especially Columbia) were left in ruins. Therefore, a great majority of former slave owners were grateful to those former slaves who'd decided to remain with them. Unfortunately, due to the war and economic situation, most of those former slave owners were not in position to pay the now freed blacks for their labor. Instead, they were given land and livestock, while some simply worked for food, clothing, and shelter.

With the arrival of Reconstruction, freed blacks were now allowed to attend school. With the passage of the 14th (and later 15th) Amendments to the U.S. Constitution, blacks found themselves able to vote as well. In fact, many blacks, throughout the South, were elected to serve in various sectors of Political Office. One of the notables was, Hiriam Revels, a black man who became a

U.S. Senator filling the seat of former Confederate President Jefferson Davis of Mississippi.

With the forming of the Freedmen's Bureau, which was established to transition former slaves into enfranchised citizens, particularly those who themselves totally abandoned with the ending of slavery, providing them food, clothing and shelter, as well.

It was also during this era, of Reconstruction, that several Black Colleges, especially across the South, were established.

Yet, all was certainly 'not' well in the South. At least, not as far as white folks were concerned. There were actually, more than 30,000 federal troops that had to be sent to the South as 'peace keepers', in what had now become considered 'occupied territory' after the War failed to deter violent Whites from mounting campaigns of terror.

It was also during this period of Reconstruction that, an infamous group of whites, primarily in the South, came into existence, labeling themselves; The Ku Klux Klan...

FIVE

MT. PLEASANT, SOUTH CAROLINA, 1869

When Andrew Johnson, a former slave owner, was sworn in as the 17th President of the United States, in 1866, he made it clear that he was not interested in the welfare of former slaves! Not only did 'Johnson' veto the expansion of the Freedmen's Bureau, he also looked the other way as southern leaders instituted "Black Codes" which restricted the freedom(s) of black people.

President Johnson also made it clear that, the Government was a Government for the White man. That being said, he put white southerners, who had formerly been banned from holding government positions after the war, back into the National Government. An act, that led to 'Johnson's' impeachment!

In 1867, Congress took charge of Reconstruction, removing it from the hands of President Johnson and in 1868, Congress also passed the 15th Amendment, which allowed Black men to 'vote' throughout the country.

Lynching's, which were rare before the Civil War, had now become common.

Whites furious with the North, and Republicans, for interfering in its Society, caused the Ku Klux Klan to wage a war on blacks/former slaves.

"I'm not sure if Emancipation was a gift or a curse for

black folks!" Ms. Clarice commented, at the same time shaking her head.

Opposed to responding, Thaddeus remained deep in thought as a result of a recent statistic he'd read, which revealed that, from 1866 to 1869 at least One Hundred black men, women, and children, had been murdered (by Whites) each year, in the South.

The racial tension had become so bad, Thaddeus, no longer intervened when Granville expressed his desire to leave the South.

"Just because my wife and I are relocating to Chicago, doesn't mean I won't be here for you if you ever need me." Granville had told Thaddeus shortly before he, Sarah and their daughter loaded their belongings onto the railway car, and departed for the mid-west.

Excluding, Albertus and his family, and Ms. Clarice, only four families decided to remain on the Addison's land in Mt. Pleasant

Of the four remaining families, Ralph Coleman and his family had relocated to New York City, only to return to Mt. Pleasant.

"When I heard blacks were able to find work in the factories, no one told me that, I'd be stuck sweeping floors. Which didn't pay nearly enough to feed myself, let alone a wife and two children." Ralph had revealed to Thaddeus upon his return.

"Glad to have you back." Thaddeus responded, considering he truly was glad to have Ralph Coleman back, especially since he'd needed as many capable hands as possible to assist in building the elementary school that he was erecting on his property.

Thaddeus, also, couldn't help being thankful that he had not fallen victim to crop damage, property damage, crosses being burnt on his property, and threats (by whites), which the majority of land owning blacks found themselves being subjected to. Then again, his relationship with the Pinkney family was no secret, therefore, he couldn't help wondering if Nathaniel L. Pinkney had placed an unspoken blanket of protection over him and his property.

"Or, is it you?" Thaddeus asked, looking towards the sky. He had always felt that his mother Arethea, was watching over him and his brothers, from heaven. How else could he explain his good fortune?

"I'm glad to see you're still around," Nathaniel Jr. had a broad smile on his face, as he approached Thaddeus.

"Where am I going? This is where my foundation has been laid." At that, the two childhood friends engaged in a bear hug.

"It's really great to see you." Nathaniel Jr. reiterated before separating.

"This young lady here, happens to be my fiancé, Melissa." Nathaniel Jr. introduced the woman who now stood beside him, to Thaddeus.

"It's a pleasure to meet you Ms. Melissa." Thaddeus extended his right hand to her.

"Actually, the pleasure is mine. I've heard so many good things about you! Melissa exclaimed, ignoring Thaddeus's hand, instead, she moved in for a hug.

Considering, it was Thaddeus's first time *'ever'* being hugged by a white woman, he wasn't sure if he should return the embrace.

Having always prided himself on knowing Thaddeus better than

anyone, Nathaniel Jr. smiled, before making his comment.

"What's the matter? Don't tell me, you've never hugged a beautiful woman before?" Nathaniel Jr's smile turned into a laugh.

Relieved, that Melissa had let go of him, Thaddeus replied. "I see you still have jokes. "

"Oh, so he was always a prankster?" Melissa commented, giving Thaddeus her full attention.

"Since childhood." Thaddeus informed her with a smile.

Nathaniel Jr's smile was still in place also, seeing how Melissa obviously had Thaddeus's approval, he thought to himself.

"Are you available to have dinner with me, Melissa, and my parents tonight?" Nathaniel Jr. asked. "We'd all love for you to join us!"

Thaddeus seriously doubted that Ruth Pinkney would 'love' to see him seated at her dining table. However, he did miss his friend who had been away for nearly nine years.

"Yes, I'll be able to make it." Thaddeus replied.

"By the way," Nathaniel Jr began, "I hear that, you and my father have accomplished some pretty amazing things over the years." He smiled.

"I wonder 'who' told you that?" Thaddeus laughed.

APRIL 11, 1870

Although, they didn't get to see much of each other these days, Thaddeus was nonetheless proud of what all Nathaniel Jr was achieving for himself. In fact, he had attended the celebration party that Nathaniel Sr. had thrown in honor of his son's newly established Law Firm, located in the City of Charleston.

Today, was Nathaniel Jr. and Melissa's engagement celebration which was held at the Pinkney's mansion. In attendance was, Melissa's parents, whom Thaddeus had learned were extremely wealthy! J.C. Lawrence, Melissa's father, was not only one of Boston's wealthiest textile magnates, but was born into great wealth. Whereas, Melissa's mother, Gloria Blythewood-Lawrence, derived from one of Delaware's wealthiest families.

Therefore, Melissa was probably worth as much as Nathaniel Jr., if not more, Thaddeus thought to himself.

"Well, Hello neighbor." Thaddeus turned to find Elizabeth Pinkney standing behind him with a huge smile on her face.

"Please do not let the smile fool you. I am truly pissed off that, we live right beside one another, yet I have to attend my brother's engagement party to see you."

She shook her head.

"It's not like that." Thaddeus replied, returning her smile.

"You and Andrew know that I am a workaholic. More so,

since I've begun building the school, and church on my property." He added.

"Yes, thank goodness I have Clarice to keep me informed."

At that, Thaddeus laughed. He could see Clarice bragging
about his endeavors.

"How are the twins?" he asked

"Raymond is the sweetest baby you'd ever want to hold.
But that Rollin!" Elizabeth shook her head. "I don't think I've
ever seen a child with such a mean streak. And, he's only two!"

"Hopefully, he'll grow out of it." Thaddeus offered.

"Is there something I can get the two of you to drink?"

"No thank you." Elizabeth replied.

Thaddeus, however, was momentarily speechless, as he
came face to face with the most gorgeous woman he'd ever
laid eyes on.

"Is there something wrong?" The beautiful black woman,
who was serving drinks inquired with a smile on her face.

"I'm sorry." Thaddeus apologized.

"Sorry for what?" She asked, with a slight smile still in
place.

"For staring, I guess." Never in his life could Thaddeus recall being at such a loss for words.

"It's not a problem Sir." She responded, adding 'Sir' because
she realized Thaddeus must be someone important seeing how
he was the only black face amongst the guest.

"If you decide you 'do' want a drink, I'll be close by." She
informed him before walking off.

Thaddeus, trailed her with his eyes.

"Why didn't you just ask her out?" Elizabeth said with a
laugh.

"Wow! I'm sorry." Thaddeus apologized, he'd totally forgotten that Elizabeth was standing beside him.

"I think you need to stop apologizing and go after her."
Elizabeth suggested, glad to finally see that someone 'did' exist,
who could capture Thaddeus's attention. She was well aware
that, Clarice had been trying to get him to date for years!

"I have to go find Andrew, so we can get out of here. Don't

like being away from my babies for too long." With that being said, Elizabeth kissed Thaddeus on his cheek, whispering, "I'm serious, you need to go after her."

Opposed to going after the woman, whom the Pinkney's had serving their guest, Thaddeus searched for Nathaniel Jr.

"Excuse me." Nathaniel Jr excused himself from Melissa and her parents, as he spotted Thaddeus.

"Would you happen to know the woman's name, whom your parents have serving the drinks?" Thaddeus didn't waste any time posing his question.

"Can't say that I do. However, she is quite beautiful." Nathaniel Jr knew exactly who Thaddeus was inquiring about.

"If Melissa wasn't so amazing," Nathaniel Jr continued, but was suddenly interrupted as Melissa made her approach.

"Well thank you!" She kissed Nathaniel Jr on the cheek. "You're quite amazing yourself."

"Thaddeus, are you enjoying yourself?" Melissa inquired with a smile on her face.

"Yes, thank you." Thaddeus replied.

"He was just asking me if I knew the young woman, mother has serving drinks." Nathaniel Jr informed her.

Turning to face Thaddeus once again, Melissa's smile broadened.

"So, I take it you're interested in Rebecca?"

MAY 6, 1872

We've come a long way." Nathaniel Jr raised his champagne glass.

"From building tree-houses, to starting families." Thaddeus responded, tapping his glass against Nathaniel Jr's.

"Thank you." Nathaniel Jr added.

For what?"

"For allowing me to be your Best Man."

"Truthfully, it was a no brainer, seeing how you're the only best friend I've ever had." Thaddeus responded sincerely. Nor was he offended, that 'he' had not been Nathaniel Jr's best man at his wedding, when he and Melissa tied the knot, mainly because it was no secret that Ruth Pinkney insisted that her son-in-law Andrew have that honor.

"Can I get the two of you something to eat?" Ms. Corice approached the two of them with a huge smile on her face, yet they both could tell that she had been crying.

"No thank you." Both men replied in unison.

"I saw you crying when I handed Thaddeus the ring." Nathaniel Jr revealed smiling.

"Seeing Thaddeus making his vow was one thing, but seeing my two boys standing side by side," Ms. Corice couldn't even finish her sentence. Both men wrapped their arms around the woman who had been friend, protector, tutor, and a second Mother, to the both of them.

"Have you seen my Wife?" Thaddeus inquired, once the three of them had composed themselves.

"I'll go find her for you." Ms. Corice offered. "Last I saw her, she was with Yvette, Sarah, Monique, Danielle, and Melissa."

Thaddeus, was elated that his brother Granville and his family had come down from Chicago to attend his wedding.

"At eight months pregnant, your wife sure looked good in her wedding gown." Ms. Corice added, before walking off to find Rebecca.

"I still can't believe you're about to be a father!" Nathaniel Jr smiled proudly. "You were single for so long, I was beginning to wonder if your Mrs. Right even existed."

At that, they shared a laughed.

"It's not just her beauty, Rebecca's just different." Thaddeus tried to explain.

"Different how? And from whom?" Rebecca inquired, catching the last part of Thaddeus's remark, as she and Melissa made their approach.

All eyes were now on Thaddeus.

"It may take the rest of our lives for me to describe or explain how, in all the ways you are 'different' from any woman who has ever been in my presence. However, I relish the thought of learning, experiencing, and enjoying, all that you are, and have to give."

That being said, Thaddeus went down on one knee and kissed her fully clothed stomach.

"I think I'm gonna cry." Melissa's eyes watered as she held onto her husband.

"Me too!" Nathaniel Jr joked, as he wiped at his eyes.

At that, they all laughed.

"I see some things will never change." Nathaniel Jr. added.

"What do you mean?" Melissa asked, looking into his eyes.

"My good friend Thaddeus, has *'always'* been a master of vocabulary."

SIX

CHARLESTON, SOUTH CAROLINA, 1874

"You mind telling me again, what made you decide to run for Mayor? Thaddeus was dismayed by Nathaniel Jr's decision. "Especially, seeing how you'd be earning significantly less money than what you're making as an attorney." He added.

"Honestly, it's not about the money." Nathaniel Jr began. "Plus, I'd still own my Law Firm."

Unbeknownst to Thaddeus, it was Nathaniel L. Pinkney Sr. who had been pressuring his son to run for public office. A suggestion, that met the approval of his mother, as well as his wife Melissa. In fact, Nathaniel Sr. all but guaranteed his victory!

"In that case, why do you feel the need to drag me down here to the courthouse?" Thaddeus inquired as the two of them were about to enter the Courthouse, in downtown Charleston.

"This won't take long. I just thought it would be quite inspiring for you to meet a friend of mine." Nathaniel Jr responded.

As they reached what was apparently a Judge's chamber, Nathaniel Jr lightly tapped on its door, before entering.

"Your Honor." Nathaniel Jr addressed the man seated behind the large polished oak desk. "This here is my good friend,

Thaddeus Addison, whom I've told you about." He smiled, as he introduced Thaddeus, who stood beside him, momentarily speechless.

"Thaddeus, it is such a pleasure to finally meet you." The Judge offered his right hand for the purpose of a handshake.

"Nathaniel, has told me quite a bit about you over the years, since he and I have been friends and colleagues for some years now. Actually, he and I met while we were both up and coming lawyers. Well, I was up and coming, whereas, Nathaniel had pretty much arrived at the top of his game." The Judge laughed, although he was serious.

Fortunately, following Reconstruction, I went on to become a Judge, in the Inferior Court, here in Charleston. As you can see, I'm now graduated to Probate Judge." He offered a smile.

"Not exactly the Supreme Court, but it's a long way and great achievement, since having to hustle for clients.

"You can say *'that'* again." Nathaniel Jr co-signed, as if he'd ever had to hustle for clients.

"In any event, I was quite delighted when Nathaniel offered to bring you by, so I could finally meet you. He told me that it was you, and a woman by the name of Ms. Corice, who not only taught him in his early years, but also how he would not have made it into Harvard had it not been for the two of you.

"I was more so impressed to learn that you and Ms. Corice were both slaves during much of that period. All that being said, it is truly a pleasure to meet you."

The Honorable Macon Bolling Allen then walked from behind his desk and extended his arms.

All Nathaniel Jr could do was smile, as he witnessed the two successful men engage in a brotherly hug.

As for Thaddeus, who had remained speechless thus far, he was still at a loss for words. Actually, he couldn't help feeling a bit choked up, upon hearing that the first and only African American Judge he had ever seen or heard of for that matter, was impressed by *'his'* story....

Once again, old man Pinkney Sr., had come through on another of his promises. Thaddeus couldn't help thinking to himself, upon receiving word that Nathaniel Pinkney Jr had won the Mayoral race, and was now 'officially' the Mayor of the City of Charleston.

Nevertheless, Thaddeus was extremely happy for Nathaniel Jr. the 'unofficial'

Godfather of his and Rebecca's daughter, Arethea, who was named after his mother.

The year following, Nathaniel Jr's victory, he succeeded in his effort to have a City park named in honor of his (late) Grandfather, Charles Joseph Pinkney. It was

Nathaniel L. Pinkney Sr., who went as far as having a bronze statue created in his father's likeness, which he (himself) took the pleasure of unveiling at a public ceremony held in the park!

One year later, Congress passed the Civil Rights Act of 1875, which outlawed discrimination in hotels, restaurants, theaters, and amusement parks. At the time, no one knew 'it' would be the last great Legislation of Reconstruction....

The following year, 1876, President Ulysses S. Grant's successor, Rutherford B. Hayes, ordered federal troops 'out' of the South!

'Hayes' accepted the promise (of Southern whites) that 'they' would protect the rights southern blacks. Unfortunately, their promise proved worthless. Basically, with no one there to protect or enforce the Civil Rights of blacks, Reconstruction was over!

The Pinkney's', and Addison's, continued to profit off their cotton arrangement long after the Civil War had ended. In fact, Thaddeus Addison, was among the wealthiest black men in Charleston.

"To what do I owe the pleasure of such an unexpected visit?"

"I'm very impressed by what all you've built out here." Nathaniel L Pinkney Sr commented, as he looked about Thaddeus's property. At the same time removing his hat from his head.

Thaddeus, however, was truly surprised to see the elder Pinkney. He couldn't remember the last time Mr. Pinkney had paid a visit to Mt. Pleasant. Especially, to visit 'his' dwellings.

"Thank you, Sir." Thaddeus replied to the man's compliment. Nonetheless, curious as to what the unexpected visit was about.

"Am I correct to assume that you have never traveled outside of the state of South Carolina?" Mr. Pinkney inquired, even though he was pretty certain that Thaddeus had not.

"No Sir, I have not."

"That's what I thought." Mr. Pinkney sucked his tooth loudly, something he tended to do more so when he had something on his mind.

"I want you to make preparations for a trip." He revealed.

"A trip to where Sir?" Thaddeus inquired with a raised eyebrow.

"Actually, I'd like for you to accompany me to the State of Pennsylvania." Mr. Pinkney revealed, before adding, "Thaddeus my dear boy, you and I are going to the City of Brotherly Love, for the Centennial Exhibition."

PHILADELPHIA, PA, 1876

Upon their arrival in Philadelphia, Thaddeus was totally blown away by the enormity of the city's streets, and its splendid buildings! What impressed him most, however, was the startling array of American ingenuity! On display before his eyes, was technology in which Thaddeus was certain would knock down age-old obstacles to progress, and literally throw open the doors of utopia!

In front of him, was the Sewing Machine, the Typewriter, and the Bell Telephone!

"Thousands of people are here, some to witness and cheer the nation's productivity and resourcefulness. Others, to simply bask in the promise of a glorious future." Nathaniel Sr spoke proudly, as if he had a hand in the creation of all the new technology on display.

As they moved along, the sudden vision of what now stood before their eyes, brought a sense of clarity to Thaddeus as to why they had actually come to Philadelphia.

"Isn't she beautiful?" Nathaniel Sr. asked, as he marveled at the sight before him.

"I've never seen anything like it!" Thaddeus exclaimed.

On display before their eyes, stood the "Corliss Centennial" steam engine!

The circular, churning 'Corliss' behemoth stood about three stories high and occupied an entire building! It was said, that it provided power for fourteen acres of surrounding machinery!

"Not only is that thing extremely well-constructed, I'm told that the 'lines' it makes are astonishing!" Mr. Pinkney offered, yet, his eyes were glued to the Corliss.

"I'll be the first to admit that, I'm not the most knowledgeable person when it applies to technology, but something tells me that thing is about to change the business of cotton." Thaddeus replied, referring to the Corliss.

"You have no idea." Nathaniel Sr responded more so to himself.

Thaddeus, took his eyes away the machinery to glance over at Mr. Pinkney, who had a look in his eyes as if he'd been allowed a glimpse into Heaven.

Up until the invent of the Corliss, nature, had basically set the ground rules. Hydraulic power brought cotton and wool 'mills' to the fixed energy sources of New England, its rivers and waterfalls, and then brought 'towns' to the mills as Urban areas rose up around smokestacks and bell towers to provide for the needs of a stationary workforce. Not anymore.

The flexibility of coal-fueled 'steam power' would enable Nathaniel L. Pinkney and 'Carolina' to replace Massachusetts as the center of American cotton manufacturer.

"Yes, I think the time has arrived, for me to build my own mills, which will enable me to manufacture raw cotton into cloth." Mr. Pinkney voiced his intentions. Yet, he kept to himself that, he would also hire his own Printers, to dye the cloth as well. All he had to do now, was figure out a way to cut out the middleman, New York and Boston, and transport his material to Europe through his own means, he told himself. All of which, he'd explain to Thaddeus on their journey home, he also told himself.

"Your plan sounds quite major." Thaddeus had to admit, yet, he was still curious as to why he'd been invited on the trip.

"Although, I am indeed flattered that you've allowed me to accompany you on this jaw-dropping adventure. Why exactly 'am' I here?"

His question, provoked a hearty laugh from Nathaniel Pinkney.

"Thaddeus my boy, I do not know or understand how you have not realized by now that, something about you has always peeked my interest in you." The older man said with a smile.

"Thank You." Thaddeus was truly flattered by the compliment.

"Throughout my years, I've had more dealings with more men than I care to think of. Fortunately, however, my dealings have also enabled me to become an excellent judge of character.

"Some of the men I've had dealings with clearly possessed great knowledge and ideas even, yet, lacked the necessary determination to make anything prosper. You Thaddeus," Mr. Pinkney looked Thaddeus in his eyes.

"Have intellect, ideas, motivation, and enough determination to get the job done." He smiled.

The compliment brought a smile to Thaddeus's face as well. Yet, he remained silent, being that he knew it was more to 'why' he had been invited on such a trip.

"In light of the above, I have decided to change your life as you know it." He revealed.

"By presenting you with an opportunity of a lifetime." Mr. Pinkney added.

"Which is?" Thaddeus inquired, holding the older man's stare.

"Never in any of my businesses, or business dealings, have I ever taken on a partner or investors." Mr. Pinkney revealed "Nor would I ever, if it isn't family. Which you already know that I have long considered you." He added with a smile.

Thaddeus simply nodded his head up and down, knowing he always felt like Nathaniel Sr. had indeed treated him somewhat like a son.

"To build my own mills and the town around them, combined with the cost of the Corliss. I'm looking to kick out about a million dollars give or take." Mr. Pinkney guesstimated.

To the average person, especially a black man in the South, in 1876, the tune of a million dollars was unfathomable! However, Thaddeus Addison, was not the average black man or southerner, therefore, the sum mentioned did not cause a reaction on his part. Instead, he continued to listen.

"I don't know what your saving are like these days, but I've decided to allow you to invest into the *'empire'* that I am about to build." Nathaniel Sr.'s smile broadened significantly, mainly because he liked the sound of the word 'empire'.

"I'm in position to invest about 10% of the million that it will cost us to get it done." Thaddeus replied, producing a smile as well, mainly because he liked the sound of the word *'us'*.

As the two of them sat back in silence, and in thought on the journey home. Thaddeus, couldn't believe his good fortune. Yet, he also knew that it wouldn't be right, on his part not to bring his two brothers into the equation.

Thaddeus knew that he was being offered the opportunity of a lifetime, however, he said a silent prayer in hope that his two brothers would realize the same, but more importantly, trust his judgement!

SEVEN

GEORGETOWN, SOUTH CAROLINA, 1878

Georgetown, South Carolina, although a relatively small town, was situated about fifty miles outside of Mt. Pleasant. The fact that Georgetown was also surrounded by water, made it a perfect location for Nathaniel Sr.'s newly established cotton mills.

Georgetown's population was also a plus, being that enough folks resided there unlike most of the small towns/counties throughout the State, meaning Mr. Pinkney didn't have to worry about mill workers having to travel long distances to work.

Majority of the lower-class whites in the area, some of whom had been land owners and planters themselves, relished the fact that the mills had come to town! Many of whom, had not yet recovered from the economic effects/repercussions of the Civil War.

Although, Thaddeus and his two brothers were 10% shareholders in 'Pinkney's' mills, Thaddeus knew and understood southern politics, as they applied to blacks better than most. Therefore, he was not at all surprised, nor offended, by the fact that millwork (particularly on the machines) turned out to be a 'whites only' occupation. Which happened to also be backed by the south's rigid segregation laws.

Whereas, Nathaniel Sr. had become a major merchant for farmers, planters, and later sharecroppers, he also established (at his mills) a commissary for its workers. The commissary extended credit to all of his workers, those who couldn't settle their bill, found themselves working longer hours, and rarely made a dime to take home!

Initially, Albertus, and Granville, were both appalled upon realizing that they'd invested money into a company that excluded blacks as machine operators.

"We have to use our profits to create jobs for our people is all." Thaddeus had responded to their grievance. Leaving out, how Mr. Pinkney was basically raping his white workers by entrapping them with his credit system.

Changing the subject, Thaddeus had informed his brothers. "I hear Nathaniel Jr. had decided to run for Governor of South Carolina."

"So, I've heard." Albertus smiled, yet shook his head.

"Is that a bad thing?" Thaddeus asked, seeing how Albertus had shook his head.

"Not at all. I simply shook my head because it appears that the 'Pinkney's' are well on their way to putting a stronghold on this entire state!" Albertus laughed.

"Well, with friends like John W. Thurmond and John C. Calhoun, I cannot possibly foresee anyone getting in their way." Thaddeus offered.

Although, Granville was back in Chicago with his wife, Danielle decided to come stay with Thaddeus and Rebecca, each of the three brothers now owned over 400 acres of land. In fact, their land stretched into the small town of Awendaw....

JULY 5, 1883

For the majority of black folk living in the south, things seemingly always tended to get worse before they got better!

The spirit of blacks was deeply affected, if not troubled, by the recent U.S. Supreme Court's ruling that reinstated 'Whites Only' hotels, restaurants, barbershops, theaters, schools, and so on.

"It's barely been a decade, since Akerman and his marshals dismantled the Ku Klux Klan. Now this?" Rebecca was livid by the courts decision. Not to mention, the fear it invoked. She was certain that the ruling would breathe new life into hate groups, who would take the position that it was 'their' responsibility to enforce this new law.

"We can't worry about all of that. Our focus is to protect our family." Thaddeus wrapped his arms around his wife.

"Why can't we move our family to Canada, or somewhere?" Rebecca asked, half serious.

"Once we've accumulated enough return on my investment, we can move to wherever you want." He kissed her between her eyes, which he often tended to do.

Although, pleased by his words, Rebecca knew that her husband's investments included much more than the money he put into the cotton mills, in Georgetown. She had been his other half for over ten years, therefore, she witnessed the blood, sweat, and tears, he and his two brothers had shed in the field, the cotton gin, and building up their land, homes, and community. With such thought in mind it was 'she' who knew she would continue to stand by her man, whether it be in the racist South, or wherever fate led them....

JANUARY 18, 1887

"I'm no longer sure that it was a good idea to allow Arethea to work for Elizabeth." Rebecca confided to her husband.

"Why is that?" Thaddeus asked, peeing over the glass of wine he was having with his dinner.

"I got the feeling that, she has a thing for Raymond Pinkney."

Raymond Pinkney was the oldest of Elizabeth and Andrew's twin boys. His brother's name was Rollin, both were about to turn 18 years old, whereas, Arethea was five months away from her 16th birthday.

Sitting his wine glass down onto the table, Thaddeus took a minute to digest what his wife had revealed.

"What gives you that impression?" He finally asked.

"Not only is it a mother's intuition. But, I've noticed how they're around each other quite a lot these days." Rebecca decided not to tell her husband how 'many' times she'd spotted the two teens together.

"Do you intend to speak with her about it?"

"Should I? I mean, it is possible that they're only friends."

"I think you and she, should definitely talk about it, regardless."

Thaddeus, couldn't even imagine his little girl having feelings for the Pinkney boy. Not that Raymond was a bad kid, unlike Rollin who was still as mean as the day he was born, Thaddeus thought to himself. Yet, he knew that the slightest possibility of such a relationship could result in serious consequences. Especially, in the South.

As far as the elder Pinkney's, Nathaniel Sr. and Ruth, they'd all but lose their minds! As a result of a Raymond and Arethea union, Thaddeus also told himself.

It didn't matter that old man "Pinkney' viewed him as a son, because they both knew that his endearment was from a figurative stand point 'not' that he literally wanted (any) of the Addison's to become an actual part of his family!

"Are you alright dear?" Rebecca inquired, seeing a faraway look in Thaddeus's eyes. Nor, had he touched his food, she noticed.

"Honestly, neither of us saw it as a big of a deal. Besides, after Clarice's passing, I guess we both knew that Elizabeth could use the help." Rebecca attempted to justify their reasoning at the time.

"Plus, I didn't see a problem with Arethea earning her own money."

Thaddeus knew his wife had made a valid point.

"We may be making something out of nothing." Thaddeus finally responded. "I say, the two of you just sit down and talk about it."

"I will have a talk with her." Rebecca assured him.

That out the way, the couple made an effort to enjoy the rest of their evening.

★★★★★

"So, when is it that you leave for school?" Arethea inquired, at the same time, kicked at a fallen leaf, as she and Raymond walked towards the huge walnut tree that stood about sixty yards off from his parents' house.

"That's not for another six months." Raymond answered, looking towards the ground as they walked.

Doing the calculation in her head, Arethea responded, "July isn't that far away you know." She looked in his direction, realizing that she'd undoubtedly miss his company.

"Tell me about it!" Raymond exclaimed, obviously unenthused about having to go away to college. Mainly, because he knew that he would not enjoy being so far away from Arethea Addison.

"Why is it, that you have to go so far away?"

"My mother told me that it was my grandfather's decision to send me to Connecticut, to attend Yale University. My brother Rollin, is being sent to New Jersey, to attend Princeton." Raymond informed her. Nor, was he the least bit surprised by his grandfather's influence over his parents. Who apparently, had no say so in he and his brother carrying the 'Pinkney' last name, opposed to their father Andrew's last name. However, Nathaniel Sr. clearly had no problem breaking tradition.

"I'm surprised that the two highly prestigious Universities even accepted my brother and I, considering neither of us possess excellent grades."

At that, the two of them shared a laugh.

"Well, if you weren't going way up to Connecticut, I could help you get your grade point average where it needs to be."

Arethea said with a smile. She prided herself on being an excellent student.

Raymond didn't doubt her potential, being that it was no secret how intelligent Arethea Addison was. It wouldn't surprise him at all to learn that she possessed a genius's IQ! Yet, instead of trying to learn or acquire some of her knowledge, Raymond preferred their discreet flirting whenever they spent time together.

Neither of them could actually pin point when the attraction began. Yet, they were both disappointed by the curve-ball that 'fate' was now throwing their way, hindering the two of them from further exploring the attraction that drew them together.

"I say instead of moping, you and I make these next six months count!" Raymond exclaimed, facing her, now that they had reached the walnut tree.

"I agree." Arethea replied, returning his smile. "But then again, haven't you and I 'already' been making our time count?"

Besides flirting, the two of them did spend a great deal of time talking about school, both their lack of friends, and how it totally sucked that there were laws in place preventing the two of them from going to a movie, library, amusement park, and so.

"Well, I can think of at least one thing that you and I have not yet done." Raymond offered.

"And what would that be?" Arethea inquired.

Opposed to giving a verbal reply, Raymond leaned in and placed his lips against hers...

EIGHT

MT. PLEASANT, SOUTH CAROLINA, 1890

"Congratulations!" Albertus pat his younger brother on the back. Truly happy to see that Thaddeus, at 47 years of age, had it in him to produce another child.

"Can I hold my little cousin?" Danielle, who was now 31, asked Rebecca, who carefully handed over her newborn.

"Oh, she is so beautiful!" Danielle dotted over baby Anne Lee, before gently rubbing her nose against the child's.

"Okay, it's my turn!" Monique, who was also turning 31, exclaimed, at the same time reaching for her cousin.

"Y'all two are gonna spoil that child rotten!" Sarah complained. Yet, even she couldn't help peering over Monique's shoulder to get a better look at the baby. "My God she's beautiful!"

"Look Arethea," Monique summoned her 19-year-old cousin. "She has your same complexion! But, will you look at these eyes?"

"They're beautiful." Arethea agreed. Truthfully, she'd never seen a black child with such light grayish eyes. Staring into the eyes of her baby sister, Arethea told herself that, if she and Raymond ever had a child their baby would have beautiful eyes as well.

"You wanna come to your big sister?" Arethea disguised her voice as she reached for Anne Lee.

Watching their older daughter cradle their youngest in her arms, brought a smile to Thaddeus and Rebecca's face. At that moment, they both realized that they were truly Blessed.

As far as Thaddeus was concerned, he's always felt that his Mother was watching over him and his two brothers.

"Now, you have a much bigger family to watch over." He silently spoke to his mother, unbeknownst to those in the room.

Rebecca and Arethea, did have their talk, some years back, regarding the attraction taking place between she an Raymond Pinkney, and couldn't help feeling her daughter's heartbreak when she'd reiterated to her that, it was no sense in entertaining the thought or prospect of a relationship that could never be!

Thankfully, she no longer had to worry, being that Raymond went away to College! Rebecca had told herself. Meanwhile, all she could do was Pray that her child would be over him, and her feelings, by the time he returned home from school.

Rollin Pinkney, unfortunately, due to his attitude, temperament, and behavior, didn't last eighteen months at Princeton University! He had been home with his parents, for nearly two years now. To say that his 94year old Grandfather was livid, would certainly be an understatement! He nearly fell over and died when the boy looked him in the eyes and said, "Who cares about an education!"

Following that conversation, Nathaniel L. Pinkney had every mind to cut the boy off, and out of his will! Instead, he summoned his son, Nathaniel Jr. to come have a sit-down with him.

"What can we do with him?" Nathaniel Jr. heard the desperation in his Father's voice. Something he certainly wasn't use to. His father had always been a Man who controlled every person, place, and thing, within his circumference, so, to see him at his wit's end, concerning his Grandson was just heartbreaking.

Nathaniel Jr, had served two terms (1879-1887) as Governor of South Carolina, and could have easily won a United States Senate seat, however, he decided he was done with politics, and decided to run his father's business.

"I can always teach him the business," Nathaniel suggested. "I am getting up in age you know. So, the twins, being our only living heirs, will have to take hold of things whether you like it or not."

"Oh hush!" His Father waved his hand in the air, as if he was swatting at a fly.

"When I was 48, I hadn't even reached my peak yet!"

"Well, politics can be extremely draining, so I certainly feel as though I've already reached mine." Nathaniel Jr laughed, although he was being serious.

"Why is it, that you and Melissa haven't had any children yet?" His father gave him that same suspicious glare he'd known so well as a child.

"Can't answer you that one," Nathaniel said. "We've certainly never stopped trying." He confided with a smile on his face.

"Since 'Raymond' is my preferred heir, I want you to bring him home from school upon completing four years, opposed to eight."

"What can I do for you Sir?" Thaddeus could not remember the last time he had been summoned to the Pinkney home, in Charleston. Nor, could he believe how much the house had 'not' changed. Then again, most of the homes in downtown Charleston was pretty antique looking, he thought to himself.

"I've seen your work." Nathaniel Sr. began. "I want to hire you and your brothers, to build two homes for me."

"My two brothers no longer work with me, but, I have a competent crew of men to get the job done." Thaddeus told him before quickly adding," To your satisfaction, of course."

As he watched this young Man, whom he'd known since childhood, Nathaniel Sr wished his grandchildren (well, at least Rollin) could be so respectful, and driven.

"I want the homes built on either side of my daughter's

mansion."

"The work, being so close in proximity to where I live, will definitely enable me to have it completed sooner rather than later."

"That's what I want to hear." Nathaniel Sr., produced a smile, before informing him," My Grandson, Raymond, will be coming home from school, in about eight months. Hopefully, you can at least have one of the homes completed by then?"

At the mention of his grandson Raymond coming home, Thaddeus grew silent.

"Is there something wrong Son?" Nathaniel Sr. inquired, seeing the change of expression on Thaddeus's face."

"I'm fine Sir."Thaddeus assured him."I can definitely have at least one of them completed by then." Although he committed himself,Thaddeus didn't like the thought of putting his crew under such pressure/deadlines. They'd really have to put in some serious work, and hours, he told himself.

"I knew I could count on you."The old man smiled. He knew Thaddeus would get it done, seeing how he'd made him and his brothers rich by bringing Thaddeus in on the Mill, out in Georgetown.

"By the way, congratulations on your new baby." Nathaniel Sr. offered. "Please give Rebecca my regards."

Thaddeus's crew, consisted of six men (Monique's husband William, whom everyone called Willie; Danielle's husband Samuel, everyone called him Sam; John, whom they called Jon Jon; Malcolm, Steven, David, and Isaiah), all of whom were brothers, better known collectively, as the 'Steed' Family, or the Steed Boys.

Isaiah, being the youngest, was the same age as Arethea. The two of them had also attended school together, until Isaiah decided school wasn't for him, and he'd much rather work! Basically, following in the footsteps of his five older brothers.

Although,Thaddeus wished for someone more suitable, for his daughter, he realized that 'time' was not on his side (being that Raymond Pinkney was due home this coming Summer), he and Rebecca went out of their way to encourage a relationship between Arethea and Isaiah. The fact that, her parents had seemed to take an interest in Isaiah was cause enough, for her to give it /him a chance.

"I don't know why you continue to allow that child to be courted by that Steed boy." Yvette, Albertus's Wife, disapproved.

"Last I checked, your daughter Monique, was married to one of the brothers." Rebecca countered, leaving out Willie's name.

"She sure is married to that fool." Sarah laughed. Everyone knew that Willie didn't possess good sense. If he wasn't telling stories or jokes, he was drinking alcohol.

"If you ask me, I think Isaiah is the best Apple in the batch." Rebecca laughed.

"I don't know." Yvette, spoke seriously. "Something about that boy's eyes just ain't right."

"Really?" Sarah watched her sister-in-law.

"I was no more than yay high," Yvette stuck her hand out, indicating about three feet. "When my Daddy wrapped that apron around my tiny waist, its' pockets filled with cotton seeds, and sent me on my way. I tell you, my little feet walked more miles, spreading those seeds, then I care to remember!" She shook her head at the memory. "I say that to say, I've been around enough black men, in my time, to know when something just ain't right with one."

"Every Black man I've ever encountered has a certain look in their eyes. Especially, here in the South, having to deal with the white man's hate, prejudice, and belittlement, all the time." Sarah justified.

"I know that's right." Rebecca co-signed her words, even though she had to admit that the Pinkney men/family had been an exception in her opinion.

"Okay," Yvette concluded. "I still feel that he's not the one for my niece."

JUNE 10, 1890

"I have to congratulate you guys, on a job well done!" Thaddeus gave praise to his six-man crew. As a result, of their (combined) hard work and determination to meet Nathaniel Sr's deadline, one of the homes was (now) complete.

"I hope a strong wind doesn't blow this thing down!" Willie joked seeing how they'd built the house in such little time.

"She's good to go." His brother Jon Jon felt confident.

"In that case, how about we celebrate with this!" Willie, produced an unopened bottle of Whiskey, with a huge grin on his face.

"Where'd you get that?" His brother Malcolm inquired, wide eyed.

"The same place he 'always' gets it from." Jon Jon laughed.

"We gone have to do this girl straight." Willie said smirking, meaning without cups nor glasses.

Thaddeus, had never been a drinker of alcohol, however they did have a reason to celebrate! Therefore, when the thick-glass bottle made its way to him, he accepted it. The small swig that he took, already had his chest burning! He couldn't understand how anyone could get used to such a taste or burn!

As the seven of them sat in the grass drinking and admiring the finished house, Willie, now drunk, asked them if they'd like to hear a joke?

"Sure, why not?" Thaddeus replied, causing the other five men to look his way. They all heard their brothers' jokes, and had to admit he was truly funny. However, Willie was the last person, anyone wanted to get started…he'd have your stomach in knots the entire day! If you let him! Which was usually the case.

"Okay, Willie began. "This is the Story of 'The Five Horny Slave Owners."

"Is it a story? Or is it a joke? Thaddeus interrupted.

"It's always a joke, with Willie." Jon Jon replied.

"Like I was saying," Willie continued. "Four, of the Horny

Slave Owners, when they weren't sexing their wives or sexually abusing their slaves, would get together (at least, four nights out of the week).

"They'd go deep into the woods to light a fire and drink whiskey.

Then one day the 'fifth' Horny Slave Owner decided to join the fold. On his first night out, into the woods they went! Once in the woods and halfway through his 'third' glass of whiskey, the new comer couldn't help noticing each of the other Horny Slave Owners (taking turns) going deeper into the woods. Half drunk, he assumed, they were each taking turns peeing!

One of them must've decided to leave early, he'd told himself, noticing the absence of one of his Horny Slave Owning comrades. Feeling a sudden tap on his right shoulder, he turned, to find one of the Horny Slave Owners standing behind him.

"Come on!" Instructed the Horny Slave Owner who was standing behind.

Following his lead, the Fifth Horny Slave Owner realized that he was being lead deeper into the woods. Once they'd come upon a lit clearing (due to the Moon's light), the Fifth Horny Slave Owner noticed the somewhat large Wooden Barrel.

"Okay," began the Horny Slave Owner, who'd led him into the woods. I want you to step up to the barrel over there. When you do, you'll notice a Hole in its' side. I want you to unzip your trousers, and put your 'thing' inside of the Hole. Doing as he'd been told, the Fifth Horny Slave Owner could not believe how "awesome" the Barrel felt!!! Returning, back to where the other Horny Slave Owners were camped out, drinking, and laughing, the Fifth Horny Slave Owner leaned into the Horny Slave Owner sitting to his right, and asked; Say, can I get at that Barrel 'every night'? Without facing him, the Horny Slave Owner replied, No not every night!

"Over hearing their conversation, the Horny Slave Owner seated to the newcomer's left, informed him; You can have at that there Barrel every night, except Saturdays, Sundays, and

Tuesdays! Taking a deep swallow from his whiskey glass, the Fifth Horny Slave Owner decided to further inquire about the Barrel. Say, why is it that I can only have at the Barrel on Saturdays', Sundays', and Tuesdays'? Before either of the other Horny Slave Owners could reply, he added, I can understand Sundays being it's the Sabbath!

"Downing the remainder of his half full glass of Whiskey, the Horny Slave Owner seated across from the three of them, gave him his answer; The reason you can't have at the Barrel on Saturdays' or Sundays' is because we spend the weekends with our families! As for Tuesdays', he smiled, Well, that's "your" night to be inside the Barrel!"

Willie's joke had them *'all'* laughing, including Thaddeus...

NINE

MT. PLEASANT, SOUTH CAROLINA, 1892

"You 'do' know, what happens when you play with fire, right?" Arethea, was so tired of her older cousins, Monique and Danielle, preaching to her about 'her' love life! Yes, she was involved with Isaiah, however, she couldn't deny that it was Raymond Pinkney who her Heart belonged to. Which she couldn't actually confide or tell anyone, being that her 'entire' family was totally against the idea of her even 'liking' Raymond, let alone being with him!!

"You better look around you, and realize where you're at!" Danielle tried to talk sense into her younger cousin. "Slavery might be over, but these White folks will still hang your behind for messing with one of theirs!" She reminded Arethea." Especially if one of 'theirs' happens to have the last name Pinkney!"

"It's not that big a deal." Arethea responded, more so, trying to make herself believe that it wasn't. "Besides, I hear that Raymond has found someone, whom I also hear he's really into." The thought alone, never mind the actual information, broke Arethea's heart.

"Good for him." Monique smiled, upon hearing that.

Danielle shot Monique a knowing look, which the two of them acknowledged to mean; that it was good for Arethea (more than Raymond) that he had found someone else....

"Do you think interracial couples will be accepted, say somewhere like New York, or Philadelphia?" Arethea asked her cousins, with a huge smile on her face.

Monique and Danielle (both) rolled their eyes at Arethea's naivety, and apparent hopelessness.

"What about Isaiah?" Danielle inquired.

"What about him?" Arethea answered her question with a question. It wasn't that she didn't like Isaiah, nor was she deliberately being insensitive towards his feelings for her, but for some reason, she just couldn't get Raymond Pinkney out of her system.... which was crazy, being that, in all the years they've been flirting, then admitting to having feelings for one another, they'd never done more than kissed!

"I know one thing," Monique looked Arethea dead in her eyes. "You better not even 'think' about laying down with that white boy!"

At that, Arethea had to wonder if her cousin Monique had an ability to read minds! Nonetheless, she couldn't hide her smile.

"So, how do you like the City of Charleston, so far?" Raymond inquired with a smile on his face.

"The City is really beautiful!" Audrey replied, she too, was smiling as she added, "I especially like the people." She couldn't help noticing the hospitality she'd received since arriving from Delaware.

"The hospitality definitely grows on you, when you've lived here as long as I have." He responded, as if reading her thoughts.

"I can tell." Audrey smiled even wider. "You're truly the gentlemen."

It was during one of her aunts', Melissa, visits to Delaware that Audrey first heard about Raymond Pinkney. "He's truly to die for." Melissa had assured her. However, Audrey still a virgin at 22, was only slightly interested.

Now, as the two-walked hand in hand (along, Charleston's battery) peering out, into the Copper River, Audrey Lynn Bowers knew that love had finally found her.

It was Nathaniel Jr., who had suggested that Melissa take the trip to visit her family in Lewes, Delaware. He had also planted the seed into his wife's head, that she should tell Audrey about their nephew Raymond. He knew that once the introduction was made, Raymond's personality, intellect, and physical appearance would seal the deal.

Unbeknownst, to Melissa, Raymond, and Audrey, it was Thaddeus who had approached Nathaniel Jr., and informed him that 'they' had more than a potential problem on their hands. Thus, he explained the attraction between Raymond and Arethea and how they'd need to come up with a plan to prevent what could never be...

Rollin Pinkney, upset that his home was only halfway finished took his attitude out on Thaddeus.

"I don't know why my grandfather hired such an incompetent group of niggers, to build my house." He locked eyes with Thaddeus as he'd said it.

Seeing the expression on Thaddeus's face, Jon Jon, put his hand
on Thaddeus's shoulder, and said, "It's not worth it."

The rest of the crew, resumed working on the house, yet, they all had heard the derogative word when Rollin said it.

"What's the matter?" Rollin continued to stare Thaddeus in the eyes. "You don't like something I said?" He smiled.

"I think you need to go find something to do, and leave us 'men' to our work." Thaddeus put emphasis on the word 'men'.

"Men?" Rollin laughed at that. "For a minute there, I thought maybe a group of monkeys were climbing my house." He looked up in Willie's direction, who was nailing siding on the second-floor landing of the house.

Jon Jon was literally 'holding' Thaddeus now.

"Remember, I'm the twin who never did well in school. So, I hope you folks aint' offended by my vocabulary.

"I think you need to go ahead and get somewhere" Thaddeus warned him. "Before I forget you're a Pinkney."

"I always heard that you was a smart nigger. However, you certainly ain't sounding very smart to me right now." Rollin heard the threat in Thaddeus's words.

Thaddeus, walked right up on the boy, until they were basically nose to nose, and said, "I assure you, I'm the last nigger you want to have a problem with. Especially, seeing how you already got one strike against you." He stared into the boys' eyes.

Somewhat afraid now, Rollin refused to back down in front of the group, who he knew were watching the two of them.

"And what's strike one?" Rollin finally asked.

"Let's just say, it does not bide well for you that the man who murdered my mother, was also named Rolland." As far as Thaddeus was concerned, it was totally irrelevant that the 'spelling' was not the same...

NOVEMBER 27, 1890

"I'm truly sorry for you lost Elizabeth." Rebecca hugged her, as everyone was turning to leave the burial. "Andrew's in a much better place now." She tried to console her with kind words.

"I know." Elizabeth tried to smile, as the two women headed towards the horse-driven carriages.

Rollin, walked up and put his hand beneath his mother's right elbow. Staring Rebecca in her eyes, he spoke. "Thank you, I got her from here." With that being said, he ushered his mother to their carriage.

Thaddeus approached his wife. "Did that boy say something disrespectful to you?" He inquired, seeing Rollin had walked off with Elizabeth.

"Not at all." Rebecca smiled up at her husband. "He's really not a bad kid."

Thaddeus, didn't bother responding to that. As far as he was concerned, Rebecca had a tendency to see good in any and every one.

As they were about to mount their carriage, Thaddeus noticed Isaiah and his daughter making their approach.

"Everything okay?"

"Yes, we're fine." Isaiah replied. "I was wondering if I could fetch a ride back with you and Mrs. Addison?"

"Of course. We'll all fit perfectly." Rebecca spoke from atop the carriage.

"I'm not coming home right this minute." Arethea informed her parents. "Elizabeth is waiting on me. I think she can really use my company at the moment."

"Are you sure?" Thaddeus asked, not liking the idea of his daughter riding 'anywhere' with Rollin Pinkney.

"Yes." Arethea smiled, then planted a kiss on her father's left cheek. As she attempted to do the same with Isaiah, he turned, giving her the back of his head as he climbed the carriage.

Thaddeus didn't catch Isaiah's action, however Rebecca did.

Raymond and Audrey were already at his mother's house when Rollin, Elizabeth, and Arethea arrived. He'd avoided Arethea at the funeral, as well as the burial.

"I think I'll go lay down for a bit." Elizabeth spoke, barely above a whisper. "Thank you for being here." She leaned over to Arethea and kissed her on the cheek, before exiting the dining room. Rollin couldn't believe that his mother had acknowledged 'her' and not the rest of them. Raymond caught the angry expression on his brothers face and said, "She's just tired."

"Arethea, I'd like you to meet my fiancé Audrey." Raymond made the introduction.

"Please to meet you." Arethea smiled, in spite of how she felt at the mention of the word fiancé.

"Yeah, I bet." Rollin spoke under his breath, yet, loud enough to be heard. Audrey, was the only one in the room who didn't have a clue as to what he'd meant by that.

"It's a pleasure to meet you as well." Audrey replied. Neither female made an attempt to cross the room for a hug, nor a handshake.

"I think I'll follow your mother's lead and go lay down awhile, myself." Arethea turned and left the room.

Rollin decided to leave as well, just before he walked out of the door, he looked over his shoulder at his twin brother and said, "I'm surprised you didn't go after her."

At that moment, Raymond wasn't sure if he was more upset with his brother totally disregarding Audrey's feelings, or, because the truth really (did) hurt. He couldn't deny that Audrey would certainly make a good wife. However, it ate his conscience (daily) that, he too, had to accept the fact that; Color-in America-set precedence over love…

JANUARY 29, 1893

Everyone has heard the phrase; Sometimes, when it rains, it pours. Today, it poured (Nathaniel Sr. passed away in his sleep, at 97 years old,) yet in the midst of the down-pour, the sun was still showing (it was also Anne Lee's 3rd birthday.)

Thaddeus made an appearance at the huge funeral. Meanwhile, his wife and family, threw Anne Lee a huge birthday party!

Albertus and Granville opted to attend their niece's party. Mainly because they wanted nothing to do with Nathaniel Sr., or his family at the moment! Thaddeus had tried, to no avail, explain to his two older brothers, that the on-coming depression had nothing to do with Nathaniel Sr! Although, many hadn't yet felt the full force of the (on-coming) Great Depression of 1893, the Pinkney's and Addison's had already loss millions of dollars! Textile and shipping had already taken huge financial loss. Albeit, cotton had an extraordinary range of practical uses (clothes, shoes, bags, etc.) just as cottonseeds-oil (potato chips, cookies, salad dressing) however food, clothing, and shelter were the main three target areas in any Economic crisis.

"I do hope you know that it is a new day, now that my grandfather is no longer here." Rollin Pinkney whispered into Thaddeus's ear (from behind) as they both waited in line to not only view the deceased, but, to pay their last respects as well….

TEN

MT. PLEASANT, SOUTH CAROLINA, 1900

As far as the Addison's and the Pinkney's were concerned the turn of the (New) Century literally meant; nothing was the same!

As for the Addison's, Albertus, died of a massive heart attack, at the age of 65. Now a widow, Yvette, (bored) decided to move into the Pinkney's Charleston mansion to work for Nathaniel Jr. and Melissa, overseeing/supervising their many servants, as Ms. Corice had done years prior. Thaddeus and Granville, had not recovered (financially) following the Depression of 1893. In fact, they both sold their interest (in the Georgetown Mills) to Nathaniel Jr., mainly because the twin brothers [Raymond and Rollin] had taken over as general managers, which was a headache in which Thaddeus and his brother were not trying to deal with. Not to mention, it had been reported that Rollin Pinkney, was stealing money from the mills that his grandfather built. Yet, it was unfortunate that Thaddeus had sold his 10% shares because the mills were no longer powered by steam, but, electricity, so the cotton business was now booming like never before! Isaiah and Arethea were married, with no kids (yet) and Danielle, and her husband Samuel, packed up and moved to Chicago, Illinois. The remaining members of the Steed Family, were still in Mt. Pleasant. Monique and Willy were still together as well, although she was absolutely tired of his (mostly inappropriate) jokes... And, his drinking!!!

As for the Pinkney's, unfortunately Elizabeth passed away (in her sleep, just as her father had,) at 74 years old. Nathaniel Jr. and Melissa, were still (happily) married. At 57, he was basically retired, letting his twin nephews run his multiple (businesses.) Apparently, 'twins' ran in their family, because Rollin was also married (to a woman named Trish,) and was a proud father of twin boys. However, Rollin Pinkney, at 31 was still as cruel, and evil as he'd been growing up! Raymond and Audrey, were also married and living in his (same) house in Mt. Pleasant. Unfortunately, Audrey had conceived (twice) but miscarried both times...

THANKSGIVING DAY, 1902

The entire Addison family, including Danielle, who had come home for the holiday, as well as, Melissa and Audrey who were considered extended family, all were joined inside of Rebecca's kitchen laughing, singing, and telling stories! While Rebecca, Yvette, and Sarah, prepared the Thanksgiving meal.

The only female, who was not in attendance, was Trish, Rollin's wife. Who informed Audrey that, Rollin had forbidden her and their children from attending.

All eyes were on 12year old Anne Lee, as she entered the kitchen with not one, but 'two' textbooks in hand.

"It smells awfully good in here!" Anne Lee commented, walked over to her mother who bent to give her a kiss, then took a seat at the huge dining table.

"Honey, why are you carrying those books around? There's no school today." Melissa commented, with a smile on her face.

"That child reads from sunrise to sunset, even on weekends and holidays." Arethea revealed to the rest of them, with a slight attitude, that none of the women detected. Except Rebecca, who continued what she was doing.

Once all conversation had died down, Anne Lee decided

to pose her question.

"Who in this kitchen, knows anything about the continent of Africa?" she asked.

It was a question, that did not receive a response, partly because it was totally unexpected.

Although, Arethea, knew a great deal about African history, she simply rolled her eyes, feeling as though Anne Lee's question was inappropriate being that everyone was in a festive mood.

"How about you tell us about Africa?" Rebecca suggested, removing the gloves she'd worn to stuff the huge turkey.

"Well," Anne Lee began with a smile, being that her mother encouraged her.

"Out of the Seven continents, Africa is the second largest. Asia, being the largest. Africa, takes up over Eleven million, Six hundred, Seventy-Seven Thousand, Two Hundred and Forty square miles of land."

"It has a population of over Seven Hundred Million people, and is the site of Four principle mountain ranges, the Atlas, the Darkensberg, the Ruwenzori, and the Ethiopian Highlands."

"It is also home to The World's largest desert, The Sahara. The World's largest river, the Nile. The World's largest swamp, The SUDD. The World's second largest fresh water lake, The Victoria. And, contains the main part of The Great Rift Valley, which runs about 3,000 miles from Syria to Mozambique." Anne Lee smiled proudly.

Rebecca, also wore a smile on her face. Anne Lee was certainly her father's child! Rebecca told herself, recalling the many hours and days Thaddeus spent over the years, teaching his little girl everything he knew. As he'd done with Arethea.

At the young age of twelve, Anne Lee was a walking encyclopedia/dictionary! Although, Thaddeus had built a school in their community, and purchased countless decent textbooks, whereas most black schools in the South used worn and outdated books, he still didn't rely totally on someone else teaching his children.

Everyone seated at the dining table, were clearly impressed

by Anne Lee's articulation and intellect. Everyone except for Arethea apparently.

"How many of you heard of a woman named Sojourner Truth?" Anne Lee asked the group of women seated at the table.

Anne Lee, not now!" Arethea interceded. "We're preparing for Thanksgiving, not a history exam." She added.

Backing away from the stove, Rebecca decided to intercede as well.

"Baby, you go ahead and enlighten everyone as to who Ms. Sojourner Truth is, as well as her story."

Focusing her attention on Arethea, Rebecca's tone became quite stern as she spoke.

"I want you to come out back with me. I can use some more cornmeal."

Once the two of them were alone outside, Rebecca had words for her oldest daughter.

"For as long as I live. I better not 'ever' hear you talk to your sister the way you did in there! You and I both know how lucky you are that your father was not in the room." Rebecca scolded her.

"When you were that same age, and equally as smart, you were the same way!" Rebecca reminded her." If you don't remember, I suggest you ask your aunts and uncles."

"You and your sister are both Blessed to be as gifted as you both are academically. Truthfully, I don't know what has gotten into you." Rebecca noticed how moody Arethea had been lately. Yet, had no clue that it was Raymond Pinkney, that had Arethea acting other than herself.

"You are the last person, who should ever take part in discouraging your sister, no matter what her endeavors are. As black folk, we have the entire system at work against our advancement."

"As for Anne Lee enlightening us all to Africa, and the struggles and achievements of women such as Sojourner Truth, and so on, I'm inclined to believe that we 'all can use a refresher in history, including white folk." Rebecca stated, knowing that it was highly unlikely that Melissa or Audrey knew the answer to 'either' of Anne Lee's questions...

By 1900, the south's 'black' population was not only suffering, but moreover, was more powerless than any other time since the end of slavery! Following the demise of Reconstruction, blacks also found themselves confronted with, and demoralized by white supremacy.

The United States Supreme Courts's decision in, "Plessy V. Ferguson" in 1896, not only reflected the emerging national consensus on race, but upheld segregation. Thus, rendering 'Plessy' an unmitigated defeat for black America!

Plessy, challenged the State of Louisiana 'law' that required railway companies to provide separate accommodations for black and white passengers. Prior to 'Plessy' segregation was basically a matter of custom, rather than law.

After the court's ruling in 'Plessy' legalizing segregation on public transportation, lynching's and mob violence also reach an all-time high. Not to mention, blacks found themselves excluded from jury service, black prisoners under the south's convict-lease system were subjected to cruel and unusual punishment, and black schools suffered even worst!

"I had a conversation with my brother Samuel." Isaiah began, avoiding eye contact with Thaddeus, as the two of them carried individual loads of Sugarcane towards Thaddeus's shed.

Isaiah, everyone knew, was not a talkative person. However, the fact that he had a tendency, whenever he 'did' talk, to begin a conversation only to pause as if he wanted the person he was talking to, to persuade or encourage him to continue.

Thaddeus, simply waited for him to get to the point.

"I told him that I was thinking about leaving South Carolina. Well, getting out of the South altogether." Isaiah added.

"How does Arethea feel about relocating?" Thaddeus inquired.

"She doesn't want to go." Isaiah confided.

Thaddeus thought it best not to respond. Mainly because he knew that Isaiah and his daughter were having marital problems. Partly, due to Isaiah's distrust and disapproval of Arethea's friendship with Raymond Pinkney, although she had not only been supportive of the 'Pinkney's during their time of loss, but had also provided nursing and encouragement to Audrey Pinkney following both her miscarriages. Not to mention, Isaiah's sudden alcohol addiction, thanks to aligning himself with Willie.

"Can you talk some sense into her for me?" Isaiah requested.

His request, stopped Thaddeus dead in his tracks. "So, what you're asking of me, is to tell my daughter, who by the way happens to be grown, to pack up all her things and move to Chicago because Isaiah is tired of the South?" Thaddeus stared at his son-in-law incredulously.

"Aren't you yourself tired of this place?" Isaiah asked.

"If I were tired of this place, I certainly wouldn't run off to a big city simply because someone expects me to take at face value that the streets of Chicago are paved in gold." Thaddeus knew first hand that Samuel and Danielle were up in Chicago struggling to make ends meet, considering he and Granville had loaned them money on several occasions.

"At least here, I'm familiar with my surroundings and know exactly what I'm dealing with." Thaddeus added, knowing that 'prejudice' was not a regional problem, but a national problem.

"I don't see how anyone in their right mind could find contentment living amongst these racist, hateful, white folks." Isaiah replied.

"And you think racism doesn't exist in Chicago?"

"No offense, but if this place works for you, which it seemingly has for quite some time, then I commend you for finding comfort in the midst of oppression. However, not all of us are meant to be accommodationist." Isaiah spoke with obvious contempt.

Putting his arm-full of sugarcane down on the ground, Thaddeus wasn't sure if he wanted to hit Isaiah or simply order him to get off his property.

"Is that what I am? An accommodationist?"

Deciding not to back down, Isaiah stared his father-in-law in the eyes.

"Yes, I think that is exactly what you are. You, and the rest

of these docile black folks here with these titles such as ministers, teachers, doctors, and so on. Who continue to allow these
white folks to have their way with you all!"

"You think because the Pinkney's invite you into their
homes, or come into yours, that they actually have love for
you?"

Thaddeus, had never heard Isaiah speak as he was speaking
to him at the moment nor did he realize that such hate and/
or disdain for white folks even existed in Isaiah. Not to say,
there wasn't good reason to dislike most whites in the south,
Thaddeus told himself. Nevertheless, he also knew that Isaiah
was going through an emotional hurt, which had the potential
to produce the worst kind of pain.

Picking his sugarcane off the ground, Thaddeus brushed
pass his son-in-law.

"I think I'm going to stay out of you and your wife's affairs.
Whether Arethea decides to join you in Chicago, or not, she
will continue to have my Blessings and support." That being
said, Thaddeus left Isaiah where he stood.

"Why are you allowing Isaiah's words and opinion to bother you?"

Rebecca asked her husband, as they laid in bed that night.

"What if he's right?" Thaddeus answered her question with
a question.

"There's absolutely no validity to what all he said. I mean,
he has a right to express his opinion, but that doesn't make it
the truth."

Rebecca knew better than anyone that her husband was far
from being an accommodationist.

"Although, I have made a good life for myself and our
family, that doesn't mean that any of us are immune from the
disenfranchisement of our people. Yet, there are times when
even I find myself asking God, what have I done to receive the
level of favor that He has shown me.

"I guess from Isaiah's perspective, it is easy for someone on
the outside looking in to misconstrue my Blessings or good
fortune as something other than what it is."

Thaddeus didn't like the word accommodist or accommo-dationist.

"Especially, since there are people out there who feel as though I should be an instigator for voting rights, standing up to the white establishment, pushing for racial equality.

"But, all I've ever known is to educate myself, work hard, build, and save.

Thaddeus was expressing things to his wife, which she already knew.

"I guess I'm the model for Booker T. Washington's philosophy, that blacks should work hard, save and stay out of white folks' way."

"You have done much more than that, and still continue to do so." Rebecca had to remind him. "Had it not been for your generosity, and wanting to uplift your people, you would not have built that beautiful, well stocked school for this community. Which happens to also have an extremely qualified teacher. Not only have you put your two brothers in position to become land and business owners, you saw to it that the Steed Family and several others around these parts became owners of their property as well. Do I even need to bring up that, we wouldn't have that beautiful place of worship had you not saw to it being built? The only Church in this region mind you." Rebecca hated the thought of Thaddeus allowing someone like Isaiah to have him second guessing himself. Especially, seeing how her husband was the primary source of employment for not only most of the blacks who resided in Mt. Pleasant, but Isaiah and his family as well.

"Is it enough though?" Thaddeus asked, in a lowered tone.

Rebecca, knew it was more than her husband's earlier conversation with Isaiah, that had him second guessing himself.

His brother Granville had mailed him a book, that he purchased in Chicago, titled; 'The Souls of Black Folk' written by W.E.B DuBois, which Thaddeus had read not once, but twice! She'd noticed.

"Besides," Rebecca began, at the same time putting her lips to his ear, in her endeavor to lighten the mood. "At our age, we need to focus 'exclusively' on taking care of each other. Let the younger folks of this new millennium take up the fight for change." That being said, she kissed his earlobe.

Neither of them, was aware that Anne Lee had been standing in their bedroom doorway, and had heard the entire conversation ....

ELEVEN

MT. PLEASANT, SOUTH CAROLINA, 1906

"Y ou have a visitor." Rebecca, informed Thaddeus, as he lay there on his sick bed. Seven months had passed, since he'd suffered a near fatal stroke. Although, he showed no interest in learning to walk again, Thaddeus did regain his speech, yet, more than some of his words came out slurred. That being the case, he rarely spoke.

Without opening his eyes, he knew the visitor was Nathaniel Jr. being that he had summoned him.

"How are you feeling?" Nathaniel Jr. asked as he sat down in the chair adjacent Thaddeus's bed.

"I'm okay." Thaddeus replied, then lifted his right hand slightly. Seeing the white envelope in Thaddeus's hand, Nathaniel Jr. reached for it.

"Is it something I should review right now?"

"No, not necessarily" Thaddeus spoke slowly. "It's my Will."

"Okay." Nathaniel Jr. understood. "However, you're such a strong man, you may out-live me!" He smiled as he said it.

Thaddeus, didn't respond to that, nor did he return the smile.

Stopping to have a word with Rebecca, on his way out, Nathaniel Jr. inquired, "How have you been holding up?"

"Some days are harder than others." Rebecca replied, producing a slight smile she added, "Nevertheless, I am Blessed and thankful that I didn't lose my husband."

Nathaniel Jr., nodded his understanding, being that 'he' couldn't even imagine losing Melissa.

"Dr. Morrison says that, with therapy and a lot of determination Thaddeus could actually walk again." Nathaniel Jr told Rebecca what she'd already been informed.

"Yes, he told me. But, it's something that Thaddeus will have to do or consider when he is ready. Although, it's been seven months, I think the realization of nearly being taken away from all of us, is still weighing heavily on his mind." Rebecca explained.

"It's certainly understandable." At 63, the same age as Thaddeus, Nathaniel Jr., couldn't fathom being taken away from his family!

"How are your mother and Anne Lee doing these days?" Raymond asked, with more than a little concern in his voice, as he and Arethea strolled his property.

"They're doing ok." She smiled, briefly looking him in the eyes, before returning her focus to the ground in front of her, as the two of them proceeded to walk.

"You too, are an incredibly strong woman." Raymond complimented her with a smile.

"Sometimes I am." Arethea replied. "Sometimes, I'm not."

"Watching her, through his peripheral, as they walked on Raymond not only knew she was referring to her feelings (for him), he also understood. Following, their second miscarriage, he and Audrey had grown so distant, to him, they felt like two strangers living in the same house. Rarely, did the two of them do things together, and 'never 'did they sleep together. He had his room and Audrey had hers. He'd assumed, his wife had shut-down, as far as intimacy, because she didn't want to go through or experience a third loss.

"So, how are things going with you and Audrey?" Arethea asked.

"Not too much better than the last time I answered that question."

Arethea shot him a look. She didn't take his answer to mean that he was being smart by the way he'd said it, but, she was more so surprised that he (and Audrey) were still having such problems.

"That was over three years ago, when you and I had that last conversation." Arethea reminded him.

"True," Raymond remembered exactly the day in which they'd had the conversation. "At that time, I told you, Audrey and I, had been having some problems for over two years."

"Five years is a very long time to be dealing with marital problems."

"Is it?" Raymond faced her now. He was aware, that she and Isaiah, had been having problems of their own for quite some time.

Arethea, acted as though she hadn't heard his remark. Picking a walnut off the ground, she tossed it as far as her strength allowed.

"Not bad." Raymond was impressed by the throw.

"Remember how we use to compete?" She laughed.

"Of course, I remember." He laughed as well, at the same time picking a walnut off the ground and hurling it as far as possible.

"Stop showing off." Arethea, couldn't believe how far it landed.

"I was a kid then." Raymond reminded her. "However, I'm much stronger now." He smiled.

"Are you?" She asked, he could see the serious change in her expression.

Raymond Pinkney, also couldn't help realizing, that the two of them were (now) standing in the exact spot where they'd shared their first kiss...

"How do you deal with Arethea spending so much time, always helping them Pinkney's out?" Willie asked his brother Isaiah.

Giving thought to his brother's question Isaiah, took a swallow from the bottle of Whiskey in which he and Willie spent the past half hour passing back and forth.

"It doesn't bother me at all." He lied. "You have to re-member, she still gets paid to maintain Elizabeth's house, even though no one lives there. So, whenever she helps out Audrey, that's extra money she makes." Isaiah, deliberately left out Ray-mond's name.

"I hear you." Willie gave his younger brother a suspicious look, then reach for the bottle. "I just don't want to see you hurt."

At that, Isaiah laughed. He knew what his brother was im-plying, without saying Raymond Pinkney's name. In fact, all of his brothers had a tendency to mind 'his' and his wife's busi-ness, opposed to minding their own. Which often upset him. Especially, being that Arethea, had sworn to him that she and Raymond had never done more than kissed and that happened when they were teenagers.

However, the thought of another man (having ever) kissed Arethea, still tended to make his blood boil, especially when he drank.......

Along with Thaddeus's will, Nathaniel Jr. had found a (one page) letter enclosed, inside of the envelope Thaddeus had handed him. Having read the will, he placed it in the top drawer of his desk. Deciding if now was a good time to open the letter, or not, Nathaniel Jr. simply sat there for a full five minutes before unfolding the sheet of paper.

Nathaniel,

In spite of living the past 63 years of my life in such a seemingly dysfunctional World, I do love this life I have led. Witnessing the Pow-er of Love has enabled me to see, and understand my Blessings. Even in the midst of so much suffering, despair, oppression, and hate, I know that it is God's love for me that has me (and my family) covered.

Whereas, I am truly thankful for having been the vehicle to bring all those, within my immediate circumference, out of 'their' despair and into an environment in which not only they wished to live, but also, for which they want their children and grandchildren to live in. Yet, I still find myself (mentally) struggling with the question of how could I have done more or been a greater participant in the liberation of my people?

At this point in my life, all I can do is hope and Pray that I have at least, played the part that was intended for 'me' to play,

Nevertheless, everyday (since suffering this stroke), I lay here re-playing the days and events of my life-actions and deeds- striving to mentally ascertain what is there that I may need and/or should be asking God's forgiveness?

I think I can speak for you, and I. Due to our combined level of knowledge and understanding, when I say; that neither of us need to be overly religious men to know that it is a true abomination to put Man's feelings, opinions, policies, and laws, above or before God's plan.

As I stated in the opening of this letter, God's favor has clearly been bestowed upon my life, obviously through LOVE! In fact, I have come to the realization that this World will 'never' be right, or healed, until we all learn to embrace it (love)....

Especially, considering, it is the "only" emotion capable of conquering Hate!

As Nathaniel folded the letter, he didn't have to read between any of its lines to realize that, he too, would have to atone for his interference...as far as his Nephew and Arethea was concerned.

TWO DAYS LATER

Nathaniel Jr., could tell by the expression on his wife's face that something was wrong as she entered his study.

"What is it?" He asked with concern, as he removed his reading glasses.

"Raymond's driver just left," Melissa began, with tears forming in her eyes.

"He came to inform us that Thaddeus passed away an hour ago.

TWELVE

MT. PLEASANT, SOUTH CAROLINA, 1907

Anne Lee, couldn't remember the last time she'd seen the inside of Nathaniel and Melissa's colonial styled mansion. To say that it was truly breath-taking, she knew would be an understatement!

Observing how the young attractive girl was looking around (obviously) in awe the male house servant cleared his throat and said, "Beautiful place, isn't it?" He produced a warm smile.

"Yes, it is." Anne Lee returned the smile.

"Mr. Pinkney will be with you in just a moment." He said, then asked, "Can I get you something to drink? Or, perhaps a sandwich?" He offered kindly.

"No thank you." She declined, still smiling.

"Okay," He nodded. "If you change your mind, I'll be in the next room." With that said, he left her to admire the family's sitting room.

"Anne Lee," Nathaniel Jr., entered the room with a huge smile on his face. Walking up to her, he wrapped his arms around the young girl. "How have you been?"

"I'm okay." Their eyes met, as Nathaniel took a step back to inspect her at arm's length.

"Have a seat." Nathaniel offered, as he too took a seat on

the couch.

Anne Lee didn't have a clue as to why he'd sent for her, yet, she decided to sit in silence. Opposed to inquiring.

"The loss of your father, still pains me to talk, or even think about." Nathaniel began, already sounding a bit choked up, Anne Lee couldn't help noticing.

"He and I were like brothers." He tried to smile. We were only seven years old when he and I met."

"He told me." Anne Lee recalled.

"I've never told anyone this," Nathaniel Jr., began. "My parents were so disappointed when, as a young boy, I was diagnosed with a learning disorder."

"You?" Anne Lee found that very hard to believe, considering he (and her father) were the two smartest Men she'd ever encountered.

"Yes, it's true." Again, he tried to smile. "It was a Woman named Ms. Corice, and later, your father, who were not only my greatest supporters, they're totally responsible for bringing out the potential in me." His smile (now) was evident, at recollection.

"Seeing all of your accomplishments, they certainly did a great job! Anne Lee produced a huge smile." I think you and my father have a most unique story."

"Yes, especially with it beginning and taking place in 1850, between a privileged White child, and a slave." He agreed. "Well, two slaves." He couldn't leave out Ms. Corice.

"I find it so unusual that your parents consented to such a relationship." Anne Lee commented.

"I certainly wouldn't say my mother 'consented' to it." Nathaniel Jr, laughed. "As for my father, I'm inclined to believe he actually encouraged it. Being the businessman, who literally craved a male heir, I think he recognized early on that Thaddeus was a good influence on me."

Anne Lee, couldn't help feeling proud to be Thaddeus's daughter. She had always felt that there was truly something special about her dad. Not to mention, the fact that, he was intelligent beyond words, she thought to herself.

"I promised your father that I would see to the wellbeing of his family, in the event, anything were to happen to him." Nathaniel informed her. "He promised me the same actually."

"He did make sure that we, his family, were okay." Anne Lee reminded him. Thaddeus's Will, pretty much left his family set for the rest of their lives.

Nathaniel Jr., knew the huge loses Thaddeus (and his brothers) had taken, because of the Depression of 1893, and whereas his wife (Rebecca) and their children felt that the 80K Thaddeus had left to them was a huge fortune, Nathaniel Jr., knew better.

"I understand that you'll be graduating in three months?"

"Yes." Anne Lee smiled proudly.

"Well, if you don't mind my intervention, I want to see to it that you further your education." Nathaniel Jr informed her.

"Continue it, as in?" Anne Lee, and her father, had many conversations regarding College, but in light of his passing, she didn't think it would be a reality.

She knew that, in certain instances, it took more than currency to make things happen. Which was something else her Father had enlightened her to.

"Believe it or not, South Carolina is home to five Black colleges." Nathaniel Jr smiled proudly, considering he had been Governor of the State.

"Claflin College, being the oldest, was built in 1869. Allen and Benedict, were both built in 1870. South Carolina State was built in 1896. Whereas, Voorhees College, being the fifth, was established in 1897." Anne Lee smiled.

"Wow!" Nathaniel couldn't help being impressed. "You certainly are your Father's child!" He shook his head, then laughed.

"You do not, necessarily, have to narrow it down to a school here in South Carolina. Although, my greatest influences is indeed within this State." He informed her.

"Attending a school, here in South Carolina, is perfectly fine with me. Actually, I prefer to be close to my Mother and Sister."

"As soon as you decide which school appeals to you most, let me know, and I'll do the rest."

"Truthfully, I think I'd like to attend the school that gave us Black folks our 'first' opportunity to earn a College degree." Anne Lee, let him know that she'd already given it thought.

"Okay," Nathaniel Jr gave an approving nod. "Claflin College it is then."

"Thank you, Mr. Pinkney." Anne Lee hugged him.

"My offer is contingent on one condition." he added, as her arms were still wrapped around his neck.

"Which is?" She asked, silently Praying the offer wasn't too good to be true.

"When you and I are alone like this, it's …Uncle Nate."

AUGUST 4, 1907

"Momma, you don't have to cry." Anne Lee hugged her Mother. "I will be home more often, then not. Orangeburg, isn't an hour from here." She informed Rebecca.

"I know." Rebecca replied. "But, you have no idea what it's like for a mother to have to let go of her baby." She spoke with eyes full of tears.

"Momma. I am not a baby anymore." Anne Lee, smiled, even though she understood. "Imagine if I were going to school in another State."

She'd undoubtedly relocate to 'that' State." Anne Lee's aunt Yvette joked. Yet, they all knew her words were probably true.

"Arethea was now 35 years old.

"No thank you!" Arethea responded to her cousin's suggestion.

Rebecca, simply stared at her niece as if she'd lost her mind! As far as she was concerned, it was bad enough to be losing one child!

"I know one thing, Sarah chided in. "Thaddeus is undoubtedly the happiest man up in Heaven right now." She smiled

"I know right." Arethea co-signed, smiling as well.

Sarah's comment, brought the first 'smile' of the day, to Rebecca's tear streaked face.

"This is truly a dream–come–true." Anne Lee, stared into her Mother's eyes as she said it.

"I know baby." Rebecca too, knew that it was indeed.

"I'll be fine Momma." Anne Lee assured her.

"I know you will." Rebecca maintained her smile. "What choice do you have? I mean, you 'are' your Father's child."

"I certainly am." Anne Lee's smile broadened even wider.

"What will you be studying?" Yvette asked.

"Everything!" Anne Lee exclaimed, then laughed, even though she was serious. "I haven't decided on a Major as of yet, but I intend to take my education as far as this opportunity will allow me."

Anne Lee's enthusiasm was enough to make each of the five Women in the kitchen, extremely proud and happy for her.

Following Arethea's gaze, Anne Lee excused herself, as the two

sisters made their way outside.

Once they were on the front porch, both of them instinctively took a seat in the swing-seat in which Thaddeus had built.

"You do know, that I'm very proud of you right?" Arethea asked.

"I do." Anne Lee replied with a smile, as she looked into the spacious yard.

"Nor, do I have to tell you, that I'm going to miss you right?"

"You don't." Anne Lee was certain they'd miss each other, more than words could even express.

"Although, I probably won't need to worry about you. I'm sure you already know that I will. Right?"

"I'm sure you will." Anne Lee answered. "But, my intellect is not all that I've gotten from you and our Dad. I've also acquired your strengths." She smiled, looking Arethea in her eyes.

With that said, the two sisters hugged for what seemed like

an eternity...

"I want you to have this." Arethea said, handing her younger sister a small string necklace. "Daddy gave it to me. He said, it wasn't much, but, it was the second half of string that his father gave to our grandmother. They both had worn them around their necks. Truthfully, I cried, when Daddy told me that our grandfather had told her, before his escape, that the string was merely a symbol and reminder that they'd forever be binded." She wiped the tears from her eyes, after securing the piece of string around her sister's neck.

"I always wanted to ask, why you always wore it around your neck."

Arethea tried to smile, as she, too, wiped her eyes. "Okay," Arethea stood.

"I think we've all done enough crying for one day." She laughed.

"Try a week!" Anne Lee laughed also.

"From this day forth, I will see your departure for what it is."

"That is?"

"My sister's going off to not only educate herself, but to potentially figure out the remedy to fix this crazy world in which we live!" Arethea laughed, albeit she was serious.

"Amen to that!"

THIRTEEN

MT. PLEASANT, SOUTH CAROLINA, 1912

Although, Anne Lee visited home at least twice a year, not counting the Summers in which she spent at home, she'd decided to stay in school and pursue her Master's Degree. The Elementary, and Middle school, that her father had built (from the ground up) she noticed was still intact. Yet, she knew once she graduated, she'd be a tremendous asset, when she came (back) to teach the children in the community from which she grew. However, it was times and /or circumstances such as these, that she didn't relish coming home. In fact, her spirit had been drastically affected, upon receiving the news that Nathaniel Pinkney Jr, her self-appointed Guardian Angel/ Uncle, had passed away....

"I'm sorry for your loss". Anne Lee, approached Melissa following the funeral service, offering her condolences.

"Thank you." Melissa tried to produce a smile.

"Nathaniel Pinkney, was like a second Father to me."

"I know." Those words *'did'* bring a smile to Melissa's tear streaked face. "He was so proud of you."

"Although, he's no longer with us physically, I will forever be grateful to your husband for all he has done for me." Anne Lee couldn't help tearing up as she spoke.

The two women exchange a long embrace.

Rollin Pinkney, shook his head, as he and his wife passed them by.

"Are you okay?" Arethea inquired.

"Not really." Raymond admitted honestly. "Not only did he teach me *'everything'* I know, my Uncle was more like a Father to me than my biological father had been."

Arethea hated to see him in such pain. Yet, she didn't know how to go about comforting him. They were the only two at his Mother's mansion, thus far, where a huge dinner was scheduled following the burial.

"I appreciate how you, and your family, have always been there for my family and I." Raymond was truly thankful for her support.

"Correction," Arethea began with somewhat of a smile. "Our families have always been there for each other," She reminded him.

At that, he nodded his up and down, in agreement.

"More times than not, it totally dismays me how or why God would take such good Men, as my Grandfather, your Father, and my Uncle away from our families.

Opposed to, taking evil people, such as my twin brother, or those who are simply unhappy. "Raymond commented before adding, "Such as myself."

Although, Arethea too, found that she was often unhappy with the cards in which fate had dealt her, she had basically accepted and learned to live with them. Yet, seeing someone whom she'd truly loved, stand before her in so much pain, caused her to reach out to him.

Raymond cried like a baby on her shoulder, as she too cried, more so for him, opposed to Nathaniel Jr. Nor, did she put up any resistance, as their lips met.

Neither of them recalled who had initiated the disrobing of clothing, however, they both knew that there was only one way (and one way only) to extinguish the fire that burned between them....

★★★★★

Over the years, Rebecca and Melissa had become quite good friends. Yet, neither of these two Women (ever) envisioned having to pursue life without their husbands.

Whereas, Melissa, came from an extremely wealthy background, and was college educated, she had been a Wife for the majority of her womanhood. As for Rebecca, being a devoted Wife and Mother, is basically all she'd ever known.

"So, where do we go from here?" Melissa leaned her head on Rebecca's shoulder, as the two of them sat in the swing-seat on Elizabeth's front porch (which was identical to the one on Rebecca's front porch).

"Truthfully," Rebecca began. "I've learned to go with the motion, of each day, as it comes and goes."

"Lord, I'd go plum crazy, sitting up in that huge house of mine doing much of nothing, as the days pass me by!" Melissa couldn't fathom such a life.

Although, she was now 69 years old, and a widow, there was 'still' a lot of life to not only live, but, to strive to enjoy, she told herself.

"I'm thinking, it wouldn't be a bad idea for me to move back to Massachusetts or maybe even Delaware, where the majority of my family members are." Melissa informed her.

"Being surrounded by lots of family sure sounds good." Rebecca smiled.

The only family she'd ever known was an aunt, Rosa Mae, who had actually brought her to Charleston, from a small town in Georgia called Wrens.

"You're welcome to pack up and come along with me." Melissa offered taking Rebecca's right hand into both of hers.

"I'm touched by such a kind offer." Rebecca smiled. "But, I can't leave my home, my daughters, or the friends I've made since coming here."

"I understand." Melissa truly did. However, she had no children, nor had she acquired any real friends (other than Rebecca and Elizabeth) since arriving in South Carolina. "I do hope, that you'll at least consider visiting me."

"The furthest I've travelled was from Georgia to South

Carolina," Rebecca laughed, considering the two were connected States.

"But, if you provide the means of travel, I'd love to come and visit you from time to time."

That, brought a huge smile to Melissa's face. She genuinely liked Rebecca (Thaddeus and their daughters), she'd told herself years prior. Truthfully, she hadn't grown up amongst the level of prejudice and/or racism that she'd observed since relocating to the South. She wasn't naive to think that it didn't exist in

Massachusetts, or Delaware, but, it certainly did not compare to South Carolina.

"Can I tell you something," Melissa began. "After Thaddeus passed, I watched you, and couldn't help admiring your strength. Nathaniel had always been impressed by you as well." She smiled.

Rebecca squeezed her hand, and said," I had to be strong, if not for me, for my family."

As the two Women looked towards the stars, they both knew that, between God's guidance, and Thaddeus and Nathaniel's spirit(s) being with them.... they'd be all right.

"My aunt, Melissa, asked if you and I would like to accompany her on her trip Up North." Audrey asked her husband Raymond over dinner.

'She decided to move back to Delaware'.

"I heard that she was thinking about moving back Up North, but I wasn't aware that she'd made an actual decision." Raymond rubbed his chin, giving thought to the situation.

"Yes, she was certain about relocating." Audrey knew that much early on. "She just wasn't sure if she'd be going to Massachusetts or Delaware."

As far as Melissa's decision to relocate, Raymond found it perfectly understandable. More times than not, he too, had contemplated leaving South Carolina. However, his reasons had little to do with a lack of family. Nonetheless, he was not interested in accompanying his aunt on her trip to her new home.

"I'll need to see to my Grandparent's home being properly maintained, and I have other business that will require my presence. So, as much as I would like to visit Delaware, and help Melissa with her transition, circumstances will not allow it." Raymond reached across the table and squeezed his wife's hand apologetically.

"I understand." Audrey did understand.

"However," He smiled. "You, can take the trip if you like. I'm sure your family would love to see you. How long has it been?" He asked, although he knew it had been years.

"Too long." She produced a slight smile. "However, I'd rather not leave you here to fend for yourself."

"Nonsense, I can take care of myself." Raymond assured her.

Unbeknownst to her husband, Audrey, quite desperately 'did' want to get away for a while. Not only had the past few years been stressful (on her mind and body), she hadn't spent much alone time with her Aunt, Melissa, let alone her relatives Up North, in quite some time. Therefore, Audrey knew that she would relish the hours that she and Melissa would have traveling from South Carolina to Delaware.

"Are you sure?" This time, it was she who squeezed his hand.

"Of course," Raymond smiled at his wife. "If I get too lonely, I'm coming to get you."

At that, they both laughed. Which was something they hadn't done in so long.

Although, their, marriage had taken some unexpected turns, and had experienced more than its share of rough spots, they did love one another. Yet, they also knew the love they shared was not enough. Whereas, Raymond, truly had love for his wife, his feelings for Audrey did not compare to what he felt for Arethea. As far as Audrey was concerned, she was no fool. She didn't need her brother-in-law, Rollin, to make implications that there was something between Raymond and Arethea, because she had sensed it from the very beginning.

She actually, didn't think that anyone could stand in a room with the two of them, and 'not' detect the chemistry exuding her husband and Arethea Addison. Unfortunately, in her case, instead of running for the hills (well, back to Delaware) where she knew her heart would be safe.... knowing what she knew, Audrey still failed to understand *why* love had found her and presented her with such a prize (Raymond Pinkney), yet, confine her to second place in his heart?

"As much as I'd like to spend time with Melissa and my family," Audrey began, staring her husband in his eyes. "I'd much rather be here with you, working on our marriage." She smiled slightly." All you have to do is tell me to stay."

Giving her words some thought, Raymond knew that the time alone would give him an opportunity to figure out what he was doing, because although they'd both wanted it, he still couldn't believe that he'd actually made love to another woman. Especially, a woman whom he knew there could never be a real relationship and/or future with.

"No." He spoke. "I really do want you to go, and enjoy your time with the people who love you." Raymond smiled.

Having her answer, Audrey, smiled as well, before releasing his hand to take a sip from her wine glass.

"While I'm away, I'm sure Arethea will check in on you, in the event you may need anything." Audrey didn't bother to look at him as she spoke.

"Arethea's presence, nor assistance won't be necessary," Raymond responded.

I've been thinking of possibly staying in Charleston, at my Grandparent's mansion while you're away."

Audrey, had not been expecting or prepared for such a response. She didn't have a clue as to why her husband would want to stay in Charleston, or what was going on between him and Arethea. Nevertheless, his answer pleased her tremendously.

Getting up from the table, Audrey walked around to Raymond's side of the table and took his right hand into hers.

"What's wrong?" He inquired, as she lightly tugged.

"Nothing's wrong my Love," Audrey smiled seductively." I just feel that it would only be right, that your wife leaves you with something to remember."

    With that said, Audrey led him to the place in which Raymond hadn't been in years...*Her Bedroom.*

FOURTEEN

MT. PLEASANT, SOUTH CAROLINA, 1917

Five years, following Nathaniel Jr's passing, things were going exceptionally well for Raymond and Rollin, as far as the Pinkney's business ventures were concerned. Nonetheless, the entire Country showed a deep concern when, on April 6, 1917, the United States decided to enter the 'Great War' taking place in Europe. For over two and half years, America had remained neutral. Yet, enjoyed a huge economic windfall produced by the enormous volume of Allied orders. Britain and France (both) needed munitions and supplies and American factories found themselves straining to fill the orders. Not to mention, the war, had cut off the supply of new immigrants from Europe. Between 1910 and 1914, over a million immigrants a year entered the United States.

Therefore, World War I, brought unexpected opportunities for Black Americans. Labor was needed in railroad construction, steel mills, the Tobacco farms of Connecticut, and automobile plants. Packard became the first automobile manufacturer to hire blacks in large numbers (Ford would follow soon after).

Two of the most visible effects the war had on Black Americans was; 1) Blacks embraced the 'War for Democracy' with the hope that White America would reward their loyalty and service. This conflict, it seemed, presented a Heaven-sent chance to strike a blow against racial discrimination in the United States, and just as the Civil War ended slavery, so might the 'Great War' undermine white supremacy. And 2) Was the drastic migration of Blacks (from the South) relocating to the North, which was considered the Great Migration. The outbreak of war, in Europe, had created an acute labor shortage in the Northern states.

"So many of my schoolmates are relocating to Northern Cities and States." Anne Lee, informed her mother Rebecca, who was not overly concerned with what her daughter's schoolmates and their families were doing, she was simply elated to have her baby girl home for the Summer recess. "How come you've never considered moving away from here?"

Anne Lee's question brought Rebecca out of her reverie.

"Why would I leave here?" Rebecca didn't see the logic.

"I'm one year away from earning my Master's degree in Education and although, my intentions were to come back here and teach, I'm thinking about moving to a big City." Anne Lee revealed.

"Why not come home for a couple of years, then move to another city?" Rebecca found it difficult to even fathom her youngest daughter moving away to a big city. It was hard enough seeing her go away to college. "The people here, especially the younger folks, can really use someone with your intelligence. In fact, you're all everyone around here talks about, being that you're the only black person in these parts to attend a College." Rebecca smiled proudly.

"I know," Anne Lee totally understood. Yet, she couldn't help envisioning herself taking part in some of the progressive movements such as the National Association of Colored Women, and the National Association for the Advancement of Colored People, both of which she'd heard and read so much about. Not to mention, the inspiration she received reading about Women such as Ida B. Wells, who was not just currently, but, had been leading a massive campaign against the crime of lynching in America for quite some years

"Like you said," Rebecca reminded her. "You still have another year before you will complete school and earn your degree. In that time, I want you to really evaluate your future decisions. Whatever they may be, I will support you." She produced a smile, even though she silently prayed that Anne Lee would reconsider her desire to leave South Carolina, and her family.

"Okay." Anne Lee responded with a smile of her own, before giving her mother a hug. "I don't know what I'd do without you."

"Make sure you keep 'that' in mind as you consider your plans for the future." Rebecca laughed as she gave her daughter a tighter squeeze.

"I certainly will." Taking a step back, Anne Lee took in her surroundings. Their kitchen hadn't changed a bit since her last visit home, she realized. In fact, nothing about her family's home or the City of Mt. Pleasant had changed over the years, she'd told herself. Although, she found neither sight depressing, however, Anne Lee also knew that she didn't want to enjoy the complacency, nor conform to the life that her Mother, Sister, and relatives seemed to relish in South Carolina. No, she needed to be where Black folks were doing things and saying things to instigate their people to stand up for themselves, and their rights. Opposed to, accepting the farce of white supremacy. She often recalled a conversation in which she had heard, years earlier, between her parents. In that conversation, Anne Lee, could feel and sense, from her father's words, that he, too, had wished that there was more in which he could have done to help the status of Black people. And, how much it had obviously troubled him to have been called an accommodist by Isaiah.

"Go ahead and get yourself situated while I prepare dinner."

"Okay." Anne Lee replied as she prepared to exit the kitchen, not before inquiring, "Where's Arethea?"

"That's a good question," Rebecca agreed. "I haven't seen her all day."

Isaiah, didn't know what the fight was about this time, he

just knew that he was not only tired of feuding with his wife, but also striving to drown his sorrows in a bottle of Whiskey.

"Man, I don't which is gonna kill you first. That whiskey, or that seemingly toxic marriage of yours." Jon Jon, approached his younger brother, at the same time reaching for the bottle of liquor. Which he turned upside down.

Isaiah didn't bother to protest as he watched the whiskey being poured to the ground.

"I'm leaving in two days," Jon Jon reminded him. "This is not how I want to remember you, on our last days together."

"You're going to the military," Isaiah spoke, staring his brother in his eyes. "Stop sounding like you ain't coming back."

"Of course, I'm coming back." Jon Jon laughed. "But, I might not be returning to 'this' place." He emphasized the word 'this' as he looked about the spacious landscape. Although, he'd never lived anywhere else, he did know, or told himself, that he was tired of the South. "Truthfully, if we win this war, I wish I could stay over there in France or England somewhere. The way Blacks are treated here in America. I'm sure does not compare to anywhere else on Earth."

"I know that's right!" Isaiah agreed with the assumption. He, too wished he'd been drafted to serve in the military, however, he nor Willie qualified. Whereas, Willie was too old, Isaiah was told that he had health issues which prevented him. The recruiter told him nothing more, nothing less, meaning Isaiah was left on his own to ascertain what those health issues were.

"Once I'm settled, wherever *'settled'* may be," Jon Jon produce a smile, "I'll send for you."

Isaiah simply nodded his head to that.

Next, the two brothers did something they hadn't done in as long as either of them could remember, they exchanged a long heartfelt embrace.

As the two brothers hugged, Isaiah whispered, "I just hope I'm still around when you send for me."

Jon Jon didn't quite know what to gather by his brother's remark, however, he decided to let it pass.

JULY 4, 1917

Nearly Two Hundred people (family, friends, and neighbors) had joined in on the festivities, which included food, drinks, games, singing, and plenty of stories and jokes provided by Willie, all taking place on Rebecca's property. Independence Day was actually celebrated on the Addison's land long before Thaddeus had passed away, therefore Rebecca was merely keeping up with tradition.

"Willie, I hope you ain't over here telling no dirty jokes to these children!" Rebecca commented, giving him the eye, as she was passing the group.

"If it ain't dirty," Willie began with a sly grin on his face, knowing

everyone, including the kids, knew his slogan. "It certainly ain't funny!"

At that, the group of youngsters laughed. As did Willie.

"Where's Monique?" Rebecca, asked no one particular, as she looked about the vicinity. She simply mentioned Monique's name because Rebecca knew that Willie knew 'that she knew' Monique was the one person who did NOT tolerate his antics, nor inappropriateness.

Although, Rebecca had moved on, Willie still didn't feel like being confronted by his wife. Therefore, he took a sip from his cup and informed the group of youngsters, "Y'all chaps gone have to excuse me a minute. I got something I need to go handle." With that being said, he stepped off as if in search for someone.

The Sun had already set, however, quite a few people lingered as if they were in no rush to end the celebration, or go home. Which Rebecca found understandable, considering she too, on such occasions, not only missed her husband, but dreaded the loneliness associated with living (alone) in such a big house.

JULY 5, 1917

The quiet, after the storm, or more accurately, the chaos from the previous night, found the entire community of Mt. Pleasant shocked, confused, angry and afraid!

Rebecca had just fallen asleep, when Monique came banging on her front door. To say that her niece was hysterical, she knew would be an understatement, witnessing her demeanor when she opened the door.

"You have to calm down Dear," Rebecca told her, as she held Monique tightly. "So, you can explain to me what happened."

"He's dead!" Monique exclaimed. With that being said, she sobbed even louder.

Rebecca, allowed her niece some time to mourn. Albeit, she hadn't the slightest clue 'whom' she was actually mourning. It wasn't until Malcolm (one of the Steed boys) entered the house, being that the front door had still been slightly ajar, and removed his hat before informing Rebecca, "It's bad."

"What's bad?" Rebeca asked, not entirely sure she even wanted to know, seeing his bloodshot eyes filled with tears.

"They killed Willie."

Anne Lee, was standing at the foot of the living room's stairwell, which enabled her to clearly hear what Malcolm had said to her mother.

"Who killed him?" Rebecca inquired. Despite being totally stunned.

"That evil white man, and some of his friends!" It was Monique who'd said it.

"Evil white man?" Rebecca repeated.

"They not only shot him, they tied a piece of rope around his neck which they tied to one of their trucks," Malcolm broke down, gathering himself, he added, "and dragged him down the road."

Rebecca was (now) completely horrified by what she was hearing.

"Who is this white man you're talking about?" Anne Lee inquired as she stepped into the foyer.

"Rollin Pinkney."

JULY 12, 1917

"You do know, that your decision is not making any sense to me."

"Truthfully, it's not making a whole lot of sense to me either, but, it's something that I realize I must do." Anne Lee told her mother.

"You have one month left before school begins." Rebecca reminded her daughter. "Unless, you're not planning on coming back to finish school?" She stared at Anne Lee with wide eyes.

"Momma please, just respect my decision." Anne Lee begged. "I just need to get away from this place."

"Okay," Rebecca backed down. "But please promise me you won't stay away?"

"The only thing that I will promise you is that, you do not have to worry about me." Anne Lee gave her mother's right hand a squeeze as she produced a slight smile. "I have friends from school, who live in New York City. Again, I just need to get away from this madness going on here. This place is killing my spirit." She allowed her tears to roll down her cheeks.

"Okay." Rebecca repeated herself. Even though, the thought of her baby girl traveling so far away was tearing her heart to shreds.

"Audrey, is driving me to the railroad station. So, let me go ahead and get my things together, she should be here in a second."

"Okay." Rebecca repeated herself one last time, as she, too, allowed the tears to fall freely from her eyes. "I love you."

"I love you too, Momma." Anne Lee assured her mother, as she released her hand. Ascending the living room's stairwell, she knew that she was breaking her mother's heart. Yet, Anne Lee, knew that her reason for leaving had less to do with maintaining her sanity in such a cruel racist environment, and more to do with the wellbeing of the *"child"* whom she was carrying along with her....

FIFTEEN

HARLEM, NEW YORK, 1919

By 1918, the end of the Great War, nearly half a Million blacks had migrated North and West, all seeking opportunities Jim Crow denied them in the South (better wages, an escape of abuse, and a pursuit of happiness, to name a few), by white America's racism.

Sadly, blacks not only found themselves faced with unmet promises during and following the war, white America was determined to keep them in their place. However, the Great Migration continued nonetheless. A migration, that would ultimately refactor America's racial equation.

Given the nationwide white racism of the early Twentieth Century, blacks did find that the social conditions -in the North- sometimes mirrored the image of what they were fleeing in the South. Many facets of Northern life involved a high degree of discrimination aimed at blacks, discrimination just as humiliating as what they'd experienced in the South. Whereas, Northern whites had previously established a sort of acceptance, even kept racial disharmony at a low, the Great Migration radically altered such feelings and conditions. Now, these same Northern whites viewed this sudden surge/racial equation in the black communities as a serious problem. Not only were these new black migrants dramatically less educated than those who had long lived in the North, they were more so viewed as rivals for the low paying jobs held by poorly educated whites. The result, was increased racial tension and more discrimination which often led to racial disturbances leading to rioting and even mass murder.

With these changes, the old equilibrium between white racism and black security disappeared in the North's cities. Blacks crowded even more closely into substandard ghetto housing, while whites conspired to keep them there. Blacks who did attempt to move into white neighborhoods found themselves face to face with all manners of violence. Just as banks denied home loans to black families. As a result, blacks found themselves relegated to the ghetto where they were welcomed.

Arriving in Harlem, Anne Lee, couldn't help noticing how black folks seemingly didn't mind keeping to themselves. It clearly appeared to Anne Lee, as though the folks whom she'd encountered in Harlem, had manufactured a World so grand and alluring, that it was obvious that they could care less what Jim Crow was denying them!

At the time of her arrival in New York, Anne Lee was 27 years old, and although, she had never traveled outside of the State of South Carolina, Her level of knowledge, wisdom, determination, and strong will, would not allow her to be intimidated by the size, and fast pace of her new surroundings.

Nonetheless, she certainly had to admit, what New York considered its ghetto, was indeed impressive considering what she'd been use-to. The structure of the Brownstone homes, the IRT Subway stations, the abundance of automobiles in every make and model, that were polished to an incredible shine, the Black-Owned businesses, the men walking around in their creased yet baggy suits, and the women were not only stylish, but wore hairstyles that caused her to stare!

On the same token, she too, had garnered her share of stares. Which she had pretty much gotten use-to, during her years at Claflin College. In fact, even women had been known to compliment her mostly, as far as her eyes were concerned.

Now that two years had passed since her relocation to the Big Apple, she was more than ready to exert her independence.

"I truly appreciate everything in which you and Bernard have done for me and Tyra, but I think the time has come for me to spread my wings." Anne Lee informed her girlfriend from college, a woman named Doris who offered her a place to stay when she first arrived in Harlem.

"Where will you go?" Doris asked with concern in her voice.

"I've been communicating with some people, who introduced me to a man named Roger who is into real estate. Actually, he is the one who found me the Brownstone that I've since purchased." Anne Lee revealed, smiling from ear to ear.

Doris, however, was quite speechless by such news

"It's located on 138th Street, between Lenox and 7th Avenue. You really have to see it, it is so beautiful!" Anne Lee exclaimed.

Before Doris could gather herself to reply, she was further blown away when Anne Lee revealed that, she owned all *'three'* floors of the Brownstone, and they were welcomed to rent out its top floor which was actually a two-bedroom apartment.

"No offense, but it's also much nicer than where you are currently residing." Anne Lee had assured the couple.

A former classmate of hers, named Cletus Robinson, introduced Anne Lee to a cousin of his named Roger E. Robinson, who was a well-known and respectable Realtor throughout Manhattan and Brooklyn.

"I knew you'd fall in love with the place, as soon as it was shown to you." Mr. Robinson had said to Anne Lee with a smile. "The floors are newly finished, and for a small fee. I have a man who will come in as often as you'd like to maintain them."

Anne Lee nodded her approval. Truthfully, they were the shiniest hard-wood floors she'd ever seen.

"I also know a woman whose specialty is in making drapes. Some of your windows, if you notice, are quite huge, which may require her expertise." he added.

The only windows Anne Lee could think of in comparison to the ones in which she now owned, had belonged to the Pinkney's Charleston mansion.

"The appliances are all fairly new as well, so you shouldn't have a problem out of any of those."

Again, Anna Lee simply nodded her approval. She had actually already purchased the place a week earlier. Therefore, Mr. Robinson's unannounced *second* visit somewhat dismayed her. Opposed to dwelling on it, out of courtesy, she listened as he continued on.

"All of that being said, I suppose you will manage quite well from here." Mr. Robinson turned slowly, then made his way towards her front door. Turning somewhat abruptly, as if finding his nerves, he inquired, "Would it interest you, maybe in the near future, after you and your daughter are situated of course, if I took you out to show you around the city?"

Giving his question, some thought, Anne Lee smiled and replied.

"Once I'm situated, I'll definitely give some thought to your offer. If it's still on the table at that point."

Producing one of the most beautiful smiles Anne Lee had ever seen on a man, Roger E. Robinson placed his Stetson on his head, then reached for her right hand (which he brought to his lips) and said, "I'll be waiting patiently."

Once he was gone, Anne Lee stood there with her back to the door. Cletus hadn't told her much at all about his cousin Roger, just that he was a successful Realtor, who didn't do shady business he'd assured her. However, he certainly didn't mention how attractive the man was, or that he wasn't married, which Anne Lee assumed due to the absence of wedding band. Nor, was she even prepared to be courted, which was truthfully the very 'last' thing on her mind.

"As handsome, successful, well spoken, and apparently eligible as you are Mr. Robinson, your way of asking a Woman out on a date did appear quite feeble." Anne Lee thought to herself with a smile. I'm just saying." She added, in her endeavor to convince herself that she was actually not interested,

As she entered her partially furnished bedroom, Anne Lee realized that there was only one person, place or thing that had her undivided attention, and complete interest.

"Someday, I 'will' get out and see the Big Apple. But, right now *'you'* are the only Apple in my eyes." She spoke softly, as she bent to plant a kiss on the lips of her sleeping daughter, Tyra Star Addison.

Although, Anne Lee never allowed her relationship with Roger, over the two year they've known each other, to become more than a friendship, she was truly thankful that he'd entered her life. The fact that he'd always respected and not once attempted to cross the 'friendship' boundary in which she'd clearly set, made Anne Lee appreciate him and what they shared even more.

Not only did Roger show her basically 'everything' New York City had to offer, its residents and visiting tourist alike, he also schooled Anne Lee to the deception, schemes, and unpleasantries of the city.

"This is not Mt. Pleasant. Everyone who smiles at you is 'not' your friend." He'd told her. "Nor, is everyone who stares at you a potential enemy."

"So, in that case, how do I know who's who?" She'd asked.

"Truthfully, in this City 'respect' is the greatest equalizer.

Meaning, as long as you give people reason to respect you, there's no need to analyze who is who. One of the things I like about you is seeing how you've created a space in which you do not allow anyone to enter." He smiled as he said it.

"I thought most men would hold that against me." Anne Lee held his stare.

"I'm not talking about in 'that' regard." Roger laughed. "I'm talking about how you don't run around with people or bring folks into your home. Or, around your child."

"Oh no, my home is definitely off limits!" She exclaimed. "My friend Doris and her husband Bernard rent the top floor of my Brownstone, but they're working people and are hardly ever home. Even when they are home, I barely ever see them."

Roger nodded his approval. He didn't know how truthful Anne Lee had been when she'd told him that her family wired her enough money each month to cover her living expenses. At least, until her daughter was old enough to enable her to feel comfortable hiring a Nanny, while she went to work.

Anne Lee, hated lying to Roger, who had been nothing but a true friend, but she wasn't about to reveal to him, or anyone else, that she was in possession of enough money to hold her (and her child) over for as long as she desired to be a stay-at-home parent. Truthfully, she couldn't wait till Tyra was old enough to actually begin home schooling. She had so much to enlighten her little girl to. At two years old, Tyra was already showing how potentially advanced she was!

Anne Lee, also knew that if it were not for her daughter, she would have -undoubtedly- given in to an intimate relationship with Roger Robinson. The man had a lot of great qualities, she had to admit. However, she wasn't ready or willing to share with anyone else 'what all' she had in store solely for her little girl. The selfishness of her intentions and desires -for Tyra- is what enabled Anne Lee to (in good conscience) not give into a man whom she felt had already fallen in love with her....

Whereas, Anne Lee was creating a new life for herself and her infant daughter, in a City that was still relatively new and still quite foreign to her, most of the big cities throughout the country was going up in smoke. Violent race riots, resulting in numerous deaths (black and whites) were breaking out in a number of Northern and Western cities. Yet, none worst then the latest that was taking place in the city of Chicago. Apparently, a young black boy named Eugene Williams was killed by a group of whites for swimming in their section of the 23rd Street Beach. It was a race riot that ensued for nearly two weeks, with the National Guard being called in (although, they mostly assisted local law enforcement in locking up mostly blacks), when the smoke cleared nearly 25 blacks had been killed and close to 15 whites.

Anne Lee, being from a relatively small town in South Carolina, could not believe how prevalent the race riots were in predominantly all of America's largest cities. As she thought about what was taking place in Chicago, she silently Prayed that the violence, rioting, and killings did not reach her cousin Danielle and her husband Samuel! Both of whom, Anne Lee hadn't heard from, seen, nor reached out to in years. With her decision to leave South Carolina, Anne Lee, also decided that it was best that she left everything and everyone behind as well.... *Including, family!*

SIXTEEN

HARLEM, NEW YORK, 1922

"W hat's wrong Mama?" Tyra asked in a concerned, yet childish and sleepy voice. Anne Lee hadn't even noticed when her five-year old daughter entered her bedroom.

Wiping her eyes, Anne Lee feigned a smile before extending her opened arms which Tyra ran into, immediately placing her head on her Mother's chest.

"I'm okay baby." Anne Lee spoke in a comforting and assuring tone of voice, as she ran a hand over the top of her daughter's head down to her back, which was the length of the child's hair.

"Why were you crying?"

Still rubbing her child's back, Anne Lee had to think of a reason for her tears, although it killed her to lie to her daughter. Not only was Tyra the brightest, smartest, and extremely understanding, child Anne Lee has ever known, she was also too young to know certain truths, Anne Lee had decided. Whereas, Tyra never asked about other family, Anne Lee never volunteered such information. However, she knew the day would present itself when She'd have to be forthcoming, if not truthful with her daughter. Yet, she had no way of knowing that, it wouldn't be until shortly after Tyra's 16th birthday that, at least '*some*' of those truths would have to be revealed.

"Unlike children," Anne Lee began, planting a kiss atop Tyra's head before continuing, "Grown folks cry when we're happy, we cry when we think about people, places, and situations. But, to answer your question," Anne Lee paused to plant a second kiss atop her daughter's head. "I was crying because I'm so thankful to be as Blessed as I am." Which was not a lie. She knew that God had been watching over her and her child, ever since leaving South Carolina.

Although, her friends weren't many, Tyra was truly Thankful for the small hand-full, whom thus far had proven to be awesome and true! She was also Blessed with plenty to eat, plenty to wear, and a beautiful home to call her own, at a time when the majority of Blacks (especially, those who had migrated from the South) found themselves struggling to maintain in a City where most were led to believe was the -land-of milk and honey! If not, the Promised Land. She knew first hand, how folks who had left the South early on, tended to write back home, telling stories, of how one could become rich simply cleaning houses, mopping floors, or working in factories. God forbid the family member and/or friend (writers of such letters) owned a nice car, nice clothes, or sent money back home on occasion!

"We are Blessed to have the life that we do." Anne Lee told her little girl. "But, my greatest Blessing is You." With that being said, she stood up from where she sat (on the edge of her bed) and took Tyra's small hand into hers as she led the way to her daughter's bedroom. Once Tyra was tucked in, Anne Lee went around to the other side of the bed and got beneath the covers as well.

"I sleep so much better when you sleep with me." Tyra revealed to her mother with a huge smile on her face. Tyra's smile was so wide, and her teeth so bright, that Anne Lee could see it even in the dark. Not to mention, her aqua greenish/blue eyes had a tendency to shine so brightly, it was no wonder her middle name was Star.

"What a coincidence." Anne Lee exclaimed, as if surprised

by her daughter's revelation. "I, too, sleep better when I'm in your bed."

At that, they both laughed, gave each other a final hug, before turning their backs to one another. As she lay there, Anne Lee willed herself not to cry. Especially, seeing how much of a light sleeper her daughter could be. It would be the night, that Anne Lee learned to mourn without tears. For her daughter's sake, she Prayed that her spirits would one day be as they were, prior to receiving Audrey's letter (earlier that day), informing her that her mother, Rebecca, passed away...What hurt even more, was the fact that, Anne Lee could only imagine how lonely her mother must have been/felt in her final days. Albeit, she and Rebecca wrote each other over the years, and her mother claimed to -totally- understand her reason for leaving and/or not returning, it nonetheless had to have been difficult for Rebecca. Especially, losing 'both' of her daughters in a sense.

It wouldn't be until after Tyra's 16th birthday that Anne Lee informed her that she had an Aunt named Arethea, who in June of 1917, decided to run off with a man named Raymond Pinkney, while his wife was away in Delaware, never to be seen or heard from again.

Leaving behind, not only two heartbroken and confused families, but also a twin brother named Rollin Pinkney, who was clearly unstable and completely on a rampage! So much so, Anne Lee had decided to never return to Mt. Pleasant and all the chaos. Whereas, everyone during the Great Migration, had their reasons for leaving the South, Anne Lee too, had hers. Now, that her only remaining (immediate) family was no longer alive, she definitely had no reason to 'ever' return. Which she had informed Audrey, as well as gave her instructions as to what she'd like for Audrey to handle regarding her family's home and property.

Once she was certain that Tyra was sound asleep, Anne Lee quietly climbed out of her bed, gave her little girl one last 'good night' kiss on her forehead, and made her way back to her own bedroom.

After completing her (second) Prayer that night, Anne Lee climbed into her bed and closed her eyes.

"Yes, I 'am' truly Blessed. Therefore, I am 'not' going to cry." She told herself, knowing that 'crying' was the very last thing her parents would be expecting of her. Between the two of them, they had instilled so much knowledge, wisdom, and strength within her, growing up, she realized (now) that God -through her parents- had prepared her for the plan in which He had for her life. Yes, she could always go back to school and get her Master's degree, but, she finally came to the realization 'why' she had to walk away from everything and everybody. Nor, was she going to give the credit to, or allow her fear of Rollin Pinkney to be the reason.

"I know you have a daughter to raise, but don't you think you should enjoy life in the process?" Doris asked, she couldn't quite understand how Anne Lee, who had been in New York City for over five years now, still refused to date, or go out on the town. Not to mention, Anne Lee was the most beautiful person, inwardly and physically, that Doris had ever met. Men literally were stopped in their tracks whenever the two of them did go outside of the house.

"Bernard took me to the Cotton Club last weekend, and girl when I tell you we had a ball!" Doris exclaimed excitedly. "Although, I only have eyes for my husband, girl them men up in there were sharp!"

"I'm sure they were." Anne Lee laughed, then shook her head.

"I've been here for seven years now, and I still find it quite overwhelming at times, seeing so many beautiful, classy and so-phisticated Black folks in one City. And the cars they drive are unbelievable. I can't wait till Bernard and I purchase our first vehicle. Anyway, but like I was saying, we try to go out at least twice out of each month, because he and I both work so hard. You know what I mean?"

"I totally understand." Anne Lee replied, every though she hadn't worked outside of her home, since arriving in New York City. Her job, thus far, has been tutoring her child.

"Where I'm from, our definition of entertainment was going to Church, having folks over for a barbecue, or maybe going out to a movie." Doris shook her head, recalling what her life had been like growing up on her family's farm in Bennettsville, South Carolina. Her parents saving up enough money to send her to college was the second-best thing that had ever happened to/for her. The first 'best' thing to happen to her was meeting and later marrying Bernard, she thought to herself with a smile. Not only was her husband her greatest supporter and source of encouragement, but even amid struggle, he'd always found ways to make her smile.

"Since Bernard and I have been going out, we've met some pretty awesome folks. And, we've seen so many performers. I've seen Louis Jordan and the Nicholas Brothers, Duke Ellington and his Six-piece band, Cab Calloway, The Mills Brothers, Dorothy Dandridge, Lena Horne, Billy Eckstine, Sidney Bechet."

"Okay, okay, okay." Anne Lee interrupted her friend. "I get what you're saying. But right now, I'm just not interested. Roger use to try to get me to go out as well, but I guess he understands what my focus is, because he's backed off considerably." She smiled being that she truly appreciated his understanding. "However, he knew that the juke joints and night clubs wouldn't really interest me anyway. Therefore, he'd suggest a speak easy, or going to a rally to hear various folks give their speeches regarding social change, racial equality, and police brutality in our communities. When the time is right, I do intend to get out there and support the NAACP, as well as a few other Organizations I feel are sincere in representing worthy causes."

When she made her decision to leave the South, Anne Lee, knew that New York City was basically a no-brainer, because she loved all the Organizations and Movements that were taking place in New York. Since arriving in Harlem, she read just about every Editorial penned by W.E.B. DuBois, a man she considered an overwhelmingly eloquent advocate in the equality for Black people. In fact, he was a man whom Ann Lee was determined to meet some day. Also, she heard and learned a great deal about a man named Marcus M. Garvey, and his Universal Negro Improvement Association. She had attended one of Marcus Garvey's speeches at Mother Zion AME Church, walking distance from where she lived, and was very impressed by not only his message, but also his spellbinding oratory. When she'd told Roger about attending the speech, he simply shook his head.

"I wasn't expecting such an expression." Anne Lee couldn't help noticing.

"You gotta admire any man, especially a Black man, who can create such a mass movement. Actually, I personally do not know of any Black person who has generated such enthusiasm or adulation as Garvey." He had complimented/commended the black leader.

"But?" Anne Lee asked staring Roger in the eyes.

"I am not critical of is ideology, or Black Nationalism for that matter. Yu do not acquire millions of followers, a lot of whom are actually dues-paying members of the UNIA, if your ideals are completely unrealistic." Roger expressed. "My problem, as a businessman, is when folks invest money in which many of them probably do not even have to spare, I mean, I totally respect the whole African Liberation movement, but, the Black Star Line was losing money from the start. A number of my friends and associates lost a lot of money in that company's stock." He had informed her, leaving out the fact that; after finding himself under federal indictment, Garvey's promotion of black nationalism not only changed to segregation, but he also commented that the Southern white man is the best friend the negro ever had! Not to mention, he admitted to holding secret discussions with the 'imperial wizard' of the Ku Klux Klan, Edward Clark, agreeing with the Klan's opposition to miscegenation.

"Speaking of Roger," Doris grinned. "Tell me a little about your Mr. Nice Guy." She continued grinning before adding, "He certainly is a handsome man."

Deciding not to comment on Doris's physical assessment,

or rather compliment of Roger, Anne Lee replied to the question asked.

"He told me that he was born and raised in Shreveport, Louisiana. His father was a farmer, and his mother a teacher. After graduating high school, he moved to New Orleans to attend Leland College. To his parent's surprise and objection, mid-way through school, he enlisted in the military. Four months after enlisting, he found himself stationed over in France. Unfortunately, he suffered an injury while fighting, and eighteen months later found himself back in Louisiana.

For some reason, he thought, the fact that he'd nearly died fighting for the United States, that he would receive a hero's embrace upon returning to the Society in which he had left. Instead, he found himself facing much worst hostility, hatred, and torment of Jim Crow. In fact, most of the whites (men in particular) couldn't stand the sight of him in uniform. So much so, he could tell they literally wanted to rip it from his shoulders, arms, legs and back.

Seeing how so many folks he had known, prior to leaving for France, had migrated to Northern cities, he too, decided to leave New Orleans. Arriving in New York City, he began working for an Uncle, who owned several grocery stores (and was also a major Numbers Runner), until Roger, who had a good deal of money saved up, noticed how a number of white families were moving out of various neighborhoods, due to the sudden emergence of blacks. Expressing his interest in buying property his Uncle introduced him to a man named Philip Patent. The rest, as they say, was history." Anne Lee smiled.

"Wow. I bet he had a lot of money!" Doris exclaimed.

"Probably does." Anne Lee shrugged, not even slightly interested in the potential of his having lots of money. More so, because she had her own money, which had grown by tens of thousands following the visit she had recently received from Audrey Bowers-Pinkney...

SEVENTEEN

HARLEM, NEW YORK, 1927

" **I** have a serious problem with you telling my twelve-year old that she should pursue her dream of becoming a doctor." Mr. Cornell T. Riley, owner of Riley's Funeral Home, expressed his displeasure.

"What my husband is really trying to say is," Mrs. Vanessa Riley interceded. "As a tutor, you have been remarkably outstanding in regard to the overall academic improvements as far as our daughter is concerned. Much more effective than any teacher she has had thus far. I must concede." She smiled approvingly. "However, my husband and I, like to instill, or rather nurture, realistic goals in our children. I'm sure you understand." Mrs. Riley held Anne Lee's stare.

Shortly after Tyra's sixth birthday, Anne Lee decided to turn the first floor of her Brownstown into a makeshift school. Actually, she had turned the huge living room into what clearly passed as a classroom, which included a blackboard, several text books on various subjects, at least two maps (a global, and of the United States,) and six desks (for the six young girls she would tutor, including Tyra.) The only reason she'd chosen six girls, opposed to it being co-ed, was because Anne Lee knew that young boys, and girls had a tendency to distract one another. Since hers wasn't a full-fledged learning facility/school (which provided guidance counselors, security, etc.) she didn't want to take on more than she could handle. She also knew that, had Tyra been a boy, it was more than likely that she'd been tutoring six males, because the whole idea started with her daughter.

"Of course, I understand." Anne Lee responded respectfully. "However, I do not think it is wise or productive to tell a child, or anyone for that matter, who and/or what they should or shouldn't aspire to become. Do I know of any female doctors? The answer is no. Yet, who am I to say that there will never 'be' a female physician or doctor. All I do know is that, the chances of it becoming a reality is far more unlikely when we, as parents, tell our children that their dreams and aspirations are unrealistic." Anne Lee explained her position.

"That being said, I do apologize for telling your daughter that she can become whoever or whatever she chooses or is determined to become. Especially, seeing how my encouragement is clearly not aligned with what she's being taught, or told, at home. Therefore, I'd truly, find it completely understandable if the two of you decided that it would be best that someone else tutored Kimberly."

Her comment, caused the Riley's to exchange a quick glance at each other, which was followed by Mr. Riley's response.

"It's not that serious, Ms. Addison," He spoke, obviously backing away from his opening remark about having a 'serious problem', as he continued. "I've just never been one to engage in filling people, especially a child, with false hope. Nor, do I wish to do so at my financial expense." He smiled shamelessly. "I'm not a fortune teller, therefore, I do not know what progress or advancements black folks will or will not enjoy in the future. All I want is what's best for my daughter."

"I understand." Anne Lee replied. Roger told her that Mr. Riley was a very self-centered man, who could care less about the status and/or conditions of blacks living in Harlem. His only concern was that they found the means to pay for his services.

"We definitely want you to continue working with our daughter." Mrs. Riley added with a smile. "Not to mention, Kimberly's quite fond of you, and the other girls whom she's met since coming here."

"She's a very bright young lady, with a lot of promise." Anne Lee complimented their daughter, who was indeed a clearly gifted young girl.

"Alright, I gotta get a move on." Mr. Riley had the nerve to smile as he'd made the comment. "You, young lady, just keep up the good work."

Anne Lee didn't really want or feel like shaking the man's hand, which he'd extended to her. As they shook hands, he discreetly used his thumb to rub the backside of her hand, which Anne Lee quickly withdrew. Had it not been for her admiration of their daughter Kimberly, whom Anne Lee had grown quite fond of over the years, she knew she'd give the Riley's their money back and send them on their way!

"And, leave the parenting to me." With that said, Mr. Riley put on his coat, followed by his Stetson, then ushered his wife through the front door.

At Ten years old, Tyra Star Addison knew the Capital City of every State in America, a great deal of African and American history, could spell just about every word inside of Webster's dictionary, and knew the definitions of more words than the average adult could pronounce.

In math, she was equally (if not more) impressive! Not only was she by far, the smartest of the Six girls Anne Lee tutored, Tyra was also the youngest. The current ages of the other five girls was between twelve and thirteen, Tyra had recently turned ten.

By the age of Thirteen, Anne Lee decided to put Tyra in a public school. The challenge, was finding a High School that not was not only suitable, but possessed a standard curriculum that would enable Tyra to advance beyond what she already knew.

"I think you should take her out of that school, and continue to work with her at home. Especially, being that Tyra's way too ahead of the classes. They already skipped her two grades, and she's still not learning anything that she doesn't already know." Doris gave a suggestion in which Anne Lee already considered.

"Apparently she's also learning that she likes having males in her classes." Anne Lee shook her head, yet, laughed.

Doris, Tyra's unofficial Godmother, simply rolled her eyes at Anne Lee's remark, before adding, "That's all the more reason why you need to get her out of there."

"I think I'll let her finish this year out, then next year apply to some Colleges. With Tyra's GPA, I doubt there's a black college or University in the country that will turn her down once her test scores are in." Anne Lee smiled. "Then again,

I'll continue to teach her until she reaches the age of Sixteen, then we'll focus on colleges."

It's amazing that we're sitting here talking college in regard to a Thirteen-year old!" Doris said incredulously. "At thirteen, I didn't even know that college existed, let alone striving to attend one. I actually thought I had died and went to Heaven when my parents told me they were sending me off to college and away from that old farm in Bennettsville." Doris laughed as she shook her head at the memory.

"Yes, you did use to walk through the school's corridors as if you were out of place." Anne Lee half joked.

"Really?" Doris asked wide eyed. "Was it noticeable?"

"Very." Anne Lee laughed at her (now) closest friend. "Seriously though had my daughter been a white child, I'm sure they'd be placing her in one of the best schools New York has to offer. It's so unfair how disadvantaged our children are. I mean, as adults, we do what we have to in order to get by or survive, but the racial discrimination and disenfranchisement of our children is an abomination. That is why I have worked tirelessly to teach my child 'everything' if not more than, what this American/Jim Crow system teaches its' so called privileged."

Although, Doris and Bernard didn't have any children, she totally understood her friend's frustrations.

Granted, the oppression, and outward or in your face racism (absence of Whites/Coloreds 'only' signs) wasn't visible in the Cities such as New York, Anne Lee was certainly not one to misconstrue the fact that racism and discrimination was not a sectional problem, but, a national problem! In some ways, New York was just as bad as Mt. Pleasant, she'd learned.

"I sacrificed a lot of what I envisioned myself doing with my time, passion, education, resources, and my life in general. So, I'll be damned, if I stand by and allow any person, place, or circumstance to hinder Tyra from showing the World her true potential." Anne Lee spoke with so much determination, Doris couldn't help but feeling as though there was something (underlined maybe) that she was missing. Nevertheless, she was certainly impressed by how Anne Lee had 'always made her precious Tyra priority number one regardless to whom or what......

"Are you sure your mother's not going to have a problem with me walking you home?" The boy Matthew inquired, as he and Tyra proceeded down Lenox Avenue, en route to her house.

"Who says you're walking me all the way home?" Tyra asked smiling.

"Well, I assumed that that was what I was doing." He shrugged.

"You can walk me to the corner of my block." She suggested.

Matthew was perfectly fine with doing so, therefore, no response was necessary.

"How come you don't have a girlfriend?" Tyra inquired.

Matthew simply shrugged his shoulders.

"I hear you have quite a bit of admirers at our school." Tyra glanced in his direction as she'd said it.

Matthew nearly tripped as he briefly exchanged their glance. He didn't know or understand what it was about her that made him tend to feel so shy, or rather other than himself. Maybe it was her strange piercing eyes, a color in which he found difficulty in describing, or maybe it was her level of intelligence, he told himself.

It was no secret that she was the smartest girl in their entire school. Nor, was it a secret that Tyra Star Addison was more than likely the prettiest as well. Combined factors, that would potentially have the average boy acting other than himself, if not tongue tied, Matthew thought to himself with a smile.

"You care to share what has you smiling?" Tyra asked

"Just being seen walking you home, will make me the talk of the school tomorrow." Matthew continued looking forward as he spoke. Yet, through his peripheral, he noticed that his reply made her smile.

Tyra conceded that he was more than likely correct, as far as the guys were concerned. However, she knew her female schoolmates wouldn't be quite as impressed, or happy by such news.

"Why do you always carry that basketball?"

Again, Matthew simply shrugged opposed to answering the question.

"You haven't answered my question." Tyra reminded him, as if he needed reminding.

"I guess you can say, my basketball is like my best friend." He answered, avoiding eye contact.

"A basketball, as a best friend?" Tyra pondered that. "Doesn't sound too reciprocating."

At that, Matthew looked in her direction. "Why do you say that?"

"Nothing really." Tyra replied. Having a change of heart, she decided to elaborate," I just think it's unfitting to have an object as a best friend opposed to an actual person. It says a lot to actually label a person a best friend, let alone a basketball, because with a true friendship comes understanding, trust, honesty, and a level of mutuality, in all things relevant."

"In that case, it sounds like I have to find me a new best friend."

At that, they both laughed. As they proceeded in the direction of her house, Tyra noticed he held his basketball firmly cuffed beneath his left arm, therefore, she reached down and took his right hand into her left hand.

"I see you really want to give people something to talk about." He smiled from ear to ear.

"Let's just say, I learned from my Mother that I can work on having a male as a best friend, without losing focus." Tyra responded happily, as they walked the remainder of the way in complete silence.

EIGHTEEN

HARLEM, NEW YORK, 1934

"*Happy Birthday to you, Happy Birthday to you!*" The party of Ten (Anne Lee, Roger, Doris, Bernard, Matthew, and the Five girls once tutored by her mother), sang to a smiling Tyra on her seventeenth birthday.

Once everyone had stopped singing, Matthew continued on. "How old are you now?" How old are you now? He laughed. Tyra playfully hit him on his arm.

"Thank you all so much!" Tyra was clearly overjoyed seeing the people who were basically her extended family. Well, all except her Mom, who was her only immediate family.

Later during the evening, after everyone except Roger (who now lived with Anne Lee, being that Tyra now lived on campus, in Washington D.C., where she attended Howard University), said their goodbyes, Tyra helped her mother clean up.

"I really appreciate everything you do for me." Tyra hugged her mother from behind as Anne Lee dried the last of the dishes.

Without turning to face her daughter, Anne Lee smiled and said. "I appreciate your appreciation of everything I do for you."

At that they both laughed. Something neither of them had

actually done since Tyra went away to school. Yes, Roger made Anne Lee smile (quite often) but, it was different from what she and her daughter had shared living under the same roof. Although, Anne Lee was a firm disciplinarian, she and Tyra had often exchanged jokes and laughter.

"I'm really glad to have you home." Anne Lee turned to face her daughter, at the same time drying her hands on her apron. "I didn't realize that I would miss you as much as I do." Although she produced a smile, Tyra could see her mother's eyes watering.

"I miss you too Momma." Tyra reached for her mother's hands. "But, like you told me, when I didn't want to leave, it's imperative that I do this. Truthfully, I'm so glad that you pushed me because college is really wonderful." She smiled." It took some getting used to, but I love it."

Her daughter's excitement, and interest in school made Anne Lee think back to how excited she too, had been in her Freshman year at Claflin, and how grateful she would forever be to Nathaniel Pinkney Jr. for his generosity. Just as, she knew Tyra would forever appreciate Roger E. Robinson for using his influence to help get her into Howard University.

"Well, as long as you're happy, I'm happy." Anne Lee assured her.

"Matthew tells me that he wants to apply to Howard, since he's in his last year of High School. But, I told him that I didn't think his attending Howard would be a good idea." Tyra informed her mother.

"Why not? I think it would be a great idea for you to have a true friend there with you."

"The problem is, I know that Matthew wants for he and I to be more than just best friends, which is also, more than likely, why he wants to come to Howard. I mean, I like him a lot, but, I'm really not interested in a relationship with anyone. I already know that the odds are totally against me, especially me being a Black woman in my desire to become an attorney. So, the last thing I need is any type of potential distraction." Tyra explained to her mother." Honestly, that's also why I haven't been trying to establish any real friendships since arriving at Howard."

"I understand." Anne Lee did understand, as well as, appreciated her daughter's determination. It was actually unbelievable how Tyra reminded her of herself in so many ways at that same age.

"So how are things between you and Roger?" Tyra smiled, yet lowered her voice a notch being that Roger was somewhere in the house.

"It took a little getting use-to." Anne Lee admitted honestly. "You have to keep in mind, I haven't been with a man or in a relationship in years."

"Why'd you wait so long? I mean, Roger has been around since forever!"

"Yes, he has." Anne Lee agreed. "However, I wasn't about to let a man, any man, live with you and me. The same way you're determined to stay focused, I was determined to make 'you' my focus. Not to mention, what kind of example would I have been if I allowed a man to move in, or be with intimately, and he's not my husband?"

Opposed to answering the question, both, mother and daughter stared down at the sparkling diamond and gold engagement ring Roger had given Anne Lee two months prior to moving in with her.

"I totally get and respect, the whole making me a priority, but I'm inclined to believe that Roger would've gladly married you a long time ago, Tyra smiled knowingly.

Anne Lee simply smiled, considering she, too, felt that to be the truth. Nevertheless, she also felt that things worked out as they were meant to. As far as Roger was concerned, yes, she'd made him wait a number of years to have her, however, at least he knew that she had preserved herself for the man who was lucky to have her as his wife, she told herself.

"How come you never speak about my father?" Tyra's question caught her totally off guard. Yet, Anne Lee knew that it was a question that would one day come up.

"Every day I look at you, or even think of you, I feel that you were a God-send." Anne Lee began with a smile on her face. "But, your father and I, unfortunately, should have never happened. We were entirely too young, and we both should have been as focused as you are, today. We were both in college, he attended South Carolina State which was walking distance from Claflin College, where I went to school. He was from New Orleans. He told me that his father was black, and his mother was Creole, which is probably where you inherited those funny colored eyes."

At that, they both laughed. Even though they both knew that Tyra possessed a pair of the most beautiful eyes either of them had ever looked into.

"It wasn't long after I revealed to him that I was pregnant, that I never saw him again. A friend of his, who was actually his roommate told me that his parents abruptly sent for him to come back home to New Orleans."

"What was his name?" Tyra asked, still in a lowered tone of voice, however, her voice tone no longer had anything to do with Roger over hearing the two of them.

"His name is Morris." Anne Lee revealed. Even though it was all past tense, she decided to use 'is' opposed to 'was' because she didn't want to imply that Morris was deceased.

Instead of making any further inquiries, Tyra gave her mother a long, heartfelt, embrace. She could only imagine how afraid and alone her mother must have felt. Not to mention, how such abandonment would have affected 'any' young person, especially someone who had as much to lose, and as much promise, as her Mother!

"*No wonder, why, she'd always been so over protective of me!*" Tyra thought to herself. Whereas, she had always loved and cherished her mother, never had she appreciated her more than at that very moment.

"How did your mother handle such news?" Tyra asks. Her face was still buried between her mother's neck and shoulder, which was both wet from her tears.

"Of course, she was a little disappointed. But, her love for me clearly superseded the situation. So, as time went on, all she talked about was how much she couldn't wait to take care of you, while I finished school."

Although, Tyra made a sniffling sound, Anne Lee could tell that her words made her daughter smile.

"I came home during Summer recess, and so much had changed in Mt. Pleasant, I noticed. The prejudice and Jim Crow had existed majority of my childhood, but my father had always protected us from most of that. To actually see the hatred and violence, reach my family's doorstep, was too much for me. Not only was I 'not' trying to fall victim to what was going on, I knew that I had to protect you, the same way my father had always protected me and my sister. So, I decided to leave."

"And Grandmother wasn't willing to leave with us?" Tyra asked.

"No." Anne Lee's heart began to ache as she thought of her mother, whom she missed dearly. "I tried to convince her to come with me, but, Mt. Pleasant was all she'd known for most of her adult life. Not to mention, she couldn't fathom the thought of abandoning all that she and my father had built."

"What about your sister? How come I've never heard you talk about her?" Lifting her head from her mother's shoulder, Tyra now stared into Anne Lee's grayish-green eyes. Although, they shared a different eye color, Roger always commented on how exotic looking both his girls were.

"Your Aunt Arethea, surprised everyone in the family, the day in which she and a man named Raymond Pinkney disappeared. As close as she and I were, she didn't even reveal to me what her plans were. As for Raymond Pinkney, he up and left while his wife was visiting her family in Delaware."

"Do you miss her?"

"More than words can express." Anne Lee held her daughter's stare. "It hurts even more, knowing that she would never get to know you. I'm more than 'sure' that she'd love you as much as I do." Her smile, caused a smile to appear on Tyra's face as well.

"What a sight." Roger, too, had a smile on his face as he entered the kitchen. "I love seeing the both of you so happy."

"Thank you," Tyra walked over to him and gave him a hug. "For everything." She added, as she took a step backward.

"Okay, I have some unfinished unpacking to do. Good night to both of you." With that said, Tyra exited to the kitchen.

"What?" Roger asked, seeing how Anne Lee was looking at him.

"How much did you hear?" She inquired, with a raised eyebrow.

"Enough to know that, the version you told Tyra, is totally not what you told me." Roger stared his fiancée in her eyes. "My question is, which one of us are you lying to?" And why?"

NINETEEN

HARLEM, NEW YORK, 1938

The Great Depression began in the United States as an ordinary recession in the summer of 1929. Its fundamental cause was a decline in spending (sometimes referred to as aggregate demand), which led to a decline in production as manufacturers and merchandisers noticed an unintended rise in inventories. The sources of contraction in spending, in the United States, varied over the course of the Depression, but they cumulated in monumental decline in aggregate demand. The American decline was transmitted to the rest of the World largely through gold standard. However, a variety of other factors also influenced the downturn in various countries.

In 1937- 38, the United States suffered another severe downturn, but after mid 1938 the American economy began to grow rapidly.

It was during the early state of the Great Depression that Roger began losing on his Real Estate ventures. A number of families, blacks and whites, found themselves unemployed, and on the verge of starving, let alone keeping a roof above their heads. In fact, had it not been for the Red Cross and other Organizations providing food and/or opening soup kitchens, as well as handed out clothing, countless people would have fallen victim to starvation or froze to death.

"Things aren't always going to be this bad." Anne Lee had said to Roger, shortly after they'd married in 1935. On several occasions they volunteered their time assisting in feeding the less fortunate, as well as donated money and clothing.

"I would hope not." Roger dreaded the thought of things remaining as critical as they were for much longer.

"Do you still communicate with Paul?" Anne Lee had inquired. Paul Mizelli was a longtime friend of Roger's uncle, who had often given Roger information regarding low cost available properties.

"Haven't spoken to him in a while. Truthfully, there hasn't been much need to, seeing how bad the economy is, and how I don't have it to invest in or purchase any new properties." Roger shook his head.

Anne Lee nodded her understanding. Later that evening, while they were alone having dinner, Anne Lee revisited the subject.

"I was thinking," Anne Lee began. "Maybe we should reach out to Paul. How about we pay him a small commission to act as a Realtor, in securing properties on our behalf. I mean of course we won't need him to purchase properties here in Harlem or various sections of Brooklyn, but I was thinking about places such as Williamsburg, Park Slope, and in lower Manhattan." She said with a smile.

"Those are predominantly white communities." Roger reminded her.

"My point exactly." Anne Lee had said, her smile still in place.

"Even during a Depression property in those areas will cost much more than what I'm used to paying. Not to mention, money in which I don't have." Reminding her of that as well.

"It isn't just folks in the black communities who are being evicted and struggling. That being said, I think now is the perfect time for us to purchase as much property as we can afford, because once this Depression is over and the economy is back on the rise white folks will be the ones to enjoy first come, first serve, on everything." Anne Lee had stared at Roger from across the dining table. "Especially, jobs."

"It makes all the sense in the world. But where will the money come from to purchase all these properties?" He asked.

"From me." She smiled, knowing her father, Thaddeus would be proud of his baby girl at that moment.

Roger simply stared at Anne Lee. She never ceased to amaze him, he thought to himself, seeing how his wife was not only the most secretive woman he'd ever known, but also, full of surprises. Just last year, she had confessed to him that she had told a half-truth (to him and Tyra) because doing so was a matter of her and her child's safety. Without going into detail, she'd asked that he accept that as an explanation and let it go. Reluctantly, Roger let it go as that.

Sitting across from his wife, Roger simply waited for her to explain.

"I have some cash put away." Anne Lee reveals. "I say cash, because I've never trusted banks."

Roger couldn't blame her seeing how the Stock Market had crashed.

"My father had left me some money. And, after my mother died, I asked a family friend named Audrey to sell my parent's house and the land in which my father left to my sister and I." Anne Lee explained. "I hope you're not upset with me for keeping all this from you?"

"Why do you feel the need to keep me in the dark about stuff. I'm your husband." Roger shook his head, clearly confused and disappointed.

"Having money and deciding not to disclose the fact, never had anything to do with you." Anne Lee explained, hoping he didn't take that as harshly as she knew it sounded. "The money has always been, and still is, a security blanket for my daughter and I. That's why I was so reluctant at first when you asked me to marry you, because I do not know how to 'not' put my child and myself first. I only include myself in that statement, because I know how much she needs and relies on me."

"But I'm your husband now," Roger spoke in a softer tone. "I'm not in this to take anything away from you, or Tyra. I just don't like all of this secrecy and distrust."

Although, Anne Lee knew he was right and deserved to know everything about her, there were just somethings she was simply 'not' willing to share or disclose, to even her husband!

"How much money are we talking about?" Roger asked.

"A little over Fifty Thousand Dollars." She had revealed.

Roger nearly choked on the sip of wine he'd taken following his inquiry. 'Fifty Thousand Dollars?" He repeated incredulously. "You've had that kind of cash laying around here all this time?" He couldn't believe it.

Anne Lee simply stared at him from across the table.

"I guess we 'can' buy up some property!" He exclaimed, producing a smile. The first one he'd produced since the start of their conversation.

Anne Lee, didn't doubt that she could trust Roger. Especially, since they were married. However, even as her husband, she had learned from her father that 'everything wasn't for everybody' therefore, she'd withhold revealing to Roger the latest and larger amount of money in which Audrey had also secured for her and Tyra...

Three years had passed since then, and to say that things were going exceedingly well with Anne Lee and Roger's (and Paul's) Real Estate business, would be an understatement!

Literally, their properties expanded beyond Manhattan and Brooklyn (thanks to Paul's ties and influence), they had secured homes in Queens and the Bronx, as well.

WASHINGTON, DC, 1939

"This is the best graduation present ever!" Tyra hugged her Mother, then Roger. "It's beautiful. Thank you so much."

"It certainly is." Cynthia, a former classmate and friend of Tyra's, agreed.

"It's Twenty-Two hundred quire feet, which is a lot of

space for just you." Anne Lee added. She had already suggested that Tyra not take on a roommate, or roommates, even though the apartment had three bedrooms. She wanted her daughter to enjoy her space and privacy. Especially, after residing inside of a dorm for the past four years.

"I'm so proud of you." Roger gave Tyra a second hug, they both were smiling from ear to ear, as Anne Lee handed Cynthia the huge camera to capture the moment on film.

Cynthia, had also earned her Bachelor's Degree, and she, too, graduated Phi Beta Kappa. Unlike Tyra, who was staying at Howard to pursue her Law Degree, Cynthia was ready to return home to Detroit, where she was more than ready to put her recently earned Degree (in History) to use, as a school teacher. Although, she came from a hardworking, middle class family, Cynthia's parents certainly could not afford to provide her the type of Monthly allowance Tyra had received through-out her years at Howard, therefore, she relished the thought of returning home to begin earning a living while doing a job she'd always envisioned herself doing, opposed to pursuing her Masters.

"Okay, I need to be getting back to my family." Cynthia stated. "It has been such a pleasure meeting you all, and spending this time together. By the way, thanks for the breakfast." She smiled at Anne Lee, then Roger, who had taken her and Tyra to breakfast that morning before surprising Tyra with her new apartment. "I know my parents should be awake by now."

"It was a pleasure meeting you as well." Anne Lee gave her a hug.

"You two can stay here and discuss decorations, while I take Cynthia back to her parents' hotel." Roger dug into his pocket for his car keys, before planting a kiss on Anne Lee's right cheek.

Once the two of them were alone, Tyra asked, "So, how's everything going with you and Roger?" She knew her Mother better than anyone, Tyra was certain, therefore, she had sensed a difference in her vibe since the day she and Roger had arrived in D.C.

"Everything is okay." Anne Lee smiled weakly, seeing how her daughter was peering into her eyes with a doubtful look on her face, which meant she knew her mother wasn't being totally honest. "Okay, I guess it's not fair to say that 'everything' is all right." She admitted.

"I'm listening." Tyra sat Indian style on the carpeted living room floor. Anne Lee decided to sit across from her.

"I guess it's true that, you never really know a person until you marry them. Or, until large sums of money come into the equation."

"You have to be more specific Mom." Tyra continued to hold her mother's gaze. "You and Roger have known each other all of my life. He's practically a father to me."

"Yes, I know." Anne Lee agreed "It's just that, one of the things I've always liked most about him was how he handled his business with so much discretion. It was years before he even filled me in, as to what all he had going on, but I respected his privacy because I wasn't too forthcoming myself. However, he's such a different person these days."

"How so?"

"Over the past year and a half, he began going out a lot. Sure, he invited me to attend places with him, but I think it's mores a gesture or show of courtesy without sincerity. He knows I'm not doing the all-night clubbing stuff." Anne Lee shook her head. "And, not only does he garner so much attention with the three cars he purchased in the last year, the tailored suits, one for every day of the week, the shoes, and hats and ties." Again, she shook her head. "But, he seems to relish all of the attention."

"That does sound quite uncharacteristic of Roger." Tyra agreed.

"It's so much more that I can expound on, but, I'm here to enjoy my time with you, and celebrate such a milestone." They both knew that such a small percentage of women, especially Black woman, were earning degrees in 1939. Therefore, Anne Lee did not want to elaborate on the facts that, she was certain of Roger's cheating (many of nights, or rather mornings, he'd come home with a woman's scent on him), nor, was she ready to disclose to her daughter that Paul Mizelli had informed her that Roger was not only manipulating the books, but had also purchased a number of properties that were unbeknownst to her.

"What are you going to do?" Tyra inquired, knowing her Mother's lack of tolerance for any sort of wrong doing. So much so, Tyra wasn't at all surprised that her mother never even mentioned re-visiting the place in which she was born and raised. All she knew, was that, something bad/wrong had happened in Mt. Pleasant, South Carolina.

"Not exactly sure just yet, but I'm sure I'll figure it out." Anne Lee replied to her daughter's question, before changing the subject which she no longer wanted to discuss. "So, what have you been up to besides graduating at the top of your class?" She smiled proudly.

"Truthfully?" Tyra stared into her mother's eyes.

Anne Lee, simply held the stare. Which Tyra knew, meant, the truth and 'nothing' but the truth.

"I've taken part in the Southern Negro Youth Congress." Tyra revealed.

Anne Lee had heard, or rather, read about the student Organization.

Veritably, the article she'd read claimed that the organization had the potential to be one of the most important Civil Rights organizations of President Roosevelt's 'New Deal' era.

"I visited Virginia Union University, in Richmond, last year. I was thoroughly impressed by how the students had petitioned the State legislature against spending cuts and racial inequality in education. I love how so many black colleges have come together to support such a movement."

Not only did Anne Lee hear the excitement in Tyra's voice, she could also see it in her beautiful eyes. At that moment, Anne Lee recalled how her father, Thaddeus, had always questioned whether he had done enough-to help others- in his old age? Whereas, she; had once vowed to herself that she would devote her life to fighting for change (until, the un-expectancy of a child changed her life and/or intentions), but seeing her daughter apply herself to such a cause/movement confirmed that an Activist seed had not only been planted, but, was actually showing its manifestation in the form of Tyra Star Addison.

"By the way," Tyra added, bringing Anne Lee's focus back to their conversation. "I've made the decision to no longer carry the last name *Addison*. I remember you telling me that it was a white man named Rolland Addison who murdered my Great grandmother Arethea, so I see no point in carrying on his name, and certainly not his legacy."

Albeit, her comment caught Anne Lee by surprise, she told herself that her daughter's reasoning definitely made a lot of sense.

TWENTY

WASHINGTON, DC, 1942

World War Two, put 14 Million American men into uniform (One Million of them were Black men), and just like the Great War (World War I) seemingly had the potential to change everything (especially, for black folks), the second World War did show greater promise. The war dedicated America to the ideal of democracy. It led to the founding of the United Nations. And it made the United States the most powerful nation in the World. Yet, unfortunately, the Second World War led to a drastic increase in racial tensions -in America- while doing very little to address the basic causes of those tensions.

"I think this march is going to be like nothing anyone has ever seen before." Tyra not only beamed with pride, she was glad that she was an actual participant in its preparations.

"I know right." Curtis agreed with a smile.

Curtis Jackson was a native of Washington D.C., and had also been a student at Howard, which is where he and Tyra had met. Although, he earned a degree in Government, he was lucky to secure a job as a Postal worker a few months after graduating. In fact, he soon realized that black postal workers were very well organized, and Curtis came to meet a number of strong minded and influential people when he joined the National Alliance of Postal Employees (NAPE), an organization that supported the NAACP.

Although, Curtis had not yet, formally, met A. Philip Randolph (an effective Union Leader, Civil Rights Leader, and former Editor), he nonetheless, idolized the man from a distance. Which was why he jumped at the opportunity to campaign (throughout D.C. and Maryland) in support of the upcoming March on Washington.

"My friend Cynthia says folks in Detroit are excited and ready to take a part in MOW!" Tyra smiled, using the abbreviation for the March on Washington, which everyone was referring to it. "Actually, my Mother, who doesn't even go out much, says it's all folks in New York are talking about as well."

Curtis simply nodded his approval.

Changing the subject, Tyra revealed, "You know, growing up listening to my mother and her friend Doris's conversations, I didn't think that either of them were too fond of Mr. A. Philip Randolph."

Her comment, received Curtis's full attention. However, instead of giving an immediate reply, he stared at her with a raised eyebrow before asking, "And why did you receive such an impression?"

"I remember their discussions pertaining to articles that were often published in a newspaper called the Messenger, which was edited by A. Philip Randolph and Owen Chandler. In the majority of his editorials, apparently, Mr. Randolph did not discriminate in his ridicule of Black Ministers and Churches, Black politicians, W.E.B DuBois, the War, and so on." She answered.

"I call that being a Realist." Curtis defended. "We need leaders who are not afraid to not only voice their opinions, but also call folks out on their words, actions, and agendas."

"True." Tyra whole heartedly agreed. "However, can you honestly trust a person who seemingly has nothing good or positive to say about anyone?" She countered.

"Not only have I heard the man give praise where it is due, but I've also heard from reliable sources, that when the Brotherhood of Sleeping Car Porters hired A. Philip Randolph as their chief organizer to unionize the porters, as well as negotiating a contract from the Pullman Company, the company that employed the porters, legend has it that the Pullman Company tried to bribe Mr. Randolph by sending him a check for a significant amount, to turn his back on the porters."

"I take it, he didn't accept their check?" Tyra smiled.

"Nope." Curtis returned her smile. "I hear he framed it and hung it on his office wall."

Such integrity and loyalty, Tyra had to admit, certainly spoke volumes regarding the man's character. Especially, considering she was inclined to believe, unfortunately, that most representatives (white or black) would have sold the porters up the river.

"We still have three months to garner more support for MOW, and you're on Spring break," Curtis stared into Tyra's eyes from across the small table in which they were dining. "How about we see for ourselves how much support and enthusiasm is really taking place in New York City?"

"I think you want to visit New York because you've never been there before." Tyra laughed.

"That too." Curtis confessed with a smile.

NEW YORK CITY, 1942

Arriving in Midtown Manhattan, Curtis was totally blown away by the large crowds of people (all of whom seemed to be in a rush), all of the traffic, and the huge skyscrapers! As they departed the Greyhound Terminal, he was certainly impressed as Tyra proceeded to give him a little detail of midtown.

"Besides the Greyhound bus station, you have three other bus stations in the vicinity. The Midtown Bus Terminal, the Dixie Bus Station, and the American Bus Depot, all within a few blocks of each other near Times Square." She informed him.

Curtis, however, was momentarily speechless. He had never seen such crowded streets, so much movement, the thick fumes left behind from the buses, trucks and cars, the obvious confusion on the faces of other (incoming) travelers, tourists, migrants, whomever they were, and just so much life in general! He was surrounded by people of all shades. Nor, did they have to walk to 34th Street to see the Empire State Building, all he had to do was look to the sky.

"On a clear day you can actually see the top." Tyra laughed.

Curtis simply nodded his head up and down, as he took in the sight.

"Since we're traveling so light, we can walk to 42nd Street, which is even busier than this area." She shook her head. "From there, we can walk to Rockefeller Center."

At first Curtis assumed that the fumes or small clouds of smoke were coming from the buses and cars, but suddenly he realized that this was not entirely the case, which prompted him to ask, "Where is that smoke coming from?"

Again, Tyra laughed, before informing him, "It's coming out of those manhole covers." She pointed to one in the middle of the street. I hear the smoke comes from cracks in the hot water system carried through underground pipes, which supply heating to the majority of the buildings you're looking at."

Rockefeller Center stood in the heart of midtown Manhattan, around it was several shops, beautiful hotels, and a sunken plaza.

"Although I've never been, the plaza area is turned into an ice skating rink during the winter months." Tyra informed him.

"I'm familiar with the story of John D. Rockefeller and how he acquired his wealth through Standard Oil, but I can only imagine how much it cost him to build all of this." Curtis couldn't hide his astonishment. Even the folks who passed them by, predominately white had a different air and style about them than the white folks he'd encountered (mostly in passing) in Washington D.C. As a matter of fact, these New Yorkers' appeared incredibly self-assured, he told himself. So much so, the City's appearance and attitude seemed totally in contrast to the fact that the country was in the midst of War!

"It is beautiful," Tyra agreed. "But, you haven't witnessed real beauty and culture yet." She smiled.

"I've heard that Harlem is the city of Black pride." He shared her smile.

"That is true." With that being said, Tyra led him in the direction of the IRT subway. Again, Curtis was speechless as they boarded the A Train, which Duke Ellington had made famous in song.

"We'll get off at 125th Street, so I can show you around. That's if your feet aren't already hurting too bad?" Tyra spoke to him over the noise, as the train made its way to Harlem.

"That's fine by me." Curtis was anxious to see as much of the place as possible!

Never mind the fact that they had made plans to stay in New York for a full seven days.

As they exited the 125th Street station, the first thing Curtis noticed was the absence of skyscrapers, followed by an absence of white faces. Black folks were certainly out and about! However, the masses weren't plentiful as they had been in midtown Manhattan. Even the style and vibe, he quickly noticed, was completely different. Nevertheless, the vibe and surroundings brought a huge smile to his face.

"So, this is Harlem USA?" Curtis commented moreso than asked. "I want to see and go everywhere!" He exclaimed happily.

"Slow down fella." Tyra, happy to be home as well, glanced his way and added, "I don't know about you, but I'm starving!"

"So, let's eat." Curtis suggested, at the same time continued to take in his surroundings.

Although two years had passed since Anne Lee and Rogers divorce, the pair remained cordial towards one another. Therefore, it pleased Tyra that Roger was ready and willing to give Curtis his tour of Harlem. Actually, he suggested that Curtis stay at his place in the Sugar Hill section.

"So, are you and Curtis officially dating these days?" Anne

Lee asked her daughter, as they enjoyed their breakfast.

"I'm not sure if I can call what he and I have a relation-ship, but we certainly spend a great deal of time together." Tyra smiled. "I don't mean in an intimate aspect." She clarified. "But, outside of my studies, I love being a participant in anything that involves social change, racial equality, or just opposing Jim Crow in general. So, it's not only Roger's energy and dedi-cation to the betterment and liberation of black people that attracts me to him, but mores, how he welcomes, trust, and obviously values my overall input." She explained.

"Nor does it hurt that he's quite handsome, and is clearly the gentleman." Anne Lee added her assessment of Curtis.

At that, Tyra couldn't contain her laughter.

Curtis was thoroughly appreciative that Roger had taken the time to show him Harlem in its entirety! Indeed, he found Roger equally impressive, as he did Harlem. It wasn't too often you met an individual who was as successful and knowledge-able as Roger E. Robinson, who was also (clearly) well respect-ed and embraced by the streets as well.

"For years, this neighborhood has been called Sugar Hill, home to just about any and every successful or famous black person in America.

"Jack Johnson lived here, Joe Luis resides here, Cab Callo-way, Ella Fitzgerald, Count Basie, Billie Holiday, Bill Robinson, Langston Hughes, and several others." Roger informed him with a smile on his face.

Curtis, stood there taking in the long row of beautiful im-maculate homes. Their large front windows, draped more than likely with Silk curtains, he assumed, enabled a glimpse into elegant sitting rooms. The streets, lined with expensive cars, mostly Cadillacs, he noticed. And, a few black faces, mostly women, walked their neatly groomed pedigree (obviously ex-pensive) dogs of various breeds. Never had Curtis observed black folks living in such style and class.

"Harlem was once a bourgeois white district, until about Thirty or so years ago, when blacks began migrating here. You still have your Italians here and there, and quite a few Puerto

Rican families living here, mainly over on the Eastside." Roger spoke as he now drove through the city.

As they made their way through Harlem, Curtis observed several apartment buildings where the windows had been busted out, covered with various objects (clothes, cardboard, wood, or sheets), or people half leaning out of them looking downward at those, mostly children playing, on the sidewalks.

"Harlem, has seen its share of ugly riots. Most of the broken windows you see haven't been repaired or replaced since the riot we had here seven years ago." Roger added.

Curtis, however, couldn't believe how poverty stricken so much of the place (now) appeared, literally, many of the blocks were in complete contrast of where Anne Lee and Roger (individually) resided.

"If it was warmer out, you'd see blocks and blocks of children playing in water shooting out of fire hydrants. They actually cut out both sides of a metal or tin can which they use to guide the water in whatever direction they want it to shoot." Roger omitted telling him how much he disliked driving through those blocks where the hydrants were turned on. Whereas, some folks relished the idea of a free car wash (driving through such blocks), Roger kept his cars polished shined, so the hydrants did more damage than good, in his case.

During his seven-day stay, Curtis dined at several restaurants, had dinner at least twice at Anne Lee's, and certainly enjoyed lunch at the Red Rooster! At least twice, he had met Tyra at Lew Michaux's, while Roger went to work. Lew Michaux's (although white owned) was not just a well know Book Store, but also a powerhouse of Black thought. Not only did blacks (young and old) engage in intellectual debates right out front of Lew Michaux's his shelves contained the writing of just about every black Author, biographies of just about every black celebrity, and blacks could go there to read or purchase black newspapers from all over! Not to mention, there was also an art gallery for black sculptors and painters. To say that Tyra and Curtis fell in love with the place was an understatement!

As they entered the front doors of the Abyssinian Baptist

Church, Curtis, nor Tyra, could believe the size of the church's interior! Or, its congregation!

"Wow!" Tyra managed to hear Curtis exclaim, even though the choir was in the midst of a selection she'd never heard.

Without speaking, a female usher made her approach, produced a smile, and led the two of them to an available seat. In all of the years that she lived in Harlem, Tyra had never once visited the church, or any other church, although she had passed by it (daily) on her way to and from school, years earlier. She knew that her Mother believed in God, because the two of them not only read/studied the Bible, Prayer was a daily 'and' nightly ritual in their home for as long as Tyra could remember. However, Anne Lee, for reasons unbeknownst to Tyra, was not a church attending woman.

"That Reverend Adam Clayton Powell Jr., is certainly a gifted speaker!"

"Yes, he is." Tyra agreed whole heartedly with Curtis's assessment of the Pastor. Seeing how impressed he had been during and after the service prompted Tyra to inquire, "Did Roger introduce you to Harlem's legendary night life?" She glanced in Curtis's direction as they walked in the direction of her motor's brownstone.

"Actually, we drove by all of the famous night spots. The Cotton Club, Savoy Ballroom, Small's Paradise, and the Apollo Theater." Curtis answered with a smile on his face. "Roger certainly knows where the fun is, I'll tell you that." He shook his head.

"So, I've heard." Tyra responded with a slight attitude. "You weren't interested in seeing the 'inside' of any of them?"

"Not at all." Curtis pretended to take in the sights as they made their way down Lenox Avenue, yet, he could feel Tyra's glances in his direction. "However, I did ask Roger to take me to Seventh Avenue and 131st Street."

"Why is that?" Tyra was quite surprised when she felt Curtis take hold of her left hand.

"I wanted to visit the Tree of Hope."

His answer made Tyra smile. As a matter of fact, her smile

turned into a delightful laugh.

"You care to share?" Curtis looked down at her, considering Tyra was a full six inches shorter than he.

"It's nothing really." Tyra replied. Although she did not believe in coincidence, she realized that they were on the very same block in which she and Matthew had been on (years earlier) when she had taken his hand into hers!

WASHINGTON, DC, JUNE 1942

"What do you mean the March on Washington is not going to happen?"

"That's the word that I just received." Curtis informed Tyra.

"You can't be serious?" She stared at him in bewilderment, waiting for Curtis to admit that he was joking, albeit she had never known him to be a prankster.

"I'm serious." He took Tyra's hand and led her over to the suede couch, which was basically the only piece of furniture she had purchased thus far, in her spacious living room.

Curtis's announcement left Tyra totally speechless. Everyone she knew (including herself and Curtis) had spent countless hours/days promoting MOW, in fact, she was well aware that buses had been hired, special trains previously chartered, not to mention all the money that had already been spent! She literally found MOW's cancellation preposterous!

"From what I hear, the President, himself, invited Mr. Randolph to the White House. At that meeting, Mr. Randolph flat out refused to cancel the march. Apparently, the President, seeing that he wasn't bluffing, shuddered at the prospect of such a huge gathering of blacks, at Lincoln's Memorial, caused him to fold." Curtis produced a smile.

Tyra, on the other hand, was still too upset and confused to share his smile.

Seeing that she was not moved, Curtis continued, "President Roosevelt issued and signed Executive Order 8802, which states there shall be no discrimination in the employment of workers in the defense industries and in Government because of race, creed, or national origin. Actually, the Government is creating what it calls the Fair Employment Practices Committee (FEPC) to investigate discrimination and recommend appropriate action." Again, Curtis smiled big. "You have no idea how happy black folks are right now. This is truly an economic breakthrough for our people!"

Whereas, Tyra had clearly heard and understood all of what Curtis had said/revealed, she nonetheless, felt that A. Philip Randolph's decision to arbitrarily abort the March on Washington, which would have undoubtedly been an unprecedented show of solidarity amongst a people (in the South, as well as the North) who have received far worst treatment -here in America- than those, overseas, whom America was fighting to protect in its so-called war of Democracy! The truth was history has shown, time and time again, how the American government has never adhered to 'any' of its policies and/or Executive Orders, nor, its so-called Re-Construction whereas it pertained to black people. Therefore, Tyra was not entirely moved or trusting, of the President's Executive Order 8802! Nor the Government's enactment of heir Fair Employment Practices Committee.

"All I'm saying is that, "Tyra began, not wanting to rain on Curtis's parade, but simply being honest. "Whereas, the President's and the Government's intentions may be good, which is actually in total contrast to what we have seen thus far by the President's refusal to support anti-lynching legislation for example, we both know that racial discrimination is too deeply rooted for black folks to be celebrating this early."

TWENTY-ONE

WASHINGTON, DC, 1949

Just as Tyra had predicted, the President's Executive Order 8802, and the Government's creation of the Fair Employment Practices Committee (both) had been put into place simply to appease a potential situation. Neither, had placed any real regard or high value on racial discrimination and inequality towards blacks.

By the age of 28, Tyra had not only earned her Bachelor and Master degree(s), both of which she had graduated with honors, but had also received her Juris Doctorate from Howard University's School of Law.

Now, at 32, her primary job was working for the Public Defender's office in Upper Marlboro, Maryland. Upon being admitted to the Bar, she was more than ready to get some Courtroom experience under her belt. Unfortunately, her being the only black female attorney with the Public Defender's office, Tyra encountered her first lessons in prejudice at the workplace. Whereas, she had graduated at the top of her class in law school. Tyra's role at the Public Defender's office amounted to that of a paralegal. Opposed to representing clients, she found herself sifting through police reports, reviewing transcripts, conducting interviews with potential witnesses, and drafting various motions. All of this, she did for attorneys whom she knew were less qualified, or well versed (in law) than she. Nonetheless, she performed her job, whatever it entailed, exceptionally.

"I don't know why you continue to stay at that job." Anne Lee spoke to Tyra over the phone. "I told you when you graduated law school that Paul has been telling me that I need to hire a property lawyer." She reminded her daughter. Truthfully, Paul probably knows several others who can use your services."

"Momma, for one, I'm not a Real Estate attorney. And two, I thought I explained to you that I didn't want to be that far up North." Tyra reminded her.

"So, you prefer the South?" Anne Lee asked. Tyra could hear the disbelief in her mother's voice/question.

"D.C. is not the South." Tyra laughed.

"Could've fooled me!" Anne Lee exclaimed. "Anywhere pass Delaware, is the South."

"You know what I mean." Tyra replied. "I'm saying, it is not the deep South. Besides, I have other reasons for staying here."

"They certainly can't have anything to do with Curtis. Seeing how he's always complaining about not getting to spend much time with you." Anne Lee revealed.

"You mean to tell me, he's been complaining to you?" Tyra asked incredulously.

"He sure has been." Anne Lee admitted. "Actually, we talk quite often. He's a good man, who I can tell really does love you."

Tyra didn't feel like discussing Curtis with her mother. Especially, being that they've had the whole 'why haven't you married him yet?' conversation, several times over the past few years.

"I love him too, but I'm not ready for a husband. I'm entirely committed to achieving the goals in which I have set for myself."

"Being married does not mean you cannot accomplish your goals."

"I understand that, but on the same token, I recall you once telling me that, the reason you refused to marry Roger, or any

other man, was because your entire focus was on raising me."
Tyra reminded her.

"It's not the same." Anne Lee responded, yet, in a much
lower tone.

"Why isn't it?" Tyra countered.

Changing the subject, Anne Lee responded, "I just wish
you would reconsider moving to New York, I pray for the day
you come home."

Although, Tyra didn't appreciate how her mother had a
tendency to change the subject any time it pertained to how
or why she had always been so overprotective of her growing
up, Anne Lee's words brought a smile to her face.

"I'll be home for Christmas." Tyra reminded her mother.

"It's not the same."

"Momma, please try to understand me," Tyra began, "I'm
not in D.C. for the purpose of this job that I am doing, and
although it is nice to be in such close proximity of Curtis,
neither is he the reason. I am establishing myself here because
there are several individuals here in DC., whom I attended
school with or have met throughout the years, who have also
been positioning themselves here. They include doctors, teachers, lawyers, and several with political aspirations.

Although, I could be wrong, however, myself and most
of my associates believe that, to achieve social progress, racial
change, and job and economic growth for black people, we
must focus on Policy and Institutional change." Tyra informed
her mother.

"Institutional change?" Anne Lee repeated. "I hope you
haven't aligned yourself with one of those Communist organizations."

At that, Tyra couldn't contain her laughter.

"Momma, I would never join a Communist group. You do
not have to worry about that." Tyra answered honestly. "However, as an advocate and public servant, there's no better place
for me to be then Washington, D.C."

"Accessibility to 'all' three branches of Government." Anne
Lee responded, indicating her understanding.

Again, her words brought a smile to her Tyra's face.

"I love you Mom."

"I love you too Tyra Star." At that, they both laughed, being that it was the first time Anne Lee had addressed Tyra by what she now considered her "full name"

"You cannot be serious! "Tyra stared at Curtis in disbelief.

"Unfortunately, I'm dead serious." He returned her stare, then turned and headed for the refrigerator to get something to drink.

"What are you going to do?" She asked, as she followed him into his small kitchen.

Turning in her direction, Curtis looked into her eyes, shook his head, then said, "It's so unlike you to ask a question that you already know the answer to." Before Tyra could respond to that, he reached for her, "I'm sorry. I shouldn't have said that." He hugged her to him.

Tyra totally understood, therefore, she wrapped her arms around his waist.

"I never thought I'd see the day that I'd be forced to fight for a Country that considers me a second-class citizen." Curtis laughed at the irony. "I can't recall being told by a Korean person that they cannot serve me, because I'm black." He shook his head.

As she looked up, to meet Curtis's eyes, Tyra was not at all surprised at the sight of his tears. They brought tears to her eyes as well.

"We'll be okay." Tyra tried to assure him.

"Will we?" He asked, holding her stare.

Tyra knew he hadn't gotten over the fact that she had, more than once, refused his marriage proposal. However, as unfortunate as his current predicament was, she was not about to allow it to change her decision.

"I love you Curtis, and I do feel that you and I can and will get through this." Tyra confessed honestly.

"As boyfriend and girlfriend, I suppose." He let out a laugh, before releasing her and exiting the kitchen.

Tyra followed suit, yet, remained silent.

"We've dated for over Six years now." Curtis looked Tyra in her eyes as he continued, "Do you think it's fair to me, that I've stuck this thing, you and I call a relationship, out faithfully. In hope that you may someday become my wife." He shook his head. "Am I not enough for you?"

"It's not about you." Tyra spoke barely above a whisper.

"It's not about me?" Again, he laughed. Then sat down on the small couch before putting his head in his lap.

"As a young girl, I always envisioned myself being a lawyer." Tyra began, taking a seat on the couch as well. "In hindsight, its actually quite funny, or embarrassing even, because I was under the impression that Lawyers had the capability to fix peoples' problems." She shook her head at the memory. "And although my Mother kept me quite shielded growing up, I was not shielded to the point that I did not recognize that countless folks, in Harlem, were suffering. In fact, I relished giving clothing, which I hadn't even outgrown, to the Red Cross." She smiled at the memory.

"Growing up, my Mother always instilled in me that, with hard work, determination, and a good education, I could be and/or achieve anything I desired for myself. Yes, I did have to work extra hard while in law school, especially whereas I was the only black woman in my class, but my determination to graduate at the top of my class was more so due to the 'belief' I had in my Mother's words."

"I understand all of that. But, what does it have to do with us? I find it incredibly hard to believe that you cannot achieve your goals, as my wife."

"I probably can." Tyra answered before adding, "It's just that I want to at least try to fulfill what I consider a personal goal, before I consider marriage."

"You sound very selfish right now." Curtis replied, as he got up from the couch and made his way to the window. "I know many people who have accomplished many of their goals, while married. People do so every day!"

"I'm sure they do." Tyra, becoming somewhat frustrated by Curtis's refusal to accept and/or respect her decision added,

"As far as I am concerned, marriage to me, is about compromise. Something I'm not ready or willing to do." Hating how cold that had sound, Tyra stood and approached Curtis from behind. "I realize that there are plenty of people out there who are committed to their spouse, family, job, their friends, and so forth, but those are not 'my' experiences. I am a woman, who has not yet learned to share my commitments."

Sharing commitments, especially intimately, is the one thing in which Tyra had never learned from Anne Lee, who had made raising her daughter her number one priority. Nor, did Tyra reveal to Curtis that, her current job at the Public Defender's office was simply a means to an end, or that she had already began her work with other black attorneys in Delaware, Maryland, D.C., and Virginia areas (as well as establishing relationships with several prominent, black and white, lawyers throughout the Country), all of whom, shared a common agenda.

Tyra, was one of many lawyers throughout the country, who became a part of a network of cooperating attorneys that worked with the NAACP Legal Defense Fund. The Fund, established by Charles Houston and Thurgood Marshall, pursued litigation challenging the legalized caste system that Southern States had imposed after the end of Reconstruction and with only a few exceptions had been approved by the Federal Courts over several decades. It was actually a lawyer by the name of Elwood Chisolm, who taught a Howard Law School, and a member of the Fund's staff (which included; Robert Carter, Jack Greenberg, and Constance B. Motley) who had introduced Tyra to Thurgood Marshall, who had also been a graduate of Howard Law School.

Tyra's spirit, although dampened by Curtis's departure for Korea, had been lifted tremendously by the recent United States Supreme Courts' ruling in three separate cases that collectively knocked holes in the Court's earlier decision in Plessy V. Ferguson.

In Sweatt V. Painter, the Court ordered the University of Texas to admit a black applicant, Herman Sweatt, into its Law

School. A hastily improvised black law school in Houston, it ruled, could not possibly provide Sweatt with a legal education "substantially equal" to that available to white students at the University of Texas. In the second case, Mclaurin V. Oklahoma State Regents, the Court ruled

that the University of Oklahoma had been wrong to admit George Mclurin as a graduate student but then require him to sit apart from the white students. In the third, and last case, Henderson V. United States the Supreme Court had ruled that 'segregated' railway dining cars were unconstitutional.

As a result of the three monumental rulings, the NAACP filed lawsuits on behalf of black parents in North and South Carolina, Virginia, Kansas, Louisiana, Delaware, and Washington D.C. seeking the admittance of black children to white schools. Which meant, Tyra and several other lawyers throughout the States had their work cut out...

TWENTY-TWO

WASHINGTON, DC, 1952

F ive of the lawsuits filed, reached the United States Supreme Court, They were consolidated under the title "Brown V. Board of Education". *Brown,* was a lawsuit filed in a case from Topeka, Kansas.

Although, Tyra did not work directly with the lawyers in Topeka, she did, however assist the attorneys/legal team that was headed by James M. Nabrit Jr., in one of the 'consolidated' cases titled "Bolling V. Sharpe" which was a lawsuit filed in Washington, D.C.

Unlike her job at the Public Defender's Office, where she'd recently been (indirectly) reprimanded for displaying what her Supervisor termed *'an overzealous appetite for justice'* in all of the cases in which Tyra has been assigned to work on. As far as she was concerned, it was not her fault that the majority of the motions in which she had filed for Bail, Suppression, or to Dismiss, where usually Granted, Tyra thought to herself, considering she was only doing her job!

On the other hand, Tyra relished the work she did for the Fund, and especially on the Bolling case, where she found herself aligned with other black lawyers who, like many of the clients they represented, had engaged in a lifelong struggle for equal opportunity while living and breathing the stifling air of segregation and discrimination.

"Tell me again, why you continue to work for this office?"

Without looking up from the paperwork, or rather, the trial strategy that she was preparing for another lawyer in the office, Tyra couldn't help produce a smile before giving her reply.

"Kelly, I could have sworn that question has been asked and answered at least a dozen times by now."

At that, they both laughed.

Kelly Clarkson, was a 29-year-old D.C. native, who was the primary Receptionist for the Upper Marlboro Public Defender's Office. A woman whom, Tyra, was not only on first name basis with, but also someone whom she genuinely liked.

"Well, considering how intelligent and gifted you are, none of the *'dozen'* reasons you've provided justifies your staying here." It was certainly office-knowledge that Tyra Star was by far the most competent and brightest *'star'* in the office.

Ironically, she had yet to be assigned a case/client, whereas, she was lead or even exclusive counsel. On several occasions, however, she did make courtroom appearances as co-counsel.

"Let's just say, I'm establishing my resume." Tyra smiled, before refocusing her attention on the strategy she was preparing.

Kelly simply shook her head, then backed out of the small office closing the door behind her.

Removing her reading glasses and rubbing her eyes, Tyra knew all the excuses she had given Kelly did not justify her staying on board, at the Public Defender's Office, especially due to the obvious prejudice in which she was unfairly subjected to considering her potential.

However, she was not ready to reveal to Kelly, or anyone else, especially those who were ranking members of the Washington D. C. and Maryland Bar Association, her true intent, or to what extent, her plight happened to be regarding the 'equalization' of African Americans and putting an end to 'legal' racial discrimination.

Moreover, she knew that, a 32 year old *'black'* female admitted to the Bar, in 1946, residing in a Capital (that was technically the South), was reason enough to be, more than, borderline paranoid, Tyra told herself, as she (again) gave thought to Kelly's question on her drive home….

★★★★★

"How is she?" Tyra asked, as Curtis approached her in the hospital's waiting room. She had been ecstatic upon receiving Curtis's letter informing her that he was coming home! Until, she reached the part about his Mother being terminally ill.

"Not good. Not good at all." Curtis responded sadly, before turning and heading for the exit doors.

Once they were inside of his car, heading back to Tyra's apartment, he filled her in as to what all the doctor had told him.

"He also said, they'll be releasing her tomorrow. They're actually sending her to a Hospice facility." Curtis shook his head, not bothering to wipe away the tears that were now streaming down his face.

"My mother has always been one of those persons who hated hospitals, to the point that, the only way she'll visit one is if she's rolled in or carried." Again, he shook his head. "This is all my fault."

"Why would you say something like that?" Tyra was thrown aback by his remark, and that he was casting blame on himself for the situation that was totally out of his control.

"The doctor said that he had never seen such metastasis in a single body." Curtis informed her. "Had I been home, op-posed to over in Korea, fighting a damn war that had nothing to do with me or my family, I could've gotten her to a doctor in time for them to detect the cancer in its earlier stage.

Although, Tyra was not well versed in medical terminology, she did know that metastasis was the spread of disease, or rather a disease producing agency, such as cancer cells, from the initial or primary site of the disease to another part of the body.

"The cancer spread to her liver, lungs, bladder, and stom-ach!"

Curtis, was in such pain and disbelief, Tyra clearly saw

157

(both) as he briefly took his eyes off the road to look in her direction.

"I'm so sorry." Tyra offered, as she reached for his free-hand. Just seeing his tears actually brought tears to her eyes as well. "But, you can't blame yourself for any of this. Instead, we have to be thankful that the military granted you this furlough, enabling you to have this time with your Mother, your sister, and me." She had hoped by including 'herself' it would make him smile, or at least lighten the mood.

They both knew that, had he 'refused' the draft, he'd more than likely be sitting in a federal prison, opposed to having this time with his loved ones.

"What would I do without you?" Curtis stared into her eyes, now that they were parked in front of Tyra's apartment building.

It wasn't the 'smile' in which Tyra hoped for, but certainly touched her heart nonetheless, seeing even a resemblance of a smile on Curtis's face.

"I want you to know that, had it not been for your letters, I probably wouldn't be here. Men have been dying all around me since day one, I arrived in Korea. It's crazy." He shook his head. "Your letters are what keeps me determined."

Not knowing what to say, Tyra asked, "Determined to do what?"

"To live." Curtis answered.

That being said, Tyra didn't asked anymore questions. Instead, she leaned across the arm-rest and placed her lips upon his.

★★★★★

The day following Curtis's mother's funeral/burial, he and Tyra accepted Anne Lee's invitation to spend the Thanksgiving Holiday with her, in New York. Tyra, knowing how much Curtis had enjoyed his previous trip to New York City, hoped that this trip would be no different. Especially, being that Curtis was scheduled to return to South Korea in three days, which meant he'd be leaving the day after Thanksgiving.

Anne Lee didn't realize so much time had passed since she'd last seen or even heard from Roger, especially considering she dealt exclusively and directly with Paul Mizelli regarding her real estate holdings/business. Nonetheless, she did know how fond of Roger, Curtis was, therefore, she was quite delighted when she reached out to Roger, who'd informed her that he'd be honored to spend Thanksgiving with Curtis, Tyra, Doris, Bernard, and herself, at her place.

"I brought with me, a vintage wine to be served with dinner." Roger smiled, as he entered the front door. Planting a kiss on Anne Lee's cheek, he added, "And this here," He handed her a second stylishly wrapped bottle, "Is a Champagne I thought we'd share after dinner."

Opposed to commenting on his last remark, Anne Lee simply said "You already know where to hang your coat." With that being said, she turned on her heels and exited the foyer.

As they ate dinner, Roger, who was now 65 years old. looked around the beautifully decorated dining room and table, before taking in the beautiful sight of the women who sat at the opposite end of the table, realizing (at the moment) how much he missed the life he'd had with Anne Lee.

Curtis ate about as much as he could, which Tyra noticed wasn't much at all, but his appetite was nonexistent. Actually, it was superseded by thoughts of his (now) deceased Mother. She too, had always made a big deal of Thanksgiving, not to mention, it was usually their home, where relatives gathered to celebrate the holiday/meal.

"So, Curtis," Roger began, setting down his wine glass, "Is it true that the powers that be, are currently in peace talks?"

Tyra shot Roger a look. The last thing she wanted to hear about, or engage Curtis in, was the conflict taking place over in Korea.

"If so, it's truly hard to tell." Curtis replied doubtful. "You know, right before I left to come back to the States, we got word that the Chinese stormed through the valley of Imjin through the Iron Triangle, up through the Eastern Mountains, mounting a major attack on allied outpost which was launched during the night. Over Ten Thousand allied soldiers are killed." He shook his head.

"Albeit, I hear that nearly Fifteen Thousand enemy soldiers were also killed, you have to keep in mind that, the Chinese-Korean armies have over one point Two Million ground troops! Not to mention, the Russians."

"I didn't know that the Russians were involved." Doris commented, not that she was following, or even interested in the conflict.

"Russia's leader, Joseph Stalin, was actually the person who approved North Korea's invasion of South Korea." Curtis informed her, then added. "Personally, I think we're on the losing end of this battle, because it seems like for every One-Hundred enemy soldiers we take out, another Thousand emerge. I'm talking about an enemy that is seemingly immune to the deadly forest, mountains, and valleys that are filled with land mines."

Roger, who had served in World War II, understood Curtis's fears and assessment of the situation being that he had experienced, or rather fought against German and Russian soldiers, both of whom had also appeared immune to Europe's deadly (cold) temperatures!

"I wish, I did not have to return." Curtis spoke in a much-lowered tone of voice. However, being that all conversation had ceased, it was not difficult for any of them to hear him when he added, "I've never been so afraid of anything, in my entire life."

Following their love making, Tyra couldn't help herself, as she continued to hold Curtis in her arms. She held onto him tighter than either of them had ever known her to. She desperately wanted to not only comfort him, but also assure him that everything would be all right, however, she couldn't even 'imagine' having to face or do battle with the kind of enemy Curtis had described during dinner! Especially, under such conditions! So, instead of verbalizing a false promise and /or assurance, Tyra simply held him close. So close she could literally feel his heartbeat.

Realizing that Curtis had finally drifted off into a deep sleep,

Tyra released him as she climbed out of bed. Once out of the bed, she did something in which she hadn't done in years... Tyra got down onto her knees and said a *Prayer*.

TWENTY-THREE

WASHINGTON, DC
JANUARY 18, 1953

About time! Tyra thought to herself, once her boss had departed the office. He had come to inform her that, she was (now) lead counsel on the *'Davis'* case. That was all he had said, nothing more, before turning his heels.

Preston Davis, was a Twenty-Two-year-old, white male, who had been arrested and charged with Aggravated Assault/ Battery for beating his Nineteen-year-old (white) girlfriend. An Investigator, for the Public Defender's Office, conducted an extensive background check on the defendant (Davis), being that no lawyer liked surprises, which revealed that; although, Davis clearly appeared Caucasian, he was actually a descendant of a White Grandfather and a Black Grandmother! A revelation, if it became public record/knowledge would certainly render Davis a *'Black Man'* not only in the eyes of Society, but also by Law.

"No wonder." Her boss had given her the case, Tyra thought to herself, after reading the investigation report.

As Preston Davis was led into the small visitation room, designated for 'Attorney Visits Only', Tyra had to admit; he certainly "looked" entirely white!

"Who is she?" Preston asked the guard who had escorted him from his jail cell

"Ask her." The guard replied coldly, then shoved Preston down into the chair in front of him, before taking up position beside the door.

"Who are you? And what do you want?" Preston asked with a snarl on his face.

"I'm the attorney who will be representing you." Tyra stated.

"The hell you are!" Preston exclaimed as he stood up, looking from Tyra to the guard, then back at Tyra before adding. "Ain't no way I'm about to let some 'darkie' represent me!"

"Is the visit over?" The guard asked, looking at Tyra, who shook her head no.

"Sit down!" The guard ordered Preston, with a menacing look on his face.

Preston sat back down in the chair.

"Thank you." Tyra said to the officer without looking up from the paperwork she'd began spreading out on the table. She was quite certain, that Preston had acted as he did, and referred to her as a 'darkie' hoping to score points with the (white) guard, however, she was indeed grateful when the guard's response/demeanor clearly indicated that he was not at all impressed by Preston's antics nor his racial slur.

"I've reviewed the Discovery Material in which the Prosecutor's office provided me thus far. I'm waiting to see if they're in possession of any witness statements, corroborating the victim's account of what 'allegedly' occurred." Tyra informed him. "I actually feel as though we have a good case. Your girlfriend, I mean the alleged victim has a pretty extensive history of violence." Tyra couldn't believe she'd actually pressed charges seeing how many times she had been arrested for being the aggressor in their previous disputes.

Preston just sat there unresponsive, staring into her eyes from across the table.

"Do you care to enlighten me, or rather, give me your version of what occurred?" Tyra asked.

Still, Preston simply stared into her eyes, unresponsive.

"At some point Preston, you are going to have to trust me. This case is winnable, however, due to recent developments it certainly has the potential to get a lot worse." Tyra was determined to wrap his case up as quickly as possible.

"Why should I trust you?" Preston finally responded.

Noticing that the guard wasn't paying the two of them any attention, Tyra leaned in, as close to her client as possible, speaking barely above a whisper, she replied, "Let's just say, you and I have something in common."

★★★★★

As she drove back to the office, Tyra couldn't help but wonder, what Preston's response would have been had she told him that 'something' was a black Grandmother! Probably not good if he had no idea of his ancestry, which Tyra assumed was the case.

However, what she 'did' know, was that she hadn't eaten anything since breakfast, which she also knew was not healthy or wise, as she conscientiously rubbed her stomach.

As soon as she entered the office, Kelly, who was on the telephone, handed Tyra a small sheet of paper that had a name and telephone number scribbled on it.

Seeing the name, Tyra hurried to her office.

"Valerie what's wrong?" She knew something had to be wrong, because Valerie was the last person she'd ever expect to be receiving a phone call from at work. As a matter of fact, Tyra couldn't recall ever giving her the office number.

As Tyra listened with closed eyes, her tears managed to escape and trickle down her face. Apparently, for a moment she zoned out, because Tyra could not recall ending their conversation or even hanging up, when she suddenly heard Kelly calling her name.

"Tyra, is everything all right?" Kelly was asking, as she stepped inside of Tyra's office closing the door behind her.

"It's my boyfriend," Tyra began, but stopped herself

mid-sentence.

Whereas, she had never (verbally) used the word *'boyfriend'* in reference to Curtis, hearing it come from her mouth, brought a sense of clarity as to why Curtis had been so adamantly opposed to its use or terminology which, to him, clearly diminished who and / or what the two of them, were to each other.

Starting over, Tyra didn't bother to wipe her tear stained face as she shared with Kelly, "I was just informed that someone very dear to me was killed in a land mine explosion, in Korea." That being said, Tyra rested her head on her desk.

Sensing she wasn't in the mood for further discussion, as well as seeing her obvious pain, Kelly quietly backed out of her office and as gently as possible, closed the door behind herself.

Being so bombarded with work, research, and deadlines to meet, Tyra had unplugged her home telephone (Thursday evening) and as she thought about it (still) hadn't re-plugged it. Which was why Valerie hadn't been able to reach her over the weekend.

In their conversation, Valerie, informed her that she was desperately trying to contact her because a military Chaplin had been calling asking what did she want to do with Curtis's body? Not being able to reach her, and clearly not ready or able (mentally) to put together or even deal with 'another' funeral/burial so soon, following their Mother's, Valerie made a request that Curtis be cremated.

Not only was Tyra's heart, totally, crushed as a result of not being available at such a time, it was also completely broken (beyond words) as the realization began to set in that she would never get the opportunity to tell Curtis, that she was Seven weeks *'pregnant'* with their child.

JULY 27, 1953

Tyra, was truly thankful that she had her Mother (and Doris) beside her, as she went through labor and her son entered into the world. She, with Anne Lee's input, decided to name him Thaddeus Curtis Star, after her Grandfather and Curtis.

As Tyra laid in her hospital bed (later that same evening), approximately five hours after her doctor announced, "It's a Boy!", she laid there watching the small black and white television set when suddenly, President Dwight D. Eisenhower came on tv to announce that, "It brings me great pleasure to inform the American public that the War in Korea is *'officially'* over!"

MAY 17, 1954

Speaking for a unanimous Court, on May 17, 1954, Chief Justice Earl Warren had handed down the decision, "In the field of public education, the doctrine of 'separate' but 'equal' has no place. Separate educational facilities are inherently unequal."

Brown V. Board of Education, destroyed the 'legal' basis for Jim Crow. Not only was it a personal triumph for Thurgood Marshall, but also one of the greatest victories for the NAACP. However, although the Court's decision ended the legality of school segregation in America, at the same time it gave notice to the Nation of wider moral bankruptcy of Jim Crow, even though not yet declaring *'other'* forms of segregation illegal.

Like Thurgood, Tyra also, was realistic enough to know that *'Brown'* merely set a precedent, and that implementation would require more lawsuits.

Yet, the NAACP downplayed the likelihood of strong [white] resistance to desegregation. In many areas, the NAACP told its branches that further legal action may not be necessary.

As Tyra entered the Legal Defense Fund headquarters, which was located on West Forty-Third Street, in Manhattan. She wasn't surprised by the festive atmosphere because of the Court's ruling. However, she also noticed the absence of Thurgood Marshall, Jack Greenburg, and Robert Carter, each of whom played a major role in 'Brown'.

"Good afternoon, Ms. Star." One of the secretaries greeted her with a pleasant smile on her face.

"Good Afternoon Marla," Tyra, like everyone else at the Fund, addressed her by her first name, before returning her smile.

"Congratulations." Marla added, knowing Tyra was undoubtedly elated due to the hard work and research she had provided and conducted.

"Thanks." Tyra only half smiled, then said, "It's a major victory, however, the Court's ruling does not conclude the School Cases. What the Court did." She began to explain, "Is separate the case in two parts. The lawyers for the Board of Education, as well as those for the plaintiffs, will have to reappear before the Justices to argue or rather, answer the Court's questions regarding remedy. Which means the filings of more Briefs."

"Wow!" Marla shook her head. "How long will that take?"

"Along with their decision, the Justices postponed the case for one year." Tyra informed her. "Therefore. we'll be preparing for 'Brown II'."

"It's always 'something' isn't it?" Again, Marla shook her head.

★★★★★

Shortly after giving birth to her son Thaddeus, Tyra, decided to take a leave of absence from the Public Defender's Office. In fact, she hadn't yet returned to Washington D.C.

As far as Anne Lee was concerned, she hoped her daughter and grandchild "never" returned to D.C. To say, she relished their company, would be a total understatement.

"You 'do' know that at some point I have to return to work, and my apartment, right?" Tyra, more so informed her mother, opposed to asking a question. "You don't 'have' to do anything." Anne Lee held her daughter's stare.

Tyra knew exactly what her mother was implying by that statement.

"It's not about having money." Tyra, responded. "I mean, I truly appreciate everything you have done for me finically, throughout the years." She smiled, as she walked up to Annie

Lee and gave her a hug. "But, what you have is what you've earned, which makes it yours to keep and to do what you choose. Not only am I passionate about what I do career-wise, and even more so in deeds, I actually like earning my own living."

"What's mines will always be yours Tyra." Anne Lee replied. Taking a step back from her daughter's embrace., she motioned for Tyra to join her on the couch.

Once they were seated beside one another, Anne Lee began to talk.

"I put off so many things, I once envisioned myself doing. Or at least, had intentions to strive to do and become, when I unexpectedly became a mother. Do I regret not pursuing some of my goals, or even dreams? I can't say that I do, because so much of my focus was elsewhere." She smiled as she held Tyra's hand.

"I beg to differ, seeing how well you've done in real estate." Tyra countered with a smile.

"Oh please, this was all Roger's idea, I simply capitalized from an opportunity.

"Well, whose ever idea it started out as, you certainly did well for yourself," Tyra responded. "I can't even begin to tell you how proud I have always been of your accomplishments."

The compliment touched Anne Lee's heart.

"Besides what all you've accomplished in real estate, you also managed to be 'my' greatest teacher, biggest supporter, and an incredibly awesome Mom." Tyra squeezed her hand.

"I wanted you to sit with me, so I could reveal some things to you, but you're about to make me cry."

"I'm sorry Mother." Tyra replied, yet, she continued to smile.

"I know I told you, what's mine will always be yours," Anne Lee began, "However, I've invested some money, some years ago, that literally belonged to you. I never told Roger about the money when he and I were married, or going through our divorce, because it wasn't 'my' money to bring up or disclose." She watched Tyra's face for her reaction.

Seeing no change in her expression, Anne Lee continued, "I know you're wondering why I waited this long to tell you about the money, but, I just wanted to see it continue to grow. Especially, since outside of your job, I had more than enough to keep you covered."

"So why tell me now?" Tyra asked her 'first' question.

"Because we're both 'older' now, especially me, and I feel the time has arrived." Anne Lee turned and looked in the direction of the small crib in which her Grandson was resting peacefully. "That you take over your inheritance."

"Inheritance?" Tyra was confused. "Who left me the money?"

"After your father passed away, a percentage of his estate went to you." Anne Lee revealed in a much lower tone of voice.

"My father?" Now, she was really confused.

"Apparently, he wrote you into his Will."

Tyra, just sat there, taking a moment to process what she was hearing.

"I guess I didn't tell you earlier because I didn't want to distract you, seeing how determined you were to achieve your Law degree, as well as pass the Bar Exam." Anne Lee added. Hating herself (still) for lying to her daughter. However, she was willing to take certain truths to her grave if it meant protecting Tyra and now her grandson, she told herself.

"I wish you would've told me." Now, Tyra was the one who spoke in a lowered tone. "Do you have any information, regarding some of his relatives? I mean, contact information that is?"

"No." Anne lee quickly stated. This is 'not' going well at all, she thought to herself. She wished the subject of money had never needed to be addressed, or brought up, but, Anne Lee knew it was inevitable, no matter how long (in terms of years) she avoided it. "I was contacted by an attorney. Which was quite some years ago."

Tyra gave thought to the last piece of information. She knew it wouldn't be too difficult to hire an investigator, several of whom she already knew and worked with, to get information she needed, or rather wanted.

"Would it bother you, if I took it upon myself to locate some of his family?"

Tyra looked into her mother's eyes.

"I'd be lying, if I said it wouldn't." Anne Lee confessed. "You have to remember, it was his family, not Morris, who made him abandon you, us, in the first place.

"I'm sure his parents are probably deceased, however, I'm just curious to know if maybe he had any other children is all?"

"It's your decision." Anne Lee stood up and walked over to the crib to check on Thaddeus. "I wish you'd leave my grandson here with me, for a while anyway, while you get yourself re- situated in Washington, D.C." She suggested.

"Remember you asked for that. Tyra smiled." I just hope you feel the same way, when I 'really' become busy and need a reliable babysitter."

"You just said, a minute ago, how awesome a job I did raising you." The change of subject, along with the thought of having her grandson for a time, brought about a smile on Anne Lee's face as well.

Just when she thought the subject was over, Tyra made one last inquiry.

"How much money are we talking? She asked.

"Excuse me?"

"You said, my father's estate left me some money." Tyra revisited.

"The lawyer gave me a check in the amount of Three hundred and Seventy-Five Thousand dollars, however, I let someone from a prominent family, invest the bulk of the inheritance. So, as of today, you're sitting on a little over Five Hundred Thousand dollars."

Although, Tyra was speechless now! In her mind, she was more determined than 'ever' to find out who this Black Man (her father) actually was, and how he accumulated such great wealth. Information, she told herself, if not for her benefit, certainly had the potential to 'influence' Thaddeus......

CHAPPAQUA, NEW YORK, 2007
12:30 P.M.

Roberta, decided to pause from her reading after page 170, considering her Mother's 'Journal' had her emotions all over the place! She was so glad that she kept a box of Kleenex tissue beside her bed.

As she laid her head back onto her stack of fluffy pillows, all she could think of was her husband.

"I can't believe Thaddeus doesn't know 'any' of this! Roberta said to herself. Truthfully, she couldn't understand why her Mother hadn't given Thaddeus her 'Journal' to read long ago? It wasn't like there was anything shameful between the pages. At least, not from what she'd read thus far, Roberta also told herself.

Opening her eyes, she sat up and reached for her cellular phone.

"Hello to you." Thaddeus responded.

Roberta could tell that he, too, had a smile on his face.

"I sent you a text message when I landed, did you read it?"

"I'd be lying if I said I did." Roberta informed him honestly.

"Is it that busy at the office?"

"I couldn't tell you, being that I decided to take the day off."

"Are you okay?" Thaddeus, couldn't remember the last time his wife had taken a day off from work. Unless, they were vacationing, or taking a trip.

"I'm fine dear." Roberta assured him.

Knowing his wife as well as he did, Thaddeus, had listened closely to her reply, and suddenly could tell that she had been crying.

"I have a meeting on Capitol Hill in Thirty minutes, but I'm going to cancel, and catch the next available flight home." Thaddeus told her, with concern in his voice.

"Please don't do that." Roberta pleaded. "Honestly, I am fine.

I was laying here reading your Mother's Journal and got a little emotional is all." She revealed.

Thaddeus, was silent.

"Are you there?" Roberta wasn't sure if the signal dropped.

"Yes, I'm here." Thaddeus answered. "I knew I shouldn't have agreed to your reading it without me."

"It's not that," Roberta replied. "Actually, it's quite amazing, what I've read thus far about your family."

Again, Thaddeus didn't give an immediate response.

"I'm not finished my reading, but I think your mother's Journal will answer a lot of questions that you had growing up."

"All right, let me head over to the Hill, I'll call you once I get checked in at my hotel."

Roberta sensed that he was suddenly rushing off the phone.

"Thaddeus," She spoke his name. "Seriously, I think you need to make it a priority to read this Journal upon your return home."

"I will, I promise." Thaddeus promised. "Okay, I have to go. I Love you."

"I Love you too."

Roberta, knew her husband, therefore she could tell that he wasn't too enthused about learning the unknown. Roberta felt it was imperative that at least one of them *'knew'* the entire story...with that in mind, she turned to page 171.

TWENTY-FOUR

HARLEM, NEW YORK, 1955

"You can *'not'* be serious! Anne Lee stared into her daughter's eyes to see if she'd lost all her good sense.

"Someone has to seek justice for that boy and his family." Tyra spoke with determination.

A determination, that Anne Lee silently Prayed wouldn't, one day, get her killed! She grew up in the South, therefore, Anne Lee knew firsthand how cruel, evil, and violent, countless white folks appeared naturally. And, without remorse.

"I understand, that young man deserves justice, and so does his family, but, when will you take a minute, at least to think about what 'your child need and deserves?" Anne Lee's concerns (now) was replaced by her anger. "Them folks down South Carolina will kill you, as sure as I'm standing here, before they allow you to come into their state in the name of Justice!"

"In every decision I make, I make it with my child in mind. If no one is available or willing to seek justice for that innocent black boy, sitting on death row, that could one day be Thaddeus's fate as well." Tyra countered, "We cannot let this racist, unjust system continue to have their way with our children!" Tyra, too, was (now) speaking from an angry perspective. Indeed, her anger was not a sudden occurrence she had 'been' angry seeing how blacks were still being lynched, regularly subjected to Police brutality, discriminated against in *'every'* sense of the word, and even though the highest Court in the nation ruled (a year earlier) that segregation in public schools was unconstitutional, relatively 'nothing' had been done, by the Court, the President, or Congress, to 'enforce integration!

Delayed and vague, 'Brown II', proved disastrous to the cause of integration. Whereas, some schools in the South complied with the Courts decision sooner than later, the vast majority (especially the Southern Conservatives), by contrast, mounted a crusade to convince [white] southerners that they need 'not' tolerate any racial change, no matter how gradual.

In fact, Robert P. Patterson, of Mississippi, organized the first "Citizens Council" in July of 1954 (two months following *'Brown'*), a movement that spread like wildfire throughout Mississippi, Alabama, Louisiana, and South Carolina! Similar organizations with different names appeared in other States.

The Citizens Council boasted over Two Hundred Thousand members, most of whom were Doctors, Businessmen, Lawyers, Politicians, Farmers, and School Superintendents, banding together to implement a multifaceted strategy designed to stop the emerging Civil Rights Movement in its tracks. They flooded the South with racist propaganda, subjected Civil Rights activist to threats and economic pressure, erected new barriers to black voting, tried to suppress the NAACP, condemned white liberals as traitors, and made 'segregation' and how to defend it, the central issue in Southern politics.

Whereas, the NAACP showed great optimism following the *'Brown'* decision, the organization was now feeling the Citizens Council's presence.

The NAACP's tactic of having local branches petition school boards for integration was now backfiring, as the Citizens council began retaliating against petitioners. One by one, those who signed, began to lose their jobs, and/or whatever business or trade they had with whites. The Citizens Council presented themselves, as God-Fearing, hardworking middle-class folk. The NAACP, however, drew no distinction between them and the Ku Klux Klan. Not to mention, the volleys of anti-segregation laws fired off by the South's state legislatures left the NAACP's litigation strategy (also) in tatters.

Actually, the Southern states launched a coordinated legal offensive, planned with care and stealth, to cripple the NAACP! They 'prohibited' state employees from advocating integration, forcing black teachers (one of the mainstays of the NAACP) to resign from the organization or face termination. In Orangeburg, South Carolina, twenty-four teachers (at the Elloree Training School) quit their jobs rather than renounce their membership. In Columbia, South Carolina, a teacher by the name of Septima P. Clark, also chose dismissal! However, several others decided to disassociate themselves from the organization.

Resurrecting long forgotten and obscure laws, State prosecutors began hauling the NAACP into court for neglecting to file its membership list with the state authorities. Which put the organization in between a rock and a hard place, if they complied with the law and handed over the list, they risked losing most of their members, for the Citizens Council immediately published the list. In doing so, whites targeted those whose names were exposed.

Many of the NAACP's loyal lawyers also found themselves under fire. Some were charged with violating professional ethics, prosecutors charged, by soliciting clients and inciting litigation. Quite a few were actually disbarred, although, most prevailed but found themselves virtually paralyzed by the costly, time-consuming, necessity of defending themselves in court.

Tyra, however, hadn't faced such opposition, residing in Washington, D.C., where President Eisenhower consequently (following the Court's decision in 'Brown') ordered the integration of every school in the District of Columbia, territory that the Federal Government not only called the shots, but also controlled. The President, also directed an immediate cessation to all remaining vestiges of segregation, of any nature, in the armed services. However, what the President did 'not' do, was personally urge the South to comply with 'Brown'.

Tyra, clearly understood her mother's concerns. Even she, had a feeling that her decision to take the South Carolina case may very well prove to be a life changing experience. Nonetheless, she told herself that whatever the ghost from her mother's past, that made Anne Lee determined to never return to the Deep South, she was 'not' about to let that deter her from taking on the "State of South Carolina V. Greene". Tyra was more than elated that the Legal Defense Fund had chosen her to handle the Appeal....

COLUMBIA, SOUTH CAROLINA

Whereas, Tyra had visited many County jails, in Maryland, and D.C., Central Correctional Institution (located in the city of Columbia) was the first male adult 'penitentiary' she had ever stepped foot into. Although, the prison basically_sat right in the heart of the city, something about its' design had caused an eerie feeling to run through her entire body. If that was the point, its' architect had certainly accomplished his goal, she told herself.

Once she had cleared the search area, where she was patted down by female correction officers, who also examined the contents of her briefcase, Tyra was escorted though a dimly lit 'tunnel' which she found even more eerie than the prison's exterior.

The relatively small visitation room, she noticed, was not much different from the others she had seen; however, it was designated exclusively for Death Row inmates, therefore, thick plexiglass was in place to separate the inmate-from-visitor.

Although, Tyra had seen picture of Reginald Greene (taken from a newspaper clipping), she could not believe her eyes as he slowly made his way into the visitation room. Greene, wearing handcuffs that were connected to a waist-chain and shackles around his ankles, did not look day over Sixteen!

"I get 'that' a lot." Reginald spoke first, seeing Tyra shaking her head. When he smiled, Tyra couldn't help noticing that he possessed a set of the prettiest white teeth she'd ever seen in a Man's mouth! Or, woman for that matter.

"What? That you look like a little boy?" Tyra asked, returning his smile, she was quite pleased to find her newest client appeared in such great spirit, despite his circumstance.

"Yes." He laughed. "Nobody believes I'm 23 years old." Reginald shook his head.

"It's a good thing." Tyra complimented. Ready to get to the purpose of her visit, she first introduced herself. "My name is Tyra Star, and apparently your family reached out to the legal Defense Fund regarding your case, and Appeal. As a result, your case was reviewed and I'm proud to say that I was chosen to represent you."

She smiled.

Reginald nodded his head up and down, opposed to giving an immediate (verbal) response.

"If I'm gonna be your lawyer, the first thing I want to establish is that I cannot read or understand sign language," Tyra informed him, then smiled, to let him know it was said light heartedly, yet, she did need for him to be vocal with her.

"Trust me, there's nothing shy about me." He assured her with a laugh.

"Okay." Tyra was glad to hear that, as she opened her briefcase and sifted through some papers, in search of one of the police reports. "Tell me a little bit about yourself while I go through my paperwork."

"What all do you want to know?"

"As much as you'd like to reveal, but mainly your upbringing. We'll get into what happened leading up to your arrest, and the day of, later. Right now, I'm more interested in Reginald Greene." She looked up and flashed a smile, before refocusing her attention on the contents of her briefcase.

"Well," Reginald began, "I was born in Sumter, South Carolina, but my parents relocated to Oakland, California, when I was Ten years old."

As she listened, Tyra was aware that thousands of black families, especially from the South, had relocated to cities out

West (as they had up North), hit hard by the Depression, most benefited from the jobs created during the military build-up of World War II, working at the bases and/or shipyards.

"My father found work on the waterfront, as a Longshore-man, and my mother was employed at a Department store. At first, it was a struggle. But, considering both of my parents worked, saved, and had only one child, things got significantly better financially, as the years progressed."

"I can't help noticing how well you articulate yourself." Tyra complimented.

"Thank you." Her words made him smile. "Growing up in Sumter, the schools weren't what I'd call 'learning' institu-tions being that most of the classrooms I've been in combined grades, lacked text books, and many of the teachers were ei-ther unqualified or basically uninterested." he shook his head at the memory.

"What do you mean by combined grades?"

"At Nine years old, it was common to have Six, Seven, and Eight-year old's sharing my same classrooms, subjects, and teacher."

"I take it, conditions improved when you moved to Oak-land?" Tyra asked, giving him her full attention now that she had found the statement in which she had been searching for.

"My initial school was okay, but I only went there for a lit-tle over a year. Once my family became somewhat settled, my parents made the decision to pay for me to attend St. Patrick's."

"Was that a Catholic School?"

"Yes, it is." Reginald confirmed. "Actually, my mother was pretty well read, and had always tried to homeschool me as much as her schedule permitted." As he thought about it, there were times that his mother worked two and three jobs at a time, yet, still made time for him. Therefore, it truly broke 'his' heart, knowing how much his current situation was affecting his parents, especially his mother!

"You got quiet on me." Tyra commented, as she maintained eye contact.

"I was just thinking about my Mother, and how this situation is literally tearing her down." Reginald shook his head.

Tyra understood, as well as 'saw' the pain written on his face. Yet, she also detected his strength, not only due to the absence of tears, but more so, in light of his high spirit, which prompted her to ask.

"Have you found religion since being incarcerated? Or, do you come from a very religious background?"

"Guys are always trying to convert you to some form of religion, or another, in here." He laughed and shook his head. "But, I do believe in God, and I Pray daily. My mother reads the Bible, prays a lot, and is always sending me Scriptures to read, but growing up, we would seldom attend Church. Especially, after we moved to California being that my parents worked almost around the clock. However, I went to St. Patrick's remember? So, religion was actually part of the curriculum.

"Did you graduate?"

"Yes Ma'am." Reginald smiled proudly. "Prior to my arrest, I was about to receive my Associate Degree in Journalism, at U.C. Berkeley." He shook his head.

Tyra, however, didn't recall reading no such thing/information anywhere in his case file. Not even in the 'notes' his trial lawyer had included in the Discovery she had received.

"Okay, let's get to the facts leading up to your arrest." Tyra was more interested in the information she didn't have inside of her briefcase. Sitting the police report aside, she placed both of her elbows on the table, joined her hands together, and placed her chin atop her hands, before asking, "So, what brought you back to Sumter?"

"My parents and I drove to Sumter from Oakland to attend my Mother's family reunion." He replied.

"Wow! I've never been to Oakland, but I'm sure that's quite a drive!"

"Including stops, it took us a whole four days to reach our destination." He laughed, and again he shook his head at the memory. Yet, he couldn't help thinking to himself, at that very moment, that he'd give anything to be (back) on that highway heading back to Oakland, even if it took a whole *'month'* to get there!

"How long were you all in South Carolina, or rather, Sumter, before the day of your arrest?" Tyra asked.

"Three days. Although, it was actually the 'fourth' day when I got arrested."

"Tell me what happened on that day?" She asked, as she listened closely.

"It was a Sunday, the day after our family reunion, that my cousin Glenwood and I, decided to go to some hole-in-the -wall that he was telling me about, where a lot of people hang out. Especially, the girls from neighboring counties." He smiled.

"Okay, "Was all Tyra said, as she listened.

"I believe, He and I were about a quarter of a mile away from the place when all of a sudden a Deputy Sheriff's car got behind us. When he pulled us over, I answered all of his questions truthfully, as well as complied when he asked for my driver's license. His entire demeanor and attitude changed when I told him that I was from Oakland, California and that the car I was driving belonged to my father."

"What kind of car was it?" Tyra was dismayed, already, by some of what Reginald had revealed. However, she kept quiet.

"He owns a 1953 Ford, convertible." He answered, which was followed by a laugh.

"Why'd you laugh," Tyra was curious.

"My mother wanted to take the railway to South Carolina, opposed to taking such a long drive. Which my father was totally against. Well, during most of the trip, my mother kept referring to him as a show-off, and all I could do was laugh, with my mother in mind, seeing how, at the family reunion, my father made sure 'everyone' in her family not only knew how much it had cost, but also that it was actually Ford's '50th Anniversary' Model!"

Again, Reginald shook his head and laughed.

Man, how he missed his Dad, Reginald couldn't help thinking to himself as well. Like anyone else, his father may have had his faults, however, not only was he a great provider, but he was also totally devoted to his Wife and Son.

Deciding to bring to light, or rather, to the conversation, one of her concerns regarding what he'd told her thus far, Tyra asked, "You say that you and Glenwood was heading to a hole -in-the-wall, the evening of your arrest. However, I've reviewed the arresting deputy's report, as well as, your trial lawyer's notes, and the transcript of your trial and nowhere did I see any mention of a cousin, or anyone else, being 'with' you when you were arrested."

Giving thought to her comment, Reginald responded, "I was quite curious myself, as to 'why' my trial lawyer never called him to trial to testify in my behalf. Especially, being that Glenwood knew I did not have a gun on me that day. And he damn sure 'know' I didn't kill anyone!"

"I take it, Glenwood is a cousin on your mother's side of the family, if that's the case. I'm sure you all don't share the last name Johnson."

Not only, did Tyra realize that it was imperative that she sat down with 'Glenwood Johnson' she was also glad that her finances were what they were, because as a result of (just) the little information she'd read and now heard, Tyra knew that some serious investigative work would have to be conducted if she intended to prevail in the first capital case of her career.

"How long have you been licensed to practice in the State of South Carolina?"

Reginald's question brought her thoughts back to the conversation.

"I am not licensed to practice in this state, nor do I intend to ever take the required Bar Exam." Outside of 'Greene' Tyra had no interest in practicing among those who had a history of proudly boasting, regarding their 'Good Ole Boy" system of Justice. Although, it was her associates at the Legal Defense Fund who had vouched for Attorney William J. Packard (the lawyer who 'was' licensed to practice in South Carolina, and whom she was required to share counsel), Tyra decided to make his office her next stop, to feel him out.

In spite of the praise she'd received in regard to her co-counsel Mr. Packard, Tyra already made up her mind that she would deal with him on a need-to-basis, she told herself.

"I had a dream recently, that my Savior would arrive. I just wasn't aware that he or she would be unlicensed to practice." Reginald laughed, even though he didn't know how to take such a revelation.

At That, Tyra laughed as well.

"If I weren't a licensed practitioner I wouldn't be here. I'm just not licensed to practice in South Carolina. That's why I have a co-counsel who is." She explained.

"I just didn't invite him to come along on this visit, because I wanted to meet you first." Tyra smiled.

"Now that I've met you, and realize there's a serious cover-up regarding your arrest and conviction, I'll definitely need to make an assessment of my co-counselor."

Licensed or not, Reginald Greene certainly liked Tyra Star's vibe. Nor could he shake the feeling that, besides God's obvious covering, he was 'finally' in good/competent hands...

TWENTY-FIVE

SUMTER, SOUTH CAROLINA, 1955

Prior to her trip to South Carolina, the furthest South Tyra had ever been was the State of Virginia. Even then, she hadn't seen a great deal of rural Virginia, or its tobacco fields/farms. Therefore, she was totally unprepared, taken aback actually, by the vast, unkept, and obviously unattended acres of land and cotton fields. Also, the sight of mostly, unpaved, dirt roads (many without street names and/or signs), and several of the homes she'd passed, more or less, displayed abject poverty.

Entering Sumter County, which was less than 60 miles from the state's Capital, Tyra couldn't help feeling as though Sumter, compared to Columbia, were like worlds apart. Unlike Colombia, absent (in Sumter) were; the Landmark structures, banks, hotels, restaurants, department stores, nor did she see even a resemblance of what could be described as a *'Business District'*. An observation, that made Tyra shake her head, as she thought about Reginald Greene. A young, educated, black man, from out of town, driving a brand new 1953 Ford convertible, through such a town!

"Unbelievable!"

Spotting a service station, Tyra decided to pull over. Not only to get gasoline, but also information. As she pulled into the small station the first thing Tyra noticed was the sign hanging above the only gas pump in sight, which read; "Whites Only". She also spotted a second sign that read; "Blacks Only", beneath the words was a small red arrow, pointing in the direction of what she assumed was the 'back' of the station. Only because, her needle indicted that her gas tank was on *'empty'*, did Tyra follow the sign's instruction.

Once she had finished pumping her gas, Tyra walked around front and entered the small building, which was no more than 300 square feet, that also served as a produce and variety store, she noticed. The inside although rather small in size, was actually quite clean. Even its produced appeared fresh. Scanning the variety of fruits and vegetables actually caused her stomach to growl, being that she hadn't eaten breakfast, nor had she stopped to grab anything to eat prior to leaving Columbia. However, she decided she'd pass on the fruit, it was 'information' she was more so interested in.

"I can tell you ain't from round here." Tyra's thoughts were suddenly interrupted by the remark, that came from somewhere behind her.

Looking around, Tyra spotted and elderly white woman, who she guessed to be somewhere in her late 70's, sitting in a wooden chair rubbing the backside of a large and extremely hairy black cat.

"However, much gas you done got for yo' self, you can just put the money on the counter over there." The woman instructed her, using her chin to motion towards the counter in which she referred to.

Tyra, complied by placing a five-dollar bill atop the wooden counter. Although, she had gotten four dollars' worth of gas, she decided not to request change, in hope that the stranger would prove to be a valuable source of information.

"So, what brings you to these parts?" The elderly woman asked.

"Actually, I'm trying to locate a family." Tyra informed her. She started to say, 'some distant family' but Tyra prided herself on her honesty, and although being totally honest, she knew, would not help her cause, she simply 'hoped' the woman wouldn't ask the questions in which Tyra certainly would not provide 'honest' answers.

"What's the family last name?"

"Johnson." Tyra answered, watching the woman closely.

"The Johnson's are a pretty big family round these parts. Matter fact, Minnie Pearl, lives right there up the road." The elderly woman turned her attention towards the only window in the makeshift store.

"So, Minnie Pearl is a Johnson then? Tyra asked, not believing her luck. She just knew she'd be searching for hours in such a seemingly deserted town.

The older woman shook her head, as if to say; what kind of dumb question is that? Instead, she replied, "She sho'liz."

Tyra, having never heard such a word or phrase, took it to mean; 'sure is'. Which was actually music to her ears, if her assumption proved correct.

"When you leave out that door there, you gone make that first right you come to, and take the road straight 'bout' 25 miles. When you come to the railway track, you 'gon' cross it and continue 'bout' another 15miles 'til' you run into a two-story brick house with a white wooden fence around the place. That's Minnie Pearl's." The woman informed her.

"That 'certainly' doesn't sound like 'right up the road'!" Tyra wanted to reply, instead, she thanked the woman and exited the store, at the same time telling herself that; the information, or rather, directions to Minnie Perl Johnson's residence was certainly *'worth'* the dollar.

Arriving at the two-story brick house, Tyra had to admit, that Minnie Pearl's residence was by far the most decent dwelling she'd observed, at least from the outside, since entering Sumter County.

From where she was parked, enabled her to see a variety of domestic and farm animals in the spacious yard. They included; at least two dogs, several cows, pigs, chickens and what Tyra assumed to be a horse, but then again, she'd never been up close to many animals (especially *'farm'* animals) therefore, it could very well be a 'donkey' Tyra told herself.

The sudden knock on her window, totally startled her!

"I didn't mean to scare you." A young girl of about Nineteen, spoke through the window, as she stood beside it. "How can I help you?"

Glad that I was the person, opposed to some wild animal, that had snuck up on her, Tyra smiled and replied, "It's all right. I'm here to see 'a' Ms. Minnie Pearl Johnson."

"I noticed you said "a" Ms. Minnie Pearl Johnson. Therefore, I suppose you and she never met? Which means she's not expecting you?" The teenage girl responded.

"No, she and I have never met," Tyra confirmed, leaving out the nature of the visit. "Are you her daughter?"

"No, I'm actually her granddaughter." The teenager informed her.

"Would you like to come inside, while I check to see if she's available?" The girl offered.

Stepping out of her car, Tyra followed the young lady into her grandmother's house. Upon entering, Tyra couldn't help noticing that, although the furnishings weren't that modern, the place was nonetheless nicely decorated 'and' spotless!

The hardwood floors were about as shiny as she'd ever seen. However, Tyra's attention, and stomach, were both, literally captivated by the incredible aroma that emanated from what had to be the kitchen area of the house. An assessment that was confirmed when a woman, whom Tyra assumed to be in her early 70's, yet, still quite lovely in appearance, approached her while wiping her hands on the apron wrapped around her waist.

"How can I help you?" The woman eyed Tyra somewhat suspiciously.

"My name is Tyra Star, and I was asked by the Legal Defense Fund to represent a young man, currently on death row, named Reginald Greene. Would you happen to know him?" Tyra replied, and asked, at the same time extending her right hand to the woman, for a handshake.

Instead of accepting Tyra's outstretched hand, the older

woman stepped closer, wrapping her arms around Tyra.

"Thank you, Jesus." Minnie Pearl gave Him Praise, as she continued to embrace the stranger who had come into her home. "You don't know how long I've been Praying for this day to arrive." She took a step back, enabling herself a better look at Tyra Star.

Tyra, was also relieved that she had obviously found the correct Johnson's.

"Can you tell me what your relationship is to Reginald?? Tyra asked

"He's my Grandson." Minnie Pearl answered, before adding, "His mother, Alice, is my oldest daughter."

"Can we sit down somewhere and talk?"

"Yes, of course. Where are my manners?" Minnie Pearl shook her head shamefully. "We can sit down in the kitchen. I'm actually preparing the majority of the meal for my Pastor's Anniversary." She informed Tyra, as Ms. Minnie led the way into the kitchen.

"I actually haven't eaten anything as of yet, would you like to join me for lunch?" Ms. Minnie offered, opening the oven to check on her baked macaroni and cheese.

The offer, was certainly music to Tyra's ears. Especially, seeing how her stomach was (now) doing summersaults! Not only, could Tyra 'not' recall 'ever' eating such a delicious meal, she honestly could not remember (ever) eating such a large portion of food!

"Glenwood's failure to testify in Reginald's behalf, was not his own doing." Ms. Minnie stated. "Between these racist, corrupt Sheriff Deputies, and his father's disdain for Reginald Sr., I'm totally surprised the boy still has any good sense left!" She exclaimed.

Tyra, decided to remain quiet and let her talk.

"Following Reginald's arrest, the Sheriff department threatened my entire family, even though they, and everyone else around here, knows that my grandson did not kill that white man! Everyone, including the law, knows that it was the brother who killed him." Minnie Pearl revealed." Over some white woman that they both were fooling around with."

Although, she didn't have a pencil and pad in hand, Tyra was nonetheless taking (mental) notes.

"Shortly after the Deputies questioned the brother and the young white girl, I hear they both just up and disappeared. Meanwhile, my grand-baby is sitting on death row for some nonsense that he had nothing to do with." Her eyes began to water.

"You mentioned something about Glenwood's father disdain for Reginald Sr." Tyra inquired, dismayed by how she had missed the fact that her client was even a *Junior*.

"Yes. Glenwood's father, Charles, has always been envious of Reginald Sr. It actually goes back to when they were young boys themselves. Basically, Charles's jealousy got much worse after Alice and Reginald moved out West, and started really doing well for themselves.

"I remember Alice sent her sister, Janice, some money, because I told her how bad she and Charles was doing. Do you know that fool made Janice wire the money back to California!" Minnie Pearl shook her head incredulously. "Worst of all, my two daughters, Alice and Janice haven't spoken 'since' all this mess with Reginald."

"What did Charles have to do with Glenwood not testifying in his cousin's behalf?" Tyra wanted to know. However, her answer didn't come from Ms. Minnie, but, from someone standing behind the chair.

"My father told me that if I testified, or do 'anything' in any way to help Reginald, he'd personally hand me over to the family of the deceased and the mob of white folk, who were demanding that the Sheriff turn my cousin over to them, so they could lynch him!"

Tyra turned to face Glenwood, who was standing in the doorway, beside the young girl she had met outside, who apparently went and fetched Glenwood.

"So, you're Glenwood?" Tyra asked, even though she already knew the answer to her question. She chalked it up to the lawyer in her.

"Yes, Ma'am." He answered.

"Do you mind having a seat, and telling me everything that happened on the day you and your cousin were pulled over by the Sheriff's Deputy?" Tyra asked.

Talking a seat beside his Grandmother, and across from Tyra, he began to tell what all he remembered from that day.

Once Glenwood was done speaking, Tyra began to ask questions.

"How do you 'know' that Reginald did not kill Jarvis Winters?"

Glenwood had already revealed that he knew the deceased quite well.

"Because Jarvis was murdered on the 24th of April, shortly after he left the Dug Out." He had explained previously, that the 'Dug Out' was actually the same hole-in-the-wall that he and Reginald were on their way to when they were pulled over. He also informed Tyra that the 'Dug Out' was one of those clubs that the whites had their night and the black folks had theirs.

"However, my cousin Reginald, and his parents, didn't arrive in Sumter until the evening of the 25th of April." Glenwood revealed, meanwhile, he continued to look down at the tablecloth.

"Are you sure that there were more than 'two' Deputies on the scene, when your cousin was taken into custody?" Tyra asked, considering she had only seen/received 'two' police reports, and noticed (from the trial transcript) that only 'two' Deputies testified at Reginald's trial.

"Yes, Ma'am." Glenwood confirmed, before giving further detail.

"The Deputy who initially pulled us over, was Deputy Wallace. When the second cruiser arrived on the scene it had 'two' Deputies inside. One was Deputy Greenwalt, and the other was Deputy Younts."

Tyra recalled the names Wallace and Greenwalt, however, she hadn't seen Younts name anywhere in the Discovery provided to her.

"What happened after the other two Deputies arrived?" Tyra prodded.

"Deputy Greenwalt, began to assist Deputy Wallace in searching my Uncle's car, while Deputy Younts proceeded to search me and Reginald. Once he realized that we didn't have anything illegal on us, he told the both of us that if the car is as clean as we are, we'd be on our way." Glenwood recalled.

"So, he didn't find anything on neither of you?" Tyra had to be certain.

"No Ma'am, he didn't find anything on either of us." Glenwood assured her.

Although, she felt he'd make a good witness, Tyra wasn't totally comfortable with the fact Glenwood hadn't once made eye contact with her, as he spoke.

"What happened next?"

"The two deputies didn't find anything in the car, but I saw them talking off to the side, and I had a feeling that they were up to no good, seeing how they kept looking our way. when they finally approached us, they made me stand in the back of the Ford with Deputy Younts, while the other two Deputies took Reginald to the

front of the car. Next thing I know, deputy Greenwalt was shouting to Deputy Younts that he found something in Reginald's pants pocket. I knew he was talking about a gun, because he was holding it up in the air, as he spoke."

That being said, Glenwood, looked up, into Tyra's eyes, allowing her to see his tears…

TWENTY-SIX

SUMTER, SOUTH CAROLINA, 1955

The Sumter County Sheriff's Department, would've certainly been difficult for Tyra to locate, due to the lack of street signs. Therefore, she was thankful that Samantha, Minnie Pearl's granddaughter offered to ride with her.

"You stay in the car." Tyra instructed Samantha once they were across the street from their destination. "I'm not sure how this is going play out."

Samantha, knowing how evil, corrupt, racist, and vindictive the all-white Department could be, was not only afraid for Tyra, but nonetheless relieved that she wouldn't have to show her face.

Entering through the front door, all eyes were suddenly on Tyra as she approached the nearest desk.

"What can I do for you?" A white woman, who was not in uniform, whom Tyra assumed to be somewhere in her mid to late 30's, asked.

"I'm here to see Sheriff Richards." Tyra informed her.

"Is he expecting you?" The woman asked.

"No ma'am. I know I should have called beforehand, but I'm actually visiting from out of town. However, if he's available, my reason for being here shouldn't require too much of his time." Tyra produced a smile.

"May I have your name?"

"It's Tyra Star."

"You can have a seat over there." The woman pointed to a long wooden bench adjacent the door where Tyra had entered.

"That's all right., I'm perfectly fine standing."

The two-woman held each other's gaze, until the woman in civilian clothing turned and headed towards an office that sat to the far left.

At least, a full ten minutes passed before the woman finally returned with 'two' deputies in tow.

"I'm Deputy Wallace, is there a problem I can help you with ma'am?"

Tyra stood her ground, as the two deputies 'and' the woman she'd given her name to, looked as though they were ready to arrest, or even pounce on her, simply for 'being' there.

"Actually, I'd like to see Sheriff Richards." Tyra repeated her earlier request. As she and Deputy Wallace engaged in a stare-down, Tyra couldn't help feeling as though she was looking directly into the eyes of pure hatred.

"Unfortunately, the Sheriff is busy at the moment." Deputy Wallace informed her, yet his tone was without apology.

"I am quite exhausted." Tyra replied honestly, between her drive and the enormous amount of food she'd eaten at Minnie Pearls, she was certainly ready for a nap. "So, I think I'll go lay down awhile, and come back later."

"That won't be necessary." The comment came from a male's voice, behind where the two deputies and the reception woman stood.

"I'm Sheriff Richards, how can I help you?" He asked Tyra from where he stood.

Taking in the man's appearance, Tyra was surprised by how tall he was. Sheriff Richards stood at least 6'5, and weighed about 250 pounds, she guessed. Although, he had a slight smile on his clean-shaven face, Tyra knew that she would not take his smile 'or' anything he said, at face value.

"Is there somewhere that you and I can talk? Tyra asked

before adding, "In private, that is?"

"Certainly, I do not know where, for dickens sake, my manners are this fine afternoon." The Sheriff shook his head. "Come right this way." He obliged, as he led the way into his office.

Once inside, the Sheriff motioned for Tyra to take the seat directly in front of his desk. Tyra, meanwhile, did a quick scan of the office (mostly through her peripheral,) noticing not only an array of medals, family portraits, and at least three rifles hanging from his wall(s).

"My name is Tyra Star, which I'm inclined to believe your reception has already informed you. I'm an attorney, who currently represents a young man by the name of Reginald Greene Jr., who is currently detained on death row, at Central Correctional Institution, but I'm also certain that you're already familiar with the name, as well as, the circumstances.

Therefore, I'll cut right to the purpose of my visit. I'm investigating my client's case from the beginning, because from what I have read thus far, it seems to me that a thorough investigation has never been conducted. So, I figure why not start with the Sheriff's department, before I sit down with the Solicitor, who prosecuted his case." Tyra produced a smile.

"I think the Solicitor is who you should be talking with, because I don't see no reason for you to be here" The Sheriff replied, not bothering to return the smile.

"No offense Sheriff, but I've learned that starting from the bottom, up, tends to be much more effective. Especially when the idea is to obtain the missing pieces of the puzzle."

"Are you making an insinuation?" The Sheriff asked with a raised eyebrow. "Because it sounds to me like you're making an accusation."

That being said, Sheriff Richards reached his right hand into his top desk draw.

Tyra watched his movement. As he withdrew his hand, Tyra was quite relieved to see the shiny pipe, which the Sheriff began stuffing pipe tobacco into.

"I hope the smoke doesn't bother you." The Sheriff remarked, opposed to actually asking, as he lit the tobacco and inhaled deeply.

Tyra didn't bother to respond as she witnessed his cheeks sink in.

"So, what are the pieces that you *'think'* are missing?" The Sheriff inquired, after filling the air with a huge cloud of smoke.

"We could start with Deputy Younts' report." Tyra watched closely for a reaction after giving her reply.

If the Sheriff was surprised by her response, he certainly didn't show it, she noticed.

"I don't believe that there exists a report made by Deputy Younts. If so, I haven't seen or heard about it." The Sheriff replied.

"How about I have a word with Deputy Younts? Is he available?"

Exhaling a second cloud of smoke, the Sheriff spoke through the cloud.

"I do not know how you people do things up North, but down here, we do not take too kindly to strangers barging in, unannounced, making baseless accusations, and requesting to interrogate lawmen."

He stared into Tyra's eyes as he spoke. In fact, he was practically leaning over his desk.

"I would hate for you to find yourself in a world of trouble, just because you feel sorry for a murderer." He warned.

"Duly noted." Tyra was determined to stand her ground. "However, I still would like to *'interview'* Deputy Younts." She repeated.

"Unfortunately, that will not be possible. Deputy Younts is vacationing with his family. I believe, they're spending time down in Charleston."

Tyra, gave him a simple nod once he was done talking. However, she could tell that the Sheriff wasn't being truthful.

"Why don't you run on back up there to Washington D.C., and I'll be sure to let Deputy Younts know that you stopped by. If he chooses to contact you, I reckon he'll do so." The Sheriff suggested, at the same time letting on that he knew exactly where she was from.

"How exactly do you know where I'm traveling from?" Tyra questioned.

"The same way I know that you have been in Columbia for the past two days, and have visited Central Correctional Institution at least once. In fact, I also know that you left Columbia this morning without so much as bothering to get gas, or breakfast." He produced a smile.

"And," the Sheriff continued, "I also know that it was old lady Jenkins, who gave you directions this afternoon, to Minnie Pearl Johnson's residence." That being revealed, he added, "Just because I'm down here in these sticks, does not mean that I'm any less capable of making things happen." Again, he smiled, as his pipe dangled from his mouth.

"Is that a threat Sheriff?" Tyra asked.

Waving off a cloud of smoke, Tyra couldn't be sure if he was waving away the smoke, or her question.

"I never thought I'd live to see the day, that they'd allow a woman, let alone a *'colored woman'*, become an attorney!" He shook his head in disbelief. "I guess 'anyone' can pass the bar nowadays." He added.

That being said, Tyra desperately wanted to inform the Sheriff that, on March 27, 1872, a 'Black Woman' by the name of Charlotte E. Ray, not only earned her Law Degree (from Howard University) but was also admitted to argue cases before the Supreme Court, in the District of Columbia!

"Put 'that' into your pipe and smoke it!" Tyra wanted to tell the racist Sheriff, however, she didn't want to find herself occupying a jail cell. Therefore, she remained silent.

"If you and I are done here, I have some other matters that need my attention." The Sheriff was basically dismissing her, without bothering to stand, escort her out, nor offer a hand, for the purpose of a handshake.

"Thank you for your time Sheriff." Tyra offered, as she stood and headed for the door.

"I hope you have a *'safe'* trip home." The Sheriff replied, not bothering to look up from the papers in which he was now sifting through atop his desk.

Upon reaching her car, the first thing that struck Tyra was the absence of Samantha!

Climbing into the driver's seat, she also noticed a small brown sack sitting on her passenger's seat. Thinking it was something that Samantha must've left behind, Tyra dug into the sack.

Whereas, she had never personally touched a 'noose', Tyra knew exactly what the knotted piece of rope was, and implied. However, it was the second item inside of the sack that made her hands begin to tremble, as she held her college graduation picture, which displayed 'her' smiling proudly with both her arms wrapped around the shoulders of her mother, Anne Lee, and Roger!

The "only" copy of the picture she was holding, hung on her office's wall, at the Public Defender's Office in Upper Marlboro, Maryland…

WASHINGTON, DC

Arriving at her office, upon her return from South Carolina, Tyra immediately knew something was wrong by the expression on Kelly's face. However, since she had a more pressing matter to deal with, Tyra strolled right pass the receptionist desk, en route to her office. Kelly, came from behind her desk and followed suit.

Opening her door, Tyra could not believe her eyes. "I had no way of reaching you, to tell you that Mr. Condon, personally packed your entire office into those three boxes." Kelly informed her.

Tyra heard the words, but her focus was totally on the three boxes that sat in the middle of the floor. She sat down, crossed her legs, and began going through the first box.

"He also told me to inform him whenever you arrived." Kelly added, at the same time hating herself for sounding as if she was a co-conspirator in 'whatever' was going on. Yet, she was certain that Tyra knew how much she actually despised their boss, Mark Condon.

"What's going on?" Kelly asked Tyra, as she kneeled down beside her.

"It's not here!" Tyra exclaimed, after going through the contents of the third and last box.

"What's not in there?" Kelly asked.

"The picture from my Graduation, that I had hanging on my wall."

Kelly knew the picture. "I didn't see Mr. Condon take anything. Well at least I don't think he did."

Just then, Mr. Condon appeared in the office doorway.

"I see you made it back safely, from your trip down south."

With that being said, he and Tyra engaged in a stare-down. When he looked away, Tyra pretty much had the answer to her suspicion.

"It's a shame, I had to find out from a source Six hundred mile away, that you've been working with the NAACP Legal Defense Fund. I have a good mind to report you to the Bar, whom I'm sure you know, does not take too kindly to under-handed practices." Mark Condon threatened.

"Kelly, would you mind carrying one of these boxes to my car? Tyra asked the receptionist.

Once Kelly was gone, Tyra shut the office door. Enabling her to be alone with Mr. Condon.

"For years, I've accepted your prejudice and discrimination, while I did my work and the work of most of the lawyers in this office without complaint. Then you have the audacity to outright threaten me with termination when I got the Preston Davis case dismissed." Tyra eyed him coldly.

"But, for you to actually 'steal' a photograph from my wall, to send to your associates, or whomever, in the South, is beyond outrageous even for someone like you. However, I do want you to know that I've been doing some investigating myself, as far as you are concerned… I'm quite sure the Bar Association would not take to kindly, that the head of the Public Defender's Office not only has a brother who's a known Klan member and is serving time in a South Carolina prison, but that you, yourself, have ties to the Citizens Council." Tyra produced a smile, basically for affect. She knew that the members of the Bar, or rather the group of white men who presided over the Bar, could probably care less about Mark Condon being related to a convicted Klansman, or whom he, himself, had ties to. Nevertheless, she also felt there were a lot more skeletons in Mr. Condon's closet, because where there was smoke there was usually fire. So, why not let him sweat, allowing him to 'assume' that her investigation revealed much more.

Once Kelly returned, Tyra handed her a second box, before exiting the office with the last one in hand.

"Don't worry about telling me that you've decided to fire me because I quit."

Opposed to allowing the photo incident to distract her, Tyra was more determined than ever to help Reginald Greene.

"What are you going to do now that you don't have a job?" Kelly wanted to know, as Tyra climbed into her car.

"Spend some time with my Mother and Son." Tyra said with a smile before adding. "Before I head 'back' to South Carolina." That being said, she drove off...

HARLEM, NEW YORK

Tyra, thoroughly enjoyed the two months she spent with Thaddeus and her mother, but she was ready to get back to work on the 'Greene' case. Which Anne Lee was totally against.

"Imagine if I told her about the noose and picture incident!" Tyra thought to herself, as she entered the Fund's headquarter.

"Marla, how have you been?" Tyra asked the receptionist.

"I'm great, even though I'm 'still' trying to get used to these New York winters." Marla blew into her hands as if she'd just come in from the cold. "Have you heard about Montgomery?"

"Montgomery?" Tyra was dismayed by the question.

"As in, Montgomery, Alabama." Marla clarified.

"What's going on in Montgomery, Alabama?"

"It isn't front page news, but something tells me it will be."

Tyra remained silent, as she waited for Maria to elaborate.

"Apparently, a black woman, by the name of Rosa Parks, was arrested there for refusing to give her seat, on a bus to a white person."

Tyra commended the woman's courage, however, she had been aware of other such incidents. Yet, none of them had made headlines, she thought to herself.

"Why do you think Mrs. Parks case will be any different from the Claudette Colvin case?" Tyra was curious.

Holding Tyra's stare, Marla produced a smile before revealing.

"Because, not only is she one of Ours." Meaning Rosa Parks was a member of the NAACP. "Something tells me, this incident is not entirely coincidental."

TWENTY-SEVEN

SUMTER, SOUTH CAROLINA, 1956

Relieved, was an understatement, in describing how Tyra felt upon finding out Samantha (Minnie Pearl's Granddaughter) was all right. However, she still could not believe that Deputy Wallace had frightened the young girl so badly that, instead of waiting for Tyra in her car (that day), she walked all the way home!

"Why would you get a hotel room in Columbia? You're more than welcomed to stay right here." Minnie Pearl asked/offered.

Tyra was touched by the woman's offer. However, she knew the danger she'd be placing upon Minnie and her family had she accepted.

"I have plenty of room." Minnie added

"I can't stay here. It will put you and your entire family at risk." Tyra explained her reason for declining.

"I don't know what the Sheriff told you, but I'm not worried about them folks, nor am I afraid of them bringing trouble my way.

"As far as I'm concerned, it is the 'Lord' who brought you all this way to bring my Grandson home, so we ain't fitna let the 'law' git in our way!' Minnie Pearl exclaimed.

Tyra simply smiled, thoroughly impressed by the older woman's courage and feistiness.

Samantha, however, stood off to the side with a hand over her mouth to contain her laughter regarding Minnie's comment.

"I'll tell you what." Tyra began. "How about you have someone point me in the direction of Deputy Younts's residence, so I can proceed in doing the Lord's Will.

At that, Minnie Pearl visibly simmered down and put a smile on her face.

"I can have Glenwood show you where he lives." Minnie stated. "He's actually not that far from here, seeing that he lives right up the road."

Tyra couldn't help laughing. She knew from experience that 'right up the road' certainly did not always mean 'not too far'.

"What's so funny?" Minnie asked

"It's nothing really." Tyra gathered herself.

"Go and get Gleenwood!" Minnie instructed Samantha with urgency.

"He'll just be showing me the place, then I'll be dropping him back off here." Tyra explained. She didn't want anyone to actually accompany her, while she conducted her investigation.

"Whatever you want dear." Minnie understood. "If you want, I can go with you." She offered.

Again, Tyra couldn't help feeling touched.

"How about I go at it alone, while you cover me in Prayer?"

"Sounds like a plan." Both women smiled, before Minnie Pearl wrapped her arms around the woman she knew was a God-Send.

At first, Tyra couldn't help thinking that maybe Glenwood had been mistaken, in pointing out the house in which he told her was the Younts's residence. Although, the outside was quite clean, the place was nonetheless (obviously) old and run-down!

When she returned, Tyra heard at least two small children inside of the home, as she was about to knock on the front door. Suddenly, she was interrupted by a male's voice.

"Can I help you with something?" He asked.

Tyra turned in the direction of the voice, at the same time locking eyes with a white man, whom she guessed to be around thirty years of age, and dressed in badly worn denim overalls.

"Yes, my name is Tyra Star, and I'm here to speak to a Mr. Dexter Younts."

Tyra learned the man's first name from Minnie Pearl, who had known him since he was a young boy.

At least, a full two minutes passed as they (both) eyed one another suspiciously.

"I'm Dexter Younts." He finally replied,

"Do you mind if I have a minute or two of your time?" Tyra asked, before adding "In fact, is there somewhere we can sit-down and talk?" She knew she'd need a written confession from the deputy if it was at all possible to obtain.

"We can talk right here where we're standing!" With that being said, He brought the double-barreled shotgun from be- hind his right leg, so that now it was in plain view.

"I already know that you're that Yankee lawyer, who Dep- uty Wallace told me was looking for me. He also told me that you'd more than likely show up at my front door." He stated with an attitude.

"Deputy Wallace and I didn't engage in much conversation the day I visited the Sheriff's department, but I guess he was right about me showing up at your front door." Tyra said with a smile on her face, hoping to ease some of the tension.

"You asked for a minute or two. What is it you want from me?" He asked not bothering to return the smile.

"As you may know, or maybe received word from Depu- ty Wallace, I represent a young man named Reginald Greene, whom I'm also sure that you're aware, is currently sitting on death row for an offense that I personally do not believe he committed,

"I say that because, of what all I've read and heard, pertain- ing to this case. I didn't get anywhere talking to Sheriff Rich- ards or to the Solicitor who prosecuted the case. But, from the background that I've uncovered regarding the moral aptitude of Dexter Younts is really the reason I'm here." Tyra explained.

"Background provided by who?!" He inquired.

"Well, for starters, a woman by the name of Minnie Pearl Johnson."

At the mention of Minnie's name, Tyra saw something shift in the white man's eyes as his right hand leaned the shotgun up against the brick siding of the house.

Making his approach, Dexter extended that same right hand to her. As they shook hands, Tyra couldn't help feeling as though Minnie Pearl Johnson, probably 'did' have Favor with God.

"Again, what can I do for you?" Dexter asked.

"My visit is not about what you can do for me, I'm solely here for the purpose of finding out what you're ready, willing, and able to do for Reginald Greene. An innocent young man occupying a cell on death row." Tyra spoke sincerely.

Closing his eyes for a moment, Younts simply nodded his head as if he knew this day would someday present itself.

"Let's go inside and talk." He suggested, as he retrieved the shotgun, looked around to make sure no one was watching the two of them, and then led the way into his home through the back door.

"I remained at the Sheriff's Department for maybe a year following the Reginald Greene incident. But, things there were never the same for me, especially after his trial and conviction." Dexter began to explain.

"I guess you can say, I became the traitor of the Department being that I refused to testify at the trial."

"Did you ever submit a written report, as to what actually occurred the day Reginald was arrested?" Tyra asked her first question.

"Of course, I did, It's protocol." Dexter informed her. "Why the defense, apparently, never received it is another story. One that I'm sure, you do not need me to tell." He shook his head.

Tyra nodded her understanding.

"What is that you do now? I mean, for a living that is?" She wanted to know, considering Tyra was still quite thrown aback as to the former deputy's living condition. In fact, she was quite certain the Younts family were not much better off than the average black family in the region.

"I do various jobs to feed and clothe my family. But mainly, I grow produce, which I sell to old lady Jenkins and several other families in these parts." Younts answered before adding, "I try to save as much as possible while the weathers' good because the winter basically puts me out of commission." He gave a weak smile. "I did try to take some of the fruits and vegetables to Ms. Minnie Pearl, just for her to have for herself, family, and the Church she attends, but she ran me off."

Younts held Tyra's stare as he added. "Actually, she made it clear that, she would never take or eat anything I had to give, even if it were the 'last' piece of fruit or vegetable on this earth."

Whereas, Tyra managed to hold in a laugh, she could certainly picture Ms Minnie Pearl going off on the Deputy in such a manner.

"There is another way." Tyra spoke.

"Another way for what?" Younts asked in dismay.

"To 'Right' a wrong." Tyra answered, knowing that he, along with Glenwood Johnson, would be her best shot at getting Reginald a new trial.

"I have a family to think about."

Tyra knew his concern was not only genuine, but moreover legitimate.

"You can always relocate." She offered in response.

At that, all Younts could do was laugh.

"Yeah right!" He finally exclaimed. "And go where? With very little money to my name, no guarantee of a job, and a wife and two small children in tow." He looked across the table incredulously, as a result of such a suggestion.

"How about you and I, narrow down what all you wrote in your report?"

Tyra took out a pen and notepad, "Then, we can focus on working out a solution to the potential repercussions afterwards."

Although, she knew Younts was bewildered by her suggestion/remark, Tyra was nonetheless pleased to see him re-writing what had actually, occurred on the day of her client's arrest. As he wrote his statement, already, a plan began to formulate in her mind...

COLUMBIA, SOUTH CAROLINA

Securing a full written statement from not just Dexter Younts, but from Glenwood Johnson as well, Tyra made her second trip to Central Correctional Institution to see Reginald Greene Jr.

"How are you?" Reginald asked happy for the surprise visit, as he sat behind the thick plexiglass with a smile on his face.

"I'm fine." Tyra replied returning the smile.

"Any good news?" Reginald wanted to know.

"Actually, I've been making great progress I'd like to believe." Tyra didn't want to get into too much detail as of yet, she knew how easy it was for clients to get their hopes up.

"I'm here because I need your permission to withdraw your motion for Direct Appeal." Tyra informed him.

"Why would I agree to something like that?" Reginald asked with a raised eyebrow.

"The Direct Appeal, in your case, is literally a waste of time. No pun intended." Tyra stated. "I say that because, on Direct Appeal, you can 'only' raise the issues in which your trial lawyer preserved during the trial. In your case, upon receiving the trial transcripts, I've noticed that your trial attorney didn't make a single objection. Which not only means that, you do not have anything preserved for Appellate review, but moreover we can clearly demonstrate that your trial lawyer was totally ineffective.

"I've been on your case a little over Six months now, and I honestly cannot believe the lack of investigation on the part of your trial lawyer." Tyra shook her head in disbelief. Yet, she knew that the average black person (male or female) rarely received adequate legal assistance and representation, which was '*why*' she wanted to become a lawyer in the first place.

Nodding his understanding, Reginald posed a question.

"So, let's say I agree to let you withdraw my Direct Appeal, what other avenue do I have?"

"That's a good question." Tyra smiled. "I want to file a motion for Post-Conviction Relief." She answered.

Again, Reginald nodded his head up and down. He'd heard of a PCR, yet, he wasn't all that familiar with how it worked.

"By filing a PCR, I can challenge everything that trial lawyer failed to do, in my endeavor to get the court to agree that he was not only ineffective, but also, had it not been for his ineffectiveness the outcome of your trial would have been different." Tyra further explained.

Opposed to nodding his head up and down, a third time, Reginald simply smiled from ear to ear.

"My grandmother told me you that you were a God-send."

At that Tyra laughed.

"I'm just doing my job. Nothing more, nothing less." Tyra replied modestly, however, she knew she was going above and beyond, simply doing her job, for the young man sitting across from her in shackles. Especially, if she could actually pull off what she had in mind for the Younts family as well, she thought to herself.

"So, is your co-counsel, Mr. Packard on the same page?" Reginald inquired, bringing her focus back to the conversation.

"I haven't discussed my intentions with him as of yet, but, he and I have come to an agreement that, I will solely make the pertinent decisions as they relate to your case." Again, Tyra smiled.

"And he's totally okay with following your lead?"

"I wouldn't put it that way. Let's just say, he's not only busy with other cases, but Mr. Packard isn't to thrilled about the potential attention this case is liable to garner, especially if I prevail in getting you back into court for a new trial." Tyra explained, leaving out the part about William J. Packard being utterly *relieved*' when Tyra suggested she'd handle majority of the defense, including research, motions, and arguments. As a resident of South Carolina. Mr. Packard, certainly was not trying to deal with the potential backlash of representing Reginald Greene, Jr…

TWENTY-EIGHT

HARLEM, NEW YORK, 1958

Although, Tyra admitted Reginald Greene's application (motion) for Post-Conviction Relief, in the spring of 1956, she knew it would be anywhere from One to Two years before a court date was set. Meanwhile, she focused her attention on what was going on in Alabama, and elsewhere.

Whereas, the Montgomery Improvement Association, led by a 26-year-old Atlanta native and Pastor of the Dexter Avenue Baptist Church, named Reverend Martin Luther King Jr. organized the Montgomery bus boycott, Tyra, nonetheless, immensely impressed, had been awaiting the United States Supreme Court's decision in 'Browder v. Gayle', a decision that was handed down in November of 1956, that said; City and State [bus] segregation laws were unconstitutional.

On December 20, 1956, the Montgomery Improvement Association ended the boycott. Tyra, like her mentor Thurgood Marshall, had felt that 'nonviolent' protest in the South had a potential to lead to massive slaughter. However, one of the striking features of the bus boycott had been the relative 'absence' of violent retaliation on the part of whites.

The Montgomery bus boycott, certainly inspired blacks in other areas of the South, Tyra had to admit, seeing how members of the NAACP's Youth Councils (in Wichita and Oklahoma City) demanded to be served at Department store lunch counters, which customarily excluded blacks. It was the beginning of what would be called 'sit ins'.

"How are you doing today Marla?" Tyra asked as she entered the Fund's Headquarters, where she often checked if they'd received word from William J Packard, regarding a court date in the Reginald Greene case.

"I have good news for you." Marla smiled brightly.

"Let's hear it." Tyra said smiling as well.

"A Senator Joseph Bivens, from Delaware, wants to meet with you. He said it was brought to his attention that 'you' were one of the lawyers who worked on the Briefs, as well as conducted a lot of the research in the *'Brown'* case." Marla stated.

"I still don't understand why he wants to meet with me?"

"He did tell me to inform you that his reason for wanting to meet with you, pertains to the United States Civil Rights Commission."

SUMTER, SOUTH CAROLINA

Reginald Greene couldn't believe how good it felt to be back in Court! Which was quite ironic, he told himself, seeing how Five years prior (at his trial), the 'court room' was the last place he wanted to be! All he could do was smile, as he looked over his shoulder into the faces of his parents, his 'many' relatives, and Minnie Pearl.

Yet, Reginald, avoided making eye contact, or even looking in the direction of the 'many' (angry) white faces, filling every single row of seats, behind the Prosecution's table.

"Are you nervous?" Tyra asked, hoping, by producing a confident smile it would help ease his tension.

"Happy, and nervous at the same time. If that makes sense?" He too, smiled weakly.

"Don't worry, we have a strong case." Tyra touched his

shoulder.

Reginald, couldn't help noticing that his other lawyer, Mr. Packard, hadn't said much at all to him since his arrival in the courtroom. He also realized, that Mr. Packard spent most of his time conversing with the Judge, and the Prosecutor and not once bothered to sit at 'their' table.

"I don't trust William Packard!" Reginald leaned in to whisper his concern to Tyra, who was shuffling through documents.

Without looking up from her paperwork, Tyra whispered her response and said, "I don't either."

"All rise!" The court officer shouted out.

Tyra knew it was a formality, however, she had never witnessed a Judge taking his seat behind the bench an hour 'before' the proceedings began. In fact, the Judge waved his hand, indicating that there was no need for the spectators to stand.

"Go ahead and call the case." The Honorable K.C. Buddy Richards instructed the bailiff.

"Is he kin to Sheriff Richards?" Reginald whispered his question to Tyra.

"Mr. Packard says he's not." Tyra answered. However, the resemblance was obvious. She also knew it would be a waste of time to ask the Judge to recuse himself, but she would certainly do an investigation to ascertain whether the Judge and Sheriff were actually related. She knew that if they were related, it would certainly mean a new hearing for Reginald. Now, she had to focus on the here and now, she told herself.

"Ms. Star, as I'm sure you're aware, the burden of proof, in a Post-Conviction Relief hearing, is on the defense. Therefore. how about you go ahead and present your case?" Judge Richards instructed.

"Thank you Judge. My first witness is Glenwood Elway Johnson."

Glenwood didn't even glance in Reginald's direction as he made his way to the witness stand. An observation, that had Reginald suddenly wondering if Tyra Star was doing the right thing by calling his cousin as a witness? A cousin. whom he had not communicated with in Five years.

"Glenwood, will you please state your full name and address for the court?" The Bailiff instructed him.

"Do you swear to tell the truth, the whole truth, and nothing 'but the truth?" The Bailiff asked.

"Yes." Glenwood spoke in a loud and clear voice.

"The witness has been sworn in, Your Honor."

"Glenwood, I want you, in the same loud and clear voice to tell the court exactly what happened on April 27, 1953. Take your time, because no one except you and Reginald were there, outside of the Deputies, so I will only ask questions when you're done." Tyra explained.

Not only did Glenwood articulately describe what happened on that day, he revealed to the court that Jarvis had actually been the only *'white'* friend he'd ever had and how his death affected his spirit (eyeing Jarvis's parents as he spoke), before apologizing to his cousin Reginald, and his parents, for not testifying at his first trial.

"Why is it, that you didn't testify?" Tyra asked

"I was afraid for my family's safety." Glenwood omitted what his father's role in his decision, not to testify, had been.

Tyra, left it as that. She knew that the Solicitor would object if he testified to any alleged threats made by any member of the Sheriff's Department. Nor did she want to put Glenwood in such a position.

"So, when exactly was it that you heard that Jarvis had been murdered?" Tyra asked.

"The night it happened." Glenwood answered.

"Do you recall what night that was?"

"April 24, 1953."

"What day was it, if you can recall, that your Aunt, Uncle, and Reginald, arrived in Sumter?"

"April 25, 1953. It was around 5p.m. to be exact."

"How is it, that you can testify with such seemingly and unequivocal certainty that they arrived on April 25 at 5pm when that was actually over Five years ago from today?" Tyra posed.

Looking over at the defense table, for the first time since taking the witness stand, Glenwood locked eyes with his cousin Reginald.

"About Three hours after their arrival, to my Grandmother, Minnie Pearl's house, Reginald informed me that he stole a bottle of Jack Daniels out of his Father's suitcase, which he wanted the two of us to go out back and drink."

"Did he say why he'd stolen the bottle from his father's suitcase? I mean, do you know if he was in the habit of stealing?"

"No, Reginald has never been a thief as far as I know." Glenwood continued to hold his cousin's stare as he spoke. "He told me that he took the liquor because he wanted us to celebrate."

"What was the occasion?" Tyra inquired.

"He said. we were celebrating 'my' officially becoming a Man."

"Becoming a Man?" Tyra asked with a raised eyebrow, as if she didn't already know where the witness was going.

"Yes, those were his exact words, being that April 25, 1953, was actually the day I turned 21 years old." Glenwood revealed, as he used his bare hand to wipe away tears that were now streaming down his face.

At that moment, the anger in which Reginald had harbored towards his younger cousin, whom he hadn't spoken to in over Five years, departed from his spirit. Nor, did he feel the least bit ashamed as she used his shirt sleeve to wipe his eyes.

Next, Tyra called the former Deputy Younts, to the witness stand.

Majority of the spectators, seated behind the Prosecutions table, shouted insults, gasped, and /or simply shook their heads, as the former deputy proceeded towards the witness stand.

Once he was sworn in, Dexter Younts told his version of what had transpired on the day of Reginald Greene's arrest.

"Do you believe that you conducted a '*thorough*' search of the defendant, Reginald Greene, after your arrival on the scene that day?" Tyra asked, emphasizing the word 'thorough'.

"Of course, I did. I conducted a thorough search of the defendant, as well as his cousin, Glenwood Johnson." Younts assured her before adding, "You have to understand, it was for officer safety. I didn't want either of my partners, or myself, to be victims of a stabbing, or even worse, getting shot by anyone."

Tyra, nodded her head up and down indicating her understanding.

"If the defendant was in possession of a weapon, which he wasn't, I certainly would've found it when I searched him." Younts added in a matter of fact tone of voice.

"Where do you think the handgun came from?" Tyra knew she was reaching by asking such a question.

"I object, Your Honor." The Solicitor was on his feet.

"Sustained." The Judge glared at Tyra Star.

"I can't say. All I know is that," Younts began to elaborate.

"I said, SUSTAINED, Deputy!" The Judge barked, staring down at the witness. As a former officer of the court, he was certain that Younts understood what 'sustained' meant.

Tyra knew she had made her point.

"Nothing further," Tyra said, as she made her way back over to the defense table.

William J. Packard, held back his smile, however, he did give his co-counsel a (discreet) wink of the eye.

"Solicitor Evans?" The Judge looked toward the Prosecutor.

"I have no questions for the witness." The Solicitor, seated at the prosecutions table, eyed the former deputy with disdain.

"Will you be calling either of the two deputies, who testified for the State, at the defendant's trial?" Judge Richards asked Tyra Star.

Finding the Judge's question rather unusual, Tyra addressed it. "Actually, I have no intentions of calling either of those deputies today. As far as I'm concerned they've had their say in court." Tyra answered, before adding, "However, Solicitor Evans is more than welcomed to do so." She faced the prosecution table.

With that said, Judge Richards simply stared at her from

the bench.

Standing, Tyra further addressed the Court.

"Your Honor, this case is by far the clearest example of a miscarriage of justice, if I've ever seen one." Tyra began.

"Unfortunately, we have no way of knowing if the .32 caliber handgun in this case is even the actual weapon used to kill the victim, Jarvis Miles. What we do know is that, we have sworn testimony from two witnesses, one of whom is a former officer of the court, who unequivocally stated that my client, Reginald Greene Jr. did 'not' have a gun on his person, the day in which he was erroneously arrested and charged.

"What I have gathered from the testimony heard here today is that, the only 'wrong' doing my client may be guilty of is stealing a bottle of Jack Daniels from his Dad."

At that, several of the spectators (even some of those seated on the Prosecution's side of the courtroom), burst out in laughter.

In his effort to regain order in the courtroom, or rather silence, Judge Richards banged his gavel quite loudly.

"So, you honestly expect me to take the word of a former Sheriff's Deputy, over the testimony that I've heard from two highly regarded deputies during trial?" The Judge asked the defendants lawyer, Tyra Star.

"It's not my place to tell you what to expect, or believe, Your Honor. But, with all due respect, the facts in this case clearly speak for themselves." Although, Tyra had spoken in calm and collective manner, she was nonetheless upset, seeing how the Judge was totally disregarding the testimony of Glenwood Johnson, as if a young black man's account of what occurred was irrelevant.

"Truthfully, I find it quite offensive, as it relates to the Sumter County Sheriff's Department, how you come in here today with your two witnesses, attempting to assassinate the characters of two of the 'finest' deputies to ever serve this county."

The Judge's stare was borderline menacing, as he spoke.

"Then, you do not even have the decency to call the two deputies into court today, to enable them to reiterate what we all, already know to be the truth."

The majority of the white folks, seated in the courtroom, cosigned the Judge's remarks by nodding their heads in agreement.

"Your actions are *'not'* how we do things around here." He added.

"In the PCR hearing, the burden of proof is on the defense. Therefore, again, with all due respect to the court, I've taken *'that'* to mean that, it is entirely up to me to present whatever evidence and testimony I choose. As well as, disregard whatever I deem to be irrelevant.

"However, apparently my co-counsel Mr. Packard clearly failed to inform me that, in the Courts of Sumter County, there's a specific procedure to adhere to or follow, when presenting a defense." Tyra complained.

"Are you sassing the Court? Judge Richards asked as he removed his eye glasses.

Opposed to answering the Judge's question, Tyra realized she needed to, literally think quick on her feet, because Judge K.C. Buddy Richards was truly a piece of work, she told herself.

"Your Honor, I honestly did not come here today expecting to get justice for my client," Tyra began. In fact, I'm confident that I've accomplished exactly what I've set out to do, therefore, I'm content with whatever the court decides." With that said, Tyra reclaimed her seat between Reginald and her co-counselor.

"Do you really mean that?" William J Packard whispered.

"Of course not." Tyra whispered back.

"And what exactly is it that you feel you've accomplished here today Ms. Star?" Judge Richards inquired.

"That the record will clearly reflect that it is virtually impossible for my client to receive even a semblance of justice, as long as he continues to pursue such, in the Courts of this State. Therefore, again, I feel the record has been established whereas the Fourth Circuit, or if we find ourselves before the U.S. Supreme Court, that my client has not only been railroaded by an incompetent trial attorney, a corrupt Sheriff's Department, and evidence that obviously disappeared while in the possession of the Solicitor's office.

"But, I assure you, I will not rest until Reginald Greene, ultimately, set a precedent that will safeguard other black men and boys particularly in this State from being unfairly targeted, under represented, and falling victim to police, as well as pros-ecutorial misconduct."

As a result of Tyra Star's proclamation, everyone in the small courtroom could see that Judge Richards was enraged.

"Court is adjourned till this afternoon." The Bailiff announced, seeing how the Judge literally stood and left the courtroom without uttering a word.

"Something clearly needs to be done about that Yankee lawyer." The Bailiff, again, spoke on behalf of what he knew the Judge was feeling, as they, too, sat with Sheriff Richards and his two trusted deputies.

"I felt that way since the first day she paid a visit to the station house." Deputy Greenwalt responded.

"She certainly presented a strong case." Sheriff Richards admitted.

His comment, caused all four of the other men to look in his direction.

"In all honesty, something tells me that, the Reginald Greene case certainly has the potential to set that precedent in which she mentioned as being her intentions." The Sheriff added for effect.

"That wouldn't be good at all." Judge Richards spoke for the first time, clearly concerned. He'd had his fair share of cases overturned by the Higher Courts, however, the mere thought of a 'Published Opinion' that would be used by every lawyer in the State of South Carolina to defend, *'guilty'* black men claiming they were being unfairly targeted was unfathomable!

"Call Solicitor Grills in here." Judge Richards instructed the Bailiff.

"Don't worry yourself Uncle Buddy." Sheriff Richards spoke in a reassuring tone, while holding his uncle's gaze. "If you decide to turn the boy loose, not only will I see to it that he doesn't make it back to California alive, I will also see to it that the lawyer lady doesn't make it out of South Carolina."

"All I want to know is," Deputy Wallace began with a devilish grin on his face,

"Can I take care of Dexter Younts?"

Judge Richards ruling certainly threw Tyra, Mr. Packard, Dexter Younts and the entire Johnson family for a loop! As for Reginald he couldn't decide whether he wanted to smile, laugh, or simply cry! Therefore, he just sat there, behind the defense table, stunned beyond words.

"Boy, why is you still sitting there?" Minnie Pearl was suddenly all over her grandson.

"Congratulations." William J. Packard extended his right hand to Tyra first, he too could not believe that Tyra Star had pulled it off, before offering the same hand to Reginald Greene. "I think you better be getting out of dodge." He warned, for good reason.

Tyra, for some reason, couldn't help feeling as though something wasn't right about the entire situation. She knew that Reginald had a strong case, even though she didn't know another 10 years would pass, 1968, before the U.S. Supreme Court upheld 'Terry v. Ohio', establishing case law that would define illegal search and seizure and the question of 'pat frisk' pertaining to officer's safety.

"I don't think we should go outside." Glenwood re-entered the courtroom, where everyone was now exchanging hugs with Reginald.

"Why not?" Minnie Pearl asked.

"I don't think I've ever seen a mob of white folk bigger than the one that's out front." Glenwood revealed. "You all can't hear them yelling 'send him out' from inside here, but that's not the only thing they're yelling." He was clearly petrified.

No one noticed that William J. Packard had slipped out of the courtroom.

Dexter Younts, had already been prepared to accept his fate by agreeing to testify for the defense, however, he was extremely thankful that Tyra had introduced him to a Northerner named Paul Mizelli, who not only bought his property above value, but also mortgaged him and his family a house/ farm in Stormville New York. Yet, he couldn't help feeling bad for Reginald and Tyra, both of whom, he was certain would (also) never leave South Carolina alive.

All eyes were on Sheriff Richards, as he walked into the courtroom sweating profusely.

"We better leave 'now' if you folks want to make it out of here alive." The Sheriff exclaimed, looking from Tyra to Reginald.

"What do you mean we?" Tyra eyed him suspiciously. As did Minnie Pearl and the rest of the family.

"Listen lady," The Sheriff began, returning Tyra's stare." I don't know who you know, nor do I care. My only concern is my wellbeing." He decided to keep to himself the Governor's exact words, as they related to the safety of Tyra Star, and her client.

"Deputy Wallace will take up the rear as I 'personally', escort you to the North Carolina border." Sheriff Richards continued to hold Tyra's stare as he spoke.

In all the years he'd known Sheriff Richards, Dexter Younts had never once seen him sweat.

"You can trust him." Dexter Younts addressed Tyra.

At that, Tyra nodded her head, meanwhile, hoping that Dexter Younts was correctly assessing the situation.

"Let's go." Tyra took hold of Reginald Greene's hand, as she headed for the door. "I'll put Reginald on a plane to California once he and I arrive in D.C." Tyra assured his parents.

Seeing that Dexter Younts hadn't followed the two of them outside the courtroom, Tyra ran back inside and motioned for him.

"We *include* you." With that said, the Sheriff led the three of them to Tyra's car…

TWENTY-NINE

GREENSBORO, NORTH CAROLINA, 1960

On February 1, 1960, four young black men (Joseph McNeill, Ezell Blair Jr., Franklin McCain, and David Richmond), college students, decided to order cups of coffee at a Woolworth's counter, in downtown Greensboro, North Carolina.

Their action, evoked an immediate response from fellow students at North Carolina A&T University. On February 2. Twenty-nine students followed their action. Within a week, more than Three hundred students decided to 'sit in'. Before long, 'sit ins' were happening throughout North Carolina, South Carolina, Virginia, and Tennessee.

Whereas, the Montgomery bus boycott had been passive, sit-ins were assertive. Students [physically] challenged segregation by placing their bodies directly in the way of Jim Crow. Even white students joined the Student Nonviolent Coordinating Committee, the organization responsible for the 'sit ins' movement.

Tyra, and countless other lawyers throughout the country, visited many of the cities to represent the students who had been arrested. In 1960 alone, nearly Four Thousand students had been arrested for offenses such as; criminal trespass, breach of the peace, and disorderly conduct.

"I think you lawyers are condoning the actions of these kids by coming to their defense, opposed to letting them sit their butts in a jail cell." The white jailer, spoke loud enough for Tyra and the other two lawyers, who were also visiting potential clients.

Once he'd ushered each of the three lawyers to their respective booths, the guard didn't even bother to inform them how long they'd have to wait to see their clients.

Each of the three attorneys, Tyra included, had spoken to no less than five clients, whom they'd informed that they would be seeing a Judge shortly, and more than likely released. When the other two lawyers left for the courthouse, Tyra had one last client.

"You must be my lawyer?" The question was posed in such a soft-spoken voice, Tyra almost didn't hear the young lady as she looked up from her paperwork in which she had been reading through.

"And you must be Katherine Grove?" Tyra produced a smile, even though she was clearly exhausted by now.

"That's me." The young woman smiled brightly.

"You're awfully high spirited for someone sitting in jail." Tyra couldn't help commenting.

"I'm here for a Great cause." The girl Katherine responded, smile still in place.

Her response, caused Tyra to sit her paperwork down onto the counter.

Katherine Grove, had been the first and only client she'd interviewed thus far, who made such a comment. The rest were totally concerned about their release, and how the arrest would affect them as far as school was concerned. And such.

"What makes this such a Great cause to you?" Tyra inquired, giving Katherine her full attention.

"For starters, I think racial prejudice is a disease that certainly needs to be cured, by any means necessary. However, I'm alright with the whole 'nonviolent' approach. Whatever works right?" Katherine gave a shrug of the shoulders. "I just hate to see anyone discriminated against."

Tyra simply nodded in agreement as she continued to hold the younger woman's stare.

"If they give you a low bond, is there anyone I can contact to come and post it?" Tyra asked.

"My parents are probably beside themselves with anger, knowing that I've been arrested for sitting in." Again, she shrugged, yet, had a smile on her face. "However, they'll be all right. "I'm totally down for the cause, even if it means having to 'sit in' jail a while longer."

Tyra was so taken aback by the young 'white' girl's attitude that, at that moment, she knew she'd be the one to post the girl's bond if need be...

HARLEM, NEW YORK

"Thaddeus, come help me prepare the table." Anne Lee, who was now 71 years old, had to literally take hold of her eight-year-old grandson's hand to pry him away from the television set.

"Why are they doing that?" Thaddeus asked. A question he directed to his mother, Tyra, who was also watching the evening news.

Turning the television off, Tyra followed her mother and son into the dining room, at the same time considering an appropriate response to her son's question.

"Do you notice that every time you and I Pray together, I thank God for giving me such a beautiful, caring, and very intelligent son?" Tyra began her answer to his question with one of her own.

"Yes Ma'am." Thaddeus answered.

"Well, I'm constantly giving thanks as far as 'you' are concerned, because unfortunately we live in a world where not everyone has a beautiful, caring heart." Tyra explained as the two of them maintained eye contact.

"Do you know what ignorance means?" She asked her son. Yet, she was certain that he did. Truthfully, she had not yet

turned Five, when her mother Anne Lee, taught her its definition.

"Yes Ma'am." Thaddeus replied.

"Well, what you just witnessed on television, was the acts
of a group of ignorant people, who clearly were not fortunate
to have been taught the true meaning of love, compassion, and
understanding."

Thaddeus, nodded his head, indicating that he understood
what his mother was saying.

"How come Demetrius says that all white people are evil?"
He asked, referring to Doris's grandson, whom he spent time
with occasionally

At that, Tyra and Anne Lee exchanged glances.

"Do you know what the word 'equate' means? Tyra inquired, not sure if it was a word in which Anne Lee had yet
taught him the definition. Thaddeus looked to his grandmother, who nodded her head.

"It means, to make equal, equivalent or comparable." He
answered.

"Correct," Tyra said with a smile. "Let's equate evil with
ignorance.

Do you think that all white people are ignorant?

"No Ma'am." Thaddeus answered sincerely.

"While I've compared evil to ignorance, it is a word that
I would never equate to an actual person. Whether they be
white or black. What you saw on television is a group of people
who simply do not know any better. They were erroneously
taught that white was superior to black, and that God did not
intend for the two races to join together as one. That's why
some of them go to such great lengths to fight integration.
Even if it means resulting to physical violence."

"I'm pretty sure God does not like what those folks were
doing to those black people in the middle of the street." Thaddeus spoke in a much lower tone, as his mind drifted back to
the graphic images that were captured on television.

"Amen to that." Anne Lee clearly heard his comment as
she re-entered the dining room with a large black roasting pan

in both hands.

Even though, Tyra watched as her mother expertly carved the large chicken she'd roasted, her thoughts had also drifted (back) to the sights that had been shown on television, which were currently taking place in Birmingham Alabama. It had also been reported that a second bus, a Greyhound, had been attacked also (earlier that day) in Anniston, Alabama.

Tyra, had been familiar with the Congress of racial Equality (CORE), and their plan to send a racially mixed group of people into the Deep South, on a Trail way and Greyhound line, initially they called it a Journey of Reconciliation, however, it was rechristened 'The Freedom Riders'.

Her thoughts were suddenly interrupted, as Thaddeus came around to where she sat and planted a kiss on Tyra's left cheek. He had already given his grandmother Annie Lee her kiss.

"What was that for?" It was Anne Lee who'd asked.

"I don't know where my manners are sometimes." He frowned, shaking his head. "I was so focused on the television, I forgot to wish the both of you a Happy Mother's Day."

At that, both Mother and Grandmother smiled.

Whereas, Tyra hadn't yet considered herself a full fledge activist in the fight for racial and social change, she nonetheless had a tendency to put herself in the line of chaos, as the attorney who was there to represent 'those' fighting the cause. And while she knew that the role was indeed imperative, Tyra was ready to apply herself in more than just the courtrooms across America.

Several of her associates, clients, and friends, often commended her for her ability, availability, courage, and compassion. However, Tyra tremendously admired women such as; Ella Josephine Baker (who she viewed as not just a colleague, but also a true friend), Fannie Lou Hamer (who had endured jail and beatings in her pursuit of voting and civil rights), Jo Ann Robinson (who played a major role in the planning of the Montgomery bus boycott), Diane Nash (a young white woman, student, and co-founder of the SNCC), and several others.

MANHATTAN, NEW YORK, OCTOBER 1960

The Kennedy campaign staged a national conference, in New York City, on Constitutional Rights. In attendance, was over Four Hundred civil rights and community leaders from Forty-Two states. It was at this conference, where a young Presidential hopeful named John F. Kennedy, spoke on the importance of Executive leadership, and went as far as stating that; Actually, so many things can be done by the stroke of the Presidential pen! Including, an executive order for 'equal' opportunity in housing.

Tyra couldn't help noticing how elated most of the attendees were at the prospect of having a Kennedy Administration take over the White House. It was public knowledge that even the very influential Reverend Martin Luther King 'Sr' had lent his support and influence among blacks to help get Kennedy elected. Not so much because he felt that Kennedy was the man who would (finally) deliver on such promises, but, it was alleged that [Kennedy's] willingness and influence to have Martin Luther Kings 'Jr' released from (albeit, unjustifiable) a prison sentence of twelve- months for driving in Georgia with Alabama license plates.

"How do you feel about the man?" Marla inquired, looking in Tyra's direction, as she, Anne Lee, and Tyra were preparing to leave.

"He certainly talks the talk," Tyra only half smiled before adding, "But, let's see if he walks the walk."

Marla could only nod her head in agreement.

"He just seems so young." Anne Lee added.

"He is quite young, but maybe that's what we need in the White House.

"No offense," Marla said, focusing her attention towards Anne Lee as she spoke, "But, you older folk have a tendency to be awfully set in your ways, opinions, and beliefs."

At that, all three women laughed. Not so much because of what Marla said, but more so because it was no secret (among the three of them at least) that Marla was *'only'* three years younger than Anne Lee!

"Excuse me Ma'am, but aren't you Tyra Star?"

Their laughter was suddenly interrupted by the middle aged white man's question/approach.

"Yes I am." Tyra replied eyeing the stranger with suspicion being that she was quite certain they'd never met.

The man however, produced a warm smile as he extended his right hand to her.

Out of courtesy, Tyra shook his hand as he introduced himself.

"My name is David Rufkins, and I'm with an organization called Americans for Democratic Action."

Tyra was familiar with the organization, yet, she remained silent while he explained his reason for approaching her.

"Actually, we work very closely with the Justice Department's Commission on Civil Rights." He revealed.

"Okay." Was Tyra's only response.

"I've been informed that you were contacted some years ago by a Senator, and close friend of mine, who wanted to speak with you regarding much of what me and my colleagues do. Unfortunately, I've been further informed that you never returned the Senator's call."

"That is true." Tyra confirmed.

"Just recently, I made an inquiry about you to another close friend of mine, by the name of Clarence Mitchell." He watched Tyra closely after dropping the name.

Tyra knew Clarence very well, being that he was the chief lobbyist for the NAACP, and had led a coalition of civil rights, labor, and civic groups in pushing for Civil Rights legislation.

"I hold Clarence Mitchell in high regards, for his efforts, as well as his accomplishments." Tyra complimented.

"However, what is it that I can do for you?"

"As with the outgoing Administration, I'm inclined to believe, based on both candidate's interest and promise regarding civil rights, we can certainly use someone of your legal experience, and knowledge, to do research and possibly prepare testimony that myself, and others can present before Congress in our endeavors to get meaningful legislation passed. "He smiled brightly.

"So, am I correct to assume that you are offering me a seat on the Civil Rights Committee? Or, even a job at the Americans for Democratic Action?" Tyra returned the smile, even though she already knew the answer to her question.

David Rufkins did not answer the question.

"I didn't think so." Tyra answered her own question. Her smile disappeared as she held the man's stare.

"I was quite all right being in the background at the Legal Defense Fund, because I understand the significant impact *'Brown'* could have on black children in the country. But, why would I agree to play an obscure role on a so-called Civil Rights Committee?" Tyra didn't even need the man to answer the question, as far as she was concerned the facts were already gathered. She had certainly done her homework in regard to the commission.

While it didn't take a whole lot of research or investigation to learn the extent of prejudice at the Civil Rights Committee, being that a man who was more than a colleague and friend, but actually another of her mentors, by the name of

Derrick A. Bell Jr. was one of three blacks appointed by the Eisenhower administration, to become an attorney in the Civil Rights Division of the U.S. Justice Department,

Derrick A. Bell Jr., Tyra was well aware, had recently *'quit'* the post because he was ordered to cancel his membership in the NAACP, which he refused to do.

"I'm very well versed in *'both'* Civil Rights Acts that have been passed and were signed into law. The both of them were just that, 'Acts' with no real substance, and certainly no enforcement of any kind to back them up." Tyra spoke regarding the Civil Rights Acts of 1957 and 1960, both of which did very little, if anything at all, to help the plight of black people.

"How many black women will I have the pleasure to be working with if I *'did'* agree to be a background player?" Tyra inquired.

David Rufkins couldn't answer that question either she noticed.

"You don't have to answer the question Mr Rufkins." She let the man off the hook, before adding, "I respectfully decline your offer. Not because I don't believe that you folks will never get it right, but I'm inclined to believe that any and all 'enactments' regarding civil rights and change, in general, will not solely come to fruition as a result of what you folks are trying to do at your organization."

Tyra knew that she didn't have to tell him that court decisions, and the passage of decent legislation weren't imperative, or that it was (actually) going to take continuous resistance, protest, and mass movements for change.

Instead, she smiled before giving her departing words.

"Good luck Mr. Rufkins, in your endeavors to get Congress and the next administration, whoever prevails, to make new amendments to your Acts." Tyra continued to smile. "However, a wise woman told me that, good intentions 'without' action means nothing." She reached for Anne Lee's hand which she gave a squeeze, as the three women made their departure...

THIRTY

ALBANY, GEORGIA, 1962

The Albany movement, which it was termed, was a broad attack against every facet of racial discrimination. Blacks in Albany, Georgia are demanding fair employment, an end to police brutality, the desegregation of bus and train terminals, parks, public libraries, and virtually 'all' public accommodations.

While the Albany Movement was locally based, the SNCC and SCLC also provided leadership. Although, it wasn't until Reverend Martin Luther King Jr. was asked to help, that the movement began to receive national attention.

Whereas, Anne Lee had constantly worried about her daughter's wellbeing, it was Tyra's involvement in the Albany Movement that had her most concerned. Especially, upon reading reports that; over Seven Hundred of Albany's Twenty-Three Hundred black residents had (already) been arrested! Most of whom were adults, which was also a first, regarding previous demonstrations and/or protest

Arriving in Albany, Tyra couldn't believe how many organizations, as well as mixtures of people were on hand. However, what she'd found most troubling was not entirely the number of people who had been jailed, but more so the fact a bail/bond fund had not been set up.

Her first course of action was going to visit as many incarcerated residents (and those who were 'outsiders') as possible. Only to learn that Albany's Chief of Police (a man by the name of Laurie G, Pritchett) had made arrangements with the court that *'all'* prisoners pay a 200 (cash) bond, before being released!

"I need help setting up a fund to get some of these people out of jail." Tyra spoke into the telephone. Although she hated involving Anne Lee, she knew that her mother had relationships with several people who possessed the kind of money it would take to set up such a fund. Even Roger (who was one of the wealthiest black men in the state of New York, his real estate holdings expanded as far South as New Orleans, where he had family. A fact that, played a part in Tyra's decision to ask for his help in locating some of her biological father's relatives, a task in which he'd informed her that he had 'no luck' as of yet, last, they spoke), and Paul Mizelli came to mind.

Unlike, Sheriff Richards (in South Carolina), Tyra, quickly realized that Chief Pritchett was a true tactician. He saw to it that the white segregationist, in Albany, *'stand down'* and allow his police force (whom he trained to employ a 'non-violent' approach toward demonstrators/protesters) to handle the situation. Also, he arranged it so that most of the demonstrators who were jailed, found themselves incarcerated in neighboring counties (opposed, to Albany), where beatings reportedly took place.

Following the arrest of Reverend Martin Luther King Jr. Chief Pritchett realized that [King] garnered more media attention from a jail cell than he did while free, therefore, Chief Pritchett had his bail posted and subsequently released the civil rights leader against his will.

Whereas, Tyra was truly thankful that she was able to provide legal and financial assistance to the demonstrators, she nonetheless began to realize that the saying was certainly true in that *'more'* was not always better! She noticed how divisions over tactics, organizational rivalries, and petty jealousies, began to cause disunity. Unlike, the (earlier) Freedom Rides, as well as the more recent 'sit ins', in terms of its' intended goals the

Albany Movement was clearly failing.

Not to mention, on July 24th, a mob of black folk began hurling bricks and bottles at the police. Acts, that were not only captured by the media, but moreover played right into Chief Pritchett's attempts to cast negative light on the so-called 'non-violent' protest. In fact, [King] found himself declaring a 'day of penance' following the violent outburst.

As far as Tyra Star was concerned, she couldn't be sure if she was more discouraged by the latest turmoil, or the fact that, it was President Kennedy who had recently appointed a known segregationist (named Robert Elliot) to the federal bench... the same Judge who was responsible for so many blacks going to jail, being that he 'granted' the city of Albany an injunction against demonstrations.

Meanwhile, in the State of Mississippi, SNCC and NAACP workers were being threatened, jailed, beaten, and even killed, as they fought for the right to Vote.

In September 1962, a young black man, named James Meredith, attempted to enter the University of Mississippi (where the court ordered integration) however, a mob of whites gathered outside of the school, and a full-scale riot erupted. The Attorney General (Robert Kennedy), had tried to persuade Mississippi's Governor (Ross Barnett) to protect 'Meredith' but his request apparently fell on deaf ears.

By the time President Kennedy decided to commit troops, two people were dead and the campus of 'Ole Miss' resembled a battlefield.

To Tyra's dismay, the 'Kennedys" refused to allow the U.S. Civil Rights Commission to hold hearings regarding the events in Mississippi.

BIRMINGHAM, ALABAMA

The 1963 surge of non-violent direct action made the maintenance of segregation, in public accommodations, untenable. Black people knew that if segregation could be cracked in Birmingham (the South's most segregated city) it could be cracked anywhere.

Between April 3rd and May 8th, 1963, Martin Luther King Jr and Fred Shuttlesworth, led blacks in a determined campaign to attack segregation in Birmingham. The protest included mass meetings, a tight boycott of downtown stores, persistent lunch counter sit-ins, and repeated attempts to march to City Hall. Defying a court injunction banning demonstrations [King] went to jail, as did 3,500 others.

Anne Lee, and her (now) Ten-year-old grandson, Thaddeus, watched their television set in awe, as *'hundreds'* of children marched out of the Sixteenth Street Baptist Church and into the lines of waiting policemen, taunting them and singing as police vans hauled them off to jail! Not to mention, the sight of blacks being chased down by police dogs, as well as drenched and pounded by high powered fire hoses.

"What in the world is this world coming to?" Anne Lee asked, to no one in particular. However, she did take her eyes away from the television set long enough to look up towards her living room's ceiling.

Thaddeus, however, remained silent as he continued to watch the events taking place on television. Unbeknownst to the two of them, Tyra, was among the 3,500(others) who were jailed!

Whereas, she had visited more County jails than she could count, Tyra, had never seen the inside of a jail cell. Therefore, she was quite surprised by how small, crowded, and hot, the cells were. She counted Twelve women in the cell that was no more than 10 by 12 feet. Eight women occupied the two small wooden benches, and the remaining four squatted on the cement floor.

"We can take turns between the benches and the floor." One of the women occupying a bench suggested.

Tyra, couldn't help noticing that the four women seated on the floor were actually quite young, whereas, those seated on the two benches (including herself) were obviously older. No one had suggested who would sit where (upon entering the cell), therefore, she concluded that it was basically a show of respect on the part of the younger females to take to the floor.

The same lady who had made the suggestion to take turns between the bench and the floor, broke the silence once again by introducing herself.

"My name is Wyllona Sharpe, and I'm from Mobile, Alabama."

After about 30 seconds, another woman introduced herself.

"I'm Emma Jean Bailey, I'm from right here in Birmingham."

Each of the 12 women began to introduce themselves, and where they were from. All eyes were on Tyra, following her introduction. Mainly, because she had revealed she was from Harlem, New York.

"Wow! I've heard so much about New York City!" One of the young girls seated on the floor exclaimed.

"Especially, Harlem." A second girl added with a smile.

Tyra, noticed that each of the four young girls had all been natives of Birmingham, and were more than likely Church girls seeing how they each wore similar skirts and shoes.

"New York may not be as segregated as the South, but like most Northern cities and states, it too, has its own form of segregation and discrimination." Tyra explained, without going into the 'housing' problem blacks were subjected to in every major city in America.

"What kind of segregation or discrimination can a black person *'possibly'* encounter in Harlem?" One of the girls asked in dismay.

Once again, all eyes were on Tyra, who seconds ago 'thought' she wouldn't be expounding on the housing issue.

"It actually goes back to the 1930's when the public housing program began under President Franklin D. Roosevelt's 'New Deal' to provide shelter for the poorest people, a so-called policy of 'racial equity' was established. Meanwhile, it did not prohibit the rigid segregation of housing projects, in basically every part of the country.

"The truth is, the official policy of the U.S. Government

was to promote racial segregation and exclusion. In fact, the government shared the private housing industry's belief that property values suffered when residents of a neighborhood were not homogenous. So, the Federal Housing Administration(FHA) issued an underwriting manual in 1938 declaring that; if a neighborhood is to retain stability, it is necessary that properties continue to be by the same social racial groups."Tyra paused, at the same time shaking her head.

"In other words, not only are blacks in New York City, and elsewhere relegated to the projects, but you have institutions such as banks, and savings and loan companies who receive federal benefits like insurance on deposits or subsidized mortgages, who discriminate on the basis of race. So, the deck has been stacked against blacks for quite some time, in every region of the country, with the federal governments support."

"I guess the devil is busy all over the world." Emma Jean commented.

A Sheriff Deputy approached the cell with a tray of sandwiches in his hands.

"Feeding time." He announced with a stained tooth grin.

None of the women stood or approached the cell door.

"You can keep your stale bread and cheese sandwiches." Wyllona Sharpe spoke for the entire group. She had been jailed during the Montgomery bus boycott simply for carpooling. Not to mention, she was a devout member of the Women's Political Council.

"Suit yourselves!" The Deputy replied before walking off.

As things calmed down, one of the older women initiated the song 'We Shall Overcome', obviously they all knew the words, as all 12 of the women joined in. Including Tyra.

The group became a lot louder, in song, as they (now) sang the words to a song called 'This Little Light of Mine', which prompted the deputy to return, banging his billy club against the cells bars.

"You folks need to hush that noise!" He barked. "None of you are going to like it if I have to return to this cell." He warned.

Following his warning, the cell grew quiet. Tyra, actually closed her eyes as she thought about her son Thaddeus. She continued to keep them closed even after one of the women began to sing a solo about 'how she was going up yonder to be with her Lord'.

The Deputy, suddenly re-emerged. However, his focus wasn't on the woman who had abruptly stopped singing.

"You, with your eyes closed!" He shouted, his comment was directed at Tyra.

Tyra held his stare, without bothering to move.

"Apparently, you've made quite a name for yourself." He produced that same smile from earlier. "Some associates of the Commissioners' must have recognized you from those television cameras. They say you're the one who got that black boy off death row down in South Carolina, and that you were instigating trouble in Albany, Georgia as well." He shook his head.

"I'm sure Eugene will show them how they should've dealt with a Northern instigator like you." The Deputy added, referring to the racist Police Commissioner (Eugen 'Bull' Conor) by his first name.

For the third time that evening, Tyra noticed that all eyes were on her.

"Wow!" You're that lawyer?" One of the young girls asked, totally impressed.

"You were part of the Albany Movement?" Emma Jean asked, also impressed.

"And I thought you Northerners' were all talk and no action." Wyllona smiled widely, "I knew it was something different about you."

Tyra, simply shook her head, before smiling herself.

"You're not concerned, that being arrested can be potentially get you disbarred?" Emma Jean asked, once everything had quieted down.

"Not at all." Tyra responded honestly. I'm just hoping that the 'end' justifies the sacrifice." She smiled.

"Amen to that!" Another woman shouted.

Just then, the Deputy made his third appearance at their cell.

"You must want to join us in here." Wyllona laughed.

Focusing his attention on Tyra, once again, he put his key into the slot of the cell door. Opening it, he announced, "I'm not sure who pulled this off, but you're free to go."

"If I go, we all go." Tyra announced from where she continued to sit.

The Deputy stared at her as if she'd lost (all) of her good sense.

"Suit yourself." He responded, locking the cell door, and then walking off.

Tyra again, shut her eyes. Not because she was tired, but because she was quite sure that 'all eyes' were once again on her!

"Yeah, this child's definitely cut from a different cloth!"

Tyra recognized Wyllona's voice by now, therefore, she didn't have to open her eyes to know who'd made such a comment. The fact that 'she' had clearly garnered the admiration of a woman who had long since been a part of the fight for civil rights, demonstrations, sit-ins, boycotts, harassment, arrest, and devoted to the Women's Political Council (under Jo Ann Robinson), brought a smile to her face.

About thirty minutes had passed before the Deputy returned once again. This time, when he opened the cell door, he simply stood to the side, leaving more than enough room for all 12 women to pass him by.

On May 10, 1963, the SCLC called off the protest. It had secured a written agreement from the Birmingham's business leaders, that desegregated store facilities, pledged the hiring of black store clerks, and promised continuing bi-racial negotiations to upgrade black employment opportunities across the board.

Tyra, meanwhile, was moreover impressed that the SCLC compelled the Kennedy administration to *finally* intervene in the crisis (something it had significantly failed to do in Albany, Georgia), and side with the Civil Rights Movement…

THIRTY-ONE

WASHINGTON, DC, 1963

The weeks and months following Birmingham, Saw an unprecedented number of black protest throughout the South, on a scale never seen before. Blacks, boldly asserted their right to use 'whites only' parks, playgrounds, libraries, movie theaters, restaurants, and hotels. They boycotted and sat-in.

The magnitude of the 1963 protest/demonstrations not only surprised (and disturbed) white Americans, but also made the Kennedy administration fundamentally 'revise' its' approach regarding the civil rights question. The entire nation's attention was on the South, where the ugliness of Jim Crow was not only being revealed, but moreover, was embarrassing the United States in the eyes of the World.

On July 11, 1963, (the same day that a white supremacist shot and killed Mississippi NAACP leader Medgar Evers), President Kennedy appeared on nationwide television, where he asked Congress to pass a strong Civil Rights Bill.

In the weeks that followed, the President conducted a series of meetings in the White House to persuade businessmen, lawyers, educators, religious groups, union leaders, and Southern Governors.

As Congress debated whether to pass the more stringent

bill, legendary civil rights leader A. Philip Randolph (as he had decades earlier) met with other leaders and proposed a "March on Washington". Appointing his longtime Protégé (Bayard Rustin), who helped him plan the 1941 March on Washington, the event was put together with meticulous attention and detail.

MARCH ON WASHINGTON

On August 28, 1963, Over 250,00 people (blacks and whites) turned up at Washington's Lincoln Memorial for the peaceful rally, to hear speeches and songs, opposed to protest. Whereas, the 'march' did little to spurge the passage of the Civil Rights Bill, it 'did' give the Civil Rights Movement a [national] platform, as well as present itself as strong, united, and determined. Which was (partly) the reason, Tyra Star, accepted the invitation for her (and family) to stand/sit center-stage. She knew that such a show of solidarity (especially, among black folk) would be an experience of a lifetime whereas 'Thaddeus' was concerned. Also, it would be a tribute to Curtis Jackson (Thaddeus's father), who played an organizing role in the 1941 'March on Washington' that ultimately did not take place.

"That Reverend Dr. Martin Luther King Jr. is 'truly' a gifted speaker." Anne Lee complimented, as she, Tyra, and Thaddeus, returned to their room at Washington's Park Sheraton Hotel.

"Yes, he is." Tyra agreed. In fact, she had never heard anyone speak so eloquently regarding racial harmony and reconciliation, at the same time sending a warning to America regarding the whirlwinds of revolt and how they would continue to shake the foundation of America.

"What did you get from the march?" Anne Lee asked, focusing her attention on her grandson, who had been relatively silent all evening.

"That the pursuit of freedom, justice, and equality, is not solely a black cause, but a common cause." Thaddeus answered. Never in his life had he'd seen so many blacks and whites coming together, especially in such a peaceful setting. It was an image, he knew would forever be ingrained in his mind and heart.

Although she didn't pose the question, Tyra couldn't contain her smile upon hearing her son's answer.

HARLEM, NEW YORK

"Yes, may I ask who's calling?" Thaddeus answered the phone. Turning towards his mother, he informed her that a Mrs. Wyllona Sharpe was on the phone.

"Wyllona, how are you?" Tyra spoke into the phone, to the woman whom she'd kept in contact with since the Birmingham ordeal.

"You can't be serious!" Tyra exclaimed, as tears suddenly began to form in her eyes.

Thaddeus, and Anne Lee, watched her with growing concern as she ended the call.

"What's the matter?" Anne Lee asked, yet, bracing herself for an answer in which she wasn't entirely sure she even *'wanted'* to hear.

"Apparently, some white supremacist, decided to plant a bomb inside the Sixteenth Street Baptist Church, down in Alabama."

"Oh, my goodness!" Anne Lee exclaimed, bringing her right hand up covering her mouth.

Looking at Thaddeus, who was (now) in the process of fixing a bowl of cereal, pretending 'not' to be listening, Tyra reluctantly further informed her mother that, "Four young black girls were killed in the explosion."

As Thaddeus sat down to the table with this bowl of cereal in hands, at the same time witnessing (both) his Mother and Grandmother crying and completely heartbroken (only 19 days following the historic March on Washington), he knew that September 15, 1963, would *'also'* be a day that he'd never forget.

The conscience of the entire nation was aroused, as never

before by the murder of Four little girls in the bombing of the Church.

America had not yet begun to heal, when on November 22,1963 President John F. Kennedy was assassinated by a man named Lee Harvey Oswald, while visiting Texas.

"I can't watch this anymore." Anne Lee said, as she got up from her living room couch, and headed towards her bedroom.

Tyra, totally understood, seeing how all the news channels continuously replayed the President being shot in the head, as he sat besides his wife in their chauffeured convertible vehicle.

"Why would someone shoot the President?" Thaddeus asked

Tyra was somewhat traumatized by the unexpected tragedy, that she totally forgot her Ten-year-old son had also been watching.

"Come on, let's go upstairs." Tyra suggested, taking his hand after turning off the television.

"What's going on Momma?" He asked, as the two of them now laid across her bed. Tyra knew her son was clearly dismayed by the sudden turn of events following the beautiful, harmonious experience they (along with over a Quarter of a Million others) shared during the March on Washington.

Placing his head on her chest, Tyra responded in the gentlest tone of voice.

"I always try to understand why people do the things in which they do, but it really isn't my place to try or to justify their actions." She knew her words were totally contradictory to what she had explained to him earlier, about some people being ignorant. But, her present hurt and anger wouldn't allow her to make excuses for such hatred and incomprehensible violence against Four, innocent, young girls.

And now, The President.

Although, she felt that President Kennedy had not always been a crusader for Civil Rights, Tyra nonetheless, felt he was a decent man. who certainly didn't deserve to die in such a violent manner.

"Is Grandma gonna be okay?" Thaddeus asked

"Yes, she'll be fine." Tyra assured him, running a hand through his full head of hair.

"Do you think the President's wife will be okay?" He asked, showing concern for the First Lady.

Tyra, was touched he'd asked such a question.

"I don't know." Tyra gave an honest answer before adding, "I certainly hope so."

At that moment, The Kennedy's two small children came to mind. The thought, further broke Tyra's heart.

"How about you go check on your Grandmother for me?" Tyra suggested.

Without any words or protest, Thaddeus climbed out of the large bed and did as he was told.

Now that she was alone, Tyra took the opportunity to reflect on everything that was going on. What troubled her most was the realization that Kennedy's Vice-President (Lyndon B. Johnson) did not have a track record for supporting anything that had to do with Civil Rights. Which, she couldn't help but feel, as though the Civil Rights Bill that President Kennedy had been striving to get passed, was (now) more than likely a lost cause.

Majority of her adult life, she'd spent representing causes and people who had been ready and willing to give up their lives and freedom for the betterment of black people. However, for every step towards progress blacks made, it seemed as though something (a potential set-back) always occurred, she thought to herself.

Her thoughts were interrupted as Thaddeus, along with Annie Lee, climbed into her bed.

"Grandma is fine," Thaddeus spoke for his Grandmother.

Tyra met her mother's eyes, as Anne Lee reached for one of her daughter's pillows.

"Of course, I'm fine." Annie Lee smiled, even though Tyra could clearly see she had been crying.

"Wasn't the President trying to fix things for black people?"

Thaddeus, caught both of them off guard with his question.

"He was trying, yes."Tyra answered him sincerely.

Sitting at the foot of the bed, facing his mother and grand-mother, Thaddeus simply gave a nod, as if to say 'that's what I thought'.

Looking from his Grandmother, to his Mother, he made his next remark.

"The two of you, or our people, need not be sad or even disappointed."Thaddeus told the two most important women in his life, before adding, "I'll fix all of our problems, when I become President."

THIRTY-TWO

SELMA, ALABAMA, 1965

To everyone's surprise, following President Kennedy's death, the man who filled his seat in the Oval Office (Lyndon B. Johnson) decided to make 'passage' of the Civil Rights Bill his first priority, in honor of John F. Kennedy. In fact, opposed to weakening the Bill, he strengthened it.

Johnson's political skill and influence, combined with continued pressure from the Civil Rights Movement, and lobbying efforts by several religious groups, spurred the bill's passage.

The 1964 Civil Rights Act, which President Johnson signed into law on July 2, went further than anyone would have thought! It banned discrimination in employment, federally assisted programs, public facilities and accommodations. The [Act] empowered the Government to initiate lawsuits to desegregate Southern School Districts, and to withhold funds from recalcitrant school boards. It set up the Equal Employment Opportunity Commission, and created a Community Relations Service to mediate racial problems. It not only prohibited discrimination on the grounds of race and color, but also on the grounds of religion and national origin. In the case of employment, it included discrimination on the grounds of sex.

Immediately following its' passage, Blacks everywhere began integrating all aspects of public accommodations. Initially, there was some doubt whether it covered bars and taverns, which the Courts decided it did. Jim Crow had finally expired.

Yet, as blacks justly celebrated getting rid of the egregious and humiliating forms of racial discrimination, the Civil Rights Movement quickly realized that the 1964 Civil Rights Act was merely [another] milestone in a long and difficult journey.

The abolition of segregated public accommodations was gratifying, but swift (white) adjustment to the change provided an ironic indication of its superficial nature. The more substantive sections of the Act, those dealing with schools and employment, were statements on intent that demanded an enormous act of enforcement. Whites continued to fight school integration, and showed little willingness to surrender economic benefits of job discrimination.

Moreover, the 'voting' section of the Civil Rights Act was so inadequate, it literally left the problem of black disenfranchisement virtually untouched. Basically, leaving the Civil Rights Movement to campaign further.

Selma, Alabama, epitomized the scandal of black disenfranchisement. Dallas County, of which Selma was a part, contained 15,000 black residents of voting age (of which 'only' 335 managed to become registered voters), meanwhile, whites, who were slightly outnumbered in the overall population, made up 99 percent of the electorate.

"You do know that, I never envisioned myself 'ever' returning to the South." Marla informed Tyra with a raised eyebrow. In fact, she still couldn't believe that she'd allowed Tyra Star to convince her in accompanying her to Alabama! Although, she was born and raised in Augusta, Georgia, Marla hadn't been back home in 30 (plus) years.

"You're here to support a great cause." Tyra replied with a smile.

"That may very well be true, however, I'm way too old to be finding myself sitting up in someone's jail cell singing Negro spirituals."

At that, both women laughed, even though Marla was dead serious.

"Don't worry, my investigation revealed that a bail fund is in place." Tyra informed her friend with a wink of the eye.

Marla simply shook her head. However, she thoroughly admired Tyra's courage, she (often) told herself. Especially, considering she was aware that Tyra Star could easily enjoy a privileged life. She had more money than most black folks, stood to inherit several properties, and had a beautiful, extremely intelligent child. Not to mention, possessed a Law degree, at a time when most black women found it a challenge to simply obtain and/or maintain even the lowest paying jobs, Marla thought to herself.

Tyra, had not yet arrived in Alabama, when on February 18th, a group of 400 demonstrators marched through a small town called Marion. Not only were they attacked by state troopers, local police, and white residents, but a black man named Jimmie Lee Jackson died as a result of the wounds he'd sustained.

Inclined to believe that Alabama's Governor (George C. Wallace) had co-signed the Marion attack, the SCLC proposed a fifty-four-mile march from Selma to Montgomery, with the aim of placing Jackson's death at Wallace's feet.

The Governor banned the march, and ordered the state police to stop it.

"I don't feel good about this march." Marla confided, being that it was no secret that Governor Wallace intended to oppose it.

"This is Alabama," Tyra reminded her friend. "We can hope for the best, however, it wouldn't be realistic to '*not*' expect the worst."

Meeting up with Wyllona Sharpe, and over Six hundred others, on March 7, 1965, walking two abreast, they set out for Selma.

Crossing the Edmund Pettus Bridge, which spanned the Alabama River, the group of marchers encountered a phalanx of state troopers, backed by Sheriff Jim Clark and his posse of *'special'* deputies, some of whom were on horseback. The marchers halted, yet, refused to disperse (or turn around), so the white lawmen attacked. In fact, they clubbed, teargassed, trampled, ran-over, and chased the marchers.

What became known as 'Bloody Sunday" unfolded in full view of the World's press/media. Everyone who owned a television saw it, and anyone who bought a newspaper read about it!

Politicians, Religious leaders, editors, and thousands of private citizens joined the Civil Rights Movement in denouncing the violence. Most importantly, the chorus of condemnation 'included' some white Southerners.

Tyra, had been hit by a billy club, and was finding it difficult to breathe due to the thick fumes of teargas. Yet, she was more concerned about her 71-year-old friend, therefore, she continued to search (through the mayhem) for Marla Jenkins.

Finally, spotting her friend, Tyra's heart sank as she kneeled down beside an unconscious Marla, who was also bleeding from a gash on her forehead.

"Somebody help us please!" Tyra shouted, yet, she knew her cry for help would be to no avail considering the commotion taking place all around them.

Suddenly, she felt the presence of someone standing over her. Looking up, Tyra squinted her eyes, not so much due to the glare of sunlight, but more so out of a sense of recognition.

"So, we meet again." The white policeman shook his head. "You just couldn't stay out of the way."

Tyra, however, remained silent as she cradled Marla's head in her lap.

"Is she dead?" The police officer inquired, focusing his attention on the older, unconscious woman.

"I don't think so." Tyra finally spoke in a low voice. Yet, she was totally surprised to see the officer from the Birmingham jail, especially since they were in a different county.

"Come on let's go!" He ordered, at the same time helping her to her feet.

"I can't leave her here like this." Tyra tried to protest going (back) to jail, and leaving Marla.

"We're not leaving her." With that being said, the husky white man (in uniform), lifted Marla across his shoulder.

"Where am I?" Was the first question Marla asked as she came to.

"You're in a hospital." Tyra informed her with a smile on her face, extremely happy that her friend was all right.

"How long have I been here?" Was Marla's second question.

"Since yesterday." Tyra answered.

Taking inventory of her surroundings, Marla finally realized that her foot and ankle was heavily bandaged.

"You broke it." Tyra informed her, seeing how she was staring downward.

"My foot?"

"No, your ankle."

"You suffered a concussion as well."

Marla simply nodded her head (which was also bandaged), remembering (now) that she'd been struck across her forehead.

"How did I get here?" Marla was curious.

"It's not important. I'm just glad that you're all right." Again, Tyra produced a smile. She knew that Marla wouldn't understand how she had gotten to the hospital, being that Tyra, herself, still could not believe that the deputy had assisted them. In route to the hospital, hardly any words had been exchanged between the two of them. The only thing he had revealed was that, he 'remembered' her (Tyra) having a very influential friend or associate.

"So, I guess Selma is a lost cause?" Marla asked with a frown on her face.

"I wouldn't say that." Tyra disagreed.

"What do you mean?" The last thing Marla recalled was the heavy police blockade, which was followed by their attack

"Folks are marching in protest of what happened here." Tyra informed her." I hear they're marching in Detroit, Chicago, Boston, Philadelphia, St. Louis, Washington D.C., Los Angeles, and New York."

"Are you serious!" Marla exclaimed.

"Yes I am." Tyra answered smiling. "Folks all over the World witnessed what happened here." She added.

As a matter of fact, Reverend Martin Luther King Jr. is here, and he's preparing for a second march across the Edmund Pettus Bridge." Tyra informed her.

"And I thought we were heading home." Marla replied.

"That's the plan." Tyra responded

"No, it is not." Marla disagreed. "I'm crossing that Bridge, even if I have to do so in a wheelchair!"

Over 25,000 people participated in the march from Selma to Montgomery (a march, 'finally' sanctioned by a Federal Judge and protected by Federal Troops), where the Reverend 'King' addressed a victory rally from the steps of the State Capital.

On March 15,1965, President Johnson addressed a joint session of Congress to propose the enactment of a Voting Rights Bill. At which time, he called 'Selma' a turning point in man's unending search for freedom. In tribute to the Civil Rights Movement, The President praised the heroism of the American Negro, whose actions and protest have awakened the conscience of the Nation. He urged Congress not to delay or compromise on the issue. And literally, astonished 'all in his closing, by stating an anthem of the Civil Rights Movement, telling his audience; "WE SHALL OVERCOME."

On August 6, 1963, the Voting Rights Act became Law. It disallowed literacy test, constitutional interpretation test, and good character requirements (all of which whites had used to disqualify blacks from voting, since the end of Reconstruction), the crowning achievement of the Civil Rights Movement the 'Voting Rights Act' re-enfranchised black Southerners and Democratized the South, officially ending the era of Jim Crow...

THIRTY-THREE

WASHINGTON, DC, 1972

Following the passage of the Civil Right Act of 1964, and the Voting Rights Act of 1965, things did begin to improve for blacks, especially in the South. However, enforcement of the Act(s) were quite slow. In the South, school systems continued to make decisions that perpetuated segregation.

Whereas, the civil rights reforms had mostly been designed with the South in mind, it appeared that things continued to get worse in most Northern and Western cities/states. Especially, in the areas of job discrimination and housing segregation. Not to mention, police brutality, which led to riots throughout the country.

No one was more surprised than Tyra Star, to receive an invitation to the White House. Not so much because such invitations had, up until that point, been unheard of as it pertained to the purpose of an 'all' Women's Conference held by the first lady, Pat Nixon. Whose husband, unlike Lyndon B. Johnson before him, was not a crusader for anything to do with civil rights.

"Is this your first time?" A Woman's voice inquired.

Turning in the woman's direction, Tyra came face to face with an elegantly dressed white woman, who she guessed to be somewhere in her age range, quite beautiful she had to admit, as the woman now stood before her with a perfectly white teeth smile.

"Excuse me?" Tyra asked.

"Is this your first time?" The stranger repeated herself before adding, "Visiting the White House, I mean." She clarified.

"Yes, it is." Tyra answered.

"I've been married now for over 30 years, and my husband has been in the Senate just as long, so I've been a guest here more times than I can actually count." The Stranger revealed. "However, Pat is the very first to open its' doors to the blind, disabled, and all those whom she feels a visit to the White House has the potential to leave a lasting impression, or possibly have an impact on."

Tyra assumed that she and the first lady were on a first name basis seeing how she had referred to her as simply 'Pat' in her compliment of the woman.

"By the way, I'm Rose Mary Bivens." She introduced herself, at the same time extending her right hand to Tyra, for the purpose of a handshake.

Accepting the woman's hand, Tyra introduced herself as well.

"I'm Tyra Star."

"I know who you are." Mrs. Bivens produced a smile. "In fact, I'm not only aware of some of your endeavors and accomplishment, I truly feel that you epitomize the true capabilities of a woman."

"Wow! Tyra exclaimed, quite taken aback by such a compliment by a woman who, up until that point, was a complete stranger. Or rather, unbeknownst, at least to her.

"Thank you for such a compliment."

"I was only speaking the truth. Which is why I asked Pat to forward you an invitation." Mrs. Bivens revealed.

Tyra didn't know what to say. What she *'did'* know was that, she had thoroughly enjoyed herself. Some of the women in attendance, she had formerly met, woman such as; Aileen Hernandez (Chair of the National Organization for Women),

Judy Lichtman (Women's Legal Defense Fund), and Congress-woman Shirley Chisholm. Several others, she had met for the first time.

"So, what did you think of the conference overall?" Mrs. Bivens wanted Tyra's opinion.

"I think it was great to see so many women come together for the betterment of Society. Although, everyone seemed to focus on a different area or topic, I feel that, whether it's racial, gender, religious, housing, employment, it's 'all' strains of the same virus."

"I agree."

"We can't attack Banks and Savings and Loans Institutions for discriminatory practices against blacks and low-income families, and not attack racial discrimination in labor and em-ployment, because who wants a mortgage when you can't even get a job." Tyra explained.

"You're One Hundred percent correct." Mrs. Bivens agreed. "That's why I feel you could have been such an asset to the U.S. Civil Rights Commission. Their job is to investigate complaints of discrimination, and if founded, to pursue litiga-tion. I recommended you because you are clearly one of the best female attorneys in the country."

Suddenly, Tyra began to put two and two together.

"It was quite some years ago, but I do recall a gentleman approaching me, I want to say it was at a convention in New York held by the Kennedy Administration. He was obviously trying to recruit me for the research and investigation purposes at the civil rights commission." Tyra recalled.

"Yes, that was David Rufkins, a longtime friend and col-league of my husbands.' My husband and I, laughed quite heartedly when David informed us how you'd not only gave him your opinion of the 'so called' commission, but also left him standing there totally speechless." She laughed.

At that, Tyra laughed also.

"He may have exaggerated the exchange to you and your husband, because if my memory serves me correctly, I politely and respectfully declined his invitation." Again, Tyra laughed.

"So how are things going up in New York?" Mrs. Bivens changed the subject.

"As far as?" Tyra asked, allowing her suspicions to kick in.

"The charges you've initiated against the Department of Health, Education, and Welfare."

"That hasn't even reached litigation stage, so how is it that you even know about that?" Tyra knew that it was not yet public knowledge that she (and several other lawyers) were targeting 'HEW' for their failure to initiate proceedings to terminate funds to the City of New York for discriminating in *'several'* areas, including the treatment of children with disabilities.

"My husband and I, know a great number of people in a great number of places." Mrs. Bivens gave in response.

Tyra simply held the woman's stare, as she digested the remark.

"Here's my telephone number." Mrs. Bivens handed Tyra a small piece of paper that had her telephone number written on it. "I would love for you and I to not only talk further, but moreover, get to know each other better." She smiled warmly.

"You seem to already know quite a bit about me." Tyra replied.

Rose Mary Bivens didn't respond to that. Instead, she leaned in and planted a kiss on Tyra's left cheek.

Tyra simply watched her, as the Senator's wife made her departure.

HARLEM, NEW YORK

The weather was unusually warm for January, Tyra noticed, as she went out to purchase the Sunday's paper. Something she hadn't done since her childhood. Over the years, Anne Lee tended to always have the latest magazines and newspapers laying around. Later, Thaddeus had taken on the responsibility of such tasks.

However, things were different now, being that Anne Lee had become quite drawn into herself (she hardly ever left her room these days), ever since Roger's untimely passing. Even though he and Anne Lee hadn't been together in years, prior to his death she nonetheless took it very hard.

"You have to remember Roger's the only man I've been with." Anne Lee had tried to explain to Tyra shortly after Roger's passing.

"Other than my father." Tyra corrected her mother.

"Yes, other than your father." Anne Lee stood corrected.

Yet, Tyra couldn't help feeling as though the 'thought' of dying had begun to weigh heavily on Anne Lees (who was about to turn 83 years old), and the fact that she no longer had Thaddeus at the house to keep her company only made matters worse, Tyra also knew, being that he was in his second year at Columbia University.

Columbia University, wasn't that far at all from home, yet, Thaddeus preferred to stay on campus, visiting his mother and grandmother maybe twice a month. However, neither of them complained seeing how hard he was studying and how well he was doing in school.

As she sifted through the Daily News, Tyra came upon an article that caught her attention. It was pertaining to the City of Wilmington, Delaware. Apparently, an attorney named Lou Redding (whom Tyra knew had represented black plaintiffs in the Delaware part of 'Brown vs. Board of Education' nearly two decades earlier) in conjunction with the American Civil Liberties Union were considering a Metropolitan lawsuit since Delaware had temporarily changed its' school district reorganization law to make it easier for districts to consolidate, but had 'barred' Wilmington from eligibility to participate.

Whereas, Wilmington had over 40 percent of all African American students in the state, it was impossible to believe that *'race'* had nothing to do with the differential treatment.

Tyra, however, was not surprised being that such practices, or rather, discriminatory abuses of authority were taking place in most major cities throughout the country. Yet, what really peaked her interest, was seeing that the journalist who had written the article included that; the *'wife'* of Delaware Senator Joseph Bivens, Rose Mary Bivens, is also a driving force in support of the lawsuit.

Sitting the newspaper down on the kitchen table, Tyra couldn't help telling herself that, she hoped the day would never arrive in which she'd regret having thrown away Rose Mary Bivens telephone number, about an hour or so after making the woman's acquaintance at Pat Nixon's Women's Conference....

HARLEM HOSPITAL, 1980

"Can we see her?' Tyra asked her mothers' doctor, as she tightly held onto Thaddeus's hand.

"You can see her, but the tubes will hinder her from being verbally responsive if she wakes up."

"We just want to see her." Thaddeus chimed in.

Although, Anne Lee's health had been deteriorating in the last four years, Tyra nor Thaddeus were prepared for the possibility of losing her.

As the doctor escorted the two of them to the Intensive Care Unit, he spoke, "Miracles happen, but, I'm inclined to believe that she may not make it through tonight."

That being said, the doctor stepped aside as the two of them entered the room. At least, they'd be able to say their last goodbye, he told himself with a heavy heart....

THIRTY-FOUR

HARLEM, NEW YORK, 1982

Having received his Bachelors, as well as Masters, at Columbia University, Thaddeus was accepted at Yale School of Law where he earned his Juris Doctorate. Although, he knew the importance of the commercial and tax courses in the curriculum, at Yale, what interested him most was courses in civil rights, international law, and Judicial philosophy.

After graduating Law School, Thaddeus found himself subsequently employed at McNeill, Locklear and Powell, one of New York's most prestigious law firms. Upon entering the firm, Thaddeus's days were occupied doing research, drafting/ preparing Briefs, and taking notes as the more seasoned attorneys presented their arguments in court.

Considering, he was already a multi-millionaire (inheriting not only his Grandmothers wealth and properties, but Roger's as well), Thaddeus wasn't entirely focused on his earnings at the firm. In fact, he and his mother gave more to various charities than what his bi-weekly paycheck amounted to. However, Thaddeus was nonetheless fascinated by the thought and act of helping others, which was why he became a lawyer in the first place.

Although, she too, was still quite busy (even at 65 years old) in her pursuit of social and economic change, as far as African Americans were concerned, Tyra still made it a priority to oversee the operations of Star Quality Properties, which was a company she and Thaddeus had put together consisting of the combined properties that once belonged to her mother and stepfather.

"For some reason, my thoughts have been on embarking on a career in public service, a great deal these past few months." Thaddeus revealed, as he and his mother enjoyed their breakfast.

Looking over the rim of her coffee cup, with a raised eyebrow, Tyra held Thaddeus's stare.

"You represent people every day." Tyra reminded him, as she sat her cup down on the table.

"Not entirely in a legal capacity." Thaddeus began. "I'm thinking politics." He smiled.

Opposed to giving an immediate response, Tyra continued to watch him.

It wasn't that she didn't think he'd be successful in whatever his endeavors were, Tyra knew better than almost anyone the effect 'politics' could have on a person's life. As she watched her only child, from across the table, Tyra truly loved the Man/person whom he was. His good heart, nature, innocence, faith in God, people, and the law, as well as his obvious lack of prejudice.

"Did you have this discussion with Roberta?"Tyra inquired.

"Not yet." Thaddeus revealed before adding, "It's your opinion that I value more than anyone else's, which is why you're the first and only person to whom I've revealed my intentions."

His response brought a smile to Tyra's face.

"Politics is a tuff business. However, you will always have my confidence, and moreover my support."Tyra reached across the table taking both his hands into hers.

"Thank you, Mom."

At that moment, Tyra couldn't help her eyes from watering, as she thought about how proud of Thaddeus her mother, Anne

Lee, would be, seeing the Man he had become. A Man, whom she was confident would achieve great success in his lifetime.

"Don't thank me yet, because you and I have some serious planning to do." Tyra finally responded, at the same time producing a smile, in spite of her watery eyes.

In the two years that passed since Thaddeus informed his mother of his intentions of becoming a politician, not only did Thaddeus prove himself as an effective/capable attorney representing numerous clients at McNeill, Locklear and Powell, he also spent time interning at the Manhattan Borough President's office, as well as engaging in numerous (one on one) conversations with the Mayor himself. Both of which, had been arranged by Tyra Star.

"I definitely need and want your guidance and input, as far as some of my decisions are concerned. But, you have to let me get out there on my own, to establish myself with the people of New York. As well as, create my alliances."

"I understand." Tyra truly did understand where her son was coming from. As much as she had loved and respected Anne Lee, Tyra couldn't even imagine *'not'* being able to do all in which she had done (over the years) in her own way.

Yet, no one was more impressed then Tyra, seeing how, since that conversation, Thaddeus began to sit down with local business owners, ministers, public school officials, law enforcement (mainly those walking the streets of Harlem), and various folks throughout the five Boroughs of New York City. What he began to love most, ironically, was the same thing that he found most troubling, which was visiting and talking to African American and Hispanics, both of whom (combined) occupied 99% of public housing (aka 'the projects') of New York City.

"Explain to me why 99% of those living in the projects are blacks and Hispanics?" Thaddeus asked the person whom he knew could provide him the best and most honest answer.

"The answer to that question goes so far back we'd be here all of today, tomorrow, and possibly even into next week." Tyra answered him with frustration written across her face.

"Since before the great migration, most blacks living in major cities found themselves in living areas that were predominantly black. However, living conditions weren't at all deplorable because a great number of blacks were able to find work, even at the lowest levels of employment they were able to take care of their families.

"During the Great Migration, you had thousands of black families entering Northern and Western communities in search of jobs and housing. Many whom, took up resident with family members or took room at boarding houses and the like. Of course, white folks had a huge problem with this sudden influx of migrants, especially realizing that it would mean potentially having to compete for jobs.

"It didn't sit well, at all, with white folks realizing that a large number of blacks were willing to work for less money, and would readily fill-in, in the event whites decided to go on strike. Anyway, things didn't become all bad until the Great Depression hit. It was actually in 1934 that Congress adopted housing legislation to counteract the effects of the depression. The idea was to help people avert the loss of their homes and to acquire new ones through low down payments and subsidized mortgages.

"Eventually, the program aided the spurt of home building after World War II, that led to burgeoning suburbs throughout the nation. However, black folks, unfortunately, were excluded from the party, being that the United States government's official policy was to promote racial segregation. So, the Federal Housing Administration issued an underwriting manual in 1938, declaring that; if a neighborhood is to retain stability, it is necessary that the properties continue to be occupied by the same social and racial groups.

"In fact, the FHA went as far as recommending the use of racially restrictive covenants, to ensure against the 'mingling' of inharmonious racial groups, helpfully including a covenant that would make the owners of FHA insured homes liable to a lawsuit if they sold their homes to someone of another race." Tyra revealed shaking her head.

Thaddeus, however, found it all totally unbelievable.

"By the end of the 1940's, the U.S. Supreme Court ruled that the enforcement of racially restrictive covenants was unlawful. Thus, putting an end to the FHA's policy. Unfortunately, the damage had already been done. Millions of white people had, by then, used the low-down payment, low interest provision of federal law to acquire suburban homes, as well as began to acquire 'equity' that would contribute significantly to their personal wealth.

"African Americans not only found themselves segregated, but effectively excluded from the new housing opportunities in Suburbia. In the wake of the assignation of Martin Luther King Jr, Congress passed the Civil Rights Act of 1968, which gave citizens the right to go to court to obtain damages or injunctions when or if they suffered discrimination in seeking housing. But, just like most of their prior 'Acts' it too, was extremely weak in its enforcement provisions.

"It wasn't until 1976, that myself and a team of other lawyers, mostly from an organization called the National Committee against Discrimination in Housing, filed a lawsuit against the Home Loan Bank Board, the Federal Deposit Insurance Corporation, the Federal Reserve, and the Comptroller of the Currency, the four agencies that regulated most of the banks and savings and loan associations, for failing to ensure that these institutions were following fair lending practices." Tyra stated.

"What was the outcome?" Thaddeus was curious.

"In 1977, we achieved a settlement. The four agencies agreed to collect and analyze racial data on loan applications, to train bank examiners to identify possible discrimination in their review of bank records, to appoint civil rights specialists, and to use the same sanctions against lending institutions for civil rights violations as were used in other areas of bank misconduct.

"Yet, in 1982, we still find ourselves dealing with such prejudice and discrimination." Thaddeus said, shaking his head.

"You have to look at the low employment rate, the percentage of young mothers on welfare raising their children alone, the number of blacks that are incarcerated largely in part to President Reagan's so-called war on drugs." Tyra shook her head. "Not to mention, most wealthy and middle class African Americans unfounded and ignorant *'belief'* that the conditions of the poor and underprivileged is a result of laziness."

As he sat there, Thaddeus C. Star realized that he'd certainly had his work cut out for him. Yet, he'd also relish the challenge, he told himself. All he needed was for the *'people'* of New York City to give him a chance...

THIRTY-FIVE

HARLEM, NEW YORK, 1985

" I am fortunate to tell you all," Thaddeus began, address-
ing the crowd that came out to celebrate his winning
the Manhattan City Council position.

"That not only am I well versed, but have a clear understanding of what led most us *'minorities'* to continue to find
ourselves at the very top of every negative statistic, yet, at the
very bottom regarding social and economic disparity." He faced
the crowd of predominately black and Hispanic faces.

"My hat goes off to my mother and those of her era, and
the era before theirs, who fought and even died for freedom,
justice, and equality, however, I'm here to tell you all that although their efforts has brought about great change, the baton
has been passed to you and I, because *'our'* fight must go on.

"We're living in the year 1985, yet, many of our living
conditions are no better than they were in 1965. Many of us
lack the proper training skills to obtain decent employment.
Government welfare programs are destroying and breaking up
our families. Our under financed school systems are failing our
children." Thaddeus paused.

"Those are just some of *'our'* problems, that required 'our'
fight. I am here to tell you all that, we can demand better living
conditions. The law provided a remedy for discrimination in

housing, we have to hold the govern accountable. We have to create programs that will teach vocational and other skills, that will make us employable, and hold the government accountable for footing at least some of the bill, seeing how it tends to do so in less needy communities. We need these programs to enable us to gain employment and let the government keep their welfare programs.

"Lately, which I will endeavor to make one of my first priorities, we have to fix our schools. This is an area in that we cannot entirely rely on government support. We've witnessed far too much political compromise, at the expense of our children. Growing up, I lived a very privileged life. Not so much, materialistically, but, in that I was fortunate to have a Grandmother who taught me beyond the teachings of whatever learning institution I happened to attend.

I realize that I have my work cut out for me, which I'm totally okay with. But, I want my time and accomplishments as City Council to be a team effort." Thaddeus looked into the eyes of a member of those in attendance.

"It's time to get rid of the divide and conquer tactics that politicians and government has been playing for far too long. It's time for community organizing to bring about community action which I'm confident has the potential to lead to prosperous neighborhoods." That being said, Thaddeus gave thanks and made his exit.

Standing in the crowd, Tyra was impressed beyond words by her son's speech, honest determination, and accomplishments, as she looked around, Tyra realized that it had been years since she'd seen so many young folks, of all nationalities, come together for a common cause.

Roberta, who had been standing on an opposite end of the crowd (from where Tyra stood), was not only impressed with Thaddeus's words, but also the feedback from those standing within her immediate circumference. Thaddeus clearly had an influence on his supporters, she could tell, nevertheless she couldn't help feeling somewhat bothered by the number of women supporters whom she'd overheard commenting on his physical appearance.

"So, how'd I do?" Thaddeus asked, once he Tyra and Roberta were (now) sitting down having dinner.

"I think you're a natural." Tyra responded with a smile.

Returning his mother's smile, he now focused his attention towards his college sweetheart.

"The *women* certainly loved you." Roberta offered, before focusing her attention on her T-Bone steak.

At nearly 70 years old, Tyra hardly ever represented individual clients anymore. Instead, she usually found herself in litigations that pertained to civil rights violations, abuses of policy, or in other words 'fighting' the system. So, her appearance before an Alabama Federal Court certainly sparked a great deal of attention.

ALABAMA 1986

The only reason she'd taken the case was because her review of the circumstances, surrounding the case, was a clear miscarriage of justice. Nor, was she surprised, upon learning that it was an Alabama U.S. Attorney, named Jeff Sessions, who had charged the civil rights activist with voting fraud.

In securing a legal victory with her client, Tyra couldn't agree more with the Court's ruling that 'Sessions' action was racially and politically motivated.

"Ms. Star, would you like to comment on your Victory?" One of the many new reporters asked, as he extended a microphone in her direction.

"No comment." Tyra replied, as far as she was concerned her job in Alabama was done.

"Do you agree that the U.S. Attorney's case was racially motivated?"

"No comment." Tyra repeated, trying to get through the small crowd.

"Do you feel as though the U.S. Supreme Court will overturn this appellate court's decision? Especially, seeing how folks in these parts don't take too kindly to such an assassination of character, as it pertains to one of our most trusted U.S. Attorney's?"

Tyra wasn't sure which reporter asked the question that was followed by such a comment. Yet, it certainly stopped her in her tracks. Facing the crowd of reporters, she spoke loud and clear for each and every one of them to hear.

"Truthfully, I am beyond ecstatic that my client and I prevailed in receiving justice here today. Moreover, I am also glad that the court recognized Mr. Sessions actions for what they were. You all can trust and defend whoever you choose, however, Mr. Session's words certainly speak louder than his character. Therefore, as far as I am concerned, the courts did not have to further assassinate the mans' character, Mr. Session accomplished that on his own when he publicly announced that the NAACP is 'un-American', and when he announced that any white lawyer who handled civil rights cases was a disgrace to his race."

That being said, Tyra climbed into the back seat of her chauffeured Lincoln Continental, and shut its' door....

HARLEM, NEW YORK 1987

"Councilman Star, can I please have a word with you?" The elderly black woman asked, stopping Thaddeus as he was about to enter his family's brownstone in Harlem.

"Yes Ma'am, of course." Thaddeus descended his front steps, and was now within speaking distance of the woman.

"My name is Viola Fortaye." She introduced herself.

"How are you Ms. Fortaye?" Thaddeus replied. "How can I help you?"

"It's about my grandson Tyrone. He's really not a bad kid, his problem is the company he keeps, all of whom have been bad influences."

"I understand." Thaddeus not only understood, but had heard countless similar situations. "Is he in some kind of trouble?"

"Well, yes. He's currently facing some legal trouble, but my husband and I have retained counsel to represent him." Ms. Fortaye explained

"Okay, that's good." Thaddeus replied, glad that the young man obviously had somewhat of a support system in place. "Since he already has a lawyer representing him, I'm not sure what is it that I can do."

"I'm confident that Mr. Zachary Flax will prove Tyrone's innocence, but I don't think he's the right person to address what happened to Tyrone just recently on Rikers Island." Ms. Fortaye's voice began to break with emotion as she explained the situation.

"What happened on Rikers Island?" Thaddeus was curious to know.

"Tyrone was assaulted by two inmates, which landed him in East Elmhurst Hospital." She revealed, as tears suddenly began streaming down her face.

"Ms. Fortaye," Thaddeus began, gently placing a hand on the older woman's arm. "You're talking about Rikers Island. Those kinds of things happen in jails throughout the country. And, unfortunately such occurrences are out of my control." He explained, nonetheless, he had empathy for the women, as well as her grandson.

"I understand that. However, it totally bewilders me how or why a 16-year-old would be housed with two 21-year old's in the first place?"

Her question not only had Thaddeus standing before her 'totally' speechless! But moreover, it certainly made a lot of sense, Thaddeus couldn't help thinking to himself.

"Please explain to me why a 16-year-old would be housed in the same general population as 21-year old's?" Thaddeus questioned the Deputy Warden over Security at Rikers Island.

"We currently have two adolescent facilities on the Island, C-73 and C-74, where we house all of our pre-trial detainees. Those who are sentenced to City Time, one year or less, are housed at C-76. As per policy, 'adolescents' are those ranging from the age of 16 to 21. Once an inmate turns 21, we transfer them to one of our adult facilities.

"Do we make the transfer on the inmate's 21st birthday? No, not all the time at least. However, we try to get the inmate relocated as soon as possible." The Deputy Warden explained.

"So, you're telling me that you think it's okay for a 16-year-old 'child' to be housed with a 21-year-old man?" Thaddeus asked in total disbelief.

"It's not about what 'I' feel, think, or believe. The fact is, I've been here almost 14 years now, and its policy that has not only been in place when I got here, but long before."

Thaddeus held the deputy Warden's stare, before finally responding.

"Well, policies are made to be amended, and I say it's time to bring to an end what I'm sure the rest of my council members will agree, is tantamount to child abuse."

THIRTY-SIX

HARLEM, NEW YORK, 1989

The Reagan–Bush administration cut welfare programs, attacked organized labor, declared 'War on Drugs', endorsed the death penalty, and encouraged a steep rise in the prison population. Not to mention, dramatic increases in military spending that devastated the budgets for domestic and social programs.

Thaddeus, like countless others, welcomed the end of the Reagan presidency. However, George H.W. Bush, who had been his Vice President was now the in-coming president, and no one was certain how much they could trust his promise of a 'kinder and gentler' political agenda.

Actually, Thaddeus at the end of his years as City Council, decided he would not run for re-election. Instead, he would run for the vacant Democratic 'State" Senate seat.

As City Council, he had met constituents not just throughout the state of New York, but in various parts of the country. Most of whom were extremely supportive of his latest decision. Especially, those such as, New York Congressman Charles Rangel, and Mayor David Dinkins, both of whom were long-time friends of Tyra Star.

By mid-1990, Thaddeus had received an overwhelming

amount of financial and community support. Each time he visited his mailbox there was a check from different organizations, or from individuals, some of whom he'd met, others were complete strangers.

Returning home from a much-needed jog, Thaddeus spotted a woman and a young man standing out front of his brownstone.

Eyeing the older woman, mores than the young man, Thaddeus was certain he'd seen or met her somewhere, but he couldn't recall where or with precision.

"May I help you?" Thaddeus asked, as he was now standing only a few feet away from the pair.

"You already have." The woman replied with a smile.

"Ms. Viola Fortaye, how are you?" Thaddeus would've given the woman a hug had he not been sweating.

Disregarding his sweat soaked tank top, Ms. Fortaye moved in and wrapped her arms around him.

As the older woman embraced him, Thaddeus made eye contact with the young man standing more than four feet away.

"You must be Tyrone."

"Yes Sir." Tyrone answered with an embarrassed expression on his face. He couldn't believe how his grandmother had literally bear-hugged the man.

"How have you been? Thaddeus inquired, once Ms. Fortaye had released him.

"I'm fine." She replied. "I'm so sorry that Tyrone and I never came by here or your office, to thank you for what you did for the both of us." Ms. Fortaye apologized.

Thaddeus, wasn't pleased by the fact it had taken almost two years, 1987, for the policy change to go into effect. Nonetheless, he was truly relieved that the age range for adolescents on Rikers Island was now 16 to 18.

"I'm just glad that you brought it to my attention in the first place." Thaddeus replied.

"Tyrone wants to tell you something." Ms Fortaye informed him, before turning her attention towards her grandson.

"Thank you for everything." Tyrone thanked him somewhat shyly before adding, "Especially, for writing that letter to my Judge.

"You're welcome." Thaddeus extended his right hand to youngster.

"That Summer Youth Employment Program in which you mention in your letter to his sentencing Judge, secured him a part time job with the Department of Environmental Protection upon his release. Now, he's working full time." Ms. Fortaye revealed proudly.

Thaddeus nodded his head up and down, clearly impressed as he maintained eye contact with the young man standing before him.

"Not only do I want you to keep up the good work, but, I want you to know that my door is always open to you if you need me."

"Thank you." Tyrone responded with a smile.

"Let me have a word with the Senator." Ms. Fortaye spoke with her grandson, who turned and began to walk off, giving the two adults some privacy.

"He is really doing great." Ms. Fortaye spoke as she watched her grandson make his departure. "He doesn't even hangout with any of his former so-called friends." She revealed proudly.

"The bad influences." Thaddeus said, recalling her reference of them from years past.

"Yes, those are the ones." She let out a laugh before putting a hand in the air adding, "Hallelujah, and good riddance."

At that, Thaddeus had to laugh as well.

"Seriously though," Ms Fortaye began, once their laughter had subsided. "I truly thank you for what you did, and what all you continue to do for the community as a whole. Anytime your name comes up, folks have a tendency to refer to you as a Godsend. A phrase I have never, at least not in my lifetime, heard anyone equate to a politician."

Although she was being serious, they both had to laugh at 'that' as well.

"If you've noticed, I referred to you, a moment ago, as Senator."

Thaddeus, had indeed noticed that she'd referred to him as Senator, when she told her grandson to give the two of them some privacy.

"The reason I did so, is because you're a special man. Truthfully, I see you reaching the top." She said with a smile.

They both knew what she'd meant by the 'top', however, Thaddeus as optimistic as he was, couldn't help feeling as though it would certainly acquire the assistance of a miracle for a Black Man, in the United States of America, to become President!

"It's not much," Ms. Fortaye continued to speak as she reached into her carry bag, but, I at least want to have bragging rights that I've contributed to the cause."

With that said, she handed him a crisp 100-dollar bill.

This time, it was Thaddeus who initiated the hug, totally disregarding the fact that his tank top was still drenched with sweat...

WASHINGTON, DC

Although, election day had not arrived, Thaddeus graciously accepted several members of the Congressional Black Caucus's invite to attend an upcoming ceremony in Washington D.C.

"I think it's actually wonderful that Charlie Rangel and others are not only grooming you, but exposing you the way they are." Tyra spoke good natured.

"Charlie?" Thaddeus eyed his mother suspiciously as she continued to fix his tie.

"Oh please!" She laughed. "Everyone calls him Charlie. Well, at least those who are friends I presume." She corrected.

"Why won't you accompany me?" Thaddeus inquired.

"Because this is entirely your time to shine." Again, she smiled proudly as she'd said it.

"Besides, you'll have company before the week is out, am I correct?"

At That, Thaddeus smiled brightly before answering.

Yes, if she's able to get the time off, Roberta will be meeting me in Washington."

"She's such a beautiful and intelligent woman. I don't know why the two of you aren't already married." Tyra commented.

"I definitely cannot see myself marrying anyone other than Roberta. I guess I just haven't asked her yet, because I'm still trying to achieve a few personal goals is all." Thaddeus explained.

At that moment, Tyra heard similar words come out of her own mouth, as she thought about the marital conversations, or rather confrontations, she'd had with Curtis, Thaddeus's father, years past.

"I don't think that there are any goals, personal or otherwise that you will not, or cannot, achieve with the right person by your side." Tyra stated. "It's totally your decision, which I respect. But my dear Son, sometimes with fate comes regret, and the one thing I never want to witness is your unhappiness."

After making her comment, Tyra lightly patted the tie in which she had perfectly knotted before exchanging a heartfelt embrace with her son.

"I've never seen so many powerful and influential people in one room." Roberta commented. She somewhat felt like a groupie when she and Thaddeus were introduced to Senator Ted Kennedy.

As he looked around, and into the faces of the (mostly) men who currently ran the country, Thaddeus knew that his role was about to become much bigger than zoning questions, finances, community planning agendas, and what all he'd done as city council. Yet, he was certainly ready to play his position.

As long as that position meant continuing to do things 'his' way.

"Thaddeus Star?" Someone asked.

Turning in the direction of the voice, Thaddeus and Roberta, came face to face with a white man about Thaddeus's age, who had a much older white woman holding firmly to his arm.

Thaddeus, recognized the face, yet, couldn't place from where he'd met the man.

"It's Nathaniel Bivens." He introduced himself. "We actually attended Yale together."

"That's right." Thaddeus suddenly remembered him. Although, the two of them had not been what either would call 'friends', nevertheless, they did share classes and a mutual respect for each other's intellect.

"How have you been?" Thaddeus asked.

"I've been great, Thanks." Nathaniel replied.

"The two of you actually have something in common." The older woman holding onto Nathaniel's arm said with a smile.

"Besides attending and graduating from Yale's School of Law." She added.

"Mother." Nathaniel exchanged glances with her. Returning his focus towards Thaddeus, he spoke, "This Beautiful, outspoken woman on my arm happens to be my mother, Rose Mary Bivens." He reintroduced her.

Thaddeus accepted the woman's outstretched hand. Just as he was about to introduce Roberta, she took the initiative to do so herself.

"I'm Roberta Johnson." Roberta introduced herself before shaking hands with the pair as well.

"What else would it be that Nathaniel and I have in common, besides Yale?" Thaddeus was curious, as he and Rose Mary Bivens held each other's stare.

"My son is actually the incumbent Democratic State Senator for the state of Delaware, whereas, it has been brought to my attention that you're currently seeking to occupy that same seat in New York."

"Yes Ma'am, I am pursuing the State Senate," Thaddeus confirmed.

"You'll prevail." Rose Mary Bivens spoke with optimism.

"Thank you for the vote of confidence."

"My sources tell me; the people of New York are very supportive of you. Especially, those poor farmers upstate New

York." Ms. Bivens revealed, once again producing a warm smile.

As for Thaddeus, he was totally dismayed as to how she'd acquired such information? He had not made it public news, that he'd traveled throughout upstate New York, visiting farmers who were being denied government assistance, whom he promised that he would make their cause a priority if he succeeded in winning the Senate seat.

"How is it that you know so much about my endeavors?" Thaddeus couldn't help but ask.

"Oddly enough, I recall your mother, Tyra Star, asking me a similar question nearly two decades ago, when she and I attended A Women's Conference right here in Washington."

Thaddeus and Roberta exchanged a look at the mention of his mother's name

"Thaddeus, it was a pleasure seeing you again, and it was also a pleasure meeting you Ms. Johnson." Senator Nathaniel Bivens spoke, indicating it was time for he and his mother to move along.

"If I can assist you in any way, please do not hesitate to reach out to me." Senator Bivens extracted a card from his pocket which had his home, and office number on it.

"Thank You". The two men/politicians shook hands.

"I'll catch up with you in just a second dear." Ms. Bivens told her son.

Roberta, could tell the woman wanted to have a word with Thaddeus. Therefore, she informed him, 'I'll go get our coats."

"Thank You." Thaddeus replied, giving Roberta a kiss on her cheek before making her departure.

Once the two of them were alone, Ms. Bivens spoke.

"My late husband and I, have followed your mother's legal battles, courtroom victories, as well as her participation and accomplishments during the civil rights movements. To say I have been quite the fan would be an understatement." She smiled.

"Your mother is truly a courageous woman, as well as an achiever. Which I'm confident the apple will not fall far from the tree."

"Thank you." Thaddeus replied to her compliment.

"You may have noticed several monetary donations, from various strangers and organizations, in your mailbox. "Here's another," She reached inside of her clutch purse and withdrew a check, which she handed to him.

"I would also like to set up an interview with you and a dear friend of mine at Time Magazine, whom I'm sure would love to do a write up on you." Ms. Bivens suggested.

"I understand your feelings toward my mother, but why would you go to such lengths for me?" Thaddeus was nonetheless curious.

"It would appear that my actions are with motive if I told you that I had a vested interest in you. So, I will just say that, I simply want to see you succeed.

That being said, Rose Mary Bivens planted a kiss on Thaddeus's cheek, using her right thumb to wipe away the small trace of red lipstick, she added, "I'm not sure if your mother even remembers me. In any event, please give her my regards."

"What an *interesting* woman." Thaddeus said to Roberta as she handed him his coat.

"I agree." Roberta replied, as the two of them watched Rose Mary Bivens make her departure.

THIRTY-SEVEN

WASHINGTON, DC 1993

At least a decade had passed, since Tyra Star's last visit to the District of Columbia. She actually, couldn't believe how fast 'time' had flown by over the last decade. But, then again, so much had transpired in her life, as well as Thaddeus's in that time, she told herself, as she (along with her son and daughter in law) listened to President Bill Clinton give his inauguration speech to the nation.

Although, it was quite chilly out, Tyra, who was dressed for the occasion, couldn't help the mental, emotional, and spiritual, warmth she felt at that very moment. Without facing Thaddeus, or Roberta, who stood on either side of her, Tyra gave a gentle squeeze considering she held (each) of their hands in (both) of hers.

Truthfully, as she listened to the president give his speech, his words of intent, promise, and solidarity, caused Tyra to reflect on how Blessed she and her family were. Albeit, the family consisted of (only) she, Thaddeus, and now Roberta, who Thaddeus had not only wed, but promised to respect, honor, and cherish, for the rest of their lives. It was a vow, in which Tyra knew he would keep.

Tyra, also hoped, in her assessment of Bill Clinton and a

few others in the Democratic Party, that the country would finally begin to see and enjoy great social and economic change. Truthfully, it was no secret the entire country shared in that hope, and expectations.

Following the inauguration, a group of democratic leaders, their families, friends and family members of the President and Vice President, several celebrities/entertainers, and a very small group of media went inside of the White House to continue in celebration.

"Are you sure you wouldn't prefer I take you back to the hotel room, so you can get some rest?" Roberta asked her mother, Tyra.

"I'm fine." Tyra's reply was followed by a warm smile.

"It's beautiful isn't it? Tyra asked, taking in her surroundings.

"Yes, it is." Roberta agreed, looking from one portrait to the next, of previous Presidents.

"Can you imagine a Black Man's portrait hanging from one of these walls? Roberta asked. Yet, her question appeared to be somewhat of a comment.

"I can definitely see it coming to fruition." Tyra answered. The fact that black men have overcome slavery, oppression, segregation, castration, and discrimination, to become Doctors, Judges, Politicians, and so on, was indication the Presidency was not unfathomable.

Considering it had been little over Twenty years, since she'd last seen her, Tyra could not say with certainty if the woman standing to her far right, talking to the First Lady Hillary Clinton, was in fact Rose Mary Bivens.

Following her mother-in-law's gaze, Roberta also spotted the two women conversing.

"That woman, speaking with the First Lady, is the mother of Senator Bivens from Delaware. She's also the woman who asked Thaddeus to extend her regards to you when we were at the White House three years ago." Roberta informed Tyra.

"I thought that was her." Tyra responded more so to herself.

"Do you know her?"

"We've met once. However, at the time, I saw no need

to pursue a line of communication." Tyra revealed. "And, I certainly wasn't looking to make new friends." The fact was, Tyra had always had a distrust of politicians, which she realized was quite ironic, seeing the career path her son ultimately chose, with her Blessings.

"She appeared to be a very nice woman." Roberta gave her honest assessment of the woman. Recalling how she had done so much, behind the scene and without motive, for Thaddeus's campaign for the State Senate.

"Yes, she is rather intriguing," Tyra replied, before turning her attention elsewhere. Yet, she was certain Ms. Bivens had spotted her looking in her direction.

"Did Thaddeus, say how long he would be?" Tyra asked, basically letting Roberta know that she was now ready to leave.

"No, he didn't say." Roberta answered, knowing how imperative it was for Thaddeus to establish himself with this incoming administration. Therefore, she certainly did not wish to rush or interrupt him.

"Give me a second mother, while I go get our coats, and leave a message for Thaddeus, letting him know that you and I went back to the hotel. "That being said Roberta walked off.

As she waited, Tyra took a seat in a nearby chair.

"May I join you?" Mrs. Bivens made her approach, at the same time referring to the vacant chair adjacent the one in which Tyra was sitting.

"Please do." Tyra responded with an inviting smile on her face.

"How have you been?" Ms. Bivens inquired as she sat down.

"I've been doing pretty well, Thank You." Tyra replied.

"That is great to hear.

"And yourself?" Tyra asked

"I can't complain at all, seeing how my Blessings have been in abundance over the years." Ms. Bivens said with a smile.

"My son, Thaddeus, recently informed me that your son, Nathaniel has been elected to the U.S. Senate." Tyra revealed.

"Yes, that is true. As a mother, I am so proud of all of his achievements thus far. He's truly a great son, and a great man."

Tyra nodded her head at that, considering, she too, knew the feeling.

"I was fortunate to meet your son, Thaddeus, some years ago. He was truly the gentleman." Ms. Bivens complimented him with a smile before adding, "From what I hear, he is not only extremely intelligent, but also, his potential is unlimited."

"Thank You" Tyra smiled proudly. "I'm surprised to hear that a source actually got it right. Especially, in regard to character assessment."

At that, both women laughed, considering it was no secret that most folks seemingly preferred to engage in character assassination.

"He did inform me that he had met you here in Washington. Also, that you had extended your regards." Tyra said, before adding, "I really appreciate all the support you've shown towards my son and his endeavors."

"My late husband, was not only the Democratic Majority Leader, but moreover a *'very'* influential man in Washington, abroad, and inside of the political arena in general. Although, he is no longer here, the favors he has done for many enables me to capitalize when it concerns family.

Tyra clearly understood what she was implying and also conceded that she too, would have capitalized from such political influence (to Thaddeus's benefit) had she been in such a position.

"Therefore, the pleasure was actually mine, as far as whatever support I was able to lend to Thaddeus." Ms. Bivens smiled.

"Something tells me that, if you were in my shoes you'd do the same thing for Nathaniel." She added, which was followed by a discreet wink.

Tyra, however, was not entirely sure as to what she meant by her comment. But, she let it pass.

"I hope you can find it in your heart to not only forgive me for trashing your telephone number." Tyra revealed honestly, "But also my failure to reciprocate your show of support and kindness towards my son and I."

"Your apology is accepted." Ms. Bivens replied, and added,

"On one condition that is."

Tyra continued to hold the woman's stare, before inquiring. "What's that?"

"That you allow me to get to know you."

Tyra, couldn't help finding the request at least a 'little' bizarre, yet, she could tell by the woman's vibe that she was sincere. So, Tyra responded saying, "It would be my pleasure for you and I to get to know each other better,"

"Am I interrupting?" Roberta made her approach with her and Tyra's coats in hand.

"Not at all." Ms. Bivens smiled up at her. "Actually, it's good to see you again. Roberta, correct?" She asked.

"Wow!" You certainly have a good memory." Roberta responded smiling as well. Nevertheless, she too, had remembered the woman's name.

Standing, Ms. Bivens exchanged a handshake with Roberta. Then turning to face Tyra, she gave her a hug.

Not only was Tyra caught slightly off guard by the sudden hug, but looking over the woman's shoulder, she saw Roberta standing there with a sheepish grin on her face. Not sure what to do, Tyra awkwardly wrapped her arms around Rose Mary Bivens…returning the embrace.

"What was all that about?" Roberta asked, as the two of them were now seated in back of their limousine, headed back to the hotel.

"Truthfully, I'm not even sure." Tyra responded

"Well, Thaddeus *'did'* find Ms. Bivens to be an interesting woman." Roberta recalled him saying so.

Tyra, however, pondered her son's assessment of the woman, before giving her response.

"Something tells me that *'interesting'* may very well prove to be an understatement." Tyra replied, seeing how Ms. Rose Mary Bivens was seemingly always in the right place at the right time….

THIRTY-EIGHT

WASHINGTON, DC 1995

At 78 years old, Tyra was no longer optimistic that the tide of change, socially and economically, for minorities and especially African Americans would greatly improve within her lifetime.

Whereas, the Reagan, then Bush administration had been laced with disappointment after disappointment for minorities that is, Tyra couldn't really see where the Clinton administration, thus far, had been much better in her opinion. Yet, countless, particularly the younger generation, of blacks and other minorities oddly gave praise to the current administration, she'd notice.

Yet, the Clinton Administration, signed a Republican-sponsored bill that ended Aid to Families with Dependent Children, failed to reform Healthcare, supported the 'Three-Strikes' law that imprisoned hundreds of thousands of non-violent minority offenders.

In spite of her disappointment, Tyra, was nonetheless thankful that the President had at least backed the "Korean War Veterans Memorial' which was dedicated on July 27, 1995.

"I can manage on my own." Tyra informed her friend and home attendant, a woman named Della Mae Richardson.

"All right, but I won't be far behind." Della Mae replied

protectively.

The Memorial, was situated at the west-end of the Mall. It was a triangular shaped stone and steel memorial that featured a multi-service formation of 19 combat-ready *'troops'* clad in ponchos with the wind at their backs.

Tyra, stared at the granite wall, which jutted into a pool of water, the 'Pool of Remembrance' it was called. On the wall, were images and names, of the men and women who died fighting the war.

"It's unfortunate that it took this long, but I am so happy that I have been Blessed to live to see the day that this country finally gives acknowledgement to you, and all those who have lost their lives defending it." Despite her tears, Tyra had a smile on her face, as she thought of Curtis. The man, whom she had loved, conceived his child, and remained faithful to even in death. Which was ironic, she thought, seeing how she hadn't been ready or willing to 'commit' to him, in Life.

"There has not been a single day that has passed, since your passing, that I have not thought of you. Truthfully, it would be impossible 'not' to have thought of you, seeing how much our son. Thaddeus, looks like you." Tyra continued her conversation with Curtis.

"I can honestly say, that you would be so proud of our son. Not only has he inherited your good heart and spirit, he is also very determined, motivated, intelligent, and is a true humanitarian. As a result, Thaddeus's Blessings are continuously flowing. However, I am sure you already know all of this, being that I know you're watching over your son from Heaven.

"Unfortunately, there has never been a gravesite in place for me to visit. Nevertheless, I'm sure you've enjoyed our countless conversations I've shared with you in Prayer. I'm truly in Love with the fact that, this Memorial has 'finally' been erected in your memory and honor. So, it is here, that I will make it a priority to visit, until you and I are rejoined in Heaven."

Satisfied, by her conversation with Curtis, Tyra turned and headed in the direction in which she'd left Della Mae.......

HARLEM, NEW YORK

"I've noticed that you haven't been very talkative since our return from Washington D.C." Della Mae spoke, as she prepared breakfast for Tyra and herself.

"I guess I just have a lot on my mind these days." Tyra revealed.

"Do you want to talk about it? You already know that I'm a good listener, who also provides great feedback." Della Mae said with a smile.

Tyra couldn't argue that point, considering her home attendant had spoken the truth.

"Before my mother passed away, she finally opened up to me concerning some of my family's history. But, I can't help feeling that there was a lot that she left out. In fact, growing up I was under the impression that Anne Lee was all the family I had. As a result, I've found myself keeping Thaddeus in the dark, while he was growing up, concerning not only my family's background but his father's as well."

"How come you never asked Annie Lee to fill in whatever blanks you felt existed?"

"I always got the impression that, Anne Lee didn't want to re-visit that time and place from her past. Therefore, I learned to respect what I assumed." Tyra answered

Della Mae understood her reasoning. She had such a tremendous respect for Tyra Star, whom she'd realized was one of the most humble, courageous, yet considerate person she had ever met.

"But, some things still don't add up." Tyra continued. "For years I've searched for my father's relatives, but haven't been able to locate a single person.

Della Mae heard the frustration in Tyra's voice.

"Did you ever consider taking a trip to Mt Pleasant, South Carolina? I'm certain it would be a great starting point in your search for answers." Della suggested

"I've visited the state of South Carolina on one occasion,

and that was to represent a client who was on death row. Following that experience, I've had no desire to return. I'm still curious as to how myself and my client made it out of South Carolina unharmed."

Della Mae stared at her wide eyed.

"Are you serious?!"

"I just knew, my client, Dexter Younts, and I, were going to be the main attraction at somebody's lynch party!" Tyra exclaimed, before letting out a laugh.

Della Mae, however, didn't see any humor in what she'd heard.

"Are you serious?" She asked a second time.

"I've never been more serious in my life." Tyra shook her head at that memory.

Changing the subject, especially since *lynching'* was a subject that Della knew she'd never be comfortable talking about.

"I'm surprised Thaddeus never asked questions about his father while growing up? Let alone, other family members."

"He probably did." Tyra replied before adding, "You have to remember, growing up, he spent a lot of time with Annie Lee and truthfully, I don't know what, or how much she may have told him."

"In any event, he certainly turned out all right." Della Mae said with Thaddeus in mind.

"Yes, he has." Tyra smiled proudly.

"I saw something on television last night about Thaddeus's being ahead by far, in his pursuit of the U.S. Senate seat." Della Mae informed Tyra with a smile on her face.

"Yes, I watched it also. In fact, I included that piece of news in my diary."

"Diary? When did you start keeping a diary?" Della Mae asked.

"It's been a few years now. However, I'm about to take everything I've written thus far, as well as the information my mother provided me about my Grandparents, before her passing, and turn it all into a Journal." Tyra revealed.

Della Mae was totally surprised by the fact that she'd been

with Tyra Star for over three years, yet had never witnessed a diary.

"Matter of fact, what's today's date?" Tyra asked.

"August 4, 1995. Why do you ask?"

"Because," Tyra began, "I have to be sure to include the exact day and time, in which you and I had our conversation."

CHAPPAQUA, NEW YORK 1995

Roberta, truly loved what the interior decorators had done with her and Thaddeus's, four thousand square feet home in Westchester County. A full week had not yet passed since the front (and backyard) had been perfectly landscaped.

Upon hearing the electric garage door opening/closing, she decided to meet her husband at the front door.

"How was your day beautiful lady?" Thaddeus asked, as he planted a kiss on Roberta's lips before she could answer his question.

Parting, Roberta licked her lips as if to savor the taste of her husband's lips.

"If there's such thing as a 'perfect' day, today has been it. Then, you come home and literally seals it with a kiss." Roberta answered her husband's question with a smile on her face.

"Wow! In that case, I should've spend my day with you!"

At that, they shared a laugh.

"Seriously, my day has been really awesome." Roberta reiterated.

"You want to tell me about it?" Thaddeus inquired. while removing his Armani slip-ons, which was followed by the removal of his Armani neck tie.

"You're making it hard for me to concentrate." Roberta replied, referring to his little strip tease.

Again, they both laughed.

"I'll tell you what, tell me about your first day. Then, I will enlighten you to what has me in such great spirit." Roberta suggested.

"My day was pretty good actually. Norman Shears believes that, it's basically cemented in stone, that you are looking at the next Democratic U.S. Senator of New York State." Thaddeus revealed with a smile.

"That is not news my dear, everyone knows that the people of New York love you and have your back, considering your actions have shown them that the feelings are mutual." Roberta replied, with a smile on her face.

"Thank you." Thaddeus responded, taking Roberta into his arms at the same time.

"You might not want to squeeze me too tightly." She whispered into his ear.

"And why wouldn't I want to squeeze you tightly?"

"Probably because we want our *'baby'* to have all the oxygen he or she needs, to assure a healthy birth."

THIRTY-NINE

DOVER, DELAWARE, 1997

Since first meeting Rose Mary Bivens, at the White House in 1972, Tyra had not made it a priority to maintain a line of communication with her. Feeling bad that she'd totally reneged on her promise to get to know each other better, a promise that was made four years prior at the President's inauguration celebration. Therefore, Tyra decided to accept the invitation that unexpectedly arrived in the mail.

"Are you certain you want to go alone?" Della Mae asked, upon entering Tyra's hotel room.

"I've put the woman off for years, so the last thing I want to do is show up with a guest." Tyra replied. "Besides, she and I both are old women, so I don't see her biting me." she joked.

Della Mae simply shook her head.

"Well, at least Thomas will be parked in the vicinity." Della Mae said, referring to their driver.

Arriving at the Bivens' estate, which it certainly was, Tyra told herself upon noticing a security guard posted outside of the gates.

Thomas let down his window and announced, 'Ms. Tyra Star.'

That being said, the guard walked over to the intercom, within seconds the gate began to open somewhat slowly.

"Must be nice." Thomas spoke somewhat under his breath. Tyra heard his remark, but didn't respond.

Rose Mary Bivens stood at the head of the long drive-way, as Tyra's car made its approach.

"How was the trip?" Ms. Bivens inquired, offering Tyra a hand as she exited the back seat of the Range Rover.

"It wasn't bad at all." Tyra replied.

"Good."

With that being said, Ms. Bivens led the way into her home, which was actually a 12,000-square foot mansion that sat on 62 acres of land.

"Your home, and garden, is breath taking." Tyra complimented.

"Thank you." Ms. Bivens responded before informing her, "My family has lived here for over two centuries. So, the place is quite old."

"Yet beautiful." Tyra added.

"We can sit out back and talk being that it's such a lovely day out."

"That's fine." Tyra responded. Although, it was indeed a warm sunny day, both woman wore thing button-up sweaters.

Once they were seated in individual high-backed, cushioned, summer chairs, which Tyra fold to be very comfortable, a young Hispanic girl made her approach carrying a silver tray that had a silver pitcher sitting atop.

"Would you ladies like some ice tea?" The young woman asked.

"I'll have a cup." Tyra replied, with a smile.

"So, will I." Ms. Bivens added. "I have a special meal being prepared. However, would you like a snack in the meantime?"

"That won't be necessary. Thank you." Tyra responded.

"That will be all Hilda." Ms. Bivens addressed the young woman by her first name.

Once the two of them were alone, Tyra began to speak.

"I've never been one to make excuses, so I won't do so now. Instead, I'd simply like to apologize for not getting back to you when my son gave me the message, he received from your son."

"No need to apologize. I guess I was somewhat pressed for a little companionship, being that I've been in and out of the hospital over the past two years." Ms. Bivens revealed.

"Oh my God!" Tyra brought her hand up to her mouth. "Are you alright? No one mentioned anything about you being in the hospital."

"I'm fine." Ms. Bivens smiled.

"Are you sure?" Tyra asked with obvious concern.

"Yes, I am sure. However, I prefer not to talk about my health. Instead, I'd like to talk about you."

"About me?" Tyra asked in dismay.

"Yes, I would love to know some of what you've been up to."

"I assure you, I have not been up to anything of interest in quite some time." Tyra informed her.

"My husband once told me that, he feared that I'd one day go into cardiac arrest worrying about you." Ms. Bivens laughed.

"Worrying about me?" Tyra was now totally in dismay.

"When you were down there in Sumter County, South Carolina representing that young man on death-row, my husband and I had to literally *'threaten'* those red-necks down there. In fact, my husband placed a call to the Governor and told him that, if a single strand of hair is touch, on your head, he will not only ruin his career, but he would also see to it that Sheriff Richards and his deputies be placed on a chain-gang." She laughed out loud.

Tyra, however, sat there completely stunned, and speechless.

"As for Albany, Georgia, Chief Pritchett was a pretty smart man, so our conversation, concerning you, was pretty civil. Meaning no *threats* were necessary." Again, she laughed at the memory.

"Why?" Tyra managed to inquire.

"Why what?"

"Why would you do that for me?"

"The same reason I saw to your immediate release from the Birmingham jail." Ms. Bivens answered.

"That doesn't answer my question." Tyra spoke barely

above a whisper, which she attributed to shock.

"I'd have to go some ways back, for you to fully understand."

"We have time." Tyra countered.

"Give me a second." That being said, Ms. Bivens stood, then headed for the house. When she returned, after about five minutes or so, Tyra noticed she was carrying a small black book.

"This is my mother's diary." She revealed. "She gave it to me shortly before she passed away."

Tyra remained silent.

Suddenly, Ms. Bivens went into a coughing fit.

"Are you alright?" Tyra asked, not liking the sound of her cough, she added, "We can go inside and talk."

"No, I'm okay." Ms. Bivens used her right hand to wipe her lips, making sure nothing was there.

"My mother's name is, or rather was, Audrey Lynn Bowers, until she moved to South Carolina and married a man name Raymond Pinkney."

Tyra was not only shocked, but totally all ears, being that Anne Lee had told her a story of a man name Raymond Pinkney. In fact, he was the man who had disappeared with Anne Lee's sister Arethea, both of whom were never to be seen again, at least that's what Anne Lee had told her.

"It took me more than a year to read the entire diary, being that it was so difficult for me to get through all of the pain and heartbreak that my mother experienced." Ms. Bivens explained.

Tyra decided to simply listen.

"Considering, we don't have the kind of time to read through the entire diary, at least I don't," Ms. Bivens made a light sniffling sound, "I'll just tell you a story that will consist of excerpts from this diary, which I'll allow you to take with you when you leave."

Seeing how Tyra wasn't trying to respond either way, she continued.

"My mother's aunt, a woman name Melissa, was not only married to a man name Nathaniel Pinkney Jr, it was she who introduced Audrey to Nathaniel's nephew Raymond.

"As far as my mother was concerned, it was love at first sight. But, unfortunately, it wouldn't be long before Audrey realized that Raymond's heart belonged to another woman."

"Arethea Addison." Tyra said, filling in the blank.

"Yes, Arethea Addison," Ms. Bivens confirmed, "Apparently, their hearts had been intertwined long before Audrey entered the picture. However, not only was theirs a forbidden love, Audrey decided to remain in the equation simply because she knew Raymond and Arethea could never be together. Plus, her heart was too far gone."

Ms. Bivens eyes began to water as she told her story.

"At some point, Arethea ended up pregnant. Yet, she didn't know with certainty who her child's father was, being that she'd entered into an adulterous affair with Raymond Pinkney, while married to a man named Isaiah Steed.

"On June 20th, 1917, Arethea went into labor. A cousin of hers named Monique, and a sister named Anne Lee, who was home from school at the time, assisted a local doctor in delivering the child. My mother's diary described the child as extremely beautiful, and when the doctor laid the little girl on Arethea's chest, it was the child's bright greenish/blue eyes that twinkled like a star, which was why Arethea named her *"Tyra Star."*

Although, Tyra sat there with her eyes shut, her tears nonetheless, managed to escape them as she listened.

"Just as the doctor prepared to wrap things up, Arethea, suddenly began to experience excruciating stomach pains. Which caused Anne Lee to become somewhat hysterical, fearing her older sister was about to die. However, it wasn't long before the doctor realized she was having contractions. In fact, Monique, nor Anne Lee, could believe their eyes as the doctor encouraged Arethea to push.

"Taking hold of baby Tyra, my mother writes in her diary, Anne Lee stepped back with the child in her arms as Monique handed Arethea her second new-born, which was also a girl. To everyone's surprise, the *'twin'* was born with skin as white as snow.

"Arethea's initial shock, was suddenly replaced by a mother's smile, realizing that, she had given Raymond Pinkney a gift in which he thought fate had unfairly denied him. It was Monique, who pointed out the child's unusual birthmark, which was located on the back of her left shoulder. None of the four adults in the room had ever seen a birth mark that clearly resembled a rose. To none of their surprise however, Arethea announced that her daughter's name would be *Myra Rose.*

"As she held her new-born twin girls, Arethea, opposed to sending for the man whom she'd married, instructed Monique to go find Raymond. As she predicted, Raymond knew exactly how to handle the situation. Overcome with joy, as he held his twin daughters, Raymond was nonetheless heartbroken as he realized that he'd not only have to let another man raise Tyra, but moreover, Isaiah would believe that she was 'his' flesh and blood.

"In order for his plan to work, Raymond had the four of them swear to secrecy. Including Audrey, who begrudgingly found herself sharing her home with a child whom she knew she could never love."

Ms. Bivens paused her story, as the two-woman sat there, in the bright sun, allowing all of what she'd said to process.

"Shortly after Raymond and Arethea were both gone, my heart began to soften and my feelings for the child, whom I previously refused to have anything to do with, also began to change," Rose Mary read from Audrey's diary. "Whereas, I once blocked out the child's loud wails during the night, I now find myself relishing the act of cradling her in my arms."

"I guess I knew in my heart that Myra Rose had nothing to do with my husband's infidelity and betrayal. Not to mention, I also realized that I needed to step up and be the child's protector, knowing that her life was potentially in danger." Closing the small diary, Ms. Bivens handed it to Tyra.

"You can read the rest yourself. I'm sure it will fill in a lot of the questions that are in your head." She added.

"What happened to Myra Rose?" Tyra thought she already knew the answer to her question, however, she wanted confirmation.

"Shortly after everything transpired, Audrey decided to re-name the child. Actually, she wrote that, at some point she knew she'd be leaving the state of South Carolina, and returning to her family in Delaware. Therefore, the decision was made in part because she never heard of a white child with the name Myra, she wrote."

At that, Rose Mary Bivens let out a laugh.

"So, she decided that 'Myra' would become 'Mary', and make 'Rose' the child's first name."

Again, the two of them sat there in complete silence fol-lowing what was an incredible revelation, as far as Tyra Star was concerned.

Finding her voice, Tyra asked a question.

"Can I see the birthmark?" Tyra requested, however, it was barely above a whisper.

Standing, Rose Mary removed the thin button-up sweater, revealing the thin straps of her summer dress. Turning, so her back was now facing Tyra, who was also standing.

Staring at the back of her left shoulder, Tyra had never seen a birthmark so unique. The resemblance of a 'rose' was so un-mistakable., it could easily have been misconstrued as a tattoo, she told herself.

As Ms. Bivens turned to face Tyra, not only was tears streaming down both their faces, but when the two sisters en-gaged in their first, heartfelt, hug… it was a 'hug' that seemed to have lasted an eternity!

HARLEM, NEW YORK

In the seven days that passed, since Tyra learned that she'd had a sister, not only did she read Audrey's diary in its entirety, but Myra Rose was all that she talked about! So much so, Della Mae couldn't help feeling slightly jealous.

"I wonder if 'she' is as delighted as you are, that the secret has now been revealed?" Della Mae inquired with more than a little sarcasm in her voice.

"You do not understand," Tyra began. "This woman, *my sister*, has been trying to get to know me for decades!"

"I understand that."

"It is entirely my fault that, so much time has gone by, hindering she and I from establishing a relationship." Tyra explained.

"You cannot blame yourself for something you were not made aware of." Della Mae countered.

"I know. However, we're much older now, so I want to try to spend as much time with Myra Rose as possible." Tyra replied, with a smile on her face. "She and I, lost our parents, whom we've never had the pleasure of knowing. However, we're truly fortunate to still have each other."

Della Mae simply nodded her head understanding.

"In fact, I have to call her. Maybe she'll be available to spend this weekend with me, when I return Audrey's diary to her."

After dialing Myra's home phone number, it was answered after only one ring.

"You've reached the Bivens residence, this is Hilda speaking, how may I help you?" Hilda inquired with a Hispanic accent.

"Hello Hilda, this is Tyra Star. May I speak with Ms. Bivens?"

There was a pause, following Tyra's request, she noticed.

"Is there something wrong?" Tyra inquired.

"Can you please hold a minute?" That being asked, Hilda apparently went to summoned Myra to the telephone, Tyra assumed, as she waited.

"Ms. Star." A male's voice spoke Tyra's last name. "This is Nathaniel, I've been meaning to reach out to all of my mother's friends and associates. However, my emotions have been all over the place these past few days, I haven't gotten around to doing much of anything."

"What's wrong Nathaniel?" Tyra asked with concern.

"My mother was diagnosed with brain cancer last year, at which time her doctor gave her six months to live. In fact, it was during that period that I asked Thaddeus to have you give her a call, as per her request. Unfortunately, we lost her five days ago." He began to sob. Although, Tyra was in complete shock, she managed to make an inquiry.

"When is the funeral?" She closed her eyes in an attempt to confine her tears, to no avail.

"Actually, we buried my mother yesterday." Nathaniel revealed before adding, "It was decided that only *family* would attend."

MANHATTAN, NEW YORK, 2007
5:00 P.M.

Roberta, was not entirely upset that she'd received her first speeding ticket (ever), while on the FDR Drive, but, what did make her angry was the fact that, the Highway Patrolman, who'd pulled her over, took nearly 45 minutes to write her ticket! Nor, was it her intentions to be rude, as she walked right passed the young hospital receptionist, Theresa Garcia, without acknowledging her. Roberta, was simply anxious to be with her mother!

Stepping inside of her mother's hospital room, Roberta, stood silently beside the door as a nurse proceeded to take Tyra's vitals.

"You do not have to stand way over there." Tyra spoke, apparently realizing someone had entered.

"I didn't realize you saw me." Roberta responded, taking a few steps closer to the bed. Yet, allowing the nurse her space to do her job.

"My vision may have gotten terrible with age, but for some reason my (hearing) ability has certainly improved." Tyra said in response.

"So, that means you didn't know that it was me standing by the door?"

"No, not until you spoke." Tyra admitted.

"Is there anything I can bring you before I continue the rest of my rounds?" The nurse inquired.

"I'm fine dear." Tyra replied. "Thank you."

Once the nurse was gone, Roberta walked up to the bed and planted a kiss on her mother's head.

"I take it you read my journal?"

Opposed to an immediate response, Roberta continued to stare into her mother's eyes.

"I guess you can also see 'why' I lost my desire to continue my writing." Tyra turned and faced the window.

"I am so sorry." Roberta offered her condolences, even

though Twenty years had passed since Myra's passing.

When Tyra turned to face her, her eyes were filled with tears.

"I've visited her grave countless times over the years." Tyra revealed. "I was not there for her when she needed me." She cried

"You didn't know." Roberta spoke in a very low tone of voice. At the same time, reaching for her mother's hand. Knowing the full story, she clearly understood Tyra's pain.

"It truly breaks my heart to know that you have carried such pain and guilt for all of these years." Roberta added, she too, was now crying.

"Myra, had literally been my Guardian Angel, yet, I failed to show up even when I 'promised' her that she and I would get to know each other." Tyra reiterated the vow she once made to the woman who turned out to be her sister. At the same time, staring into Roberta's eyes as if 'they' were the place in which forgiveness laid.

"You have to stop blaming yourself." Roberta countered. "You cannot be held responsible for that in which you did not know."

Tyra gave no response.

"In fact, I read how Myra held on for nearly two years, in spite of her doctor giving her Six months to live. Obviously, she was determined not to go on to Heaven, until you knew the truth." Roberta explained.

"I can assure you, she is now resting in peace." She added with a smile on her face, despite her tears.

Tyra continued to hold her daughters stare.

"What does surprise me is the fact that, neither of your parents tried to locate you or Myra over the years." Roberta said in dismay, somewhat changing the subject.

"Our parents?" Tyra responded confused.

"Yes, didn't Raymond and Arethea disappear shortly after you and your sister were born?"

Tyra closed her eyes, as it suddenly dawned on her that, Roberta hadn't read Audrey's diary. Therefore, she didn't know the entire story.

"I should have given you Audrey's diary also." Tyra told her.

"I read in your Journal, several excerpts from Audrey's diary."

"No, you do not understand." Tyra began. "Our parents never abandoned us."

Roberta, did not know how to respond to that.

"My sister and I were born on June 17th, 1917. As you've read in my Journal, my father Raymond Pinkney, swore everyone who was present at the time of Myra and my birth, to secrecy. However, Monique failed to keep the secret.

"Apparently, she told her husband, Willie Steed, who in turn revealed to my mother's husband, Isaiah, one day while the two of them were drinking, that Raymond Pinkney was my biological father.

"In Audrey's' diary, which I still have, she reveals in graphic detail, the night Isaiah stormed into the home that she shared with Raymond, before entering their room with a sawed-off shotgun in hand. Words were exchanged between the two men, and the next thing she knew Isaiah pulled the trigger. Killing Raymond instantly."

Roberta, stared at her mother wide eyed, totally speechless.

"Audrey, further wrote that, opposed to being afraid for her life as well, the irony was that, as she stared into Isaiah's eyes, she identified with his pain, confusion, and betrayal. In fact, she had totally lost track of the time, as well as her surroundings, as Raymond's corpse laid there beside her, their mattress absorbing his blood like a sponge."

Roberta, couldn't help feeling somewhat nauseated as she listened.

"That same night, Isaiah used the same shotgun to kill my mother, before turning it on himself." Tyra recited the excerpt from Audrey's diary with closed eyes.

"Oh my God!" Roberta finally spoke. A part of her was glad that Tyra had not given her Audrey's diary to read.

"Two days after Isaiah embarked on his murderous spree, which happened to be the Fourth of July, Rollin Pinkney, along with a group of white men, abducted Willie Steed, who apparently revealed the entire story before meeting his death. As a result, Rollin Pinkney made a vow to kill 'both' myself and Myra." Tyra further revealed.

Suddenly, it became clear to Roberta, why Anne Lee not only fled the South with Tyra, but moreover 'why' she had basically led a secluded life, as well as kept so many secrets!

"My grandmother Rebecca, and Audrey, gave my aunt Anne Lee a fairly large amount of money, and suggested she take me somewhere where I'd be safe, not to mention, she'd raise me as her own."

Roberta, bent down to give her mother a hug.

"I suppose, Audrey wasn't very afraid of Rollin Pinkney, being that she stayed in Mt. Pleasant for quite a few years before ultimately returning home to Delaware. Actually, it was she, who had sold Rebecca's house and property following her passing, at Anne Lee's direction.

"In fact, some years later, she and Anne Lee, had decided that Audrey would sell Raymond's shares in Pinkney's Enterprises, to Rollin Pinkney, who gave Audrey the sum of One Million Dollars, although the company was worth nearly Fifty Million by then.

"Anyway, Audrey took 250,000, which she split with Anne Lee for the purpose of raising Myra, and I, the remaining 750,000, Audrey invested into her family's business. The money was Myra and my inheritance."

Roberta, now realized where the 375,000 came from, in which Tyra mentioned in her Journal. In fact, Anne Lee had revealed that it was now a half Million when she turned it over to Tyra.

"It's unbelievable, Thaddeus doesn't know 'any' of this." Roberta thought to herself. "I read that Raymond Pinkney attended Yale University." Roberta wanted to lighten the mood, if at all possible.

"So did his two grandsons." Tyra added, producing a slight smile, with Thaddeus 'and' Nathaniel Bivens in mind.

"You 'do' know what this means?" Roberta asked.

"Yes" Tyra responded.

"I've already called to confirm that Senator Bivens is currently at home, in Delaware." Roberta revealed.

"Isn't Thaddeus out of town until late tomorrow?" Tyra inquired, remembering he'd said as much during their visit the previous day.

"Yes. However, this is a trip that I will be taking by my lonesome." Roberta further revealed, before adding, "It would be extremely helpful if I had a copy of Audrey's diary to take with me."

"I figured as much." Tyra produced a smile before adding.

"Therefore, I requested that Della Mae bring it to me this morning." With that being said, Tyra reached beneath her pillow for the diary, which she handed to her daughter....

DOVER, DELAWARE

"Senator Bivens, I am so glad you agreed to meet with me on such

short notice" Roberta thanked the Senator, at the same time taking his outstretched hand into hers.

"Nonsense." Senator Nathaniel J. Biven replied with a warm smile on his face. "I've known you and your husband for quite a long time, in fact, I consider the both of you as friends. Therefore, whatever I can do for you, I will certainly give it my all."

"Thank you." Roberta returned his smile. "However, I am not here for a favor, nor assistance."

That being said, the Senator became somewhat dismayed as to the nature of her visit.

"Please," He said, allowing her to lead the way into his office.

Once they were both seated, Roberta began to get right to the point.

"Senator, I really don't have a lot of time being that New York is a Three-hour drive, and I'd like to be home when my husband returned from his trip to Washington D.C."

"Okay." Was the senator's only reply. As he continued to hold Roberta's stare.

"I brought with me, my husband's mother's Journal, as well as a diary that was written by a woman whom I'm sure you know."

Certain that, there was no skeletons in his closet, nor a woman out there who could potentially drag his name into some sort of scandal, the senator asked, "What is her name?"

"Audrey Pinkney."

The mention of his grandmother's name caused the senator's stare to become quite intense, Roberta noticed.

"Why would you have a diary that belongs to my grandmother?"

"Actually, she gave it to your mother, Rose Mary, who shortly before her passing gave it to my mother-in-law." Roberta explained.

"I see." The senator replied, although he was clearly confused.

"Again, Senator Bivens, it is not my intentions to use up too much of your time." Roberta reiterated. "However, I'd like to leave with you 'both' my mother-in-law's Journal, as well as your grandmothers diary, in hope that, you will make it a priority to read them both at your earliest convenience."

"Of course." The senator agreed, turning his focus towards the two relatively small books that sat in her lap.

Roberta stood, placing both books onto his polished desk.

"I'll be sure to return these to you once I am done reading them." The senator added, leafing through Tyra's Journal.

"Is there a particular order in which I should read them?" He asked as a final thought.

"Something tells me, you'll get a better understanding if you start with 'A Rose beyond a Star'," Roberta suggested as she made her way towards his office door.

The senator didn't even realize that she was on her way out, considering he was already halfway through the 'prologue'.

"One question," Roberta began, turning to face him.

Looking up from the Journal, the senator acknowledged her.

"What's that?"

"Would the possibility of becoming Vice President interest you?"

Senator Nathaniel J. Bivens stared at her a moment before finally giving his answer.

"I do not know anyone who wouldn't enjoy the prospect of such a position."

At that, Roberta smiled.

Without anything else being said, Roberta let herself out. At the same time, shutting the door behind her, allowing the Senator his privacy to read....

EPILOGUE

JANUARY 20TH, 2018

My name is Roberta Johnson Star, whereas, my mother, Tyra Star, decided to do a 'Forward' to her Journal "A ROSE BEYOND A STAR" I have taken it upon myself (being that my mother is no longer with us) to do the "Epilogue' to such an incredible story.

I am sure that the majority of you are familiar with me, more so, as former First Lady of the United States of America! Yes, not only did my husband, Thaddeus C. Star, prevail in his endeavor to become the Commander in Chief, Nathaniel J. Bivens, I am proud to say, served as his Vice President!

Together, they served the American people for 'two' terms.

One of their greatest achievements was making Health Care affordable for 'Millions' of Americans! In fact, I am also sure that you all are familiar with all of the ACTS and Legislation, in which my husband succeeded in having passed through Congress. Some, he took upon himself to pass, by way of Executive Orders.

It was on this day, January 20th, 2009, that my husband stood before the entire world, to give his historical Inauguration speech. Not only has it become a day that will forever be a part of history, and a defining moment, especially for African Americans, but it was also a day that I am proud to say, my mother, 'Tyra Star' lived to see! Unfortunately, she died Four days after her son's 'second' Inauguration.

It was also on this day, January 20th, 2017, that my husband graciously left office. Leaving behind, not only an incredible legacy, but more so, inspiration and the realization that, in this land of the free, and democracy, 'nothing' is impossible...

ACKNOWLEDGEMENTS

First and foremost, I have to give Thanks to Jesus Christ (My Lord and Savior), without an unwavering Faith in You, I totally believe that nothing I do, or touch would prosper!

I also give Thanks to my Parents Alfred Adams Sr. and Dorothy Jean Adams. My Father has been a true "Entrepreneur" my entire life (before I even knew the definition of the word!), and my Mom (who continues to be my inspiration of Higher learning/Achievement) although you are no longer here with us (in the physical) you will "Forever" be my Role Model!!!! Especially, witnessing how you absolutely refused to allow any person, place, thing, or situation to prevent or hinder you from achieving the [many] degrees you have earned in your lifetime...including a Ph.D! Therefore, it's no wonder where and from whom I've acquired my love of reading, writing, and being creative in general!

My family and friends consist of many. Far too many to individually acknowledge in my Debut! However, I promise you all that; with the [many] incredible stories that I intend to release I 'will' strive to mention/acknowledge you ALL! Because each and every one of YOU have brought something special to my life. Nevertheless, I do have to take this opportunity to give a special 'Thank You" to the [many] ANGELS... (Lorraine, Myra, Tarin, Jessica, Della, Prim Rose, Sylvestre 'Toot', Uncle Tee, Wolf, Harold, Robert, Timothy, Darae, Shaborn, and several others) who continue to watch over me!

And to my ADAMS FAMILY PRESS Family/Team, let's take this story-telling/amazing content to the next level!! To my supporters/readers......Enjoy the Ride!!!